HIDDEN BODIES

CAROLINE KEPNES

HIDDEN BODIES

a novel

EMILY BESTLER BOOKS

ATRIA

NEW YORK LONDON TORONTO SYDNEY NEW DELHI

An Imprint of Simon & Schuster, Inc.
1230 Avenue of the Americas
New York, NY 10020

This book is a work of fiction. Any references to historical events, real people, or real places are used fictitiously. Other names, characters, places, and events are products of the author's imagination, and any resemblance to actual events or places or persons, living or dead, is entirely coincidental.

First Emily Bestler Books/Atria Books hardcover edition February 2016

Book design by Natalie C. Sousa

Manufactured in the United States of America

10 9 8 7 6 5 4 3 2 1

Library of Congress Cataloging-in-Publication Data has been applied for.

ISBN 978-1-4767-8562-2
ISBN 978-1-4767-8564-6 (ebook)

This book is for you, Mom.
Thank you for life.

1

I buy violets for Amy. Not roses. Roses are for people who did something wrong. I have done everything right this time around. I'm a good boyfriend. I chose well. Amy Adam lives in the moment, not in the computer.

"Violets are the state flower of Rhode Island," I tell the guy wrapping up my flowers. His careless, dirty hands graze the petals, my petals. *New Fucking York.*

"Is that so?" He chuckles. "You learn something new every day."

I pay cash and carry my violets outside to East Seventh Street. It's hot for May and I smell the flowers. *Rhode Island.* I've been to Rhode Island. I went to Little Compton last winter. I was lovesick, petrified that my girlfriend—*R.I.P. Guinevere Beck*—was in jeopardy because of her emotionally unstable friend—*R.I.P. Peach Salinger*.

Someone honks at me and I apologize. I know when something is my fault, and when you walk into a blinking crosswalk, it's your fault.

Just like it was my fault last winter. I go over the mistake in my head a dozen times a day. How I was hiding in a closet upstairs at the

Salinger house. How I had to pee but couldn't leave. So I pissed in a mug—a ceramic *mug*—and I put the mug down on the hardwood floor of the closet. I ran when I had the chance, and there is no way around it: I forgot the mug.

I'm a changed man because of that day. You can't go back and alter the past, but you can go forward, become a person who *remembers*. Now, I'm committed to the details. For example, I recall with total precision the moment that Amy Kendall Adam returned to Mooney Rare and Used, to my life. I see her smile, her untamed hair (blond), and her résumé (lies). That was five months ago and she claimed she was looking for a job but you and I both know she was looking for me. I hired her, and she showed up on time for her first day with a spiral notebook and a list of rare books that she wanted to see. She had a glass container of *superfruits* and she told me they help you live forever. I told her that nobody gets to live forever and she laughed. She had a nice laugh, easy. She also had latex gloves.

I picked one up. "What are these?"

"So I don't hurt the books," she explained.

"I want you up front," I countered. "This is just a basic job, mostly stocking shelves, manning the register."

"Okay," she said. "But did you know that there are copies of *Alice in Wonderland* that are worth over *a million dollars*?"

I laughed. "I hate to break your heart, but we don't have *Alice* downstairs."

"Downstairs?" she asked. "Is that where you keep the special books?"

I wanted to place my hand on the small of her back and lead her down to the cage, where the *special books* are preserved, boxed, saved. I wanted to strip her down and lock us inside and have her. But I was patient. I gave her a W-9 and a pen.

"You know, I could help you go yard-sale-ing for old books," she said. "You never know what you're going to find at yard sales."

I smiled. "Only if you promise not to call it yard-sale-ing."

Amy smiled. The way she saw it, if she was going to work here, she was going to *make a dent.* She wanted us to travel uptown to estate sales and hunt library clearances and jam our hands into empty boxes on the street. She wanted to *work together* and this is how you get to know someone so well, so fast. You descend into musty vacated rooms together and you rush outside together to gulp the fresh air and laugh and agree that the only thing to do now is get a drink. We became a team.

An old woman pushing a walker looks up at me. I smile. She points at the violets. "You're a good boy."

I am. I thank her and keep walking.

Amy and I started dating a few months ago while we were on the Upper East Side in a dead man's parlor. She tugged on the lapel of the navy blazer she had bought for me—five bucks—at a tag sale. She pleaded with me to drop *seven hundred* on a signed, wrinkled edition of *The Easter Parade.*

"Amy," I whispered. "Yates isn't big right now and I don't see a resurgence on the horizon."

"But I love him," she begged. "This book means everything to me."

This is women; they are emotional. You can't do business like this but you also can't look at Amy with her big blue eyes and her long blond hair out of a Guns N' Roses song and say no to her.

"What can I do to change your mind?" she wheedled.

An hour later, I was the owner of an overpriced *Easter Parade* and Amy was sucking my dick in a Starbucks bathroom in Midtown and this was more romantic than it sounds because we *liked* each other. This was not a blowjob; this was *fellatio*, my friends. She stood and I pulled her boyfriend jeans to the floor and I stopped short. I knew she didn't like to shave; her legs were often bristly and she's all about *water conservation*. But I did not expect a bush. She kissed me. "Welcome to the jungle."

This is why I smile as I walk and this is how you get happy. Amy and I, we are sexier than Bob Dylan and Suze Rotolo on the cover of *The Freewheelin'* and we are smarter than Tom Cruise and Penélope Cruz in *Vanilla Sky*. We have a project: We are amassing copies of *Portnoy's Complaint*. It's one of our favorite books and we reread it together. She underlined her favorite parts with a Sharpie and I told her to use a more delicate pen.

"I'm not delicate," she said. "I hate delicate."

Amy is a Sharpie; she's passionate. She fucking loves *Portnoy's Complaint* and I want to possess all the dark yellow copies ever made and keep them in the basement so that only Amy and I can touch them. I'm not supposed to overstock a title, but I like fucking Amy near our yellow wall of books. Philip Roth would approve. She laughed when I told her that and said we should write him a letter. She has an imagination, a heart.

My phone rings. It's Gleason Brothers Electricians about the humidifier but it can wait. I have an e-mail from BuzzFeed about some list of *cool indie bookstores* and that can wait too. Everything can wait when you have love in your life. When you can just walk down the street and picture the girl you love naked on a mound of yellow *Complaints*.

I reach Mooney Books and the bell chimes as I open the door. Amy crosses her arms and glares at me and maybe she's allergic to flowers. Maybe violets suck.

"What's wrong?" I ask, and I hope this isn't it, the beginning of the end, when the girl becomes a cunt, when the new car smell evaporates.

"Flowers?" she asks. "You know what I want more than flowers?"

I shake my head.

"Keys," she says. "A guy was just here and I could have sold him the Yates but I couldn't show it because I don't have *keys.*"

I toss the flowers on the counter. "Slow down. Did you get a number?"

"Joe," she says, tapping her foot. "I love this business. And I know I'm being a dumb girl and I shouldn't tell you how into this I am. But please. I want keys."

I don't say anything. I need to memorize it all, lock it away for safekeeping, the low hum of the music—the Rolling Stones' "Sweet Virginia," one of my favorites—and the way the light is right now. I don't lock the door. I don't flip the OPEN sign over. I walk to the other side of the counter and I take her in my arms and I dip her and I kiss her and she kisses me back.

I'VE never given anyone a key. But this is what's supposed to happen. Your life is supposed to expand. Your bed is supposed to have enough room for someone else and when that someone comes along, it's your job to let her in. I seize my future. I pay extra to get ridiculous theme keys, pink and flowery. And when I place these pink metallic things in the palm of Amy's hand, she kisses them.

"I know this is huge," she says. "Thank you, Joe. I will guard these with my life."

That night, she comes over and we watch one of her stupid movies—*Cocktail*, nobody is perfect—and we have sex and order a pizza and my air-conditioning breaks.

"Should we call someone?" she asks.

"Fuck it," I say. "It's Memorial Day coming up."

I smile and pin her down and her unshaven legs scratch against mine and I'm used to it now. I like it. She licks her lips. "What are you up to, Joe?"

"You go home and pack a bag," I say. "And I'm gonna rent us a little red Corvette and we're gonna get out of here."

"You're insane," she says. "Where are we going in this little red Corvette?"

I bite her neck. "You'll see."

"You're kidnapping me?" she asks.

And if this is what she wants, then yes. "You have two hours. Go pack."

2

SHE shaved; I knew she had it in her. And I did my part. I really did rent a red convertible. We are *those assholes* and we're cruising through the woodsy part of Rhode Island. We are your worst nightmare. We are happy. We don't need you, any of you. We don't give a fuck about you, what you think of us, what you did to us. I am the driver and Amy is the dream girl and this is our first vacation together. Finally. I have love.

The top is down and we sing along to "Goodbye Yellow Brick Road." I picked this song because I'm taking it all back, all the beautiful things in the world that were corrupted by my tragically ill girlfriend Guinevere Beck. (I see now that she suffered from borderline personality disorder. You can't fix that.) Beck and her horrible friends ruined so much for me. I couldn't go anywhere in New York without thinking of Beck. I thought I'd never listen to Elton John again because his music was playing when I killed Peach.

Amy taps my shoulder and points at a hawk in the sky. I smile.

She isn't the kind of asshole who needs to lower the volume on the music and discuss the bird and read into it. God, she is good. But no matter how good it gets, it is always there, the truth:

I forgot to take the mug.

That fucking mug haunts me. I understand that there are consequences. I am not unique; to be alive is to have a mug of urine out there. But I can't forgive myself for screwing up, like some girl "forgetting" a cardigan after a one-night stand. The mug is an aberration. A flaw. Proof that I'm not perfect, even though I'm usually so precise, so thorough. I haven't hatched a plan to retrieve it, but Amy makes me wish I had. I want the world clean for us, Lysol fresh.

Now she offers me her scratched sunglasses. "You're driving," she says. "You need them more than I do."

She is the anti-Beck; she cares about me. "Thanks, Ame."

She kisses my cheek and life is a fever dream and I wonder if I'm in a coma, if all this is a hallucination. Love fucks with your vision and I have no hate in my heart. Amy is taking all of it away, my healer, my Bactine beauty. In the past, I had a tendency to be intense; you might even call it obsessive. Beck was such a mess that in order to take care of her, I had to follow her home and hack into her e-mail and worry about her Facebook and her Twitter and her nonstop texting, all the contradictions, the lies. I chose poorly with her and suffered the consequences. I learned my lesson. It works with Amy because I can't stalk her online. Get this: She's off the grid. No Facebook, no Twitter, no Instagram, not even an e-mail address. She uses burner phones and I have to program her new number into my phone every couple of weeks. She is the ultimate analog, my perfect match.

When she first told me, I was flabbergasted and a little judgmental. Who the fuck is offline? Was she a pretentious nutcase? Was she lying? "What about paychecks?" I asked. "You have to have a bank account."

"I have this friend in Queens," she answered. "I write my checks over to her and she gives me cash. A lot of us use her. She's the best."

"'Us'?"

"People offline," she said. "I'm not alone here."

Cunts want to be snowflakes. They want you to tell them how nobody in this whole world compares to them. (Apologies to Prince.) All the little fame monsters on Instagram—look at me, I put jam on my toast!—and I found someone different. Amy doesn't try to stand out. I don't sit alone and scroll through her status updates and home in on her misleading photographs of staged joy. When I'm with her, I'm with her, and when she leaves me, she goes where she said she was going.

(Of course I've followed her and I occasionally look in her phone. I have to know that she isn't lying.)

"I think I smell salt air," Amy says.

"Not yet," I tell her. "Couple more minutes."

She nods. She doesn't fight about stupid shit. She's no angry Beck. That sick girl lied to the people with whom she was closest—me, Peach, her fucking fellow *writers* in school. She told me her father was dead. (He wasn't.) She told me she hated *Magnolia* just because her friend Peach hated it. (She was lying. I read her e-mail.)

Amy is a nice girl and nice girls lie to strangers to be polite, not to people they love. Even right now, she's wearing a threadbare URI tank top. She didn't go to URI; she didn't go anywhere. But she always wears a college shirt. She got a Brown shirt for me, just for this trip. "We can tell people that I'm a student and you're my professor." She giggled. "My *married* professor."

She digs up these shirts at various Goodwills all over the city. Her chest is always screaming *Go Tigers! Arizona State! PITT*. I tend to the stacks and eavesdrop as people who come into the shop try to connect with her—*Did you go to Princeton? Did you go to UMass? Do you go to NYU?*—and she always answers yes. She makes nice with the women and she lets the dudes think they have a shot. (They don't.) She likes a conversation. She likes a story, my little anthropologist, my listener.

We are nearing the road that takes us to Little Compton and just when I think life can't get any better, I see flashing lights. A cop is coming at us. Hard. His lights are on and his sirens are blaring and the music is gone. I brake and I try to keep my legs from shaking.

"What the fuck?" Amy says. "You weren't even speeding."

"I don't think so," I say, keeping my eyes on the rearview mirror as the cop opens his door.

Amy turns to me. "What did you do?"

What did I do? I murdered my ex-girlfriend Guinevere Beck. I buried her body in upstate New York and then pinned it on her therapist, Dr. Nicky Angevine. Before that, I strangled her friend Peach Salinger. I killed her less than five fucking miles from here, on a beach by her family's house, and made it look like a suicide. I also did away with a drug-addled soda jerk named *Benji Keyes*. His cremated body is in his storage unit, but his family thinks he died on a bender. Oh, also. The first girl I ever loved, Candace. I put her out to sea. Nobody knows I did any of these things so it's like that if-a-tree-falls-in-the-woods question.

"I have no idea," I say, and this is a fucking nightmare.

Amy rummages around the glove box for the rental's registration, takes it out, and then slams it shut. Officer Thomas Jenks doesn't take off his sunglasses. He has round shoulders and his uniform is slightly too large. "License and registration," he says. His eyes burrow into on my chest, the word BROWN. "You heading back to school?"

"Just going to Little Compton," I say. And then I cover. "Eventually. Taking my time."

He doesn't acknowledge my passive-aggressive defense. I was not fucking speeding and I am not a Brown asshole and this is why I don't wear college shirts. He studies my New York driver's license. A century passes, and then another.

Amy coughs. "Officer, what did we do wrong?"

Officer Jenks looks at her, then at me. "You didn't signal when you turned."

Are you kidding me, motherfucker? "Ah," I say. "I'm sorry."

Jenks says he needs "a few minutes" and he plods back to his car, breaking into a jog and he shouldn't be jogging. He also shouldn't need "a few minutes." As he opens the door to his cruiser and slips inside, I think of my prior offenses, my secret activities, and my throat closes up.

"Joe, relax," Amy says, putting her hand on my leg. "It's just a minor traffic violation."

But Amy doesn't know that I killed four people. I am sweating and I've heard about things like this. A guy gets pulled over for a minor infraction and somehow, through the sadistic magic of computers and system, the guy is pinned for all kinds of other shit. I could shoot myself.

Amy turns the radio back on. Five songs play and twenty minutes tick by and Officer Thomas Jenks is still in his automobile, holding my personal information. If he's issuing me a simple ticket for failing to signal, if that's all there is to this, then why is he on the phone? Why does he keep pushing buttons on the computer? Does my freedom end at the beginning of *the season* when my iPhone shows sun and the sky above is swollen with rain? Because I do know a cop in this state. His name is Officer Nico and he thinks my name is Spencer. What if he saw my picture in the computer? What if he recognized me and called *Jenks* and said, *I know that guy.* And what if—

"Joe," Amy says, and I almost forgot she was here. "You look like you're having a panic attack. It's not bad. It's not even a speeding ticket."

"I know," I say. "I just hate cops."

She strokes my leg. "I know."

She reaches into the cooler and takes out a peach. A *peach.* Of course it kills me that we are moving backward. She is eating a peach and I am obsessing about Peach Salinger and my mug of piss.

That mug.

I try to believe that it's gone. I picture a maid swiping it, disgusted, scouring it clean, dousing it with bleach. I picture a golden retriever—people with summer homes, they love their great big dogs—and he's sniffing around, pawing at the mug, and he knocks it over and his master calls and he runs and my urine seeps into the floorboards and I am safe. I picture a Salinger child playing hide-and-seek. The mug gets knocked over. I'm safe. I see a Salinger cousin, cunty, texting, absentmindedly throwing shoes into the closet, losing her shit when a full mug soaks her precious Manolos, her Tory Burch sandals. She trashes the shoes. I am safe.

I hear the door slam. Jenks is on foot. He might ask me to step out of the car. He might lie to me. He might try to trick me. He might ask Amy to step out of the car. He wears cologne, poor guy, and he hands me my license and the rental registration.

"Sorry about the holdup," he says. "You know, they give us these computers and half the time they're jammed up."

"Technology," I sigh. Free. *Free!* "It's the end of us all, right?"

"All the more reason I'd like you to use that blinker," he quips.

I smile. "I'm truly sorry, Officer."

Jenks asks us if we live *right in the city* and I tell him it's quieter in Brooklyn and everything is going to be okay. I am blessed. I smell Jenks's hopeful body spray. I see his small life, it's all in his eyes, unlived, dreams he didn't chase, dreams he won't chase, not because he's a pussy, because he simply doesn't see his dreams in detail, the kind of details that drive a person to pack their shit, to move. He became a cop because of the simplicity of the uniform; you don't have to think about what to wear every day.

"You have fun," he says. "Be safe."

I pull back onto the road and I'm relieved that my day, my life, doesn't end here. I have one hand on the wheel and I maneuver the other under Amy's cutoffs. I see our turn up ahead, the one that leads to Little Compton. I don't want the police anywhere in my future and I accept that I fucked up, that I left one loose end, and I will never, ever do that again.

This time, when I turn, I use my fucking *blinker.*

3

WE stop at Del's Lemonade and sit at a picnic table, toasting with lemon slushie cups. Amy shrugs. "It's fine," she says. "But honestly, this isn't *that* good, you know?"

I love her contrarian way. "People think everything is better when they're on vacation."

"Yelp Nation," she says. "Miserable people want to call it a one-star slushie and insecure people want everyone to be jealous of them and be all, 'best slushie everrrr.'"

Sometimes I wish she could have met Beck. "Wow," I say. "You just described my ex to a T."

She smacks her lips. "Which one?"

It's vacation, so I let loose. I tell her a little about Beck even though you're not supposed to talk about your old girlfriend with the new one.

"So she was an Ivy League chick?" she asks. "Was she snobby?"

"Sometimes," I say. "But mostly she was sad."

"You know, most of the people who go to those schools, they are psycho because they spend their whole childhoods *trying* to get into those schools. They can't live in the moment."

I will fuck her on this table right here, right now. "You are so right," I say. "Did you ever date anyone like that?"

She shakes her head. "You can show me yours, but I don't want to show you mine."

She is the only woman left who knows the value of mystery. She tosses her slushie into a trash bin and we lie back on the table, watching the branches above us sway.

"Talk," she says. "Tell me."

I start at the beginning, in the shop, Beck without her bra—Amy says that's attention seeking—and Beck buying her Paula Fox—Amy says that was to impress me—and this is where Amy is so beautiful and unusual. She doesn't interrupt me to tell her own story or slip into a jealous rant. She listens to me and she is a sponge. It's cathartic for me to describe Beck's viciousness, and this is why you need to get in a car and go sometimes. I don't think we could have had this conversation in New York. I feel so aware with Amy, and she just gets it when I tell her about Beck Tweeting from Bemelmans Bar, the way she had to look up *solipsistic* in the dictionary. When I tell her that Beck referred to Little Compton as *LC,* she kicks the air. She gets it. All of it. I am known. She turns her head.

"You guys came here together?" Her voice is higher, suspicious.

"No," I say. And technically I'm not lying. I followed Beck here. There's a difference.

I tell her about the way Beck cheated on me with her shrink.

"How terrible," Amy says. "How did you find out?"

I held her prisoner and broke into her apartment and found the evidence on a MacBook Air. "I just had a feeling," I lie, because it's also sort of true. "So I asked her and she told me and then that was it. We broke up."

She strokes my leg. I tell her to Google Nicholas Angevine and she does and she scans the headlines and she looks at me, horrified. "He killed her?"

"Yep," I say. And it's impressive. I framed him for the murder so effectively that I don't even *exist* in the Wikipedia page about the crime. "He murdered her and he buried her near his family's second home upstate."

She shudders. "Do you miss her?"

"No," I say. "I feel sorry for her, of course. But it wasn't good between us, you know? And when you came along, I mean, it sounds sick, but that was like, well, then I really didn't miss her anymore."

She bumps her knee into mine. "That's sweet." She promises me she won't cheat on me with a shrink. She is wary of physicians and psychiatrists, "people who thrive on other people's pain."

God, I love her brain, all pink and mushy and suspicious. I kiss her.

"I'll be right back," she says and she leaves her purse with me and crosses the parking lot to the restroom. She walks for me and she turns back and winks, same way she does in the shop. When she disappears into the restroom I take her phone out of her purse.

I'm never afraid of what I'm going to find when I look through her phone. I just want to know everything. It's like that guy in that old Julia Roberts movie who loves to watch her try on hats and dance around to "Brown Eyed Girl." Nothing in Beck's phone ever made me smile, but rummaging through Amy's always reaffirms the way I feel about her. The first item in her Google search history is *Henderson sucks.* She is reading recaps of his talk show *F@#k Narcissism*, the one we hate-watch a couple of times a week, where he sits on the couch and the guests sit at the desk. The hook is that he's sitting on the couch because he's a *narcissist* who only wants to talk about himself, but every interview obviously devolves into talk about whatever shitty movies the *guest host* is promoting. She says Henderson's success is proof that our culture is edging toward a cannibalistic apocalypse.

"What are you doing?"

I startle and nearly drop Amy's phone. I look up guiltily as her shadow falls over me. She's standing, arms crossed, eyes narrowed.

Fuck. I swallow. I am caught.

"Amy," I say, clenching her phone. "I know what this looks like but this isn't that."

She holds out her hand. "Gimme my phone."

"Amy," I plead. "I'm sorry."

She looks away. I give her the phone and I want her to sit with me but she crosses her arms again. Her eyes are wet. "And I was literally just thinking how happy I am with you."

"I'm sorry," I say again.

"Why are you snooping around?" she demands. "Why are you ruining this?"

"It's not like that," I tell her, reaching out.

"No," she says, waving me off. "I get it. You don't trust me. And why should you? I'm the one who showed up with a stolen fucking credit card the first day I met you. Of course you don't trust me."

"But I do trust you," I say, and how strange the truth sounds. "I'm looking in your phone because I'm fucking crazy about you and when you go in the bathroom I miss you." I get onto my knees and grovel. "Amy, I swear. I have never been so crazy about anyone and I know this is crazy. But I love you. Even when you're in the bathroom, I just want more."

At first there is nothing. She is blank. And then she sighs and scruffs my hair. "Get up."

We settled back on the bench as a family emerges from a minivan, loud, sandy. Five minutes ago, we would have been cracking jokes about them. Now we are somber. I nod toward them.

"You and I didn't grow up like that and we're a little messed up because of it," I say. "It's hard for people like us to trust each other, but I do trust you."

She watches the mother squirt lotion onto the kids. "Okay," she says. "That's fair. About the shitty childhoods and the trust."

I hold her hand as we watch the father try to reason with his unreasonable four-year-old son, telling him he can't have another slushie because he won't have any room for hot dogs at the barbecue. The kid shrieks. He doesn't *want a hot dog—he wants a slushie.* The mother comes around and squats and hugs the child and says *please tell Mommy what you want.* The child screams *slushie* and the father says the mother is spoiling the child and the mother says it's important to communicate with kids and respect their own desires. It's like watching TV and when they disappear back into the minivan, the show is over.

Amy puts her head on my shoulder. "I like you."

"You're not pissed at me?"

"No," she says. "I'm the same way. Sometimes I can't believe how alike we are."

I stiffen. "You've looked in my phone?" *CandaceBenjiPeachBeck-MugofUrine.*

She laughs. "No," she says. "But if you would ever leave your phone, I totally would. I'm not very good at trusting people either."

I nod. "Look. I don't wanna be that guy. But we can get better."

She squeezes my hand. "I might fuck up."

Being together is the best feeling in the world, better than sex, better than a red convertible or that first *I love you.*

"Yeah?" I ask.

"Yeah," she says, and mimicking is a sign of love.

This was a good idea, this trip. We get more slushies for the road and get back into the 'Vette. There's been an atomic meltdown and we're the only two people left on Earth and this is why people shouldn't commit suicide, because maybe, someday, you might get to sit in the shade with someone who is *refreshingly different!* I make her laugh so hard that she has slushie spilling out of the corners of her mouth. And then we drive away and find a quiet spot and I eat her out and when I finish I have her spilling out of the corner of *my* mouth. Your vacation is not the best vacation ever. Mine is. I earned it. She caught me sneaking around in her phone and still she spread her legs.

When we get to the hotel, she gasps. "Wow."

And when we walk into the room and onto the terrace, I don't gasp. I knew we were close, but I didn't realize I'd be able to see it so clearly—the Salinger cottage, twinkling, lit by fireworks, full of people. People who may or may not have seen my mug. Amy nods toward the house. "Do you know those people?"

"One of them," I tell her. "They're the Salingers."

I tell Amy about Peach's dysfunctional friendship with Beck and her inevitable suicide. Amy wraps her arms around me and if this were a cartoon, I could stretch my rubber arm all the way across the beach, into that house, up those rickety stairs, into that bedroom, reclaim my mug of urine, and then, then I would have it all.

4

THE next day we hit the beach with Ralph Lauren towels. We sit near the Salingers'. I figure maybe, *maybe,* I can ask to use their bathroom. *We* can ask to use a bathroom. Nobody is going to say no to Amy and while she's making small talk I can go upstairs. It's a reach but it's all I've got.

"Whoa," she says, shielding her eyes with her hands. "He looks *pissed.*"

I turn. A Salinger man whistles and storms toward us. My balls crawl back inside of me. Amy groans. "They're as bad as you said."

"Let's be calm."

But he's not calm. He's spitting. "This beach is private," he snarls. Families fascinate me; Peach is dead, but there is her nose, her frizzy hair. "You need to be on the other side of the sand."

You can't be on the other side of the sand and Amy peels off her shirt like she's Phoebe Cates in *Fast Times at Ridgemont High*. "I'm so sorry," she says. "Did you want to let us know about anything else?"

She smiles at him and he's staring at her body and she's a fucking genius. He skulks back to his ugly wife and Amy laughs. "Can we get in the water already?"

"I need to warm up," I say, but really I need to do recon on the Salingers. There are so fucking many of them, romping on their *trampolines* on the water, on the sand, as if the sand and the waves and the *cottage* aren't enough. Children scamper and older Salinger men in madras shorts with short-sleeve shirts talk Vineyard Vines, golf courses in Ireland, reunions. The women bitch about nannies and salesgirls and a waitress they all think is after their chubby husbands. You would never know that this family lost their *daughter*, their *sister*, their *auntie*. They are on vacation in every sense of the word and their only purpose is to alert passersby that they can't use the trampoline or sit too close. I have never seen such a family of cunts, living for barricades. We've already been yelled at and I am not getting in that house today.

So fuck it.

I grab Amy and throw her over my shoulder and she screams and the Salingers glare, jealous of us, young, poor, in *love*. I carry her toward the water, the same water where I disposed of Peach, the same shore where she washed up months later after her tragic so-called suicide. Amy wraps her legs around me and envious Salinger men watch, wish, drink. We stay like this, glued in Peach's ocean grave and by the time we get out of the water, most of the Salingers have retreated into the house. It's colder now and we put on sweaters and Amy reaches into her beach bag and pulls out a children's book called *Charlotte & Charles*. "This was my favorite," she says. "Can I read it to you?"

"Of course."

She leans into me and the story goes like this: Two giants, a man and a woman, live on a desert island. The woman is lonely but the man feels safe. Humans arrive and while the woman is excited, the man is hesitant. The last time humans were there, everything went to shit. The humans tried to kill them. Charlotte wants to try again and Charles complies, but sure enough, the humans are ringing bells, the sound of which will kill Charlotte and Charles. But Charlotte and Charles wear earplugs to protect themselves.

There's an earthquake and Charlotte and Charles help the humans, then swim away to a new island. The second to last page of the book is a picture of the giants on an island together at night. Several years have passed. They look at the stars and Charlotte wishes that more people would come. Charles says that the people would do the same fucking thing and screw them over. Charlotte concedes that this is possible. But she also reminds him that he could be wrong. And in the corner of the page, there is a ship. People are coming.

Amy closes the book and smiles up at me. "Well?"

"That's one dark fucking book."

She smacks my leg. "You can't swear at *Charlotte and Charles*." She spins to face me. "Tell me what you think."

"I liked it," I say.

She nudges me. "Come on. What did you *think*?"

This feels like a test and it's supposed to be a vacation. I shrug. "I want to let it sit awhile. I don't like this culture of reading a book and spitting out an immediate reaction."

She tilts her head like a schoolteacher with a slow kid. "I see that," she says. "I've read it a hundred times and I've had my whole life to think about it." She shivers.

"Are you cold?"

She shoves the book into her bag and we leave the beach. I failed to retrieve the mug and I failed to understand *Charlotte & Charles* and walking on sand is just no fun. Ever.

Back at the hotel, we shower together, I put my Charles in her Charlotte, and she helps me write back to the BuzzFeed guy. We bring Cajun scallops and buttery lobster rolls and cannolis to our room. We eat in the bed and we fuck in the bed and we laugh in the bed and we wake up bloated, happy.

I fuck Amy in the shower and in the *soaking* tub and on the balcony—her favorite, she tells me during what she calls *blueberries in bed*—and I fuck her on the sofa and then I fuck her on the love seat. I memorize her face, her trembling lips, *Oh Joe,* her legs quivering, clinging. She opens her mouth, my little seal. I pop a blueberry into that hole in her face, the one that takes my dick in a way that no mouth ever did before.

She winks. "Good shot."

We live here now, in this room, in these sheets, like a fucking John Mayer song come to life. We joke that they will cordon off this room when we go because nobody will ever occupy it the way we did. I love her more now than I did five minutes ago, more than I did five hours ago. I break the rules and tell her this because she is not like other girls.

"I know," she says. "Isn't it weird the way most people only get *more* annoying and you only get *less* annoying."

I jab her with a pillow. "I'm not annoying."

She shrugs teasingly and we bash each other with pillows and she pins me down and drops blueberries into my mouth and I plant my mouth on hers and we eat together, one mouth. I ask her about *Charlotte & Charles* and she tells me to forget it and I mark her body all over with my pulpy blue kisses. They'll have to throw away these sheets and when she comes, she screams and she throws a pillow across the room. It goes out the window, over the balcony.

She giggles. "So I guess that was what you call a one-pillow orgasm."

For a brief moment, I see Beck, the way she humped a green pillow. I smack Amy's ass. "By the end of the day, there won't be any pillows left in here," I say, ready to go again.

But she puts her hand on my chest. "Whoa," she says. "Joe, we do *have* to go out."

"We don't *have* to do anything," I say, and it must have been so much easier in the dark ages, before restaurants, when there was no fucking *Little Compton Coupon Guide* designed with the explicit purpose of interfering in our fuckfest.

"Here," she says, flipping through the coupon guide. "Scuppers by the Bay. They have a band."

"Do they deliver?" I try, and it's a waste of time.

She's out of bed telling me that I'll be thanking her after I've had a good meal. And that's how you know you're in love. You put on *slacks* and feign excitement over oysters and *live light rock* and you grab the keys and leave.

Scuppers by the Bay is overstuffed with assholes. The lot is jammed and the valets look stoned. There's a sixteen-thousand-piece cover band tooling away in the back—murdering Tina Turner's "What's Love Got to Do with It"—and the clamor in the kitchen is matched by a screaming spoiled baby at a nearby table with spoiled parents fussing over skewered scallops. We don't have a reservation and the coupon is not valid tonight and we are told to wait at the bar for one hour, maybe two.

I suggest we go but Amy nods toward a couple at the bar. They're overdressed, he's swishing his wine in his glass and she's drinking something blue. I don't want to talk to them but when Amy whispers to follow her lead I start to get hard. She dabs gloss on her lips. "Okay," she says. "We're gonna pretend to be other people and we're gonna glom onto them."

"Seriously?"

Her eyes flash. "You be Kev and I'll be Lulu."

We really are the same. I like fake names, but I'm used to it being a means of survival or escape, like when Officer Nico believed that I was Spencer Hewitt because of my Figawi hat.

"I don't know, Amy," I say, fucking with her. "Lulu sounds pretty fucking made-up."

She claps, excited, and we decide to be Kev and Mindy from Queens. "I'm a chef and you're an aspiring actor."

"An actor?" It stings. Why not a director? Or doctor?

She cups my chin in her hand. "Well, you're too hot to do anything else, honey."

I would like to take her into the handicap bathroom and fuck her brains out but she has already started in on the *nice* couple. When a woman wants to socialize, no penis in the world can replace meaningless conversation about iPhone autocorrects—*ducked! Hahahaha*—and rental car *snafus.* So we pair off with Pearl and Noah Epstein. They're also from New York—*that's so crazy!!!*—and they're both lawyers and they're actually likable, funny. When we shake hands, Noah says, "Hi, that's Pearl, I'm Noah and we're what Grammy Hall would call real Jews."

We talk about Woody Allen and then we also meet Harry and Liam Benedictus. Harry is short for Harriet—yawn—she's a financial planner and he's a broker. They have *two under three* and they're uptight, but they're also full of compliments. Liam *freaking loves movies* and wants to hear about my career. We talk small—*how funny is it when your mom texts?!*—and I make up shit about my kooky mom sending me Crock-Pot recipes. Amy talks about how *her* mom thinks LOL means Lots Of Love, and our new friends think we're *so freaking funny.*

The conversation drifts to terrible places at times, the ups and downs of the NASDAQ, but we survive. In this bar, lying to these strangers, there has never been more honesty between us. We are closer with every lie, undercover together, fusing. Amy talks about her imaginary father, the one who sends her articles about Rachael Ray. She is vulnerable and we needed this, pretending to be people with parents, parents who text and call and love and ask for help with attachments. The hostess says we can sit now if we're all willing to squeeze into a booth and I want to squeeze my dick into Amy and she is clapping. She *loves* booths. All women love booths.

On the way over, Amy whispers, "Wasn't I right?"

"Yes," I say. "This is a fucking blast."

I get to sit beside Amy, our legs pressed together. She raps her knuckles on the table and starts a game. "Okay, okay," she says. And every man in this restaurant would trade his woman for Amy. "Favorite movie sex scene. I go first. *The Town.*"

I've heard this all before, how much Amy likes Ben Affleck and Blake Lively together. I slide a hand underneath her skirt and she doesn't object and I move that hand underneath her panties, onto her ass cheek.

Noah worships that British newsy from HBO—how surprising—and sends the undercooked scallops back to the kitchen and Pearl knocks over her *Chablis* and says it's because she has *schpilkas*. Harry *crafts* jewelry and sells it on Etsy. The waiter returns with scallops and I take the first bite and I nod. "They're ducking perfect."

Everybody in our party cackles at my stupid, easy joke and we could be friends in real life. It would be a long Swiffer commercial with dogs and potlucks in Park Slope. I start to wish they didn't think of me as an aspiring actor named *Kevin*. But then if they knew that we were both high school graduates who never went to college, if they knew we worked in *retail*, these people wouldn't be friends with us anyway. I squeeze Amy's thigh; that's what's real, my take-home.

Amy says I'm *for sure going to make it as an actor* and Pearl says I have *one of those faces*. Her husband laughs and Amy's eyes glisten and she got a little too much sun today. I wish I could hit PAUSE and stay here in this moment, with the light fading. This is what all the love songs are about, the moment when you find your own way forward with someone and there is no turning back.

Amy winks at me and gets out of the booth to request a song—"Paradise City" by Guns N' Roses—and the band doesn't know it and she's pouting while our new fake friends are discussing the menu. I kiss her cheek. "You're sweet."

"What's that for?"

I stroke her thigh and move my hand up to where the jungle used to be. "I get it."

She is puzzled. "Huh?"

"'Paradise City,'" I say. "Guns N' Roses, like the first time, when you welcomed me to the jungle."

Her face is blank. Pearl wants to know if we prefer calamari or clams casino and Amy says *both* and she doesn't remember our Guns N' Roses connection. She's not as smart as I am, but maybe it's better that we're a little different.

When it's time to deal with the check, Amy pulls the valet ticket out of my pocket. She excuses herself to go to the bathroom and then I pretend to get a phone call and step outside. We latch onto each other and the valet delivers the 'Vette and we're gone and it's like we were never even there.

"I do feel kind of bad," I say. I liked Pearl & Noah & Harry & Liam.

"Oh please," she sighs. "When you split a check like that, it's almost easier if half the people disappear, you know?"

When we get back into the room, she brings her blueberries into the bed and she fellates me with her superfruit mouth and I smush blueberries on her tits. I want to talk about our lies and our parents and *Charlotte & Charles* but she says we should sleep because of the drive back tomorrow. I know she's right but at the same time, I can't stand the idea of being asleep and missing one second of our life together.

While Amy snores, I walk out on the deck and see the lights on upstairs at the Salinger house. Fuck that mug. It doesn't scare me anymore. I have a partner now, and this time, I'm leaving it behind on purpose.

5

THE ride home is always different from the ride out. We're both a little burned out, a little hungover. We don't want to stop at Del's for slushies and we agree that lemon ice is precisely the sort of thing that sounds great when you start the vacation, but not what you want on the way home. We hit traffic. We laugh about our fake friends and we forgot to find out the brand of the sheets at the hotel. She holds my hand randomly, as if to say, *I can't believe you're real.* This is love, this is Sunday, and when we get back into the city, she strokes my neck.

"Will you hate me if I just kind of want my own bed?"

"I could never hate you," I respond.

We make it to her street and I signal with my blinker and she laughs and that will be a running joke for us, that time we rented that red Corvette and got pulled over for not using a fucking *blinker.* I can't wait to be old with her. I put the car in park. She kisses me.

"Thank you," she says. "I hope you know how wonderful you are."

I hold on to her and breathe her in. Someone behind us honks. I wave the asshole around and Amy climbs out. At the rental joint, the guy asks me if I had any trouble with the car. It is with great pleasure that I tell him *we* had absolutely no trouble at all. He looks at me like I'm crazy and it's okay because I am. I am crazy in love.

The next morning, I can't get to the shop fast enough. I can't wait to see Amy. I can't wait to tell her that I found Pearl & Noah & Harry & Liam online. I can't wait to find out if she watched *F@#k Narcissism* last night and if so what she thought of Kevin Hart. I wonder what panties she's wearing today and I'm excited to see if this shaving business continues.

I quicken my stride and I reach the shop but the music in my head ends abruptly. The door is slightly ajar. If Amy came in early she would have closed the door and Mr. Mooney hasn't been to the store in years. I yank the door open and step inside. I see dust particles in the air and my nose adjusts to the shop, the way a place smells different when you return after a few days. My senses are on fire and we've been robbed and I don't want this kind of distraction after such a good weekend.

The violets I bought Amy are on the floor, scattered, dry, the vase in pieces. There are papers everywhere, books tipped over. My laptop is gone. I tip-toe around the counter and quietly remove the machete from my hiding spot below the main entrance. I haven't held it in a while and it's heavier than I remember.

I am not calling the cops—they are not all Jenks and I've learned my lesson. I creep toward the back of the shop, checking the stacks to my left, to my right. I move past FICTION and BIOGRAPHY and at the back of the shop, the basement door is ajar too. The silence of the shop bears down on my brain. They are long gone, I think. But if they are still here I'm slicing their throats. I clench the machete as I descend the stairs slowly, soundlessly. When I reach the bottom step, I gasp and drop it. I don't need it anymore.

There is nobody here, but someone *was* here all right, someone who eats *superfruits.* There's a bowl on the floor next to the gaping hole where the yellow wall of *Portnoy's Complaint*s used to be.

Amy.

She stole every last copy, didn't even leave one for me. She took the Yates first edition too, the one she blew me for, the one that started it all. There's a blueberry-stained copy of *Charlotte & Charles* on the floor, right next to my computer and the pink keys, the ones I made for her. I grab my phone and call her and of course this number is now dead, out of service, gone, just like all the others.

I drop to my knees and scream. She left me. She stole from me. I bought that bullshit about her needing her own bed and she must have come here right after I dropped her off. I throw her superfruits at the wall. *Supercunt.*

I pick up *Charlotte & Charles.* I understand the meaning of that fucking book now. Don't trust women. Ever. I open it and there is a message scribbled inside:

Sorry, Joe. I tried. But we really are the same. We both hold back. We both lose control. We both have secrets. Be good to you. Love, Amy.

I haven't made a comprehensive list of everything she took, but so far, I estimate $23,000 in rare books. She knew what she was doing the day she walked in here, and I fell for it. I should be dragged into a field and shot for being so fucking stupid, dick-blind, cock-sucked. *We're the same*, she said. Fuck me. Fuck her.

She pulled the wool over my eyes with her latex gloves and her dick-sucking eyes. This was never love, not on the beach in Little Compton, not in this cage, not in my bed. The bitch came here to trick me, to rob me, and I made her fucking keys.

I grab the laptop and get the fuck out of this fucking cage and I lock it—a little late, asshole—and I trudge up the stairs and I lock the basement door—what a fucking asshole I am, I should lock *myself* in the basement—and that's when I see another mess. Amy ransacked my least favorite section of the shop: DRAMA. She stole acting manuals:

An Actor Prepares

10 Ways to Make It in Hollywood

How to Make Them Call You Back

Monologues for Women Volume IV

Are you fucking kidding me, you lying thieving hairy-legged beast? My head spins. Amy was not an untrained sociologist, wearing college paraphernalia to experiment on human behavior. She was not lying to Noah & Pearl & Harry & Liam. She was *acting*. Why else would she steal those manuals?

I sit down at the counter and wake up the laptop. She claims to be so *off the grid* and above this computer shit, but she managed to erase the recent search history. My cheeks sting at the idea of her on that floor, trying to block me, trying to clear the search she conducted on *my* computer. Well, she should have learned a little bit more about how these machines work, what they can do for me. Chrome isn't that simple. She only cleared the last hour of her time on my computer, not the whole fucking history. I know my recent searches—rare books and motels in Little Compton—and it's not exactly difficult to shine the light on her key fucking words:

UCB, cheapest headshots, free headshots, UCB classes cheap, Ben Affleck, top dollar used books, selling rare books, Philip Roth price, auditions, casting calls, blond girl next door audition, sublet Hollywood

She also didn't clear her fucking downloads and I bring up her application to an Improv 101: Improv Basics class at Upright Citizens Brigade and a script for some short fucking film with a cover page that references a Craigslist ad. So the bitch has run away to try to make it in Hollywood. *Making It in Hollywood* is the most disgusting phrase in the English language. It's more disturbing than *prolific serial killer* and *rare terminal illness.* I can't wait to catch her and tell her what a deluded loser she is.

I print her search history and there is nothing more terrifying than realizing that the one who knows you best loves you least, pities you even. She knew I was fucked up and alone. She knew I wanted a blowjob and a girlfriend and she knew I wanted these things so badly that I would let her watch *Cocktail* fifty times a fucking week in my bed, that I would give her a fucking a key. I did that and I can't undo it. But I can find her. I can eliminate her.

And I will. She doesn't get to walk around thinking she got away with this. Fuck no. She doesn't get to think that I'm a sucker who you can fuck over and dump with *Charlotte & Charles.* I lapped her nipples with my tongue and I ate her hairy bush and she used me. She is evil. She is dangerous. She is incapable of love. She is a sociopath. Worse than a borderline. That's why she uses fucking burner phones. She's a criminal.

She thinks she's so smart but if you erase an hour, it doesn't mean shit, not unless you erase the weeks leading up to that hour. She thinks life is better off the grid. Yeah. She'll die thinking that. Cunt. I call JetBlue. I buy a ticket. Sorry, Amy. You lose.

6

IF there's one thing I learned from that horny charlatan Dr. Nicky Angevine and his patient/mistress Beck, it's that you can't control what other people do. You can only control your thoughts. If there's a mouse in your house you have to make it your business to remove that pest, set the traps, check the traps. Amy is my mouse, but this is *my* house and I'm deep into the extermination process already. I called the UCB and claimed to be a guy named Adam checking on my registration. This is how I was able to confirm that there is a girl named *Adam, Amy* reserved for an improv class.

I gave notice on my lease. Fuck that shithole and it's time I got the hell out of here, out of my apartment where I bring the wrong women into my bed, cold city girls—their hearts are hard and pale—and I can't become one of those New Yorkers who lets the city win. I won't sit behind the counter of that fucking shop the next time some chick walks in and bats her eyelashes at me. I'm fucking done.

It's June and the city is ripe with meaningless fecal heat. It will be a different kind of hot in LA, the kind that made the Beach Boys all tan and giddy, a heat that doesn't harass you in the shade.

I get on the train and begin my last humid, smelly ride to Mr. Mooney's. I thought about writing him a letter or calling him, but it's been too many years. I owe him a good-bye. My trip ends, finally, and I leave the train where a mariachi band sets up and hoochies take selfies. Good-bye, subway people.

A guy in a suit emerges from a deli across the street with fresh roses, running, trying, believing. Idiot. I walk into the butcher and pick up Mr. Mooney's favorite sausages. I hope he doesn't cry. I hope he doesn't try to lock me in his basement. I turn the corner and knock on his door.

He doesn't smile. "Don't tell me we got robbed again?

"No such luck, Mr. Mooney." I laugh. He was almost happy when I called and told him about the robbery. He said that insurance money is *the most beautiful kind of money there is in this world.*

"Well, what's wrong then?" he jabs.

"Nothing," I insist. I hold up the sausages. "You hungry?"

He pushes open the screen door and waves me in. His house smells like kitty litter and old ladies and he doesn't have a cat or a wife. He has two eggs on the stove and the radio on.

He puts my sausages in the old fridge. "You want some coffee milk?" he asks.

Nope. "Sure!"

He shakes the powdered concoction and sets a small chipped glass down on the table in front of me. He talks about a pillow he bought off an infomercial, how the dame on the phone said he couldn't return it because thirty days had passed. He talks about the eggs at his local market. They used to be cheaper but now they're ridiculously priced because they're from some farm nearby. "In which case, they should be cheaper," he rails. He waves his saggy arm. I don't want to be like this someday, alone, frying eggs, eating local food in a stingy rage. But at the same time, I can't imagine ever loving anyone ever again.

Mr. Mooney finishes frying the eggs and sits down with me at the table. The eggs are overcooked, glistening. I think he used a pound of butter and I don't think he's cleaned the skillet since 1978. "So to what do I owe this honor?" he asks.

I drink my coffee milk. By some miracle, I keep it down. "Well," I say. "I've decided I need a change. I'm moving to Los Angeles."

He burps. It's wet. Flappy shards of eggs fly out of his mouth. "What's her name?"

"Whose name?"

"The girl," he says. "Nobody moves anywhere unless it's about a girl."

I hesitate, then tell him about Amy, her desire to be an actress, the way she kept it from me. I don't tell him that she was the thief.

"I knew there was a girl." He dips his finger into the ketchup on his plate and licks it off. "You might be wiser to let her go."

I shake my head. "This is something I have to do."

Mr. Mooney sighs. "Tip the world over on its side and everything loose will land in Los Angeles."

"Frank Lloyd Wright said that."

"He was right." Mr. Mooney rises from his seat and tosses his rank sponge in the sink. "Los Angeles is the seat of evil, Joseph. It's the womb of idiocy. It's where everything bad comes from, the peak of the volcano of this nation's stupidity. It's no place for an intelligent man. That's why there's nothing to watch on the damn television set. You're better off here." He'll never say it but he's going to miss me.

"I'll give you my e-mail address so we can keep in touch."

He takes my plate and stacks it on his. I know if I offer to do the dishes he'll be pissed. "E-mail is baseless," he dismisses me. "Just promise me you won't waste your life on a damn computer."

I say I'll see him again soon and a cockroach scampers by and he stomps on it with his boot. "You don't know that," he says. "There's no way you could know that." He tells me to lock the door on my way out. "Goddamn Girl Scouts are pushier than ever."

MY apartment is empty. Everything I'm taking with me is in my dad's giant duffel bag, the one I've never used because I've never gone so far away, never had an occasion to pack up everything I want, my books, my clothes, my pillow, my computer. There's a knock at my door and I don't check the peephole, figuring it's the landlord to complain about the damage. But no. It's Mr. Mooney, in sunglasses. I can't see his eyes.

"Word of advice," he begins. "Get your dick sucked."

"Okay."

"Get your dick sucked," he repeats. "Don't sleep with actresses. Don't waste your time with In-N-Out burgers. Don't watch too many movies. Don't eat too many vegetables. Don't refer to vegetables as veggies. Don't go in the pool. It's cold and dirty. Don't go in the ocean. It's cold and dirty. Don't have a child. Most born there become whores."

"I got it."

He stares at my unplugged refrigerator. "Is the shop locked up?"

"Yes," I declare. "Bolted, shut down."

"Good," he says, and he smiles. "Maybe I'll run away too."

"Do you want to come in, have a seat?"

But there's nowhere to sit. He reaches into his breast pocket. He pulls out a thick envelope and hands it to me.

I protest. "I can't take this."

"Yes, you can," he says. "You'll need it."

He ambles down the stairs, and I realize I might never see him again. I gather my things and slip the key under the door. A fat kid on the first floor asks where I'm going.

"California," I say.

"Why?" he asks.

"To make the world a better place," I answer. I give the kid some books, none of them rare, all of them important. The kid is grateful and I'm noble and it's true. I am gonna make the world a better place. That kid is already leafing through *Lord of the Flies*. Next up: Amy, hog-tied, sinking to the bottom of a swimming pool. *California.*

7

I don't read during the flight to LAX. I don't watch a movie. I fuck around on Facebook—I finally joined for real, as Joe Goldberg, as me—but it's not what you think it is. I *have* to fuck around on Facebook. I'm a hunter going on a wild safari and I need guides on my trek through this small segment of the foothills of Hollywood known as Franklin Village. I need camouflage. I need *friends* and it's not the worst thing in the world to need people. I am inspired by the *Fast & Furious* movies where the heroes Toretto and O'Conner can't hunt the bad guys without first assembling a team. I need help finding Amy, the same way they need help finding a corrupt Brazilian drug lord. And I can say this for the aspirings in the Upright Citizens Brigade: They're an open bunch. They accept *Joe Goldberg, writer* as a friend, and these people talk a lot. About the dry cleaner and Tinder and their shoes and their auditions. And *yes*, they talk about someone they refer to as *Amy Offline*.

The best resource so far is a guy named Calvin, who works at a used bookstore right next to the UCB. He posted a job listing for someone to pick up shifts and I wrote to him. I think I have the job; none of the other *dudes* he knows have experience with a register. I ask him about rare books, if he ever sees any original editions of *Portnoy's Complaint.* Maybe Amy already started moving her inventory. He writes back:

LOL dude we get like one valuable book a year. Mostly people who live up Beachwood dump their moldy shit when they move or their parents die or whatever. Or like people on the block are broke and they try to sell stuff but it's supereasy mostly it's like you get like a couple bucks it's superchill dude.

In addition to Facebook and Twitter, Calvin has a website where he reveals everything you could ever want to know about him. He's an aspiring writer-director-actor-producer-sound designer-comic-improv player. Can you imagine yearning for attention so badly that your identity required all those hyphens? He worships Henderson and Marc Maron and suspenders and beards and pictures of beards and Tinder and bacon and *Breaking Bad* and things from the '80s. In Brooklyn this guy would be working at a branding firm. He would be playing poor and checking his 401(k) late at night. But Calvin has a PayPal account where "fans" can help him pay rent. I could never respect Calvin, but he's easy and grateful that I'm willing to fill in when he needs to audition.

I order a Sprite Zero and vodka. My second most useful Facebook friend is an older aspiring stand-up comic named *Harvey Swallows.* I applied for an apartment near UCB in a building called *Hollywood Lawns.* Harvey's the manager, and when I e-mailed him about the apartment, he responded with a Facebook friend request and invitation to be his fan. *Angelenos.* Harvey is the West Coast equivalent of my old coworker Exclamation Point Ethan. Harvey is another open book with his website: He changed his name to Harvey Swallows and moved to LA to be a comic at the "ripe young age of fifty-seven." His catchphrase is *Am I right or am I right?* He's big into *#ThrowbackThursday* and he's shared so many photos of his old life in Nebraska, when he was married and selling insurance and growing sick with aspirations. Note to self: Do *not* get sick with aspirations. They eat your brain and trick your heart and you wind up on a stage in a basement saying unfunny things and waiting for someone to laugh.

Nobody is laughing and/or paying Harvey to say funny things, so he manages forty-five units at Hollywood Lawns. The place is a nice change of pace for me. I get off Facebook and look at pictures of my new home. There is a pool—I could hold Amy under the water—and there is a hot tub—I could boil the bitch—and there is a *game room*—I can choke her with a pool stick—and it's within walking distance of everything I could ever want. Including, of course, Amy.

She may not be on Facebook but you can't pursue an acting career in LA without the Internet. A girl like Amy, a brand-new sociopath with no agent, no connections, she would start looking for work on Craigslist. Anyone can post a casting call on the site and actors submit their pictures and résumés *constantly*, according to Calvin. So I write a casting call, specifically designed to appeal to Amy's overweening ego.

SUBJECT: Are you taller and more beautiful than the girl next door?

BODY: Indie feature seeks lead actress. Stunning & blond. 5′7–5′11. Age 25–30. Reply back with photos/résumé.

I am astounded by the speed of it all. Within a few minutes, I have dozens of girls sending me pictures. My hands shake every time I open an e-mail from a girl. Some are *naked*, some are ugly, some are even gorgeous, but none of them are the supercunt.

I order another vodka and Sprite Zero and the two girls across the aisle talk about *the Bar Method*—they love it—and *carbs*—they hate them—and *directors*—they want to know them. I wonder if Amy would become that kind of person in LA if I don't kill her first. Part of me wants to tell her about the assholes on the plane but more of me wants to scream at her, to hold her accountable for everything she did but I can't, not yet. I open a Word document and write to myself.

> *DEAR Supercunt, You are a vile evil thing and I wish you never walked into my life with your gloves and your bullshit.* Cocktail *is crappy because the protagonist is ultimately rewarded for being a shallow, gold-digging prick. You think that you're headed for something good. You're not. You're callow. Even when you shaved, your legs were stubbly. You were wrong to steal from those people in Little Compton. They're better than you. Blueberries are disgusting and you will die no matter what. You need a haircut. Your legs are too long. Your skin is a waste of space because there's no heart inside of you. You're too much of a pussy and a phony to be on Facebook. You suck a good dick. But you're not special. You're dead.*

The older woman next to me knocks on my tray table. She points at my screen. "Are you a writer?"

I save my document. I close it. "Yes. It's a monologue in this thing I'm writing."

She points at the headshots. "And directing? You're casting, right? I see pictures."

"Yep!" Boundaries: Where did they go? "Here's hoping."

She nods. "You know," she says. "If you're casting something, my niece lives in North Hollywood and she's *very* talented. You can see her at Gretchen Woods dot com."

So that's how it is here. I tell her that I'm making an adult movie and she gasps and whips her head toward the window, and maybe now she won't go around telling random guys how to find her niece online. But she's given me an idea. Being a writer is a great cover during my expedition. I'll say that I'm working on something called *Kev & Mindy Forever* and it will be about me and Amy and our last weekend in Little Compton. It will begin with Amy telling me that she can't sleep in her own bed and I know how it ends: me killing Amy.

I order another vodka and Sprite Zero and go back on Facebook. One of Calvin's friends, Winston Barrel, has requested my online friendship. He doesn't even know me. I accept friendship with Winston. I immediately receive an invitation to a comedy show along with 845 other people. This is good. When I pull Amy's extra-long body into an infinity pool and make it look like an accident—dare to dream!—I will be okay because I will have become a Facebook guy, a normal dude. We live in an era where people who don't have 4,355 friends are considered nefarious, as if socially entrenched citizens aren't also capable of murder. I need friends so that when Amy disappears, my *friends* can roll their eyes at the idea of handsome, gregarious Joe *killing* someone. I can't be that guy who "keeps to himself." That's too in-line with the dated but pervasive stereotype of a "killer" reinforced by biased TV "news" shows no matter how many happy-go-lucky husbands go and murder their wives. We all want to fear single people. It's endemic. It's American.

I click through my new Angeleno friends on Facebook. I love them; they are like kids, the way they just fucking *hope.* I hate them; they are like kids, the way they just fucking *hope.* I envy them. They don't sacrifice their bodies for bookstores and they don't waste their lives underground, riding subways and exposing themselves to chemicals and old shit. People move to LA to *make it.* They dream harder than people in New York and believe that ferociously socializing is critical, that life is all about "who you know."

And honestly, I don't hate Facebook as much as I thought I would. (Suck it, Amy. Sorry, Beck.) Once you're a member, there's a network in which you are the center, it's empowering. Humans are entertaining, fun to look at. So are cats. People are so lonely, they spend their birthdays on the Internet, thanking people for wishing them a happy birthday, people who only know it's their birthday because Facebook told them. I "Like" *Fast & Furious* to establish myself as a fun guy and then I write to Amy: *Dear Cunt, Facebook is only people trying to help each other from being lonely. Fuck you. Love, Joe.*

The pilot says we're almost here and I lean forward and see Los Angeles through the tiny window. The city is a grid, and like Amy's bush that first time I saw it, the thing fucking sprawls. I can't help but smile. Amy thinks she's *off the grid* but she has extremely traceable rare books and aspirations that require online socialization. I'll find her. I wish I could break open the window right now and parachute into Franklin Village, where I know she is, but then she might see me coming and that would be like whispering to the deer, *psst, I'm here*, right before shooting it.

8

THE first song I hear in LAX is that ditzy fucking Tom Tom Club song about getting out of jail and it sobers me up, hard. A UCLA brat bashes into me with her oversized suitcase. People are pushy and tourists are slamming into me, all of them on an exodus to get pictures of Sean Penn, who is in baggage claim. In New York, people fight to make a train to get home or to make it to the squished aisles of Trader Joe's. In LA, people fight to smell an actor, an old man.

I've received two electronic communications since I landed.

One is from Harvey: *Wow! You have perfect credit! Most people who move here have horrible credit!*

It is my destiny to know people who abuse punctuation. The other one is from Calvin: *We have a Blu-ray so bring any movies you wanna watch during shift.*

You aren't supposed to watch movies in a bookstore and I get into a cab and the driver taps the address of Hollywood Lawns into his GPS and I wonder if Amy took a cab or a shuttle. I wonder when the wondering will stop. I hate this part of the split, when that girl just *lives* in your head. I need to get laid and we take La Cienega and the city gets glitzier as you go north and I see women in nighttime dresses walking around in the day, like this is okay. I see homeless people like from *Down and Out in Beverly Hills* and I see the Capitol Records building and my heart quickens when we reach Franklin Avenue—Amy, Amy, Amy—and when I emerge from the cab I step into dog shit.

"Fuck," I seethe. My head pounds, the sun, the excessive vodka.

The driver laughs. "People in LA, man, they like their doggies."

Hollywood Lawns looks like the building in *Karate Kid* and the dogs trapped in the small hot apartments bark as I walk up the stairs. The FOR RENT sign beams: MONTH TO MONTH. I wonder if Amy lives here, in this very building. You never know. She is just the kind of lying transient who would gravitate toward this; her sublet in New York was *week to week.* I should have known then, but your dick makes you blind.

Harvey looks older in person, waxen, arched eyebrows. It's hard to look at him and I let him talk to me about his act and I agree to get drinks with him. He tells me my apartment is on the first floor, right by his office, and I brainstorm future excuses to avoid time with him. He warns me about ridiculous shit. "One thing you gotta know about the 'hood, newbie," he says. "This isn't New York. You can't be jaywalking. They will ticket you and those tickets will add up."

"I knew LA was an anti-walking city but that's fucking ridiculous," I say.

Harvey smiles. "You sound like me when I see Joe Rogan on TV. Downright ridiculous. Am I right or am I right?"

Conversations about Joe Rogan are not a part of my life so I don't encourage him, the way you don't laugh at a child who swears. "Hey," I say. "I saw the sign outside. Do you get a lot of people moving in all the time?"

"World's full of dreamers," he says. "Do you have friends looking?"

"Yeah," I say. And this is where I have to tread lightly. I don't want to say that I'm *looking* for Amy Adam because then, when she disappears, I will be a suspect. I am careful. "I know this girl looking," I say. "But she wants a share."

Fact: Amy has never had her own place. She's a leech.

Harvey nods. "If I had a nickel for every hot babe who moves in here to sleep on the couch and pay half the rent . . ." He shakes his head. "I'd be able to paper the walls with nickels! Am I right or am I right?"

Harvey introduces me to another guy in the building, Dez, entitled, thug-light. He lives on the first floor too, and he looks like an extra in an Eminem video circa 2000. Dez has a dog, Little D, and some advice for me.

He looks at me hard. "Do. Not. Fuck. Delilah."

I nod. "Word."

I need someone like this on my team, someone fluent in California '90s moron douchebag language who no doubt has access to Xanax and various narcotics.

Harvey digs up the keys to my new home and tells me that Delilah is just *sweet* and *friendly* and I know this means *desperate* and *slutty* and he says a lot of the guys in the building are crass. "It's kinda like I'm the talk show host and everybody comes into my office to work out their bits," he says. Why must everyone want to be Henderson?

"So you come by anytime, work stuff out. It's like a Seth MacFarlane vibe in here, ya know, Broseph?"

"Sounds great," I lie.

"Am I right or am I right?" he asks, as if he has a contract with himself to spew out his own catchphrase at least twice an hour.

My apartment smells like rotten oranges and chicken and it's full of pink furniture, girl furniture. The former tenant *Brit Brit* moved out suddenly, against her will.

"Her parents showed up here all upset," Harvey says, turning on a pink bubble-shaped lamp and illuminating a Kandinsky poster. "She spent half the money they gave her on a nose job and the rest on *nose candy* and then she wound up in a hospital cuz her *nose bled.*" He shakes his head and pats the hot pink futon. "I know there's a joke in there. Funny things come in threes. I'm gonna find it, I swear. Anyhoo, the good news is you scored, Broseph. The futon, the chicken in the freezer, the TV, it's all yours. Her parents wanted us to dump it."

At least I don't have to go to IKEA. "Great."

Harvey picks up the trash can. "I know one thing you don't want is *old* chicken. BRB, Broseph!"

It's the first almost funny thing he's said. I pull a Rachael Ray knife out of the new knife block on the counter. These are useful, sharp, though I wish the handles weren't orange. I flop onto the futon and the cover is stained, Sriracha and semen. That taped-up Kandinsky makes me miss New York. I miss sex. There is a knock at the door and then a girl barges in. She is like one of the girls I saw on the street. Full makeup and a bandage spandex dress that's one size too small. She is hot but not as hot as she thinks. I want her on my team, possibly on my dick.

"Relax," she says. "I'm Delilah and I'm just here for the blender."

I almost tell her that her nickname is Don't Fuck Delilah, but she is talking too much for me to get a word in edgewise. She is late to work—gossip reporting—and she lives directly upstairs—*apologies for noises you hear in the future, the walls are paper thin*—and that *fucking coke whore* promised her a blender. She's opening the closets, slamming them.

Delilah is full of rage. Maybe she knows there is a building ordinance against her vagina. She points at the Kandinsky. "Technically that's mine too," she says. "But I think you'll appreciate it. You look like you might even know who that is."

"Andrew Wyeth," I say.

She nods. "Nice," she says. "Brit Brit had no idea who that was. Did Shut-Up Harvey tell you about her?"

Everyone has a nickname. "A little," I say. "Sounds like a sad story."

Delilah tells me that Brit Brit came here to *act* and wound up hooking. "She would go to Vegas with guys and come back messed up," she says. "And she kept trying to get me to go with her, talking about how *amazing* these guys are and how you don't have to pay for anything and you stay at the Cosmo and have the time of your life."

"Hmm."

"Exactly," she says. "So I pack a bag to go with her. I mean, I know I'm not *actually* going but I wanted to see them all at the airport in case there was anyone famous in there, anyone I could write about. And at the airport, in one breath, she's like, 'Oh, by the way, you have to fuck at least two of them but you get to pick which two and it's not bad I swear!'"

"So which two did you pick?" I ask.

"Ha," she deadpans. "No. I told her I was gonna call the cops and her parents if she got on the plane."

"And did you make those calls?"

"Hell no," she says. "She flew back the next day and I picked her up and took her to Baskin-Robbins and let her cry."

I go to the kitchen and find the blender in the cabinet above the fridge. She looks me up and down. "So do you have a name?"

"Joe Goldberg," I say. "Do you?"

"I told you," she says.

"I know," I say. "But what's your real name?"

"Ugh," she says. "Melanie Crane. But not anymore. Melanie Crane is the girl who fucked up her master's in journalism by falling in love with a married guy at the *New York Times.*" She shudders. "That feels like a century ago. That's what I love about LA. It's all new. I'm an undercover reporter and a ghostwriter now. It's possible here to literally *leave* your past behind."

They all think this, these girls—Amy—that they can *leave your past behind.* Don't they know it's not that simple? It's not the past if it's not finished.

"You should give me your number," Delilah says as she cleans the blender. "I get so many invites to parties. You can be a plus one sometime, get off the block." She points at me. "Warning: You have to get off the block. People live here and they go to Birds and La Pou over and over again and there is so much more to this city." She sighs. "I mean it's important to get out there."

She explains that Birds is a bright, friendly dive bar and La Poubelle is a dark, hip French bar and that everyone in the Village skews one way or the other. I am reminded of the *Office* episode where B. J. Novak says he does not want an identity at work. And then he burns a pizza bagel and he has one: "Fire Guy." I am not a Birds guy or a La Pou guy, but I type my number into Delilah's phone. I may need her.

Delilah laughs. "I am being a bit of a hypocrite," she says, and I wonder if people in LA think out loud about themselves the way New Yorkers do quietly, in our heads. "I mean, I go to Birds almost every night and I even have a tattoo inspired by this song they play there. But the thing is, I go *late night*, after I've been other places, you know?"

She bends forward and rolls up her dress and encourages me to come closer so I can see her leg—close shave, self tanner—and there are words engraved on her inner thigh. Journey lyrics. As if they need to be on her thigh after they've been used in *The Sopranos* and *Glee* and every bar in America.

"I know it's lame," she says and she pats my head, ordering me to stand. "But you can't live here unless you believe."

Delilah is almost special, and it's a hard thing for a girl to be, not beautiful enough to be beautiful, not smart enough to be smart. Amy has it easy; she's taller, hotter, smarter. There's something so unsure about Delilah and she would never be friends with someone like Amy, who gets to cross her legs and eat blueberries with her greasy hair. Delilah is a girl who tries. Amy is a girl who takes. At the end of the day, trying is better. I know that now.

There's a quiet moment where Delilah and I could run away together and our dynamic would be set: I would inspire her to let go of the aspirations that are holding her down, *marking her body*. She would get me off Amy. But I want revenge and Delilah wants her blender. She waves. She goes. The end.

I download Journey. I picture Delilah's thigh pressed against my face and I jerk off on my pink futon. Afterward I shower and put on jeans—I refuse to wear shorts—and a T-shirt. I throw away Brit Brit's food (diseases, cocaine residue) and I stop by Harvey's office. He is taking a selfie and the trash can he didn't bring back is sitting there. This is so different from New York. I could go months without seeing a neighbor in my old building. But Harvey's office is a glass box. Everyone here wants so badly to be watched, noticed. And the upside is that the desire to be watched is a blindfold. Harvey doesn't even notice me as I walk by the door and begin my hunt for Amy.

9

THE self-serving sociopathic greedy little bitch wouldn't go a fucking *day* without her superfruits, so my first destination is the neighborhood grocery store, the Pantry. But this is not a grocery store. It's a modern art museum, part neon, part busted fender metal, and part repurposed wood signs. The floor is spongy and the font on the price tags is curly and the lighting is nonfluorescent. The music is louder than it is in a normal grocery store and the songs are all over the place, a true mixtape—Donny Hathaway and Samantha Fox and the Everly Brothers and DMX—and I Shazam it all because I want a record of this.

This is a grocery store if Cameron Crowe made grocery stores and the lighting is good, dim and clubby. Every aisle has a funny name. There's an aisle of *books* (BEFORE THEY WERE MOVIES), snacks (BAD THINGS ☺), spices (ROSEMARY & THYME), and processed cakes and cookies (SCRUMPTIOUS EMPTY CALORIES). The pet food aisle is jamming and that's called UNCONDITIONAL LOVE and the baby food aisle is called SEMI-UNCONDITIONAL LOVE.

Most of the girls here are like Amy, tall and scraggly with messy hair and baskets full of superfruits. This is where I'm going to find her. I know it. But I don't find her in the organic produce section (BECAUSE ME) or the section of cheaper produce (BECAUSE RENT). Fatboy Slim's "Talking 'Bout My Baby" comes on and when the hell do you hear that in a *grocery store*? I don't think you could ever get annoyed in here and maybe I could like LA, or at least this one part of it.

The flower section (I'M SORRY/I LOVE YOU) is a desert and maybe nobody loves anybody in LA. There are orchids and roses and then I see violets, more electric and purple than the ones I got for Amy.

A little rotund Mexican woman in a pale blue smock smiles. "They are painted, sir." She laughs. "God doesn't make these."

Of course He doesn't; these flowers are the botanical equivalent of breast implants. I thank her and move on and everyone in here is so *happy*.

My phone buzzes. Six consecutive texts, all of them images, all of them from Delilah. I open them one by one, screen grabs of invitations to Hollywood parties, complete with home addresses, parking instructions, corporate-sponsor logos, and dates and times. One of these parties is at *Henderson's* house. *Henderson!* I will kill the broken part of my brain that wishes I could tell Amy about this. I text Delilah: *Thanks. I'll let you know.*

She texts back: *Have fun with Calvin.* ☺

I stop moving. This isn't right. I didn't tell her where I'm working. I type: *Huh?*

She writes back: *We're buds. I saw him on the way to work. He's cool. Have gun!*

She deliberately left the typo so she could text me again ten seconds later: *Have gun. Ha. FUN. I love autocorrect.*

Ugh. I don't write back to Don't Fuck Delilah. I walk to FREEZER BURN, the aisle where they keep the single people servings and the yuppie flash frozen vegetables, and standing there in front of the premade meals is Adam Scott. It's my first celebrity sighting and I fucking love him in *Stepbrothers* and *Burning Love* and *Friends with Kids* and my palms get damp and maybe I really am becoming an Angeleno because this actually feels important to me.

And I'm not alone. An aspiring actress is looking at him while typing into her phone and so is a dorky guy holding a pack of frozen asparagus. A couple of high school girls giggle and take a picture of him and that's when it hits me. The good thing about social media and celebrity spottings is that the net is cast wide, all over the world, twenty-four hours a day. Facebook isn't enough; I need to use all of it.

I pull out my phone and download Twitter and Instagram and it's the most difficult thing I've ever done. *CandacePeachBenjiBeck* don't touch this because this is me surprising myself, doing something I never thought I'd do. I follow Adam Scott on Twitter, then search for his name. Sure enough, people have tweeted and apparently Joshua Jackson and his unfairly pretty girlfriend are also here.

Omigod literally just saw Pacey Cole Witter Lockhart #dawsonscreek #pantry #needaffair #ilovela #idie

How hot is Adam Scott? He's so hot the frozen foods are all melting at the grocery store right now. Not saying which one. #Greedy

Diane Kruger is too pretty. #notfair #celebritysighting #cantijustgetgroceries

LA, where you can't get groceries without feeling like a #loser #pantry

#adamscott #joshjackson #dianekruger #ihaventbookedanythingin4months

I look at the counter and there he is, Joshua Jackson. He's laughing. He's close. People here aren't just shopping for overpriced fruit, they're looking for celebrities, just like I'm looking for Amy. I approach a guy unloading peaches. "Bruh," I say, because I'm *going native.* "No offense, dude, but are they serious with the prices?"

"I know," he says. "Dude, don't tell 'em, but I'm all about Ralph's. The one on Western. You can buy like, fifty burritos for five bucks."

"Yeah," I say. I lay my trap. "My girlfriend, though, she's supposed to go to Ralph's. But then she comes here and blows all my money on *berries* and Wolfgang Puck. She swears she doesn't but we work opposite schedules so I can never catch her."

He laughs. His name is Stevie and he's an actor slash drummer and he asks what Amy looks like. "Stone cold fox," I say. "Long blond hair, blue eyes, she always wears random college shirts and denim cut-offs and big bright sneakers. You can't miss her." Zebras stand out in the grass and she is nothing like the LA cunts in their maxi dresses or their I-don't-have-a-job-and-I-just-sweated-a-lot outfits.

He says Amy *sounds familiar, especially the sneakers*. "When did you think you saw her?" I ask.

The wheels are turning in Stevie's chemical-addled brain. He holds up a hand. "Dude," he says. "She was in here like three days ago with this other chick and they were drunk and eating blueberries and I was like, 'You ladies gotta pay' and they ran."

Yes. "Who was the other girl?" I ask.

He shrugs. "I mainly saw yours," he says. "She was *fine.*"

Stevie and I high-five and he wants to text me if Amy comes around. I tell him no, that's cool, but he's got his hands full here, I see that. But he insists. He's bored as fuck and he can totally *snap a pic* of Amy on the *down low*.

I test him. "Seriously, bruh?"

He nods. "Word."

"To the mother," I confirm, surprised that there's no irony at play. We exchange numbers and I fill my cart with Rice Krispies and milk and Wolfgang Puck salad and deli turkey.

When I am cashing out, the woman smiles, giant. "Ray and Dottie send their love."

"Who?" I ask.

The Botox mom in back of me *awws*. "You are too cute," she says. "You're new. They're the owners," she says. "That's a Pantry thing. Ray and Dottie send their love."

I look at the cashier. She nods.

Ray and Dottie are fucking geniuses. What better way to win over a city of rejects and desperados than by creating a business where the last thing they do before they take your money and send you away is give you *love*.

My tour continues and I pass the dilapidated bookstore where I'll be working. A sign in the window reads BACK IN FIVE OR TEN and I continue toward the UCB theater. It's smaller than I expected, like a storefront. Posters cover the glass begging for my attention and a chubby girl holding a clipboard asks me if I want a ticket.

"Yeah," I say, *improvising*. "Does the beginner class have a show soon?"

"Which class?" she asks. Someone inside pounds on the window and she waves her clipboard. "Did you want a ticket for the Master Blasters at five?"

No I do not want that. She burrows back into the building and I keep walking. I'm almost home, near the corner of Franklin and Tamarind and walking here is uncomfortable, not like strolling in New York. I take out my phone and check Facebook and *fuck it all* because someone's commented about Off-the-Grid Amy dropping out of her UCB class. My head pounds, the heat, the news. Fuck.

And then it's that phenomenon, where you're thinking about someone and they suddenly appear. Because right there, in the window of Birds Rotisserie Chicken Café & Bar, is a photo of Amy. It's a surveillance shot, grainy black and white, but it's her, down to the long blond hair and STANFORD SWIMMING T-shirt. Beneath the photo are the words: *Window of Shame.*

I go into Birds. I sidle up to the bar. When the hot bartender chick asks what I want I tell her to surprise me. I smile. This woman has to want me. That's how I will get her to tell me about Amy.

She winks. "I hope you like pineapples."

I fucking hate pineapples. "Love 'em," I say. "Bring it."

Her tits are hard, fake, harsh like her, strapped against her chest by her black tank top. Her name is Deana and she is what happens when the hot girl in the Guns N' Roses video grows up. It's real now and she tells me how Amy made it onto the *Window of Shame.*

"She started coming in a couple weeks ago," she says. "She was a pain in the ass from day one, asking for *blueberry vodka* and sending back drinks claiming they were weak or not what she wanted. Totally shady. Like, bitch, I saw you water it down. Then she just walked out, didn't pay her bill."

"The worst," I say. "Did you call the police?"

Deana stops shaking my drink and looks at an old guy with slick red hair. They laugh in an inside joke sort of way. "Did we call the police?" she repeats.

"How many minutes ago exactly did you move here?" the man asks.

"Earlier today," I say. Deana gets excited and rings a bell and grabs a megaphone and I get a free shot of Patrón.

The man introduces himself to me. His name is Akim, and Deana says they didn't call the cops because this is Hollywood. She shrugs. "They have better things to do than chase down girls who run out on checks."

Deana says that Amy is allowed at La Poubelle because it's different there. "Guys buy drinks for chicks like that, model types." She doesn't mask her disgust. "Personally, I don't go anywhere where I can't pay for my own booze. Self-respect."

I stay at Birds for hours, drinking that pineapple shit, making things right with Deana, laughing at her jokes, letting *her* be the one to tell me that she doesn't date customers. I leave a fat tip and bring my groceries home and change and rush over to La Poubelle, the place where Amy should be. It's a long dark bar, like the hull of a Parisian pirate ship. I sit in the back corner. I stay until two, waiting for Amy to get there. I buy some Xanax off Dez. I'm sure that I'll find Amy within twenty-four hours, forty-eight at the most. She doesn't have class. She'll be here. She will.

10

BUT she wasn't there. She didn't go to La Pou that night, or any night. And now it's been a month and I've tried everything—hiking, Craigslist, breaking into Harvey's occupant database, even Pilates—but I still can't fucking find Amy. All I have to show for it is a farmer's tan and a bunch of new muted button-down shirts that I never would have bought in New York. My brain hates me for all the stupid casting calls I've posted. None of it works. I stay optimistic. I listen to "Patience" by Guns N' Roses and I think of hunters and explorers who spent countless nights in the wild, unsure of where they were, or if they would find what they were looking for. But LA is fucking monotonous and it's wearing on me, the way I keep not finding her. And when I try to talk to people, everyone says the same thing: Tinder!

Fuck them. Amy's not on Tinder. She's too smart. Too phony. Too old-fashioned. *We are the same.* I get so mad that I can't sleep and Dez laughs—*you do like your downers*—and I collect Percocets, just in case I need to drug her.

I hate it here. Everyone is wrong. Delilah is bad at flirting. Harvey is too aggressive about drinking. And every day is actually three days, a freezing morning, a blistering day, and a cool night. You need a lot of clothes. And every day is the same day, which is why it's important to hang a calendar. I see why people move here and wake up one day scratching their heads, wondering when they turned forty or what year it is.

It's claustrophobic and I have no car and I hate Amy for not being on Facebook, for not having an e-mail I could hack. I live almost exclusively in this one giant square of earth bound by Tamarind Avenue on the west and Canyon Drive on the east. In New York, you can walk for hours and go unnoticed and you can follow a woman for several blocks without her knowing. But the cliché is real and people don't walk here unless it's to improve their precious fucking bodies or to reach another form of transportation, a car, a bus, a Lyft. They put on sneakers and carry silver canteens around and what I would do to just have one hour on Seventh Avenue in the middle of the night. I miss being invisible. I think I might be getting fat too.

Every day some awful noise wakes me up, Stevie from the Pantry accidentally texting me instead of his girlfriend, Harvey practicing with his ukulele, or people showing up to shoot piece of shit shorts in the building. I am not a snob, but the average person here is just, well . . . it's not New York. I stare at my popcorn ceiling and think about my beautiful old apartment. I check up on Pearl & Noah & Harry & Liam; I live vicariously through them now. Sometimes I think about friending them and confessing everything. Maybe Amy mixed up and told one of the girls something that would help me find her. But she's a professional. She knew what she was doing.

AT the beginning of July I sign a rent check and hand it over to Harvey.

"Don't look glum," he says. "They say it takes about ten years to settle in here. You gotta stay positive. Am I right or am I right?"

I give him the thumbs-up he wants so badly and he claps and I flee and I'm so sick of the stupidity of it all, Harvey and his big fucking smile, my boss Calvin, who is a whole other kind of annoying.

It's nothing like Mooney Books and Calvin is one of those people who is better on Facebook than he is in real life. He would be wiser to evaporate and live exclusively online with his telegenic swath of thick, dark hair. I want to wipe it the fuck off his forehead and take his stupid oversized eyeglasses too. I feel that way a lot here, like I want to tear people's clothes off their bodies in a nonsexual way, shave their heads, line them all up for *Silkwood* showers. Calvin keeps all his passwords on a piece of paper in his wallet, fucking moron, and there's always a movie playing in the bookstore, as if this is a video rental store in the '90s. Today it's *True Romance* so that Calvin can tell me for the fiftieth time that they shot part of it up the street on Beachwood.

"Sup, Joe-Bro?"

"Sup, Calvin."

Something is *always* up with Calvin and he launches into a story about his manager that sounds made up. In the past month I've learned that there are many Calvins, dependent on which drugs he's on. There is Cocaine Calvin, amping up for a *Better Call Saul* audition. There is Marijuana Calvin, chill and watching Tarantino and dreaming of being in a Tarantino movie and laughing out loud at jokes that are meant to make you smile. There is Reject Actor Calvin, gut protruding through a tight purple T-shirt, glasses on, reeking of hair products, telling me to be quiet because he's *visualizing*.

Some days, Calvin is a writer. He puts his hair in a ponytail. He works on something called *Ghost Food Truck*. Some days it's a self-aware campy teen horror flick about a haunted food truck. Some days it's a pitch for IFC about a food truck that is run by ghosts. Offbeat, he likes to say, as if this somehow means a TV show doesn't need a *story*. Still other days *GFT* is a pilot script—possible HBO or FX but *never* network—about a serial killer who roams the country killing people and making burritos out of them. The thing is, *Ghost Food Truck* is like Calvin and like everyone here, so flipping *flimsy*. It changes depending on what he watched last night. On what his friends watched.

At least today I'm dealing with the good kind of Cocaine Calvin. He's dancing and pounding his chest and telling me about *True Romance* again and he's best like this, getting hyped for an audition, wearing himself out like a toddler. He leaves to try and *make it in Hollywood* and I post another useless casting call on Craigslist—*tall blond beautiful*.

My listings are getting more uninspired as time goes by and every day that Amy doesn't submit a headshot to one of my imaginary castings, I feel like a detective in one of those shows where they hit you over the head with the fact that a missing child becomes almost impossible to find when twenty-four hours pass. It could drive you nuts, searching for someone in LA, and that's why people here are so miserable. It is fucking hard to find things. Fame. Love. Parking spots. Cheap gas. Good inexpensive headshots. An agent. A manager. A happy hour where the nachos don't suck. A tall blond con artist named Amy.

It's been a long month without rain, without clouds, without a sighting. And it sickens me to look back because I've done my part. I set my traps. I assembled my team. Calvin knows to text me the second anyone walks into this place with a copy of *Portnoy's Complaint* and Amy should have been in by now. How does she pay for her fucking superfruits?

Harvey knows to tell me if any new girls show up, tall blondes in college shirts. Dez too. Deana from Birds quit, but I set better traps there, as well as at La Pou and all the places in between. I bought bottles of prenatal vitamins and told the bartenders that my estranged girlfriend is pregnant. I worked up some tears. The female bartenders at Birds said we're all *family* in the Village and they couldn't get over how sweet I am, carrying vitamins around. The guy behind the bar at La Poubelle was empathetic. He looked me in the eye and lifted the bag and promised me he'd be on the lookout. I had so much hope. So why the fuck haven't I found her?

Calvin comes back all coked up, hooting and hollering and doing a stupid jig he does after he *nailed it*. He goes on Tinder.

"Jesus," I say. "Didn't you just hook up last night?"

He nods. "That's not what I'm doing now. I'm working it, Joe Bro. Tinder is the most important casting database in the world," he raves. "The place where *every* actor and actress is hanging out, like what the club used to be, or the drugstore soda fountain was in, like, the fifties." He burps. "Fucking Tinder, dude. My buddy Leo, he got cast off Tinder last week."

"But isn't it just dating and shit?" I protest. I don't want this to be true. I don't want to join and I don't want Amy to be on there *Tindering* around.

Calvin burps. "Swipe. Fuck. Book."

I have no choice. I join. I swipe. And twenty-four hours later, I think my eyes are broken and my head is so full of faces that I worry the visual part of my brain might run out of room. There are so many girls. And they're all here. It's an infinite database and when girls on Tinder wander into my five-mile radius, I can see them in my phone. Now Tinder is taking over my brain and every time I swipe, I picture Amy in a USC shirt, yawning and strolling out of my radius and I can't stop swiping because I have to find her. I don't sleep at all for two fucking days.

It's the most pathetic move yet and I think California is getting to me. I call Mr. Mooney. He has no patience. "I told you," he snaps. "Get your goddamn dick sucked."

So I try. I meet a girl named Gwen on Tinder and it's like ordering Chinese food. In the pictures, Gwen is shiny and rested, glistening like pork-fried rice. Gwen shows up and she isn't as shiny in person, same way the pork-fried rice is always greasier than you want it to be. Her skin is puffy. She is pale. She is proof that they can't all be *California girls* and she tells me about her acting class and her last bad Tinder date. She drinks red wine and looks at herself in the mirror. Her teeth stain. She sneezes. I say God bless you. I drink vodka and search the bar for Amy. It's different being here with a woman instead of Calvin. I'm staring at people and Gwen notices. "I was the same way my first month," she says. "Everyone's just so much *prettier* here. Even the men."

Naturally, while I'm at the bar with Gwen, I see the most attractive girl I've ever seen in my life. And I can't put my finger on it. She is not classically beautiful by any means and she is hardly young. Her off-the-shoulder soft sweatshirt showcases the right amount of her boobs, like two scoops of ice cream, soft and creamy. Her hair is cotton candy. Her legs are caramel. When the bartender brings me the glass of water I asked for an hour ago, the candy girl and I reach for it at the same time.

"I'm so sorry," she says.

"Take it," I say.

She smiles. It would be a dick move to hit on her in front of Gwen and I am not a dick. This is why I agree to see Gwen's new apartment. She lives in a guesthouse by a pool in Los Feliz. It's depressing and small and there are pictures of Madonna everywhere. Gwen humps me and I close my eyes and picture the candy girl. We use each other. She sucks my dick.

I spend the night in Gwen's guesthouse and this is where it's true when the deluded aspiring actors say that the business is all about timing. The *one fucking night* I leave the Village and fall asleep in Los Feliz, I wake to three texts from Calvin:

Dude girl here with Portnoy Complaint

She's being weird about money wants cash not direct deposit you want to buy it off her?

All good, she was in a rush so we worked it out got it 4 u

My hands are shaking and this guesthouse smells like soup and I am out of the squeaky bed and I am looking for my shoes and fuck. This is my fault. I lost my focus. I have to get out of here but I can't find my fucking shoe and I look under the bed and it's nothing but dildos and stilettos and acting manuals. Fuck my shoes. I don't deserve them.

My Lyft is one minute away and I step out into the overbearing, in-your-face, moronic sun and I duck my head and here are my shoes, lined up next to Gwen's, as if she wanted the people in the big house to know about this, about us.

I get into the Lyft and the driver wants to know if he should take Franklin or Fountain and he doesn't have sunglasses and the AC is broken and he misspells the name of my street in his GPS. The phrase *one-night stand* is a misnomer. There is no such thing as a one-night stand. Sometimes, what you do for one night destroys your future.

11

IT'S not a book. It's a *screenplay*. White, thin, single-sided pages bound by brass tacks. Calvin rubs his eyes. Stoned. Sucking on a kale smoothie. "Dude, you said *Portnoy's Complaint*."

I am livid. "The *book*."

"Yeah," he says. "Right thiggity there."

"This is a *screenplay*," I hiss. "Who collects *screenplays*?"

"JoeBro, don't take this the wrong way, but you need to chill. Have you ever done a juice fast?" He hits a pack of American Spirits against the desk. "You get so intense. That gets your cortisol going. Cortisol is not cool."

This is like getting pulled over for not using your blinker and I could kill Calvin. I could kill Amy. I could kill everyone and put them in a blender and make them into a smoothie. *Fast Five* is on the TV and I watch Dominic Toretto and RIP Brian O'Conner assemble a team. My team fucking sucks.

"JoeBro," Calvin says. "You got Tinder banged and you look all miserable and shit."

"I rushed over here for the book."

"Well, like, the screenplay is *about* the book, so, like, it's kind of the book, only in different form, like the way iced coffee is still coffee even though it's cold."

I can't help it. "Fuck off, Calvin," I snap.

"Dude," he says. "You need to chill."

Toretto never *chills* because you don't get anywhere in this world by being *chill* and Calvin is going on about a Flaming Lips *LP* and food trucks and Big Bear and bacon, about how *wasted* he was last night. I wish I had Cocaine Calvin. Pothead Calvin is impossible, a no-talent Duplass brother, smug and slow. His *buds* are texting. They're at some fucking market downtown and they can bring us lunch and Calvin still doesn't get that I don't drink vegetables or care about *dope food trucks in K-Town.* I care about books.

I tell him I'm not hungry and he says I need to laugh and he gives me his iPad and commands me to watch a *killer Henderson video.* I tell him I don't want to watch the video but he says that I have to. "Henderson is on," he says. "He goes *off* on his new girlfriend and this dope is gold. This gold is dope. Genius."

Everyone here calls everything *genius*. "Calvin."

"JoeBro, you need to chill," he says. "Watch. Chill. Be."

But how can I be chill when Delilah is texting, clinging, and Calvin is yammering about pitching *Ghost Food Truck* to Comedy Central or IFC. He might *get weird* with it and go to Adult Swim and he's banging the vaporizer that never works against the counter and his ego swells and *Ghost Food Truck* would *actually* be mellower on HBO and maybe you could even put John Cusack *in* that truck and maybe he would pick up girls and disappear and look for the girls and *never find them, because like, it's a Ghost Food Truck and he's a ghost and he doesn't know it.* I give in and tell Calvin it's *genius* and he texts his *writing partner Slade* and I would bet my nuts that Calvin and Slade will never write *Ghost Food Truck* the cartoon, the movie, or the HBO series. People in LA talk about writing but they don't actually do it. It's the LA equivalent of going to the Cloisters or the Met in New York. You say you're going to do it but at the end of the day it's Saturday or it's too hot or it's too cold or you could just as easily watch TV.

But then what the fuck makes me so superior? I can't even find Amy.

"I'm popping next door for another kale smoothie," he says. "You want?"

"No, thanks," I say.

"JoeBro," he says. "You got to get out of your head, brother. Watch the H man."

"Calvin, I'm pretty beat."

"The video is two minutes."

"I actually hate Henderson."

"Nobody hates Henderson," he says. "You crack me up, JB."

I give in again and I watch Henderson on *F@#K Narcissism.* He's on his couch, in one of his trademark laugh-at-me T-shirts (#BOOBS), talking about a girl with a *dirty vag.* I don't like that abbreviation; it's a pussy or it's a vagina but it's not a *vag.* He calls the girl an *organic pig* who smears *superfruits* all over his sheets and her *vag* is hard to reach because of her *bush.* My hands start shaking and I turn up the volume.

"Blueberries," Henderson rails. "I tell her to keep the blueberries in her vag and I think this is a reasonable request. I get hungry. I take a bite. But these sheets, my sheets, these are high thread count sheets, people. Okay, I'm sorry to be that asshole, but I did not just get a deal from Comedy Central. I got a *deal* from these idiots. So these sheets are not cheap. And she is gonna make it up to me, you know, a little lovin', but then my show comes on and she wants to *watch it.* Do you believe this shit? So now I got blueberries, I got blue balls, and I'm my own cock block. You sit on your shitty futon in your shitty apartment and you dream about having the girl and the sheets and the money and then you get it and hello. Can I get laid in my own bed? Hell, no! I'm my own cock block!"

The crowd roars. He looks at someone in the audience. He shouts: "Love you, Amy baby. Super kisses, baby, it's all good, right?"

My heart thumps and my throat closes. The camera does not pan over to Amy and I rewind the clip and he says it again—*Love you, Amy baby*. She's sleeping with the enemy, *my* enemy, *our* enemy. Vile duplicitous cunt, and in *Crimes and Misdemeanors*, Mia Farrow pulls this shit on Woody Allen. They watch movies together and bond over their disgust for a television producer played by Alan Alda. Woody is smitten, sweet, noble, and in the end, Mia Farrow chooses to marry the *producer.* She tells Woody that he's not so bad. When I wrap my hand around Amy's cum-stained throat, she'll say the same thing about Henderson, tell me to lighten up. In this moment, at the counter in the bookstore, having found Amy, I have to do something vile too. I have to text Calvin: *This is genius.*

Calvin rushes back, maybe he did a little Adderall, and he's *stoked* that I have seen the light and join him in worshipping at the altar of Henderson, funnier than Richard Pryor, smarter than Jerry Seinfeld—*Did you know he didn't even go to Harvard? He never ran the*

Lampoon *like Conan!*—and yet Henderson is a genius—*Literally, his IQ is like 10,000*—and he deadlifts and he wrestles and the man can do anything. Right now he's in Malibu, surfing and Instagramming *while* riding waves. I could go to Malibu and drown him and smash her head against rocks but with traffic and bus schedules, I wouldn't make it by sundown.

"Does he live at the beach?" I ask.

"No, he lives up in the hills," says Calvin. "He has these Friday night workouts where he fills the house with people and jams on new material, you know the way comics show up randomly, he likes to do it in his home."

It's Friday. My heart might explode with Rachael Ray knives. "Cool," I say. "You wanna go?"

Calvin shrugs. "I don't know, JoeBro. I'm, like, in the writing zone and I used to hang out with his crew. I mean I've met him, but, like, I'm trying to keep it all about the writing right now, you know, get back into the scene when my shit blows up instead of just hanging out and stuff."

Oh, but Calvin, you're never blowing up because you are never finishing anything. I breathe. I reason. "Well, that's great, but sometimes, the thing you need is to get back in touch with people, you know. I bet if you told him about *Ghost Food Truck* he would go nuts."

Calvin sighs. "True, but like, I feel like I'm entertained by him and I love him but he would just *not* be the right producer for *GFT*, you know?"

Because there is no such thing as *GFT* and I am going to move back to New York someday—I promise my brain, I will—but I say this:

"Honestly, Calvin, you are a funny dude. Like, *GFT* could be a one-hour, but picture Henderson and his people chomping at the bit for it and then you use that ammo to go to your one-hour places."

I will sit here and tell lies all day long to get Calvin to commit to this party. Amy will be there. I need to be there. But I cannot show up alone. I cannot be *that guy* and I cannot bring Harvey because the only thing creepier than a guy alone at a party is a guy with an *old guy* at a party.

Calvin hesitates. "I don't know the password."

I am so close. I've won him over with my compliments and there's no choice. I need that password. I need it now. I text Delilah: *Random question. Do you know the password for Henderson?*

She writes back: *Jim Walsh's Hooded Bathrobe*

I write back: *Thanks*

She writes back: *Best one ever right? I love his passwords. Love old 90210.*

I don't write back. She writes more: *I might go. Are you going?*

But I can't have Delilah around. After I show up with Calvin, I will slip away, some bullshit about meeting a girl, and then I will find Amy and get her alone and I can't have Delilah following me around asking me who I'm looking for. It's vicious, it's cruel, but there's only one way to stop her from showing up at Henderson's. I write back: *Actually fuck it. Do you wanna get a late dinner, 10 or 11? I wanna go to Dan Tana's. Yeah?*

She writes back: *YES*

Calvin is playing music, going into party mode, raving about Henderson's *guac*. And I'm sure Delilah is in her apartment, bouncing up and down, deciding what slutty dress she's going to wear for me tonight, not realizing that she would look much better if she covered up, if she teased me.

I imagine Amy is on her knees sucking off her *boyfriend* and I bet she doesn't have to do anything to get ready for their big party tonight. I bet they have maids.

12

YOU don't go to a party empty-handed and my reusable Pantry bag is stuffed with rope, my Rachael Ray knife, rubber gloves, plastic bags, duct tape, and Percocets from Dez.

I spent all afternoon looking for pictures of Henderson's house online. Sometimes it's easier to plan the crime if you know a little bit more about the scene. But I couldn't find pictures of Henderson's house online and I went a little crazy trying to figure out what to do.

If Amy loved me, it would be different. I could make eye contact and signal for her to meet me outside and we could whisper to each other about our regrets and our unresolved feelings. I could tell her to make an excuse and we could slip off together and drive into the mountains or the beach. Los Angeles is full of places to hide a body, but when the person inside the body doesn't love you, it's not an easy thing, turning that breathing person into a dead one.

I bought a ton of Percocets off Dez, figuring this is Hollywood. People overdose all the time. But then I realized that Henderson's in love with her and if she passes out, he will be all over that shit and call an ambulance. So I Lyfted to Home Depot, where I bought random stuff, rope and duct tape, plastic bags, cable ties, and plastic gloves. The girl at the register winked and said she's also a big fan of *Fifty Shades* and this is what has become of our society. Fucking and killing are the same damn thing.

Now I walk outside with my bag and Delilah texts: *Not stalking but have fun grocery shopping.* ☺

I ignore it. For her own good. I want her to learn to be less available.

At La Poubelle, Calvin is already semi-wasted, practicing hashtags. "Which do you like better?" he asks. "House of Henderson or Henderson's House?"

I start planting the seeds for my alibi and tell him I invited this girl from Tinder. He says cool, and he better remember this in the event of an investigation. Calvin orders an Uber and three of his *buds* show up—fuck fuck fuck—and we pay our tab to meet them outside. The guys all brought beer and they toss their sixers in the trunk, and they give me shit because I insist on holding my reusable Pantry bag on my lap. It's too crowded and Calvin's friends are too loud and they won't let up about my fucking bag.

Pissant one: "Is your makeup in there?"

Pissant two: "No, his dick is in there."

Pissant three: "I heard about those retractable dicks. You get a lot more done every day."

Calvin: "Guys. If you give JoeBro any more shit about his retractable dick, he's not gonna tell you where you can get one."

These guys are pale and puffy with ostentatious T-shirts under wrinkled flannel button-downs and they hate Woody Allen and they love Wes Anderson. They dismiss *Crimes and Misdemeanors* as wordy and I think they never even watched the whole thing. I wish it were socially acceptable to brandish a knife. But the driver is an innocent bystander and I wouldn't subject him to any additional torture. We are close, and I still don't know how I'm going to kill Amy.

Pissant one: "Americans aren't funny enough to get *Parks and Rec.*"

Pissant two: "*Parks and Rec* isn't American enough to get Americans."

Pissant three: "I'd fuck Amy Poehler."

Pissant one: "I'd Poehler Amy Fuck."

Calvin: "Is that because she's your Poehler opposite?"

Calvin nudges me; he did too much coke. "JoeBro, come on," he says. "You're the one who wanted to go so bad. Get into it. People would fucking kill to be going to this party right now."

We continue up into the hills and this country needs a draft; these assholes should be challenged, beaten down. The Uber driver is unassuming and blank and I wouldn't be surprised if he kills us all. People disappear in Los Angeles; this is a sad place, haunted. We are still driving, up, up, up, and I am not a pissant in Pumas and these idiots won't shut up.

They brand Chelsea Handler a slut and Jimmy Kimmel a sell-out and Jimmy Fallon a lucky motherfucker and they are wrong about so much in the world and *are we there yet?* I don't aspire to slave away and live up here. These hills are glum and neutral, even as we climb, and my ears pop and I should have come alone. I don't have a plan and these hills aren't even the right hills, the glamorous sparkling mounds that hover above Chateau Marmont. These are the hipster hills, where lazy people in cool clothes pretend they never wanted to be *gross rich* but only wanted to be *comfortable, you know, chill.*

My phone alarm goes off because it's ten thirty. I text Delilah: *Some shit going down, hang on, maybe late night drink instead of dinner.*

She writes back: *That's cool. Let me know! I can bring booze!*

The world is too extreme with Delilah and her lack of self-respect and Amy with her big fat ego. I will deal with one girl at a time and I put my phone in Airplane mode. We slow down. We are here. The driver says he is *not* available to shuttle us home later and he gets to leave, the lucky bastard—and my throat is tight and my underwear shrunk—the dryers at Hollywood Lawns are no good—and my teeth chatter. I was starting to think I'd never get here and now this is it.

I follow the pissants into the house where Bobcat Goldthwait lived for a few weeks in the late '90s (like I give a fuck). There is a security camera by the *open gate* and a sign over it that reads STICK YOUR TONGUE OUT AT ME I'M FAKE. The thing about Californians is they think fearlessness is cool; there isn't a single security measure intact, which is great news for me.

We cross the overgrown lawn where hipsters idle taking selfies and talking about making it to *Mecca.* We give the password and enter through the oversized mahogany door—motherfucker—and I smell eucalyptus and cucumbers and money. I don't see Amy. I grip my bag.

"Calm down," Calvin says. "Look around. Lord Henderson is the freaking honey pot."

I let him go find the guac and then slump onto a couch and I'm annoyed that I *like* the couch. I haven't been anywhere nice in so long. If I had money I would have a house just like this, and I can't believe Amy is Henderson's girlfriend. She lives here, with all the fine things and I was deluded to think that she would be holed up in a shithole with a sisterhood of competing aspirational climbers. My head spins and I get up. I will not sit on this couch, knowing that she has *sucked Henderson off* on this couch.

I walk toward the kitchen and Calvin joins me. He still doesn't have any guac; he ran into some buds. He took something. I can feel it. He's morphing. He's pushy. He reaches for my bag. I flinch. "I got it."

"It's cool," he says. "Everyone is putting the booze they brought in the kitchen. Henderson has a whole bar set up."

"I got it," I insist.

And then I realize it all might begin now, before I even have a drink or a snack, because here comes Henderson. He's shinier and leaner in person and the smile on his face would be more at home on an action figure. Amy's not with him, but she probably approved of his fucking shirt, a yearbook picture of Louis C.K. The quote underneath reads "Van Halen Sucks" and schmuck after schmuck slobbers—*best T-shirt ever, dude that is bad ass, dude that is it, dude Van Halen* does *suck*—and Henderson says *you're welcome*, like he made the joke, like he made the T-shirt, like he has a tenth of Louis C.K.'s talent. There is nothing genuine about Amy's boyfriend with his gleaming skin. It's true; when you make it in show business, you make a deal with the devil. The more pictures they take of you, the less there is inside of you (unless you're Meryl Streep) and Henderson is a ghost, all muscle, no fat, all outside, no inside.

"Get it, boy," Calvin says. "Get at this guac before it's all gone."

"Dope guac," says some asshole, and I pick up a Dorito and shove it into the guac. There is nothing remarkable about this *guac*, about any *guac*, and California needs to calm the fuck down. They're just avocados. Guac is guac and while sometimes it's slimy and disgusting, it's never *delicious.*

I look for Amy and I don't see her and where is she? Don't hanger-on girlfriends have to hang on to their boyfriends at times like this, when random girls are pouring into the house? A fan asks him about his girlfriend. I stop moving.

"She's up north tonight with my mom," he says.

Girlfriend. Up north. No. No. I didn't consider that she wouldn't be here. I try to calm down but it's loud and Cards Against Humanity isn't *that* fucking funny and droll girls wear bold, old clothes with deliberately '50s hairdos. *Dear Women of New York: You are superior.* I go room to room looking for Amy even though she's *up north*. I pour wine into a glass and Calvin raves about Henderson.

"Steve Martin retweets him every time he tweets," Calvin exalts. "Like no matter what he says. How cool is that?"

Henderson swoops in, scooping Skittles into his mouth full of veneers. "Pretty fucking cool, bro."

"That's dope," says Calvin. "Mad dope. Hey, this is Joe, he works for me over at Counterpoint."

Henderson nods and a girl with a microphone warbles and Henderson asks if Calvin still lives in *The Village.*

"I'm up on Beachwood," Calvin answers, fawning like a girl at a New Kids on the Block concert. "Joe's in Hollywood Lawns."

Henderson looks at me. He doesn't have any pores and his eyelashes are too long. "Birds," he says. "I fucking *love* that place. All those ripe, drunk girls. Oh man, I used to go there the way you go to Mickey D's. *Feast.*"

Henderson *feels it* and he climbs onto a chair and then onto his marble island and he whistles and the room goes silent. "You guys mind if I grab this here mic and maybe work out this bit I've been hashing out on my own?"

Cheer. *Yes. We love you, Henderson.* And then the chanting: *Set! Set! Set!*

Henderson tells us that he's seeing someone. (Cheers.) He says it's going well. (Cheers.) He says her name is Amy. (Cheers.) He says Amy is out of town. (Biggest cheers yet, offers to fuck, suck, etc.) Every woman in this place yells something along the lines of *I-will-fuck-you* and if you want to see the opposite of feminism, go to a comedian's house.

He goes on. "When the cat's away, the mouse will masturbate on the sofa and RSVP no to dinner party invitations." The *hooting*, and I don't think a New York crowd would laugh this hard. "But the thing is, I'm happy. I'm in this. When Kate Hudson texts to meet in the CVS parking lot for a quickie, I'm like, no, dude. Go get new tits."

Again the women are laughing and this is not right.

"I'm so fucking happy that I can drive by an elementary school without feeling profoundly bitter that I never got laid once the entire time I was in elementary school."

It's not funny, making fun of child molestation. Henderson doesn't understand how good he's had it.

"Earlier today, I had these Japanese hookers, and I was like, 'I'm so happy in my relationship that you don't need to suck my dick, just fuck each other.'"

More laughter.

"My girlfriend would *hate* me if I admitted this so you all have to hold hands across America and promise me that you are not going to tell on me."

Calvin pledges his allegiance along with all the other followers.

"I think my balls are uneven."

Girls scream out. "Your balls are *sweet*."

"I think my dick is too big. For a Jew." Again there is laughter, as if a Jewish man analyzing the size of his anatomy is funny at this late stage in humanity.

"So you can imagine how good it feels for me that this girl I'm dating now, God, wow, saying that, *dating*. Like I can't believe that? Can you guys believe that?"

He shakes his head. *F@#k Narcissism.*

"Well okay, my girlfriend, when we're fucking, she gets *really* into it and I mean like—you guys, you gotta *swear* this is just between us—where's the camera? Who's got a camera?"

Everyone has a fucking camera and he knew that, the arrogance of the man who gets onstage and thinks he doesn't need a punch line. He's gyrating. Mocking Amy, the way she yelps. He pretends to finish and he grins. That fuck-face grin and he takes a bow.

"So afterward I'm like, no offense, but I've been fucking for a while now and I know that I'm not very good at it. So I ask her if she's faking it." The crowd goes *ooh* and Henderson raises his eyebrows. "And you know what she says to me?"

He smiles. How awful it must be to be him, to be brimming with viciousness. "'You have to understand. I have this ex—and, well, let's just say I never loved him and he was bad at sex.'"

The Spanish tile floor collapses into the basement and *This is the End* and my insides go quiet as Henderson shares with the world what Amy said about me.

I back out of the living room and go upstairs and I barge into his bedroom, where Amy fucks him and whispers vicious things about me. Well, fuck *you*, Amy. She used me and then she used *us* to entertain her new *boyfriend*. He knows about me so I deserve to know about *him* and I search for his box of secrets—everyone has one and people with no imagination keep theirs under their beds—and sure enough, he has a box of shit about his ex-wife: journal entries, newspaper clippings, pictures, ticket stubs.

Her name was *Margie* and she went to Birds with him, sat on his lap, laughed at his bad jokes, and took naked selfies on their shitty futon. They saw Billy Joel and had terrible seats. He was puffier and once upon a time he had a heart. He got divorced when he started to get famous, when he was on the way *up*. Margie lives in Lake Kissimmee now and has three kids with a *salesman*. She doesn't look bitter. *Never loved him, bad at sex.* He can't be happy without her, clearly, and I will put him out of his misery. Downstairs, the laughing only gets louder. Someone needs to stop him from poisoning the world.

I grind up four of the Percocets and empty them into the reusable metal water bottle by his bed, right next to his bottles of Xanax and prescription sleeping pills. I take his box into his *walk-in, live-in, fuck-in* closet and I text Calvin that I'm Lyfting with the Tinder girl. I text Delilah: *Sorry to do this at the last minute, but I have to bail.*

I get why Calvin likes improv. There is something kind of exciting about having so little control. I didn't plan to kill Henderson, but then, when you go on TV and whine about your girlfriend's *bush* and stand up in your home and say mean things about Kate Hudson and brag about your masturbatory habits and open up your home to strangers—the password was all over Twitter ten minutes after we got here—well, Henderson is gonna learn the hard way that you can't go around making fun of people you've never met before.

13

IT takes a long time for the party to end because most of the guests are dirt-poor fan boys who need this night to stay juiced about their own flailing careers. I listen to their American Apparel conversations and the way they analyze their expressions—*even your teeth look stoked*—and I wonder what will become of them all. There aren't enough mansions and jobs to go around.

Hiding behind Henderson's suits is uncomfortable and my neck hurts and it occurs to me that I could walk out on all of this, everything, and go back to New York. But I need closure. Henderson's fucking act changed everything and now I have to know why Amy said those terrible things about me. I can't leave this house and go on with the rest of my life wondering if I'm bad at sex. And I can't lose the chance to talk to the one person who actually knows where Amy is.

There is a loud *boom* downstairs and that was the remote-controlled blinds going down all over the house. There is an emptiness in the house now, the sound of Henderson pouring cereal into a bowl, watching a little recorded *Seth Meyers* before turning it off and locking the doors—that's a good boy—and heading upstairs. All lonely men are the same and he's no different from Mr. Mooney as he plods up the stairs. My heart beats. I stand at attention, listening as he gets ready for bed.

Fortunately, his nighttime regime only involves brushing his teeth and rubbing potions all over his precious face. I hear him walk into his bedroom, the unmistakable *click* of the metal bottle I spiked with Percocet, the *plip-plop* of the sleeping pills into his hand, the *plip-plop* of the Xanax, another sip of his Percocet water. And then his lights go out. He jerks off, and within minutes he is asleep.

He is snoring now. I open the door. He doesn't move—thank you, pills. And thank you, Henderson, for being the kind of asshole who waxes his entire fucking body. I cuff his arms with cable ties and though it's demeaning—I miss my cage, where I didn't have to be reduced to this kind of thing—I pull off the covers and cuff his legs at the ankles. I cover him up with the buttery duvet and then I slap his face. Nothing. I slap him again. Nothing. This goes on awhile until it doesn't, until everything in the world, every last bit it of it, is in his eyes, in his scream. He is the ultimate toddler and I put on his Beats headphones and wait for him to accept his circumstances. These headphones are powerful; they *do* block out the noise and I turn on his bedside iPod—*Jersey Boys* soundtrack, not very hipster chic of him—and wait while he thrashes, a dying shark.

When he finishes fighting, I take off the headphones and I pick up his iPad. I ask for the password. He begs me—*no no please no*—and I approach him with my Rachael Ray paring knife and he caves: "Margie19."

"Who's Margie?" I ask innocently.

"My wife," he says. I look at him. He corrects himself. "Ex-wife."

I am in his iPad and now I need to contact his maid.

"What? Why?" he protests. "Please, you tell me what you want, anything. Anything, just let me go."

"I told you what I want," I say. "I want your maid's name."

"I can wire money to you." His forehead is already slick with sweat. "I can sell this house for cash and you can have the cash and I can go away." He sobs. "Dude, please."

He won't stop negotiating, offering me all kinds of fabulous prizes if I would just let him go. "I don't want your *money*," I say. "I want to know the name of your maid."

He gets it. "Jennifer," he says. "She's in Contacts."

I find Jennifer—JENNIFER MAID as opposed to JENNIFER TITS and JENNIFER BIG TITS and JENNIFER NO TITS—and I write: *Jennifer. You have the day off. Calling in big guns for this one. Sorry for the late notice.*

Jennifer gets the text and responds immediately: *You are so kind!*

And now it's time for the real fun to begin. I tell him to stop bellyaching and he asks me to let him go and I tell him that's not going to happen and he screams again. I sit down in his white modern throne of an office chair. "Tell me when she said it."

"Let me fucking go."

"Tell me when she said it."

"I don't know what you're talking about but there is fifty K in the safe."

"I'm talking about Amy."

"Who?"

"Amy," I snap. "Don't say *who* like you don't know who I'm talking about. You talked about her on your show and you talked about her tonight so don't sit here and tell me that you don't know who Amy is."

He swallows. He nods. "What do you want to know?"

"I want to know when you met her."

His lower lip trembles. "Is this . . . are you from the network?"

I look at him. Could he possibly be that stupid? "No," I say. "I'm from the world."

He cries again and he squirms and I focus on the future. I imagine the online melee that will ensue when Henderson's untimely death hits the news. Someone will leak the details about the box of pictures of his first wife and psychologists will say that comedians are notoriously depressed. People will be stunned that Henderson killed himself at the peak of his career. I can hear the funereal battle cry clichés already. Everyone's a philosopher after a suicide.

It just goes to show you, money isn't everything.

Maybe if he was married, things would be different.

At least he didn't leave any children behind.

What a shame that he didn't even have any children yet.

His poor mother.

And to think he just told those people how happy he was.

Finally Henderson stops moving. He breathes, sweats. "What do you want?"

"I told you," I say. "I want to know when you met Amy."

"Are you her boyfriend or something?"

"I said I want to know when you met Amy."

He nods. There is not one single blueberry stain on the duvet but

I bet he's so rich that he has tons of duvets. These sheets are softer than the ones in Little Compton, the ones she liked so much, back when I was good enough. "I met her at Soho House," he says.

I shouldn't be surprised, but it hurts to think of her with her legs crossed at a private club where rich people like to sit near other rich people and talk about things rich people talk about. It's the kind of place frequented by girls like Delilah and guys like Henderson, gold diggers and deep pockets, almost like a brothel, less honorable. "Okay," I say. "And then what?"

"She was at the bar and she was checking me out and I asked her what year she was."

I dig my Rachael Ray knife into the armrest of his stupid white chair. "What do you mean?"

"She was wearing a Peter Stark T-shirt and I know a couple people who did that program," he says.

"Who's Peter Stark?" I ask. *Ugh, Amy.*

He is smarmy even now as he raises his eyebrows. "The Peter Stark Producing Program at USC," he says, as if I should know this, as if entertainment makes the world go round.

I picture her the day she got here, learning about the Peter Stark program, finding a shirt, taking it.

"Dude," he says. "She's not worth it, okay? This is not worth fifty K."

"And then what happened?"

"I don't know," he says. "What ever happens? I bought her a dozen drinks and I got her number and . . . and then I don't know. I have a driver. I blacked out."

He's an alcoholic and I bet he doesn't remember most of his

life but he better try. I want to know it all. "Did she go home with you?"

"Dude," he says. "This is really not cool."

Angelenos. As if *not cool* is the correct way to describe being tied up and interrogated. "Did she go home with you?"

"What?"

"Don't act like you don't do this five nights a week, Henderson. I'm asking the questions. You answer the questions."

"And then you'll let me go?" he asks.

"Yes," I say. Dummy. "Then I'll let you go. So yes or no, did she go home with you?"

He looks at the wall. "I told you I don't know."

"Henderson." I stand. This is fucking ridiculous. "It is very simple. You met her at Soho House. You asked what she year she graduated. Finish the fucking story."

He growls. "Okay, fuck it! Fuck it! There is no story to finish because she's not my girlfriend. I made it up!"

I stare at him. "You just pointed to her the other night. You said '*hi, Amy.*'"

He laughs, patronizing. "It's a *TV* show," he lectures. "I pointed at a plant."

People in this business; all they do is make shit up. "You mean, you're not with her?"

He sneers. "She never even wrote me back, kid. I sent her a dick pic. She must be a prude. Or a lezzie. Or a fucking nut job."

"So why the hell are you out there telling people she's your girlfriend?"

He writhes. "Because that's my job! I can't go out there and talk about banging hotties every night! Because sometimes they want your bits to be about relationship shit! Because on TV you make. Shit. *Up.*"

"You never slept with her?"

He laughs. "I told you. She's a lezzie or a prude."

I stab the chair. He's the same annoying fuck he is on the show; not *everything* is made up.

He whistles. "Yoo-hoo, buddy! Can we fucking move on from this shit already?"

I'm sick of California with the lies and the jagged earth and the hills and the monotony. I walk into the bathroom. And no, we can't *move on from this shit*. It doesn't add up. *Blueberries.* I bolt out of the bathroom.

"If you didn't sleep with her, why did she say her ex was bad at sex?" I demand.

He heaves. "This is fucking *tired.*" He chomps and snorts and he's a dog, a spoiled dog. "Okay," he says. "Let's break it down already. I met a chick named Amy. She said she hated my show, which obviously made my dick hard because most of the time girls are just throwing themselves at me." This, at least, is good to know. He continues. "She wouldn't go home with me. She said she's not that kind of girl but, you know, the ones that say that, they're the ones who will do just about anything a day later, right? So I got her digits and sent her a picture of my dick."

Revolting. All of it. The idea of dicks in Amy's phone. "And?"

"And nothing," he says.

"How did you know about blueberries?" I ask.

He laughs. "She said the best sex she ever had was with some guy, some blueberries, I dunno, bar talk. I told you. I make shit up. I turn it around. Nobody wants to hear me go off about how my lady's ex is, like, the shit in bed. It's called a fucking comedy routine, son. It's called, *comics make shit up.* It's called, let's get you paid."

He really thinks he's getting out of this and I walk into the bathroom. I turn on the water. *Best sex she ever had.* Still, she ran away from me, from love, from all the good we shared. She would rather sit in a bar and lie to strangers than be with me. *Charlotte & Charles.* Bullshit. She makes Tinder Banger Calvin seem like John Fucking Sweetie Pie Cusack and I get it now. I'm too good for her. Way too good for her. My hands are too good at grabbing her ass and my dick was too appetizing to her and she loved me so much she couldn't stand it.

I check on Henderson. He's revved up again, moaning and thrashing. "Can we get the show on the road?"

"Hold on," I say. "We're not done just yet."

"Dude," he says. "Go get her back. Fuck me. Fuck this."

I look through his phone but there are so many fucking Amys in here: Amy Toronto and Amy Chubby and Amy Bad Nose and Amy Tits and Amy Ass.

"Who came first?" I ask. "Amy Tits or Amy Ass?"

"Dude," he says. "You try meeting this many people. You have no idea what it is to be in my position."

"No," I say. "But I guess Amy Gym and Amy Chateau and Amy Marmont and Amy Blowjob know about positions."

"Stop it," he says. "Don't act like there's anyone in there that didn't wanna be in there."

"Even Amy Fat Ass?"

"Especially Amy Fat Ass," he says. "Stop it. Come on."

"Tell me," I say. "Did Amy Blowjob get on her knees before or after you put her name in your phone?"

"I have *four* women writers on my staff," he boasts. "And I only banged two of 'em."

I look at his phone. "Which one did you bang? Amy Fish Lips or Amy Sponsor?"

"That's private," he snaps. "Neither. Fuck. Stop it. Seriously."

But there are so many more. "Does Amy Sponsor One know about Amy Sponsor Two?"

"Kid," he says. "You quit now, you get paid. You fuck around, you don't."

"Who gives better head, Amy Sponsor One or Amy Sponsor Two?"

"That's an AA thing," he barks. "I was in that for a while, and that's that."

"But I guess that's not how you met Amy Grey Goose and Amy Tequila."

I laugh but he struggles. "Dude," he says. "I don't lie to these girls. I'm not the bad guy. This is fucking beat, kid. You gotta stop."

"Did you meet Amy Bellagio after you boarded Amy American Airlines or before?"

"Fuck off," he snaps. "I'm serious. Cut. Stop. Enough."

"Oh, come on," I say. "This isn't your show, Henderson. Do you not get that by now?"

Frankie Valli continues to croon in the background, lecturing adolescent men about their juvenile posture. Henderson meanwhile screams and I search for Amy Blueberries. She lives here too, and I never felt so betrayed. My girlfriend, his phone. She looks foul here, lumped between Amy Blue Balls and Amy Bradley Whitford Party. I want to kill her. I want to kill Henderson. I dial Amy Blueberries and it brings me to a familiar recording. This phone's not in service anymore; fucking Amy.

Henderson howls, red and enraged. He wants out of his shackles. Five seconds ago he was talking to me about *getting paid* and you really can't trust anyone here. No wonder Amy thought she'd feel at home.

I search his phone for communications with Amy Blueberries. I feel like I'm going to get diseases just from looking at these texts and I am so disgusted with him, his abuse of power. I bet Jack Nicholson never did anything like this and I bet Paul Newman never asked women to *come over bring two other chicks I want to watch you eat each other out.* All his requests are honored. The girls come over. They bring other girls. It's all horrifying and pornographic and he is one of America's favorite men and this isn't Bill Clinton falling for an intern and this isn't Hugh Grant bumbling with a tranny on Hollywood Boulevard. This is revolting. He doesn't delete any of the messages and the girls are always writing to him gushing about his dick—it's HUGE and HOT—even though he ignores them once he gets into their pants. He is a loveless narcissist and only interested in the *new.* Just like on his show, the way he makes fun of our *nostalgic fucking culture* and brings on one soulless noisy band after another, all of them disposable. Then he gets home and rocks out to the *Jersey Boys* soundtrack and obsesses over pictures of his ex-fucking-wife. It's the easiest thing I've ever done, honoring his request for water. I turn off my music.

"Let's get you hydrated," I say.

He stops screaming. He nods. "Dude," he says. "Believe me, brother, I know this city makes you crazy, okay? I get it. We can work this out. You might even be onto something here. You know, and if that's what this is, if this is a pitch, we can talk about that. Fuck it. We're almost there, right?"

He says this like it's a good thing and I'm glad the water is strong and deadly. This man is no good for this world. He brings out the worst in women and his fifteen minutes have gone on too long. I pick up his metallic water bottle and pour the Percocet water into his mouth. He coughs and sputters. But he drinks. A lot. His pupils shrink and his breath grows shallow and his eyes roll around. I tie a plastic bag around his head. I go to the bathroom and write down the names of all of his skin care products. Everyone will remember him for his stupid fucking talk show but I will remember him as the man who made me realize that I need to take better care of my skin. I also remember that I have to cut his cable ties.

By the time I've catalogued the products in my notebook app, he's dead. I say a mourner's kaddish. I'm not sad. Henderson got a fuck of a lot done here on earth. Better he die now than unknowingly pass on an STD to some hopeful girl with low self-esteem or become fat and irrelevant and begin the inevitable landslide toward the cancellation of his stupid fucking show, his deterioration into *that guy who had that show*. It's just basic physics. He was too high. He came down.

Downstairs, the house smells like guac and beer. Somebody threw a pizza at the print of John Belushi's face. I don't know if it was intentional or accidental but I do know that nobody bothered to clean up the mess. *Assholes.* All of them. But at the same time, I'm grateful that people are pigs. I glove up and gather leave-behinds—lipstick-stained cups, sweaters, a *bra* from the office, and bowls of M&M's—and I take them upstairs to make a DNA sex party in the bed. We all know how many fingerprints there must be in a fucking bowl of candy, on a bottle of wine, and this will look like some classic, deviant Hollywood orgy gone awry. I seize the headphones (they are mine now) and I leave his *Jersey Boys* soundtrack on. Let the world know that the man didn't bring his new and cool work home with him. Let them know he had an old heart. I take two of his brand-new T-shirts, tags on, then I send an empty bubble from his Twitter account. His last word is silence.

His final Tweet blows up, with people retweeting and favoriting it even though it means nothing. I get it. His silence is an invitation for others to project their voices onto him. Overthinking cultural critics will elaborate on this tweet in *Salon*, in *Slate*. The man who never stopped tweeting sent an empty bubble minutes before he died. The symbolism! His tragic sex-death will move the masses and people will learn from him, and in this way he's a lucky guy. If there's a heaven, he's probably going in spite of what he said about me.

On my way out, I buy the *Jersey Boys* soundtrack on my iPhone; it's a long walk down the hills and I needed this. We are built to walk. Not to SoulCycle and jog and hike. Walking is mental. You sharpen your thoughts and process your emotions.

I didn't kill Amy, but I found her. *Soho House.* Of all the places. I should have known that she'd go west. She'll never stop going west, looking for someone richer, someone better. She has a disease, like an animal that can't stop roaming. But I'll stop her soon, after I shower, after I rest.

I turn up Bronson and it's so early that nobody else is up except for a couple of joggers. I debate going into the Pantry, but I go there too much. It's time to mix things up. I cross the street and Hollywood Lawns is in sight. A police cruiser veers around the corner, the red and blue lights flashing. It pulls up onto the sidewalk and suddenly the cop is out of the car, pointing a gun at me. I set my reusable Pantry bag on the pavement and I hoist my hands into the air. And I don't fucking know how, but I'm caught.

14

A bitter piece of shit named *Officer Robin Fincher* grabs the headphones off my head. He has shitty Bakersfield blond hair, the sort better off concealed beneath a dirt bike helmet. His eyes are too close together. At some point, someone in his bloodline fucked someone he wasn't supposed to fuck and the genes were compromised. His skin is rough and he's bad at shaving and the world is not fair. Even with all Henderson's products, this Fincher would still be a cretin.

"Shut it and turn around," he grunts.

I don't know what he wants with the headphones and I don't know how he found me and I don't know what he knows. But I do know that Henderson's shirts are in my bag. I'm aware of them, as if they were flashing lights.

"Turn around," he commands.

I obey. I stand here, fucked. It's that time of day when the sun is a zombie from a '50s horror movie, slowly intensifying, creeping up on me, my exposed cheeks, my nose. My stomach clenches and my palms sweat but I did my job up there. I left no prints. I left no mug of piss.

"Officer," I say, projecting innocence, *fake it till you make it*. "Can you tell me what this is about?"

Fincher walks toward his car, his footsteps heavy on the pavement. "This is about you being a fucking prick, so shut it and wait like I said," he calls.

He didn't say this was about a murdered millionaire in Los Feliz, but he walks back over and grabs my arm and I'm pretty sure you're not allowed to do that.

"Gimme your license."

I give him my license. He huffs. "New York," he says. "Fucking figures."

I will not let relief appear on my face. But I am relieved. This is not about that dead man in the hills. If this were about that dead man up there, this cop would be cuffing me, not bashing Manhattan. I get my bearings as my reactionary adrenaline subsides.

"Walking around like you own the place," he sniffs. "Fucking typical."

I wish he could meet the nice cop in Rhode Island and see how it's done. People think cops are bad and this fucker should be fired because of all the *good* cops out there who follow the rules and risk their lives to serve and protect people.

He sneers. "You live here?"

"Yes, sir."

"You live in this hood?"

"Yes, sir," I say. "I live in Hollywood Lawns."

"Then why the fuck do you have a *New York State* license?"

Are you fucking kidding me? "Well," I say. "I'm just here for a little while."

"You a hobo?"

Hobo? "No, sir," I say. "I'm a writer."

He swallows and I know; this man is an actor. Calvin gets the same look when someone, anyone with the potential to hire him, enters the shop. "On a show or some shit?"

"No," I say. "I'm just trying it out."

He spins away and I step toward him. "Officer, can I ask what this is about?"

"Did I tell you to move?"

"No," I say.

"And are you deaf?"

"No," I say.

"And are you a fucking 'tard?"

Who the hell says that? "No," I say. "I'm not a fucking 'tard."

He storms up to me and gets in my face. "You think it's okay to verbally assault a police officer?"

"No," I say through clenched teeth.

"You think you're some tough-ass New York scum bag transient hobo motherfucker and you can cross state lines and flap your ugly gums at a California State policeman?"

"No," I manage.

"Yeah." He laughs. "I figured you for a New York wigger pussy."

Wigger. This is why they need cameras on police cars and he finishes writing me up and it's a *jaywalking ticket,* just like Harvey warned me about. I have to pay three hundred seventy-five dollars for crossing the street while the crosswalk was blinking, while there was not a single car in sight. This is wrong and the motherfucker says he's keeping the headphones.

"Because you're a fucking tool bag," he says. "This city doesn't belong to you. This city belongs to the cars and you can't walk around here with your goddamn head up your ass."

"That's not fair," I say but I can't fight with him. Not after I just killed fucking Henderson.

"Oh and you better go to the DMV and register," he says. "Fuckers like you, showing up here, refusing to register with the state, you're no better than the beaners who think they can just come on over here and take our jobs."

Officer Robin Fincher spits at me as he gets into his cruiser with my headphones and I picture me joining forces with all the mentally delayed Americans and all the undocumented Mexican workers. We storm the shithole apartment in the Valley where he undoubtedly eats egg whites and spinach—he had something green stuck in his teeth—and lifts weights—his arms were unnecessarily jacked—and watches *COPS.*

After I get home, I hide my Pantry bag in the top right corner of my closet. I shower. I dress. I go to Harvey's office and tell him about this fucking cop and this fucking jaywalking ticket.

He chuckles. "I told you to watch out," he says. "Am I right or am I right?"

Nobody has ever been so ready to leave Franklin Village as I am right now, but as soon I get into my apartment, Delilah barges in wearing last night's Band-Aid dress. She's sobbing and she flops onto my futon, hysterical, and fuck, I forgot I blew her off. I go to her and kneel. Mascara paints her face. Tears flow. She shakes. She drops her purse. She yanks the front of my shirt. There is something phony about her sadness because it *feels* like a display, like she could have taken a deep breath before coming here, like she wanted me to see her in this state.

"Delilah," I say. "Breathe."

But she sobs. I close the door and her teeth chatter and she doesn't use words. She slips out of her pointy shoes and settles into the nook under my shoulder.

"Delilah," I say. "I can't help you if I don't know what's wrong."

She rubs her eyes. She reaches into her purse and unlocks her iPhone—1492—and hands it to me. The headline reads: HENDERSON HOUSE OF HORRORS. I clutch the phone. Details are scant, but so far it seems like a *sex party gone wrong.*

She leans into me, crying again. "I loved him," she says. "I can't, I can't."

I hold her. I stroke her hair. But there is no way I am going to fuck her out of her celebrity death depression. If she came to me because her mother died, maybe, but this is ridiculous. She blubbers: "Will you take me home?"

Home is upstairs and I pick up Delilah and carry her into the hallway and into the elevator and over the threshold into her apartment. "Over there," she says, pointing to her bed, which is directly above my futon. I try to let go of her but she kisses me. Bold. "Make me feel good," she says. "Please."

And before you know it, I'm fucking Don't Fuck Delilah. Why not make things as bad as they can possibly be? Why not bang the stalker upstairs?

"Joe," she says. "Open your eyes."

I am inside of her and on top of her and I look at her. "Hey."

She pulls me closer. "My mom is coming next week," she whispers. "She wants to meet you."

I stop pumping my dick. "I'm pretty busy."

She grabs my ass. "That's cool," she says, smothering my neck in Franklin Village slobber. "I get it."

We get back into it and it's better than it was with Tinder-Gwen and I needed this release after the last hellish twenty-four hours but Delilah isn't coming and I'm ready.

"Come," I say, and I don't want to meet her mother and she claws my back, nothing.

"Come," I say, and I tug her hair and I bite her neck and thrust my thumb against her clit.

"Come," I say, and I pull her hair and I try not to notice the *High School Musical* promotional plates on her kitchen counter. Then I get it. She's not coming unless I agree to meet her mother. She needs the hope of Sunday dinner with me, with her mom, family, *Fast & Furious.* "I can do dinner," I whisper.

Delilah comes, garbled and clingy and I get off her and stare at her ceiling, as unfortunately retro and shoddy as mine. She curls up to me and my arm is in a painful sleep under the weight of her heart, her postcoital rundown of her family, her know-it-all married sister, her fun-drunk mother, the one who wishes Delilah would just get married, as if that's going to make everything all better.

"You know, you're good," she says. "I've been with some *pretty famous guys* and you're really good."

I go into Delilah's bathroom, a carbon copy of my bathroom, a windowless vestibule, hell within hell. I take a shit. I don't flush. I leave. An hour later, she texts me: *I love that my bathroom still smells like you.*

My television set turns into an international funeral for Henderson. I killed Henderson and nobody knows it but everybody knows it. America mourns; his brother is *in the service* so this means that all the people who would usually take umbrage with coverage of a useless *celebrity* are on board. Not one bitter assistant comes forward to call him a douchebag. Hours pass. Delilah wants to come over that night; I tell her I'm sick. It's impossible not to search for Amy on TV when the intrusive helicopters hover over Henderson's house, even though logically I know she's not there.

Delilah writes back: *Gotta get better for my mom. She can't wait to meet you. Sunday Funday. Xx*

I remember telling Amy about my mom, how maybe we would find her and go to dinner. I wanted that the way you crave samosas at four A.M. for no reason. I hate love. I hate LA. Delilah leaves a care package at my door: kale soup, a *Los Angeles Times*, and a pack of Emergen-C.

I want pizza and a *New York Times* and coffee. I order a large pepperoni and it's late and cold and dry and overpriced. All the pepperoni fell to one side and the delivery guy says he could bring another, but it would take hours, *timing is everything, bruh.*

He's wearing a goddamn *RIP Henderson* T-shirt and life moves too fast. I killed him a few *hours* ago. The delivery guy smiles. "I got this at this joint on Vermont," he says. "Cool, right? I mean, the shirt, not, you know."

"Yeah," I say, realizing the weight of what I have done. Nobody made shirts for *CandaceBenjiPeachBeck.* Those people don't have fans. In trying to assassinate the invisible, elusive Amy, I have killed a *celebrity*. The others I killed faded away the way grandparents recede into the old photos or pets just disappear. A famous person never disintegrates from the collective consciousness. Henderson is on TV, on T-shirts.

Dr. Nicky Angevine is constantly trying to get out of prison and his sister-in-law has a website trying to raise public awareness, proclaiming his innocence. The American public doesn't root for a shrink who cheated on his wife with a patient.

But they do root for the comedian who set them free, who told them it's okay to be narcissistic, to be a permanent guest. *Me, me, me*. It would be nice to have something alive to hold on to right now, something to love me, something with a beating heart that I can feel, something to be with me as I sit here, in hell, trying to figure it out. "Am I right or am I right?" I say aloud.

But there is nobody here to answer the fucking question and this is why people have small dogs, why they trap them in their efficient apartments, because sometimes you need another living thing, you need eyes on you, even if the eyes belong to a fucking Pomeranian.

15

THE people who *make it in Hollywood* throw their new money north, up in the hills where they settle in mansions, where they can look down on everyone. But no matter how big you get, how high your house is, you can't escape from the rats. Rats climb; they're mobile. They aren't bunnies. They don't have a biological drive to burrow.

Amy is a rat, scrounging, the kind of girl who bats her eyelashes on her first day of work and wants to know where the *Alice in Wonderland* worth a million dollars is. So of course Amy met Henderson at Soho House. I was wasting my time on Craigslist, at Birds. She got here, she got the fuck out of here, closer to 90210, to Soho House and that wealthy Westside dick she wanted so bad. And no doubt she's still out there looking for it; that Peter Stark shirt is all ratty by now, but I bet she's still wearing it.

The traffic is hell and my driver just moved here yesterday so he took Sunset.

"You maybe want to take a left, get on Fountain?" I ask the driver, the kid.

He winces. "I'm really not good with left-hand turns and we have to make one when we get there."

Even this kid who just fucking moved here has that *me me me* disease and I let it go. At least I have an in. While the club is private, they do have *events* that allow common po' folk like me to stream in. Today, for example, there is an audition for an indie film. The casting call is ridiculous, second person cuntiness:

You are beautiful but you are ugly. You are life but you are death. You are the center and the outskirts. You are a paradox. You are mother and child and you are the reunion. You are TARA.
SAG/Non-SAG
Blondes, bring headshots

The driver turns on his blinker and I get a pit in my stomach. The idea of seeing Amy after all this time is mind-boggling, to think of her, midhunt for rich dick, or possibly here auditioning for this movie, trying to be *mother and child.* Bite me.

I emerge from my Uber and I do not take off my sunglasses and I move past the security guy and he doesn't flag me. I am in the elevator. I made it. Three slinky Scandinavian girls pile in with me and they are giggling and they are my ticket so I smile.

"Good morning, ladies."

The tallest one doesn't blink. "Are you an actor?"

"No," I say. "I'm an agent."

They giggle more. The doors are closing but we are bombarded by two guys who *are* agents, smug, loud Muppet men.

"I told him to fuck off."

"You told him to fuck off."

"I fucking ended that."

"Before it began."

"Before it existed."

"Before it was in the womb."

"Before it was in my *dick*," says the alpha, also in his sunglasses. He nods at the women. "Ladies."

They explode into giggles. The one who spoke to me looks at him. "Are you an agent too?"

"Not right now, honey," he says. He looks her up and down, then looks me up and down. He returns his gaze to her. "If this guy is telling you he can make you famous, believe me when I tell you he's lying. His shoes can't make anybody famous."

The elevator doors swing open and we are at another roadblock. There is a meager-eyed man at the desk. He recognizes the two fuckers from the elevator and greets them, deferential. The main one whistles with his fingers.

"Hey, Paco. My shades ever show up?"

The obsequious servant hangs up the phone and apologizes for failing to find the shades, for failing to find the people capable of finding the shades. He apologizes for being on the phone and he apologizes for the stairs being slippery and he apologizes for holding the man back from his meeting and he apologizes again for not having the shades. The sluts in front of me watch the assholes disappear up the marble stairs.

The desk slave sighs and looks at the girls. "Do any of you have a membership?"

"No," the lead one answers as she shakes her head. "But we have the password for the audition. For the movie."

He groans. "What is the password?"

"Aniston," she says.

He waves them on and asks them to take the elevator instead of the stairs. He looks at me. "You're a guest?"

"I'm a victim," I say. "My girlfriend is sick with aspirations of becoming an actress, meaning that she left me this morning to come here and audition, which makes me evil for not following her along to support her."

He laughs. "They're upstairs in the main hall."

"Okay if I stop by the bar for a drink first?" I ask.

He nods. "Just say that Ricardo okayed it. I have to admit that I'm sick with aspirations, too," he whispers, and fakes a cough. "Alto. Dancer. Epic stud."

I laugh and it feels good to be *that guy* laughing with the servant as the doors open again and more guests arrive. I leave the blue walls and the art and begin my ascent on the marble stairs.

On the second floor there are lanky beautiful people lounging self-consciously, stomachs sucked in. I go onto the terrace and see all of Los Angeles and it looks good from up here. There are small, clean love seats and small, clean people sitting in them. There are beautiful *old novels* on small shelves.

This is the path to Amy, I know it, but she isn't seated at the bar, sipping a *mojito*, and she isn't mulling over dessert, and she isn't marveling at the flowers. I go back inside, where there is a line of doors off a long hallway. I try the first one. It opens, and the lights are out but a woman is sitting in an overstuffed chair facing a monitor. She is barely visible beneath a cashmere blanket and her Beats headphones.

"Hello," I say, but she doesn't hear me.

She is bigger than Beck but smaller than Amy and I hate the way my mind puts all girls between those two. I try again. Louder. *Hello.* Nothing. I step toward the girl and I'm close enough to see the monitor she's watching so intensely. A girl is auditioning for something on the screen. Ah, so this is the girl *in charge* of the auditions.

"Hello."

Still nothing. I step closer and now I see her tanned feet, bare, naked, crossed at the ankles. I see her cotton candy hair and my heart beats faster. I know her. It's the La Poubelle candy girl who took my water.

Running into the candy girl when I was looking for Amy. This is fate. I touch her shoulder and she sees me. She gasps. There was a study that said all relationship dynamics are determined by the first interaction. Ours is this: me scaring her.

But she is laughing. She gestures for me to sit and I do.

Her toenails and fingernails are painted iPhone white—Amy's were painted nothing—and her hair is gathered at the top of her head, falling, a ballerina. She shifts and the blanket slips and her legs are honey brown, more buttery soft than Beck's, tauter, more defined than Amy's. The girl onscreen finishes reading and the candy girl pulls a yellow legal pad out of her notebook.

She writes: *?*

She holds out the pen and I wheel my chair closer and it's that time before you've fucked someone and every single movement is penetrative. My body is all dick. I take the pen. Our fingers don't touch. Not yet.

I write: *I'm looking for someone.*

I hand her back the pen. Our fingers still don't touch.

Who?

She has fat diamonds on her earlobes. I take the pen and this time our fingers touch, barely.

That wouldn't be fair. She's auditioning.

A security guard barges in. She waves him away. It was that easy. She saved me. She is the boss. She motions for me to stay.

I owe you a water. ☺

So she remembers me too. I write: *La Poubelle.*

She writes: *Yes.*

I write: *Yes.*

She picks up an extra set of headphones and I move my chair even closer and there is sex, so much sex, inside everything she does. Amy and I bantered. This is hotter. This is purer. She scratches her elbow and I want to slap my fifty dicks against her elbow. She sneezes. I write: *God bless you.*

Thank you.

My turn: *I'm Joe. You?*

She licks her lips. *Hi Joe. I'm Love.*

There is heat generated by our legs, parallel, our forearms, close. I write: *Love?*

She covers her mouth with her hand. *My parents are crazy. It's a fun name though. Like any name after a while. You grow into it and your name is just your name. But then yes. It's weird, being love. Hello, narcissistic asshole, right?*

Love is funny. *Hello, narcissistic asshole.*

She smiles and it's on, a spontaneous nonverbal blind date. I crack jokes. Love takes pictures of my jokes about the actresses and texts them to someone. A waiter comes. I write down my order: *cheeseburger medium well fries grey goose soda.* Love bites her lip and looks at the waiter and makes a peace sign. *Two.* She is an easy, breezy, beautiful CoverGirl. I actively promise myself that I will not think of her as healthier than Beck and more fun than Amy. I won't let old, broken down, dead, bad, thieving love be in the same room with new, sweet, honey-legged Love. I am here, now.

She snaps her fingers and points at the monitor. I continue to make Love laugh and when the waiter comes back with our burgers. I reach into my wallet and Love reaches over and grabs my arm. She shakes her head no. She signs for the burgers and I crack up when it occurs to me that everyone knows that sex is better when you're in Love. She sees me laughing and she writes one word: *Pervert.*

She doesn't look away when I stare into her eyes. Amy would have hit me or squirmed or made it all into a cynical joke. Beck would have pouted and brought up something boring like the etymology of the word *pervert*. But Love's eyes remain fixed on me and I know. She's a pervert too.

16

I don't believe in love at first sight. But I do believe in electricity, the way it can recharge you. I am healing. When Delilah texts, I write back: *Went away for a couple nights, visiting my uncle.*

Love picks up a container of Ice Breakers Ice Cubes gum. She pops the lid and offers the box. I open my palm, expecting her to tip it so that a cube rolls into my hand, but she writes: *U can put ur hand in my box.*

Everything would be perfect if she had used *you* instead of *u.*

I reach into her box and I pull out a piece of the gum. I have learned from our notebook exchanges that Love is a producer on this movie. She is working with some guy, the guy she keeps sending my jokes to. I tell her that I came by to look for my neighbor who is nervous about her audition.

Love does that thing girls do when they like you, where they find out you're single and they can't smile and look at you at the same time so they stare at the floor and their cheeks turn red and their eyes crinkle and *yes.*

I write that my neighbor is *really tall. Blond. Did you see anybody like that?*

Confident Love shakes her head no. *We're looking for someone more petite. I don't remember any tall blondes, no remarkable ones anyway. Do you have a picture of this girl?*

I shake my head. *But it's fine. It doesn't matter anymore.* Her grin widens.

All first dates come to a brutal, nasty end and ours does when a voice blasts into our headphones. It's a man. He is loud and fast: "Forty to Love, Forty to Love. Checkity checkity breakity breakity."

I write: *Is that your boyfriend?*

She laughs. She shakes her head no.

That was it, my answer, my prompt, my cue, my *yes.* I yank off my headphones and Love does the same. I kiss her. She kisses me back. It is the warmest kiss of my life. Love's mouth is Soho House, velvet and marble, *members only.* I don't try for anything more than this and I pull away first. She says hello to me, and her voice is at once pornographically suggestive and judiciously blunt, like she has been on trial, been recorded, part of that generation that was instructed to *use your words.*

She shakes her head and laughs. "It's so weird to hear your voice when you haven't heard it for a while."

She's right and I'm laughing and she smells so damn good.

"Come meet my brother," she says. "He's the one who wrote the ridiculous fucking casting call, but you know, he has a vision."

She explains that their parents used to be obsessed with tennis, watching it more than playing it. Love doesn't play much (yes!) and Forty isn't much of a jock (who cares?). It's funny what girls think you want to know. We walk through the main room and she waves hello to random people. Love is a passport; she's Ray Liotta in *Goodfellas* and Julianne Moore in *Boogie Nights*, a hostess, a leader. With her, I can go anywhere. She looks at me before she opens the door marked SCREENING ROOM.

"Bear with me," she says. "Forty can be a *lot*."

She's not kidding. The room reeks of cigars and lobster. Forty's on the phone and he motions for us to be quiet while he *humors his agent.* Contrary to popular belief, Philip Seymour Hoffman is not dead; he's alive and well, camping out in Forty Quinn. Forty is bowlegged and blond, in madras shorts, a Steve Miller Band T-shirt, with a giant boy smile. Love tells me they're twins but Forty looks a hundred years older. His skin is leathery from sun, cocaine, and court-ordered community service. His hair is the opposite of his skin, shiny to the point of silken, possibly transplanted from a doll, yellow and conditioned and parted in the middle.

"He's intense," she whispers.

"Are you guys close?" I ask.

"We're twins," she says. She didn't answer the question and she tucks her hair behind her ears and begins organizing his mess. We only ordered two cheeseburgers and Forty ordered everything on the menu. I try not to react to this mess of wasted food. I will not fuck this up.

Forty has a cigarette hanging out of his mouth and he pops the cork off a bottle of Dom. "I did *not* feel the Groundlings girls," he says into the phone. "I need more heart in a woman, you know? Nancy is going to hear from me because I specifically told her *do not* bring me funny unless you bring me honey."

He hangs up, growling, and Love reels him in. "Forty," she says in a kindergarten teacher tone. "Calm down. It's gonna be fine."

"It's *not* fine," he says. "We didn't find her."

"We will," she says. "But right now, Forty, this is Joe. Funny Joe."

Forty puts down his bottle, stubs out his cigarette, and claps. "Old Sport. You fucking cracked me *up.*"

I extend a hand and I like this guy not because he is complimenting me, because he is right. I am funny. I am talented. I am *Old Sport.*

The three of us settle into *club* chairs and talk about the actresses and it's oddly easy. All my life I've struggled to fit in. I can't stomach Calvin's wannabe posse and I can't sit with Harvey and listen to him work out his bits and I could never go through life as Delilah's plus one. But this feels easy.

Love leaves to pee and Forty throws a crumpled napkin at me. "Just be good to her."

"Hell, yes," I say. "So, you guys are from here?"

He looks at me like I'm insane. "Are you serious right now?"

I look at him like he is sane. "Yes."

He cackles. He claps. "Dude," he says. "I love you for not knowing where you are right now. That is fucking epic." His eyes darken. "Unless you're full of shit."

"God, no," I say. "I came here looking for someone and I bumped into your sister. That's it."

Love returns and asks what she missed. Forty throws another crumpled napkin at her. "You missed the part where my heart was made whole again," he says. "The part where I learned that your new friend Joe has *no idea* who we are."

Love crosses her arms. "Forty," she says. "Come on."

"It's fine," I say. "I'm not with the government."

Forty laughs too hard and Love picks up the napkin and throws it away even though she doesn't need to do that. "You have to forgive my brother," she says. "He's deluded sometimes and he thinks we're famous. But we're not."

"But we are," he says. "Joe, you ever hear of the Pantry?"

"Best grocery store ever," I say. "There's one right by my house."

"In Brentwood?" he asks.

"No," I say.

"Santa Monica?" he asks.

"No," I say.

"Dude, you full time it in the 'Bu?" he asks.

"I live in Hollywood," I say. "In an apartment building."

Forty steps back and it's like at school when they find out you get free breakfast and lunch. "Cool," he says. "Holly would if she could, right, bro?"

"Our parents own the Pantry," Love says, and my mind is blown and I don't try to hide it. "Which does *not* make us famous."

Everything is hazy as Love and Forty squabble over whether or not they're famous. I can't believe Love owns the Pantry, my special place, my haven. Ray and Dottie have been trying to send me their *love* since the day I got here.

"So, will you be joining us and the moms and the pops at the big C?" he asks.

I look at Love and she smiles at me. "We're going to Chateau," she says. "Will you come?"

"Sure," I say, and it was on my list of places to go but I don't want to act like a fucking tourist.

Forty strokes his chin and stares at me and Love asks what his problem is and he sighs. "I'm gonna guess that our new friend doesn't have a jacket and I'm gonna suggest a pit stop along the way to amend this unbearable injustice. Yes?"

I look at Love. I say yes.

17

I'M at home in Love's Tesla and I was born for this. We pull out of Soho House and I show her my Pantry playlists in my phone, my Shazam search history too. She wants to see *my* most played songs and she is perplexed. "This is a lot of stuff from *Pitch Perfect*," she says. "Do you have a girlfriend?"

I tell her she's funny and I make up some shit about watching it on Netflix in the middle of the night and liking the swimming pool mash-up. Then I bring it back to us, to the Pantry playlists. "I just can't get over it," I say. "I *love* those playlists. I go in there just for the music."

She gets all excited and her knees bump and she drums her elbows on the wheel. "You don't understand how I am about to blow your mind," she says. "I *make* those playlists."

And she's not kidding. My mind is blown. Love is the *music designer* and she is the person letting "Valerie" by the Zutons melt into Gregory Abbott.

"Nobody ever notices," she says. "And I mean I *think* about this music, I *obsess* over this music. I think it's because of my name, but I have like, ten thousand pictures of me posing in love songs, like 'Stop! In the Name of Love,' you know, me in front of a stop sign."

I think it's okay to touch her and I pat her knee. "Don't worry. Your dorky little secret is safe with me and I'm not gonna jump out of the car."

She has so many different smiles. This one is impish. "You can't," she says. "You're locked in."

"Good," I say. She put me in a cage already. I tell her I love the funny names the Pantry has for each section.

"I *named* those when we rebranded," she says. "I came up with Procrastination Nation when I was in college freaking out about my thesis."

"I can't believe this," I say.

I ask if she studied drama in college and she tells me she's not an actress. "I mean, I don't think you grow up here without thinking about it, but I have a charity called Swim for Love, where we give lessons to at-risk kids. That's my main focus. These movies Forty and I try to make never come together, which is fine. But I'd rather do that than *audition*. Wasn't it so sad?"

I tell her my zombie-aspirations theory, that fame is the antidote, the issue of supply and demand. She says I sound like a writer and I say I'm a bookseller. But enough about me. "Tell me about the Pantry. Everything."

She says her great-grandparents helped build California—one Pantry to start an empire—and now they own dozens of *markets* in California. They own acres of land and malls and holy shit, the girl is loaded.

"I'm not telling you to tell you," she says. "I mean, I'm not bragging."

"I know," I say. "And I mean it when I say I would be excited if you only had the one store. I love it there."

She laughs. "I'm starting to get the picture. And we have to thank your friend, the one who auditioned." She taps my shoulder. "The reason we met." Love is bold; Love is horny. "We should send her flowers. Or candy. What was her name again?"

"Nice try," I say. "I'm not telling."

She slaps the wheel. I laugh. "I still can't believe the way your parents have been telling me about you and I had no idea."

"Well, that *send our love* thing, that was my dad's idea," she says. "My parents, they're kind of grossly in love. And after I was born—after *we* were born—my dad was like, 'Let's spread the love. Let's make that a part of our every day.'"

"I think it's sweet. My parents hated each other and our grocery store had fucking *rats*."

She has a loose high laugh. She says that Ray and Dottie are middle school sweethearts. Dottie's father was a butcher. Ray's father owned the Pantry. They fell in love as children, stayed in love as teenagers, and they're still *nauseatingly in love* now. I laugh. Love says that I won't be laughing in an hour when we're all at Chateau together. "It's just not normal," she says. "It's like they never got over each other. They act like they're in high school."

"That's unusual."

Love says it kind of sucks and sighs and says she believes in laying it all out there. She blames her parents' happiness and her given name on her proclivity for relationships. She's been married twice.

"Twice?" I ask. I hold my phone up to the window; my service is bad and I want to Google her.

"Use my iPad," she says. "The password is Love."

The password is Love and I pick up her iPad and she tells me about her husbands. She met Michael Michael Motorcycle in Vegas—*total asshole*—and she was young and stupid and resentful *and on blow.* They lasted eleven months.

"Eleven months?" I say. "That's impressive."

"You gotta try," she says and sometimes I can't tell if she's being earnest. She married her second husband, a black doctor named Dr. Trey Hanes, eight years ago. "He was my heart."

I go into Safari and look at her search history: *boots puppies boots snow boots puppies Labs chocolate labs black dog booties over the knee boots yellow labs.*

I don't see how this can be it. Maybe it's some rich person privacy setting where no matter what you look up, it just says *boots puppies*, because the girl searching for boots and puppies can't be the insightful woman here in the Tesla, the one telling me about her marriage to Trey. "We were both twenty-seven," she says. "We were crazy in love."

Boots and puppies. "Uh huh."

"But then he got sick. Cancer," she says. "People always talk about the fight but Trey didn't get to fight. We didn't get to, you know, I didn't have the chance to clean him up after chemo or shave my head to go along with his."

"He died that fast," I say. And maybe *boots* and *puppies* are a defense mechanism. "That's horrible."

"It wasn't cancer. He drowned when we went surfing, right after he got diagnosed." She grips the steering wheel more tightly. "My mom would *kill* me if she could see me right now. She says I talk about this stuff way too early. But you know how your brain has sort of a baseline resting thought, a thing you talk about with yourself?"

MugofUrineCandaceBenjiPeachBeckHendersonMugofUrine. "Yeah."

"Well, mine is always about Trey," she says. "I think he killed himself. I think he felt so bad about me having to watch him die that he killed himself. And not in a coroner poison kind of way. I mean, did you ever read *Flesh and Blood*?"

"Yes," I say.

"Well, you know the guy who's gay and he can't deal with it and he swims out to die?"

"Yes," I say again and I can't believe *Boots and Puppies* is talking to me about Michael Cunningham.

"Well, I think that's what Trey did," she says. "He couldn't handle the idea of me and my family dealing with it. My parents are all about *good* things. But bad things . . ." She shakes her head. "Is this too much? Should I put on some music or something?"

I hold her hand on its way to the dash. "No," I say. "So, is your brother married?"

"Ha," she says. "That's our family joke. I was married *twice* by thirty and my brother can't even date one girl for more than five minutes. The best role models can be the worst role models."

Love tells me that it's impossible to live up to Ray and Dottie's relationship. She doesn't even know why they *had* kids, they're so in love with each other. "You hear about moms being like, fuck my husband, I love my babies now," she says. "And my mom, I mean she loves us, but she loves my dad so much more. Are your parents together? You said they fought, but some people, that's just how they communicate."

Ah, rich girls. "No. My mom left. They weren't a model for anything."

"If only you got to choose your model," she says. "But we get what we get."

Love is thirty-five now, which will make her the oldest woman I've ever slept with, and I realize how badly I do want to sleep with her. She uses her blinker. She is kind. She says she's *sort of also* from New York. "We have a couple places there," she says. "But I never last more than a few months. It sounds lame, but I think I'm just too sensitive."

"How so?" I ask.

Love grew up *mostly in Malibu* but was homeschooled, with biology trips to the Galápagos and immersion semesters in public schools and she loves Los Angeles. She used to want to be a lawyer.

"This is a problem we have," she says. "A family thing. My dad is like, 'I got these two kids and one wants to make movies and one wants to defend the bad guys and nobody wants to run the shop.'"

"Is that how he really sounds?"

She slaps my leg. "You'll see."

Love doesn't believe in bad people or good people; she believes in people. Her September 11th goes like this: Love was in her first year of law school at NYU. "And in all honesty, I *hated* it," she says. "I wasn't getting along with anyone, you know? I was in my room watching *Legally Blonde*, wanting it to be more like that, and I mean the bad part, when Elle Woods doesn't even have any friends. I was miserable."

"Weren't you a little young?" I ask. Love is five years older than I am, many years older than Beck and Amy. But she is not *that* old.

"Well," she says. "Remember, I was schooled independently and my dad, well . . ." Her voice trails off and I suspect a lot of her stories have holes filled by money. "So I was up all night at this divey bar whining to my friends about how I wanted a sign."

"A sign?" I ask.

"You know," she says. "A sign that it was okay to leave law school." She honks at someone who tries to pass her. "And then we're still fucked up, just walking it off, and it begins. The Towers, the hell, and the world goes insane, and my friends are like, holy shit. There's your sign."

"Wow," I say. I will not judge her. Instead I think about her nipples.

"Please be horrified," she says, mind reader. "I realize how *assholey* that all sounds, to say it was my sign. It sounds stupid and selfish and solipsistic to say that September Eleventh was my get-out-of-law-school-free card."

"That's harsh." Beck had to look up *solipsistic* in the dictionary. Amy did not own a dictionary.

"But when you're young, you need all that validation and you read your horoscope and you say things like, 'If the guy at the bar gives me two cherries and not one it means I'm supposed to leave this bar and go somewhere else.'"

"I get it."

Love wants to know where I was on September 11 and we are stuck in the shitty part of Sunset where it's all strip malls. I tell the truth: I got in trouble at work. Mr. Mooney locked me in a cage in the basement. I missed it. By the time I got out, the smoke was clear.

"Wow." She drums on the steering wheel. She says she loves eccentric people. She loves old people. She loves a good story. She says we have really good September 11th stories and that we could make a good movie out of them. She likes the idea of a *New Yorker who missed New York.* She asks how old I was.

"Sixteen," I say. Too quickly.

She laughs. I want to eat her candy pussy. "Joe," she says. "One thing about me, I don't give a *shit* about age. I am not one of those girls. You can be younger than me all you want."

Her mother calls and Love talks to her about tennis balls and *Net Jets.* I can tell that Love likes me by the melody of her voice, by the way she tells her mother she's *bringing someone.*

When Love finishes up with her mother, she zips into the valet at Hollywood & Highland. "Will you think I'm a horrible princess if I say I can't deal with this traffic and I'm dying for a drink and I would rather just get you a jacket somewhere here?"

I don't think Love is a horrible princess and I don't let her pay for my clothes at Lucky or the Gap.

"Almost ready?" Love asks.

"Almost," I say.

When I emerge from the dressing room, Love is wearing new clothes too, a tiny little white dress with slits on both sides. "Wow," she says. "I can't believe that jacket's from *the Gap.*"

I can't believe she's wearing a nightie to dinner, but I rip off the tag like she asks. My mom always said, *the rich are different.*

18

I live here now, at this particular table, on this particular night, at Chateau with these particular people, my people, the Quinns. I am born again a Quinn, unofficial son-in-law of Dottie and Ray—the Dottie and Ray who send me their love at the Pantry!—and they know how to hug, how to talk. They are round, happy people and we talk current events and they don't understand the *hoopla* about Henderson. "I'm old school," Love's father declares. "Give me Johnny Carson or Jay Leno at his desk. Hell, I'll take Jimmy Fallon because the kid dresses well but don't give me this punk on his *couch.*"

"Dad, don't be so harsh," Love admonishes.

"No," I say. "I see where he's coming from. I think Henderson was poisoning us all. There's honor in asking people questions. There's honesty in it. Curiosity. It's intellectual. Earlier generations, they were more comfortable as listeners and Henderson promoted an idea that we could all be the center of attention all the time. But if everyone is onstage, who's in the audience?"

Everyone stares at me, and this has happened a couple of times tonight, when I questioned the value of organic vegetables and expressed my opinion on *kale*. But I own them and I win again when Ray claps. "You are a breath of fresh air, Joe."

Dottie beams. "So smart."

Love rubs my thigh. And she is right; Ray and Dottie do seem in love and they love me. Ray wants to know if I like boats and Cabo because he's got a new *Donzi* he's dying to get in the water and a *place* in Cabo. "*La Groceria*," he says, enthralled with his terrible accent. "The neighbors, they thought we were nuts, but I like a good name. Why shouldn't I call it *La Groceria*? Everything sounds better in Spanish."

I Google Donzi. It costs around $500,000.

Ray and Dottie insist I eat and drink whatever I want. "Your first time at Chateau is a special thing," according to Ray. "Lives are made here, Joe. This is the *mother ship*. This is our family tradition and when you're with us, you're family. You understand?"

Love laughs him off but he is right. Chateau Marmont is a country that doesn't allow extradition, a safe zone, a haven, and everybody *cares* about me. Is my chair soft enough? Is my drink to my liking? Is it too hot? Too cold? Do I need a heat lamp? Do I eat shellfish? I have never been so nurtured and Love whispers—*my parents, not so bad, right?*—and I have a new respect for aspirations because this is a great way of life.

Forty breezes in and hugs me like we're best friends. Ray huffs. "You see *all* those girls today for your audition but somehow your sister is the one who comes away with a new fella."

Forty brushes it off. "She's got the love, Pops."

"Your father and I just want to see you happy," Dottie adds.

"I know, Mom," Forty says. "And I assure you, when I finish casting and finalize the rewrites and get my agent the bio he needs for that pilot shooting in Sedona and get him the rewrites he needs for that *other* pilot shooting in Culver, I assure you, dearest parents, I will meet a very nice girl and get married and pop out two perfect children. Maybe even twins."

Love laughs. "You're horrible."

But Forty's not done. "Because it's very easy to meet available beautiful babes while I'm heading up five projects at once." He knocks back a shot of tequila. "But tonight, to Mom and Dad, on Dad's half birthday."

In my navy blazer over a plain T-shirt, I pass as one of these people at Chateau. Ray tells stories about the good old days, running around the first Pantry, working doubles for pennies—his parents gave him nothing, that was a different time—and Dottie says the past is the past. She says you can't pretend you have nothing when you have so much. She squeezes my arm. "See, his father was the *owner* and my dad was the *butcher* so it's only because of me that he knows what it was to be poor."

"I understand," I say.

"Of course you do," she says. "You're from *New York.*"

Love keeps her hand on my inner thigh. This is a *family* and Ray and Dottie like me because I *work for a living.* I could live like this but *Westward Ho!* is, by definition, about expansion and our party is larger all the time. Friends come by this half-birthday party and Love has to go *be nice.* Forty slaps an arm on my back.

"You don't work in the business, right?" he asks.

"No," I confirm. "I get a kick out of it though."

"Your notes were of value," he says. He tears into three packets of artificial sweetener. "Which is precisely what this business *needs*."

He wants a high five and I'm there and he's talking about *Almost Famous* and he vents. "People here don't like to *think*. They're afraid of it, like if they do it there's no turning back. But you're a *thinker*. You're like that statue. I can tell. I see that."

"Thanks," I say.

Ray leans in. "He's a *professor*."

Forty nods. And this is a nickname I can handle, *The Professor*, and Love returns, dangles her arms over me, and whispers in my ear, *Professor*.

"No," I say. "It's *The* Professor."

Ray claps and here comes our unofficial guest of honor, producer Barry Stein. Everyone rises for *Barry Stein*, and then Bradley Fucking Cooper—Chateau!—is hugging him, inviting him to sit. And now, Barry is coming for us. He's so West Coast that he could have been in *Ocean's Eleven*. He wants us to *sit*. He doesn't smile. He's too cool to smile. Dottie is *devastated* that he's come on his own.

"The wife and nanny are in the dumps over Henny," he says, and that's a new one, *Henny*. He switches gears, not unlike Delilah, and slings an arm around Love. "But Dottie, if it pains you to see me all alone, I'll gladly take this one right here."

Fucking pig but Love's father laughs and Love excuses herself for the ladies' room with a kiss on my cheek. Stein sighs. "All the good ones are taken."

Dottie smiles. "This is Lovey's new friend *Joe*. He's brilliant."

Ray endorses me too. "This kid's got the goods, Barry."

Barry says it's nice to meet me and I don't like him and I don't like the rich, blond motherfucker approaching this table. His hat says VINEYARD VINES and his T-shirt says FOUR SEAS ICE CREAM and when I wanted to come here in a T-shirt and jeans, we had to go shopping. Love returns from the restroom and hugs this man. "Milo, it's so good to see you."

The waitresses makes room for him and Dottie *kisses* him and invites him to dinner and Forty elbows me. "Don't waste your time turning green," he says. "Milo is just our brother from another mother."

I tell Forty I'm fine and then I'm on my feet, extending my hand. Milo opens up for a hug. "Fuck that," he says. "Bring it in."

Milo's eyes are too big, his smile pandering. He's overly gracious with the waitresses, too complimentary of the cake that Dottie got for Ray. He's a fucking liar to the bone. He's a *television producer.* "By trade," he says. "But my heart is in the theater."

I want to know if his dick has been in Love and she says that he's way too self-deprecating. All people have a blind spot. Love's is Milo. She doesn't understand that he deliberately undersells himself so that she will gush over him. "Milo is amazing," she raves. "Unlike me, he *stayed* in law school." He looks down bashfully and immediately I know that they were fucking on September 11th. Love goes on. "And Milo isn't just a producer, he's *the* producer. He's the reason *New Blood, Connecticut* won all those awards. He just *knows* so much."

Milo smiles. "The lady doth exaggerate. Please, be a friend, tell me about *you.*"

But Love cuts me off. "Joe," she says. "Milo is also a fantastic writer. He's just back from Martha's Vineyard where his movie played at the festival, right?"

"Actually it was Nantucket," he says. "And I think Uncle Barry might have had a hand in that. And it's just a short."

I look at Barry Stein, who just shakes his head. "All I did was watch the movie, officer. I swear."

We all laugh as if this is funny and it isn't and Milo tells everyone about his short fucking film and Love pays attention to him, not me. I am not involved in this conversation and I slip away to find out a little bit more about this fucker. I go online and learn that Milo is Barry Stein's godson, not his nephew. I learn that he and Ben Stiller posed for photos together less than twenty-four hours ago. I learn that his short is a *based-on-fact retelling of the most searing event of Milo Benson's childhood, when his older brother shocked Darien, Connecticut, by murdering Milo's father, hedge fund owner Charles Benson, in cold blood.*

Fucking Republicans. They kill each other over money and then the liberal boy left over takes all the cash and makes a career out of repurposing this *one* event from his childhood, first into a book of *drawings* and then into a *Vanity Fair* essay and then into his TV show.

I head back to the table, where Milo and Forty fight for the attention and approval of Barry Stein, who says Milo's ideas *have tremendous potential* but pats Forty on the back and tells him that his ideas *need work.* These are two very different statements, which is idiotic because at the end of the day, either you have something or you don't. Milo orders an *açai bowl* and Forty orders a Patrón double. I nudge Forty and tell him that last idea sounded good.

Forty nods and Ray raises his glass. "To family, to food, to fun, to the fast and furious."

Ray and Dottie are proof that money *can* buy happiness and Forty groans—*Dad, enough with those movies*—and Love laughs. "Joe," she says. "Something you have to know about my dad, he is obsessed with *Fast and Furious* movies."

I smile. "That's fine," I say. "As long as your father acknowledges that *Fast Five* is the most brilliant one, an affirmation of family values that simultaneously points the finger at our corrupt judicial system even as it endorses traditional American values like Sunday dinner and loyalty."

I am fucking on tonight and Ray claps his hands. "Right again, Professor."

Love groans, she prefers *little movies*, and Forty is drunk now and quoting *The Big Chill*, as if his knowledge of acclaimed movies will convince Barry Stein that he has something of his own to say. Ray doesn't like his son like this, drunk and trying. He doesn't like it when Barry Stein motions for Milo to move closer and save him from Forty and I bet sometimes Ray wishes he and Dottie never fucked it up and had kids.

It's an ugly thing, the inside of a family, the disappointments, the disgust, and I am relieved when Dottie tugs on my arm. "*Professor*," she says. "I still can't get over that you read all those Jonathan Franzen books. I loved *The Corrections*, but I couldn't get through it. Everyone in my movie club was so excited for *The Corrections* to become a film."

"Movie club?" I ask.

"We were a book club," she concedes. "But we couldn't get through this one book that had us all stumped, something about Haiti, I don't know, it was so long and so sad. And Haiti? It's a reach for us, honestly. I wish I were worldlier but I'm small at heart. Anyhow, now we watch movies. But maybe if we had a *guide* for which books to pick . . ."

"You should ease back in with something more relatable," I say. "Maybe *Portnoy's Complaint*?"

And I choke on my drink because I didn't even realize Amy was still on my mind and she is, clearly, or I wouldn't have suggested that fucking book.

"Hey, Professor." Forty leans in, only to be interrupted by a waitress who lays a hand on my shoulder. She is sorry to trouble me, but she has an urgent message. I look around for Love and Love is gone and the waitress slips me a napkin.

Order: Joe Goldberg

Deliver to: Suite 79

When: Now

19

LIFE is kind of like one of those Barry Stein movies where everything works out. I take my orders and I find Love's wing and I knock on the door. She is slow to answer and I take in the luxury of it all, the detail, the panels on the walls. Even the abandoned room service trays look like high art—flutes, cheese knives, truffle fries. The door opens and Love furrows her brow, looking at me blankly.

"I'm sorry," she says. "I didn't order any room service."

"Love," I say. "I know you didn't order any *food*. I got your note, you know, at the table—"

She cuts me off. "I said I didn't order room service," she objects. Then she winks and it's like *that*. She tries to close the door and I stop that from happening with my foot. Love is kind, love is patient but also, mainly, above all—*yes*—Love is perverted.

"Miss," I say, as if I've done this a million times. "It's a courtesy from the hotel, a token of our gratitude."

"This is sort of inconvenient," she simpers, running a finger along her collarbone. "My butler just drew a bath."

I tell her I wasn't planning on getting wet and that I have *strict orders* to service her. She opens the door and it's like stepping into the vault of a fucking bank, it just *feels* like money, the parquet floor, staunch hardwood—*hard, wood*—Love's little silk shorts and her matching teddy and her buttery skin, slightly darker than the creamy walls. The bed is through French doors and she could have shut those doors but she didn't and I look at those sheets, white, crisp, and I look at her, white, crisp and she shakes her head.

"I told you," she says. "My butler drew a bath."

She motions for me to follow her into the bathroom and it's an obnoxiously spartan design, a sink you could find in a walk-up in Reseda, unremarkable chipped tiles on the walls, exposed pipes and a dull shower curtain out of a porno movie, pulled aside to reveal the full tub. But it's not full of water. It's *yellow* and she giggles.

"Don't tell my dad," she says, breaking character. "I don't do this all the time."

"Is that *champagne*?" I ask.

"Veuve Clicquot."

I bite my lip. Why must something always go wrong? I never should have come up here and I don't want to get into a tub of champagne. She could have said it was fucking André and I would have been irritated because I do not *need* a bathtub of money. First she wants to pretend that I'm her servant and now she wants to rub her money on my cock, *literally*, she wants me to soak in her wealth. We are young and new to each other and this is the *good* time, the new time, and we don't need a tub of money and she knows that I can't afford to fill a tub with *Veuve Clicquot* and I don't need to do that because my dick alone is good enough.

She slips out of her shorts and a proper lady would have taken off her shirt first. She is bare as I expected she would be; no jungle there. She moves one strap over her shoulder, exposing one of those Love tits I've wanted to see and she lifts that round Love tit and licks her tongue against that firm Love nipple and the shirt collapses onto the floor. She steps into the tub and sinks into the money water and I don't move and my head explodes with bad Love word play:

Is this Love is all you need is Love for real?

"Come on in," she says. "It's so good in here."

But I won't *come on in.* Of all the fantasies she could have gone with, she had to make me into a *servant.* She could have opened that door and pretended that I was a CIA operative or the hotel doctor or an escaped convict. But in her fantasy, I'm servile, a have-not, and she's a princess. This is not my fantasy and she is not the boss and I tell her to get out.

"Joe," she says. "What's wrong?"

"Get out of the tub."

"This is for us."

"Drain the tub, Love."

"This is twenty-five thousand dollars' worth of champagne," she argues. "Why don't we just get in?"

I step closer. "Drain the tub."

She doesn't want to drain the tub and she grinds her teeth. "Why?"

I look at her. "Because I don't need twenty-five thousand dollars. Of anything."

"I thought it would be fun," she pouts. She stands, parts of her body obscured by bubbles, and she hits the drain. The money begins to disappear into the sewer system and I tell her to dry off. I slam the door. Fuck her if she thinks she can buy me.

I kick off my shoes and peel away my clothes. I hear her snag one of the many plush towels. She's drying up—fuck you, symbolism—and she's pissy, slamming cabinets and draining the tub, ashamed and lecturing me about waste. Yes, the girl who fills a tub with *champagne* is gonna teach me about conservation. This is good, she *should* feel ashamed, that money could have fed a lot of poor kids. And this is my room now and I am in charge and she yanks the door open and she's wrapped in a towel.

"What the fuck is wrong with you?" she asks. "Really, I want to know."

"Take off that towel."

She looks around, as if I'm the kind of asshole who would record something this intimate. I tell her the rules. "No talking." She nods. I'm going to re-create what we had in the room at Soho House. "We're gonna play Joe Says." She opens her mouth. "Joe says no talking." She smiles, complicit. She drops her towel.

"Joe says hand on pussy." She slaps her right hand over her vagina.

"Joe says *left* hand on pussy." She switches hands.

"Rub your clit." She looks at me. Our eyes are locked and I step even closer.

"Kiss me the way you did in the room." Her lips quiver. "Feel how wet you are down there. Now feel how hard I am for you." She looks down at me. "Push me onto the bed and climb on top of me and ride me until you can't take it anymore. Tell me what you want, exactly what you want, and make me give it to you how you like it."

I reach for one of her taut, ripe nipples. "Let me start by licking your tits as I feel you up." She spreads her legs and now we are so close that our eyelashes could touch. "Cum as hard as you can because you don't need any fucking champagne when you're fucking me. Show me that you know that. Take me." She huffs. "Own me." She puffs. "Joe says, 'fuck me.'"

We are on the bed. I don't even know how we got there, I just know about skin meeting skin—*Love is all you need is Love*—and this sex is a circle, it never ends. We are animals and she is loud. *Joe says don't stop, fuck me* and when I'm not possessed by the pure *rapture* between her legs, between the sheets, I laugh. *Joe has Love.* I have never known this kind of wetness, the stuff of pornography, *sopping*. I want to eat her but I hold back—I am not a *servant*—and I nip at her belly and she pulls me on top of her for more, and she is silent, demanding, and she pulls me inside of her and it's like Chateau: The Body Version. I belong in here, in Love.

I want her to taste me—*Get your dick sucked*—and I tell her and she turns into a different person. "Oh. I kind of don't do that."

If there were music it would stop. "Oh," I say. *Kind of* is the most useless phrase in the English language. "Well, I could do it to you."

She squirms. "I just like it better like this," she says. She kisses me and her pussy envelops me, quicksand, and it's impossible to argue about blowjobs as she rides me like a Donzi on the water, bump, bump, bump, and it would be perfect, my best performance yet were it not for that little voice in the back of my head, a warning, a caution.

Get your dick sucked.

It's almost as if she heard Mr. Mooney and she knows I need more. She looks at me. "There's a Coke in the fridge," she smiles. "Will you get it?"

I bring the glass bottle of Coke to Love and she shakes it and sprays it all over my chest and yes, it's on my dick and yes, *kind of* was just foreplay and she is licking the Coca-Cola off my midsection, she is nothing but a tongue, a set of eyes, *hands.* She is below my belly button and she is stroking my inner thighs and now she has me in her hands but somehow there is new cold Coke on my legs. She rises and her eyes meet mine. "Fuck me," she says.

"Joe says, 'Suck me,'" I say.

"Love says, 'Fuck me.'" She takes over and I give it to her and I know she's never had it like this before because she tells me she's never had it like this before. We finish together, bliss. Natural symphonic *mastery* of sex. I am thirsty, spent. I swallow the last drops of Coke and we laugh about our sticky bed.

"Now I'm thirsty," she says.

"I think there's some Coke left," I say—on my dick—and I grin.

"Nah," she says, and my joke goes right over her head. "I'm good."

She pinches my nipple. Soon, she is asleep and I am awake. The sex, the *sex.* I ate Amy's *superfruits* but it was never worth getting her jungle stuck in my teeth. It's just right with Love's pure, classic Coca-Cola pussy, and I will block out the critical part of my brain hissing that the Coke was tainted by the champagne. *Fuck you, brain.*

I dig around the room for Love's panties. I am a hunter. I want to smell Love, taste her. I find them eventually and they're in the *trash*, mixed in with a banana peel, numerous price tags from Neiman

Marcus, and a half-full jar of face cream. I move the trash bin across the room so she'll see it when she wakes up and I fall asleep too.

I wake up the next morning to her laughing.

"What's so funny?" I ask.

"I see you figured out my little indulgence," she says. "I never wear the same panties twice. I know."

"You throw them away every day?"

She kisses me. "But now that I have you, you can keep them all and you can sew them together and make them into a quilt."

"I'm not sewing your fucking panties, Love."

"Oh, yes you are."

"Oh, no I'm not."

We kiss. She licks my earlobe. "Ya wanna take a shower or ya wanna fuck?"

I WANT A BLOWJOB GOD DAMN IT. *#mydayinla #chateauproblems #cantgetmydicksucked*

"Joe says let me taste you."

She pulls away. "Joe," she says. "Is this gonna be a problem?"

"There is nothing even remotely resembling a problem in this room," I say. "I was just playing around."

I can feel a story coming and I'm right. Love has never been *comfortable* with anything oral. Her mother claims *she* never gave Love's father a blowjob and she told Love that if a man loves you, truly, he doesn't need that.

"Wow," I say. "I can't believe you talk about this stuff with your mom."

"We don't really have boundaries."

"Huh."

"What?"

"Nothing."

"Joe."

"Don't take this the wrong way, but they met in middle school. Do you *really* think your dad has gone his whole life without getting his dick sucked?"

She shakes her head. "That's the part of the story I'm getting to," she says, and then she tells me about the year she and Forty had their sweet sixteen, a giant Beverly Hills bonanza with hundreds of people. She got a horse as her present and Forty got a massage. "And Forty gets home," Love says, "And he is *messed. Up.* And I am like what's wrong? And he is like, I can't tell you. And I am like, you have to."

"And?"

"And my dad's masseuse *sucked his dick.* And she told him she did that for my dad once a week."

"I'm sorry, but that's fucked up."

Love shrugs and says that we can play Joe Says all day long but she'll never do anything oral with me. Or anyone. "I know you want to know if I did this for Michael or Trey," she says. "And the answer is no."

I strategize. "I'm just thinking, you know, it's different for everyone," I say. "What your mom doesn't like, you know, maybe you would like."

Love says that she is thirty-five years old and she knows *exactly* who she is. She kisses me and grabs a room service menu. We order *eggs benny* and coffee and pancakes and we both look at *mimosa* on the menu but champagne is a sore spot. I tell her I like her. She says she likes me too.

We sink into the bed together and this is what it is, sex, then a knock at the door, then food, then rest, then movies, then sex, then we think about leaving the room and we don't leave the room, then sex, then sometimes we get in the tub, then movies, then food, then sometimes a song, then sex, then Joe Says/Love Says. Love has a butler named Henry and she texts him and he shows up with Animal Style In-N-Out burgers. We half watch movies on TBS (Love's favorite station) and when *Bride Wars* begins, she says she never cheated on either of her husbands. I tell her I never cheated on anyone either.

"But you were never married?" she asks.

"No." I don't want to tell her about Beck or Amy. That's what feels so unique about this room, this thing with Love. I've been trying to find Amy for so long and now to break away from all that hunting, to rest. In this room, in this bed, I rarely think about the mug of piss in Rhode Island. It's as though there are invisible guards outside, like nobody can get us, our DNA, our pasts. It's only been five meals, maybe two days. I genuinely don't know. Love is a drug. The more she opens up about her life, the less I want to share my own stories with her. My life feels too small, too gritty.

"Okay," she says. "You'll let me know when you're ready."

Love is patient. She doesn't push. It's actually fun to watch *Cocktail* with her because, unlike Amy, she takes it for what it is. Love likes *Hannah and Her Sisters* but she doesn't love it the way she loves *Crimes and Misdemeanors.* Just when I think she might be perfect, she claps for the opening credits of *Dirty Dancing*. She hits the MUTE button. "Let's not have any sound," she says. "I've seen this so many times I don't need to hear it to watch it."

I blindfold her to see if she can watch it without hearing it or seeing it and I kiss her all over her body, underneath her knees, her elbows, her inner thighs. I do not eat her out. I make her come without touching her vagina. She says that's a first.

"Does this place have a pool?" I ask.

It does and Mr. Mooney was wrong; the pool is not *cold and dirty*. The pool is a giant blue oval, as welcoming as Love's vagina. My phone falls inside of it and Love swan dives to the bottom and emerges with it in hand. Her butler puts it in rice. I'm tempted to ask him to throw it away. Love says my broken phone is a sign that I'm supposed to relax. And maybe I am because it's hard to care about my life before Love.

This is why people go west, smashing rocks and hoping to spot something shimmering in the creek. Dip a pan into the rocky water and lift it and strain it and then feel solid gold in the palm of your hand. Everything I did was worth it because it led me straight into Love's arms.

20

I can't decide what I like more, this bed or these sheets or this view or the balcony or the jam and toast that were waiting here when I woke up. Chateau is Adult Disney World, the kind of place where they're one step ahead of you. I didn't have to ask for my phone. It was here when I woke up, in a little basket by the bread, by the silver coffee pot, so much more elegant than Keurig. Love's still sleeping and I put on a robe and pour my coffee and spread jam on my soft, blond bread and walk out to the balcony.

I am awkward at first, not used to having toast and a balcony and a robe. I'll have to look in the mirror after I finish my breakfast because I'm curious to see if I look different, if all this luxury closed my pores. Maybe I don't even need to buy Henderson's skin care products. I'm happy and they could evict us right now and I wouldn't care as long as they let me take that dirty little minx in the bed. Even the no blowjob bit; I'm a man. It's good to have a goal.

I lean on the balcony rail and turn on my phone. When it finally boots up, it proceeds to buzz like it's having a heart attack from trying to keep up with all these texts from Delilah.

Hey! What do you think about tomorrow?

My mom says hi LOL

My mom loves Dan Tana. Seems good, right?

Hey

Joe?

Asdjkasdkasdsda

Hey are you ok? Harvey says you never came home. Calling hospitals.

My mom is only here til Monday . . . this is fucked.

Going to Birds?

Going to Birds. See you there?

Asdbsjkdaskd yes?

Knock knock

La Poubelle?

At La Pou!

FUCK OFF

Hey Joe are you ok? Look I know I shouldn't have asked you to meet my mother but it's not what you think. She's cool. I didn't mean it in a meet the parents kind of way. So you don't have to disappear on me.

There's a picture of Delilah's tits, real, pert. There's another text:

If you're not dead, I'm never speaking to you again. I don't need this. I have a lot of great things in my life and a lot reasons to be happy and I don't need you blowing me off like this. So do me a favor and just leave me alone. Okay? Okay.

And now it's Calvin's turn. He wrote to me, just eighteen minutes ago: *Dude. Hot chick in store. She's got a Portnoy's Complaint. Book not screenplay.*

I thought I was done, that it was over, but my beating heart and shaking hands tell me it's not. Amy. *Finally.* I write back: *Hold her. On my way.*

Calvin writes back: *How?*

He wants to be a writer but he can't come up with a fucking plan to make a girl wait twenty minutes? I send my orders: *Tell her that your supervisor is in yoga and you have to wait for him to get out so you can get his approval.*

Calvin writes back: *Cool.*

He should have said *smart* and with shaking hands, I scribble a note for snoring Love—*Gotta run, be back soon*—and I nearly fall over trying to get out of the fucking robe and into my clothes. I shut the door and step into the hallway, into reality—I don't have a key, this isn't *my suite*—and I kick a discarded room service tray. Lazy, unhungry fucks tossing out lukewarm, high-end pancakes and I don't belong here, I had a *purpose* and a goal and I need closure and FUCK.

I hail a cab on Sunset. The world is uglier than it was before and I feel hungover even though I wasn't drunk. Calvin texts: *She asked what kind of yoga. I said hatha. FYI.*

I write back: *I'm close.*

And I am. This is it. I am queasy and the cab is fast and we are here. Across the street, I see her in the shop flirting with Calvin. *Cunt.* The crosswalk is flashing red but fuck it. This is *Fast Five* and I have my target in the crosshairs. I will risk another jaywalking ticket. I get out of the cab, I run. I make it to the double lines before the driver wails on his horn.

"You need to pay me!" he screams.

I forget to pay because I'm so used to Uber and technology is killing our instincts. I look into the shop. Amy and Calvin must have heard the horn because they look up, and Amy's eyes widen. The driver wails on the horn again and now the light is green and more people are honking. Range Rovers want me out of the fucking way and a woman in a Prius *enjoys* laying on her horn, taking out all that rejection rage on me. Even if I did run out on this cabbie, which I can't—the mug of piss—I would miss Amy. She's out the door and she's on foot. She's around the corner, into a waiting car, a passenger, not a driver, and she's gone.

I don't get hit by a car but if I did I don't think it would matter. My nerves are shot. I've gone from the high of Love to the adrenaline of Amy to the crash, to forking wrinkled tens out of my wallet to pay this cabbie as he bitches about *you kids and your Ubers* and to know that I was so close. All the nights I spent in this Village waiting. That bitch knew. She had to have known. The cabbie goes, disgusted, as if his shitty day compares to mine.

I walk east to the corner of Franklin and Bronson and wait for the crosswalk to turn white. I plod across the street and into the bookshop and Calvin looks like a different person. He shaved. His hair is short. He's wearing a #IWasThere T-shirt.

"Dude," he says. "I did everything I could, but she had to jam. She said she'll be back."

I don't bother telling him how wrong he is. I just slump into a chair behind the counter.

"So where've you been?" he asks.

"I was in West Hollywood," I explain, and I can't believe I missed her.

"Did you have a meeting?" he asks, as if that would matter, as if I didn't move here to kill Amy, to find Amy. I tear into one of Calvin's thinkThin bars.

"Yeah," I say, deflated.

"A two-day meeting?" he asks, all hopped up now, as if this might mean he gets to ride along. "Delilah said you haven't been around."

Delilah and I sigh. "Yeah," I say. "A friend in town, a meeting, no big deal."

Calvin picks up his iPad. "She was filthy hot," he says. "The Amy chick."

"Yeah," I say, but Love is prettier and softer and Amy has fucked me over again. I groan. Love does not know my phone number and never seeing her again is possible. I ran out on her and this is what Amy did to me and Love might think I used her for her body and her bed and her truffle fries. Life is better when it's simpler. If I could just kill Amy, I wouldn't have to worry about her. She wouldn't get in the way of things. If Amy were dead, I would know Love's phone number.

Calvin rubs his forefinger and pointer finger on his iPad, the way he always does when he sees a hot girl on Tinder. He smiles. "You can almost see her nips," he says. "Wanna see?"

I don't want to look at *nips* but he pushes the iPad at me and these nips I *do* want to see because they are Amy's nips. "How did you get this?"

"I pretended I was taking a selfie and I got a picture of her," he says. And Calvin missed his calling. I could hug him.

"Did you get anything else?"

"Don't be pissed," he says, holding up his hands.

"Okay . . ." I say slowly.

"Well, I tried to tell her that the owner was coming back." He laughs. "The hatha yoga shit, but then I said something about kundalini and she caught onto my bullshit and she was like 'What are you *really* trying to do here?' and I was like, 'I'm trying to get to know you' and she was hot for me, Joe. I'm sorry but you know, it was like some classic sitcom shit where the friend tries to get the girl to stay for the friend but then the girl likes the friend."

My heart beats again. I toss the thinkThin bar in the trash. "Did you get her number?"

"No," he says. "But I did get her address. I told her I would send her a flyer for this show I'm doing."

"You got her address?"

"Yeah," he says.

I reach for his iPad and he pulls back. "And this show, it's called *Back in the Day* and we're totally analogging it, you know? We're gonna, like, not promote on Facebook or Twitter or—"

"Calvin," I barge in. "What's her address?"

He squirms. "Can I say something?"

Fucking A. "Sure."

"I kind of can't."

"Why the fuck not?" I snap.

"It's property of my improv group and technically she gave it to the group."

I take a deep breath. I will not lose my mind. "That's cool," I say. "But you know, I won't tell her how I got it."

"Yeah," he says. He smoked an ounce of weed today. Fucker. "But like, *I'll* know that I gave it to you and I'll feel shitty about that."

Calvin, who Tinder bangs one girl after another, Calvin, who won't look Delilah in the eye when he runs into her at Birds, Calvin, who won't watch *Enlightened* because he just can't *get into a series with so much chick voiceover*, this guy is now gonna talk to me about boundaries? Keep me away from Amy Fucking Adam? God, she's a manipulative beast. But I'm better. I hop off my chair.

"Smoothie?" I offer.

"Always," he says. "Kale."

I go next door and order the kale smoothie and I go into the bathroom and crush three more of Dez's Percocets. Twenty minutes later, Calvin passes out. At last. I reach into his pocket for the password cheat sheet he keeps in his wallet and I get into his iPad and into the database for his improv group and boom.

The building is around the corner on Bronson and Amy *did* settle into this neighborhood. Maybe she got a wealth hangover and maybe she's still the girl who tells the guy she's using that she misses her own bed and maybe she's back in it right now, freaking out about seeing me, eating frozen chicken and waiting for the truffle oil to evacuate her pores and ooze out of her body.

I go to the Pantry and buy violets—the painted ones. Then, I go to Bronson and buzz apartment 326. Nothing. I buzz apartment 323. Nothing. I buzz 101 and 101 is female and 101 is awake.

"Hello?" she says, husky.

"Flowers!" I say.

The girl in 101 doesn't ask who they're for because everyone likes to get flowers. Woody Allen knows this; Anjelica Huston gets murdered in *Crimes and Misdemeanors* because she wants flowers and lets a stranger into the building. My breath quickens when I enter the lobby and I have to dart into the stairwell because apartment 101 is just a few feet from the front door. In the stairwell, I freeze. I am shaking. The flowers rattle, *swish swish.* I don't have to do this. So Amy is harassing me. So what? I could just slip out of this building and run back to Love. I prefer Love. She's sweeter. She knows music and she's ready for me. So what am I doing in this stairwell, jeopardizing my future with Love?

"Fucking closure," I mutter. If only *Eternal Sunshine of the Spotless Mind* were a real thing and it's such an asshole Angeleno thought to have, unoriginal and bratty. I can't erase my memories of Amy. But I can stop her from fucking around with my future.

I begin my ascent toward her apartment. This stairwell is concrete and white and every time I step it echoes. Everyone in this building is sleeping; Angelenos need beauty sleep. They need energy to make storyboards for web series and *hike* and talk about movies they'll never make and walk their dogs that hate them. My heart pounds and I reach the third floor and I turn the doorknob and it squeaks and I flinch and I bet nobody was ever murdered here before.

I jimmy the "lock" of 326—nothing is built well anymore—and the front door opens directly into the living room, which is awash in bras, bowls of cereal, empty bottles of Corona Light, and *US Weekly*s. There is one sofa, covered in frayed blankets, and a small TV. To the left is a galley kitchen with a sad little countertop meant to facilitate socializing.

The TV is off and the apartment is quiet, but there's an open box of Cocoa Krispies on the counter, like someone just made a bowl of cereal and wandered away. I pass the counter and walk past the Pier One barstools into a narrow hallway. The walls are white and there is a bathroom at the end of the hall and the door is open. A closet door to my left is ajar, which means that the door to my right leads to the bedroom. Amy's bedroom.

This is it. I put my hand on the doorknob and push. The room is small and dark. Marilyn Monroe hovers above the bed, a breathy beacon in white, immortalized on the wall (*why, hello, Joe*). Beneath her is a rumpled comforter, covering the faint outline of a body. Hair peeks out from those covers, blond, greasy. My breath is short. I count down. I flex. I clench my jaw. And in one fell swoop I peel away the blanket.

There's a shriek and a kick and a little ninja, a foot shorter than Amy in a black tank and black panties, springs up as I fall onto my back. The floor is hard. Wood. Her foot is a weapon and she knows it. She kicks me in the crotch. I scream and roll to my side and that foot gets my kidney. I fold into myself and now she gets my tailbone and I retreat and now that fucking foot jabs me in my belly.

"Stop!" I beg.

She kicks me again. Harder. And I deserve this because I didn't find Amy, because I don't know Love's number, because my balls have been kicked into my intestines.

She jumps on the bed and stands in karate chop mode. She yelps, "Don't move." As if I could turn over. As if my body isn't a collection of throbbing, busted places. I breathe. This was supposed to be Amy. That was supposed to be me on the bed, in control. I open my eyes. She perceives my eyes as a threat and she jumps off the bed and kicks me in the head. Everything goes away now, the pain and the fear and the anger and the lukewarm blood.

Blackout.

21

"DON'T move," the girl says again.

I can't move. She's being redundant. While I was out cold she went to work on me. She tied my limbs together with resistance bands. I'm a mermaid flat on her white shag area rug. I can't talk. A resistance band is wrapped around my head, cutting through my mouth and jamming my tongue. The girl paces. She grips her cell phone and I wonder when she called the cops, what's taking so long, how bad this is going to get. Fuck these fucking resistance bands and I have only one move.

I cry.

In the big way. For everything bad, the starving kids and the way Harvey refreshes his YouTube videos, for Calvin's body, how confusing it must be, the pot and the coke, the acting and the writing. I cry for Mr. Mooney and his eggs and for Marilyn Monroe, framed here too; she is everywhere and yet she is dead. My captor picks up a pair of scissors and kneels beside me. Ferberizing a baby is no easy thing. She pulls the band from my cheek and cuts it.

"Enough!" she screams.

I blubber. I work my lower lip. I drool. "My God, thank you."

She grabs a hand towel and wipes my face. "Stop it."

"I—I'm sorry," I stammer. "I won't move, I promise. I know the cops are coming."

Her eyes flash to the left and she did not call the cops. She grunts, throws the hand towel on the floor, and she is still holding her scissors and her phone. "I said stop it."

I nod. "Sorry."

She paces and there is a reason she did not call the cops. Anyone would call the cops. That mysterious reason is all I have and I wish I knew what it was because if it goes away I'm fucked. "Sometimes they're slow," I assure her. "But they'll be here."

She stops moving. "I said, stop it."

"I'm sorry."

"Stop talking."

"I will," I say. "There's just something I want you to know before they get here."

She groans. She looks at me.

I blurt, "I was looking for my girlfriend."

"You broke in."

"No," I say. "The door was open."

"No, it wasn't."

"Go look," I plead. "I swear to you. The door was open, just like Lydia said it would be."

The girl storms across the rooms, her thighs are hard, shiny. She opens the door. She examines the knob. She slams it. I *do* know how to pick a fucking lock. She returns to me. "Well, who the hell is Lydia?"

"Do the cops have your code?" I ask. I am *#TeamGirl.* "You should call 911 and make sure they know the access code."

"They have it," she lies. She grimaces. She gets a text and she reads and types and it's probably her best friend, who is like *call the cops* and this girl is like *I got this* and the friend is worried like *you need to call the cops sweetie this is cray.* I can smell the dynamics and I know I have a shot at freedom.

This girl doesn't want to bring in male authority figures; look how many resistance bands she has in her possession. She was training for something like this. This girl is a vigilante, like the renegade hotel manager in *Red Eye*. I can't make sense of the Marilyn Monroe pictures and the West Elm furniture; they don't match up with her rock-hard thighs, her resistance. But I do know that she would rather have me tied up in her possession than in a holding cell in a part of town she doesn't like. She could have rolled my unconscious body out the door and onto the street. She could have done a lot of things but she knew how to beat me without breaking me. She tosses her phone onto the sofa.

"Is everything okay?" I ask, subtly instructing her that we are equals, with each other's best interest at heart.

She doesn't like it and she comes at me and jams the scissors toward my face, stopping a few inches away. "I'll ask the questions, fucker."

"Okay, yes," I say. "You're in charge."

She crouches over me. I wish she would put on some fucking pants. "Who are you?"

This matters, what I say to her. I have to be someone she wants to set free. This is the most important question I will ever answer and I swallow. "I'm Paul," I begin, my mind whirring.

"Okay, Paul. What else?"

"I swear to you, I am not a sicko. I didn't come here to hurt you."

"You didn't bring a weapon," she concedes. She pulls the scissors back, the tiniest bit.

I nod. "I'm a mess right now." Girls want men to be messy.

She takes the scissors away. I sigh. "I'm taking a semester off from law school. I want to be a prosecutor."

"Uh huh," she says. "Is your girlfriend in law school too?"

"I don't have a girlfriend," I answer.

She raises her scissors. I was too quick. I fucked up. "You said you were looking for your girlfriend. You specifically said that. *Lydia.*"

"I'm sorry," I say. "I'm freaking out here."

She purses her lips. She puts down her scissors and picks up her phone. "I should call the cops."

I nod, like a Republican promising to lower taxes before a live national audience. "You should," I agree. I play hard. "I don't blame you if you do. I would have called the second you knocked me out. I show up in your *bedroom.* It's a fucking nightmare. I can't believe I went to the wrong place. If I were you, I mean, I would have done the same thing. And I'd call the cops. I mean this is fucked, I know it."

She doesn't dial 911. She looks at me. "But it's not like they're going to resolve anything. They'll just throw you in jail and let you out a day later."

"True," I say. "But then, when you fuck up like I did, you deserve a night in jail."

She still does not dial 911. I'm becoming human, becoming Paul. Her allegiance is shifting. "I know I should call," she says. "As a citizen."

In a neighboring apartment "Shooting Star" by Bad Company comes on, blasting. A moment later it disappears as suddenly as it started. We both laugh.

"Every morning," she says. "Alarm clock."

"That's one hell of a way to start the day," I say. "He lives alone, I presume?"

"He's a she," she says, and I've got her now; she's opening up. I can see it happening. "Anyway, you're right," she says, and it's an important sentence.

"I'm gonna call 911," she promises, but no she isn't. "This isn't about you or me," she rationalizes. "This is just what you have to do in these situations."

"Yes," I declare, unafraid. "It's the right thing."

She slides the unlock button on her phone. I watch her fingers, unpainted short nails. She enters her passcode. I listen to the neighbor trudge. She hits the number nine. She hesitates. I go in for the final swoop. "Don't feel bad," I say. "Believe me, I know I got myself into this."

She stops pushing numbers. "What *is* your deal?" she asks.

And I win. Now I launch into my elaborate story. I tell her that a few months ago, my girlfriend cheated on me. During my first year of law school, which has been very stressful.

"Where do you go to law school?" she asks, and God bless women, curious, mysterious creatures, mutating from one mood to another.

"UCLA," I answer, and now I get to the good part. I tell her that I was devastated and depressed and I went on Casual Encounters on Craigslist. "That's where I met Lydia," I explain. "And Lydia and I had coffee and she had this fantasy where she wanted me to show up and surprise her in her bed."

"Ew," she says. She sits on her sofa. "Does she live in this building?"

"She did," I say. "Or I got the address wrong. But I would have to look at my phone. She had said that she only locks her door when she's with someone, that I was welcome any time. Anyway, I know it all sounds disgusting. But your door was unlocked and I thought this was the place."

She springs. She can't believe she forgot to lock her door and she blames herself now. She hits her head with her phone. "I need to get better at living here," she says. The air changes now. She's all about herself, her own failure to lock the door after *this guy* left. She isn't afraid of me anymore. She's afraid of what would have happened if someone truly dangerous had shown up here. She tosses her phone on the sofa again and picks up her scissors.

"Hold still." She cuts the resistance bands that bind my arms together and now we get to know each other. Rachel is a nanny. She was the head of the rape crisis center in college and she still teaches self-defense to women. I caress my wrists. "That explains your moves."

Rachel works for a rich family and this apartment belongs to them, which is the *real* reason she didn't call the cops. "They're so paranoid," she says. "If I called the cops and the cops called them, I mean, it would be a whole thing." She puts down her scissors. "They're kooky LA zillionaires," she says. "You can tell how completely sexist and backward they are by all this Marilyn Monroe shit and all the fluffy rugs. It's what an old man thinks a young woman wants, you know?"

"Well said," I agree, still her prisoner, her yes man. "Are they famous?"

She says they are but she winces. "I signed a nondisclosure," she reveals. "I can't talk to friends or tabloids or anyone. My *mom* doesn't even know who I work for."

"Wow," I say. "That's crazy."

"Eh," she says. "Hopefully I'll be outta here soon. Anyway, are you gonna call the Lydia girl?"

I don't understand women in Los Angeles. The fearlessness. I could be anyone. I could have been lying—I *am* lying. I could be a pervert, one of the rapists she is trained to combat. Why is she smiling at me and coyly asking about my imaginary Craigslist hookup? How did she recover so completely, to the point of flirting?

"No," I say. I rub my wrists. "I think this is a sign that I should lay low."

"Right," she says. "You'll get out there when the time is right. I went to this amazing seminar on solitary expansion last month. Life-changing stuff." She is such an *alum*; she graduated ten minutes ago and thinks everything can be solved by rallies and communication and banners and hope. She beams. "Coffee?"

I don't want her to call the cops so I say that I want coffee. She directs me to sit on the sofa while she pours coffee grinds into an old-fashioned coffeemaker. She starts talking about herself. In addition to being a nanny and a self-defense instructor, she is an SAT tutor and she doesn't understand rape fantasies.

"I did Women's Studies at UCLA," she says. "So many of the

women who study that shit are *crazy* into rape fantasies. Explain it to me while I freshen up."

She walks past me into her bedroom and she does not close the door all the way. I can see her as she moves around her room, trying on Victoria's Secret PINK sweatpants and kicking them off and slipping into jeans and getting out of those too. And here I sit, waxing fake intellectual about rape fantasies and control issues and Craigslist. Nanny Rachel emerges in a tiny black cotton skirt and big fat UGG boots and a tiny gray half T-shirt. She's wearing lip gloss. Lots of it. She brushed her hair. She sprayed perfume. She got dressed up for me. I broke into her home and found her in bed and *she got dressed up for me.*

"Well, I see what you mean about the thrill of giving up control, but I feel like I give up enough control every time I walk out of my apartment. In the bedroom, I want to be in charge. But I guess you figured that out."

She pours coffee into chipped IKEA mugs that scream LOVE in all caps. Life is cruel and the word *love* shouldn't be plastered all over the fucking place. She smells like cigars. "You look like a black coffee guy."

I nod even though I want cream. "Thanks."

She looks out her window at the middle parts of the palm trees. "I do love this place though. And the baby is easy. He doesn't know he's an asshole yet." She sighs. "But the commute is awful. The family's in Brentwood and Malibu and I was commuting from Eagle Rock so the dad was like, why don't you stay here? You know how it is here, the way people are either broke on unemployment or giving out free apartments."

"Cool," I say. And I need to know if Amy lives here or if she pulled this address out of a hat. "So, do you have a roommate?"

"Not since I was in college," she says.

Amy picked this address randomly. And because of that bitch, I came here, got beaten, tied up, and forced to drink bitter coffee out of a cracked LOVE mug. I tell Nanny Rachel I have to go. I don't agree that we should exchange numbers. She looks crestfallen.

"Good luck with school," she says.

"Thanks," I respond. "Good luck with the rich folks."

She laughs. "Thanks, Paul."

I cross Franklin. I fucked up my chance at a brand-new life with Love and I take the long way around to avoid Calvin and I reach my building and Harvey's not in the office. So there is a God. But Delilah is standing at my door and her arms are crossed and her eyes are narrowed and then she says it:

"I know about your problem, Joe."

So maybe there isn't.

22

THIS is not my lucky day. Delilah is pacing in my apartment. When I stood her up, I pissed her off. And unfortunately, she didn't dive into a quart of Ben & Jerry's. Instead she went on a research mission. She's been obsessing about that night I *stood her* up. She won't say what she knows, but she is building a case against me.

"Explain that," she snaps. "We had *plans*."

"I know," I say, placating. "It was Calvin."

"You're a grown-up," she snaps. "You're not ten. Don't talk to me about fucking Calvin."

"You asked me what happened." I will my forehead to stop sweating.

"Your answer can't be Calvin," she says. "You have to take responsibility for your actions, Joe. Your actions have consequences and you ditched me and that was wrong."

"I know it was."

"Do you?" she asks, and here we go again.

She's downloaded some app that will stop her from texting me in the future. But never mind about the app because *I'm* the one who led her on and she thinks there's *something up* with me.

"There is nothing," I protest. "I flaked."

"You haven't lived here long enough to use that excuse," she says. "You're supposed to be a New York guy."

"Delilah," I plead. "Can you please let this go?"

But she can't. She has more to tell me. She knows that I told a bartender at Birds that I knocked up a girl. (I did but I didn't.)

"It's complicated."

"That's bullshit," she barks.

"Delilah," I say. "Can we not do this now?"

"Why?" she asks. "Do you have somewhere to be? Is it time for you to go freaking wander around the Pantry like a zombie?"

"I don't wander around like a zombie."

"Ask Calvin," she says. "He'll tell you otherwise."

"You just said to leave Calvin out of this," I remind her.

"Don't change the subject." She comes back at me, arms crossed. She says she found out from Calvin that I was at Henderson's and that it was my idea to go to the party. "I know you were there. I have proof." She shows me a video on YouTube and there I am in Henderson's fucking kitchen. I want to erase the Internet. "Calvin said one minute you were there and the next minute you were gone. So where did you go, Joe?"

I forgot how small this apartment is, how thin the walls. She is trying to put me in a cage and I won't let her. "Delilah, this is not cool."

"No," she says. "It isn't cool to let me suck your dick and then turn around and shit all over me. That is not cool. And I wanted you to man up and explain to me why you haven't been to work in several *days* and why you were at Henderson's party when you *told* me how much you hate him. But if you won't do it, if you won't just tell me . . ." She trails off and takes a deep breath. She sits. She points at the floor.

I sit. "What?" I ask.

She rubs her hands together. She repositions, Indian style. She's enjoying this. She wants this, whatever the fuck this is. "Look," she says. "I know."

I don't say anything.

"I know." She says it again and I don't like it. *I know.*

She knows I don't like this and she reads me well. She really is an investigative fucking reporter and her hand goes on her chin and her chin lowers and I wish she would disappear, into thin air. Poof. And depending on what she says next, I might have to make that happen.

She breathes in. "I know about your pill problem."

Are you fucking kidding me right now? I exhale and unclench my fists and she has no idea she saved her own life just now. She sits by me and links her arm through mine and begins to act out some sort of rehab *Rush* fantasy where she can save me from my addiction. She strokes my back and talks to me about Promises and halfway houses and the craziness of LA. "Dez told me how many Percocets you've been buying," she says. "And the way you disappear and wander, I mean, I put two and two together." She blames the apartment. Brit Brit fell apart too in here. She stares at the Kandinsky. "We can get you better," she says. "We can. You just have to want it."

I need her to think she's right and I tell her I want to do this on my own. "I think I need some time," I confess. *Ha.*

She pats my leg, all business. "Do you have insurance?"

I tell her that I do and she says she has an idea and she leaves and returns five minutes later with a fucking board game. "Chutes and Ladders," she says. "Sometimes you just need to like be a kid again, you know?"

I don't know but I push the spinner and feign interest in her tedious anecdotes about celebrities and about the time that George Clooney "sort of flirted" with her. She swishes down another chute and the game is never ending and this is what you deserve when you fuck Don't Fuck Delilah. I should have known it would come to this but I was a fool.

She wanted me to meet her mom and I should have gone and placated her. But stupid me, I thought I could fuck Delilah. I thought I understood her in a way that other morons in this building don't, that there was nothing to fear because she's incapable of loving someone like me. She's a star fucker and a gold digger and while she claims to put on her Band-Aid dresses in the name of work, in the name of gossip, she is putting on these dresses because Nicolas Cage married a waitress, because Matt Damon married one too, because George Fucking Clooney promised his dick to a hot lawyer.

Even if I had shown up and met her mother and told her I loved her and bought her flowers for no reason and asked her to move in and started talking rings and babies, even then, it would never last. She would continue "working" and squeezing into dresses and going to Golden Globes parties and trying to spill drinks on people like James Franco—this is how Calista Flockhart got Harrison Ford—

and she would leave me for James Franco if she got the chance.

But I did not see the whole picture. I was starved from not getting my dick sucked. I was paranoid because of Henderson and I was lonely and I didn't see the loophole. There is something that Delilah loves more than famous cock: research. And she doesn't know the real story, but she knows too much.

"My mom says hi by the way," she sniffs.

I push the spinner. "Tell her hi back," I say and I wonder if Love is awake, if Amy is alive.

She checks her messages and says she might be getting into an Ed Norton premiere tonight. She wants me to beg her to stay. I don't.

She runs her finger along a chute. "So how did you get into Soho House?"

I look at her. "Huh?"

"My friend Ethel saw you there."

"Who is your friend Ethel?"

"Just a friend," she says. "She knows who you are. She's seen you at Birds."

"That's kind of creepy." I am being stalked. This is *Fast & Furious* and Delilah has her own fucking team and does she think she can trap me into being her starter husband, her pre-Franco fuck doll?

"Joe," she says. "Where have you been these past few days? Were you on Skid Row?"

"No."

"You need to tell me where you're getting stuff," she says. "I know it's not just Dez because he didn't hear from you these past few days either."

"Delilah," I say. "It's not like that."

"Then tell me who you were with."

I look at the Kandinsky.

"Joe," she says. "I'm trying to help you. But I can't help you if I don't know where you're getting your drugs."

She's too smart. Technically, I should eliminate her. But if I were to bash Delilah over the head and go out and buy acid and reduce her body and dispose of it, I would attract the wrong kind of attention. Her parents would miss her. She's been asking around about me so I would be a suspect in her murder. And then, when I find Amy, I will have a harder time killing her because I will be under suspicion. There's no way around it: Delilah has to live. And the only way to get her off my back is to break her heart.

I pat the Chutes and Ladders board. "Delilah, I haven't been completely honest with you. There's someone else."

She swallows. Her cheeks bloat or maybe they just turn red. I tell her I'm sorry. I tell her I went to Henderson's party to see this other girl.

"But she's enabling you," she pushes.

I shake my head. "The pills aren't for me."

She pulls away. "Then who are they for?"

"This girl's mom," I say. "She has cancer. Esophageal."

Delilah closes the board.

"I'm sorry," I say.

"Whatever," she says, turning her back on me.

I tell her I'm horrible. I tell her she is beautiful. I tell her it's my loss. I hold her. I tell her I am a terrible person and I don't deserve her. I tell her she is beautiful again. I tell her she is smart, she could run the world with her connections and her tech savvy. I tell her she is going to wind up with someone *much* better than me and this is when she hugs me harder. This is when she forgives me, when I tell her, without a doubt, that I will be knocking on her door someday, when she's living in a big house up in the hills with marble floors and security. I'll be wishing I was in there with her, but I won't deserve to be.

"Okay," she says. She shakes my hand. "Just do me a favor, don't talk shit about me with Dez and Harvey and these other fucks. They're all just horrible."

"You got it," I say. Delilah packs up her stalking devices—she *has* to go to the Polo Lounge to spy on someone—and when she's gone, I find the YouTube video with me at Henderson's. I look through the comments.

User AA212310 writes:

Murderer in the house right there

User AA212310 does not respond to any of the many people who have asked what she means about *murderer.*

Thought it wuz suicide

Do u know something????

Was he killed?

Thought it was orgy

I will not fixate on the fact that the username contains the initials *AA.* AA means Alcoholics Anonymous and AA could be anyone and it's absurd to think it's Amy when Henderson has millions of fans, many who are deranged, possibly in the AA program with time to spare to go on YouTube and comment. I will not think about Delilah reading these comments, wondering, investigating. I will not fall down the rabbit hole. I did not get caught. I am fine. I am free. The only thing I ever got caught doing is jaywalking.

Then my phone buzzes and I get something I've never gotten before. A Facebook message from Love: *Ok I am a total stalker but I found you here. I'm going to Malibu. It's too hot and I think it would be wrong of me to leave you here in this heat. So this is my good deed of the day. In?*

It's like she knew about my day, my Village nightmare. Like she sensed that all I wanted was a way out, a break. I write back all caps *YES*. She responds: *Literally in front of your building. #psychokillercesquase*

She writes again: *My French spelling sucks but my French kissing is good hahha*

I write back: *Nothing about you sucks.*

And of course it's the truth.

I pack a bag and think about Delilah's vacuum mouth and Amy's hungry-hungry-hippo, all-hands-on-deck enthusiasm. I will not be getting my dick sucked in Malibu but I won't have to deal with Delilah. I bring my clothes and my underwear and my computer. I picture Harvey explaining to some new Angeleno that this apartment is cursed. The first girl took off, jettisoned her furniture. The next guy, one day he was here and the next day he was popping pills (allegedly) and then poof, gone. Still, I can't be too needy; I take out a few pairs of jeans.

Outside, I search for Love's Tesla but it's not here. I hear honking and she's down the street, waving from a Ferrari. I walk to her and she smiles when I get in. She isn't mad that I bailed on her this morning because of a *work thing*. She doesn't see it that way at all. "I know you have a life," she says. "We were in the zone. I had to send like a million e-mails this morning so believe me. I get it. Did you get your shit done?"

"Yep," I say.

"Good," she says. "Then you can focus on this Pantry mix I made for you."

It starts with Charles Mingus and I feel like a Fresh Air kid on his way out of the ghetto as we pass Hollywood Lawns and head toward Malibu. I text Calvin: *I'm gonna need a few days. I feel like shit. Sorry I was such a dick earlier. Delilah, ugh. You know the drill. Anyway I gotta take off for a while. Let me know if anything happens with GFT. Fingers be crossing, C Money. Talk in a few.*

In New York, when I ran a bookshop, if anyone talked that way to me, they would have been fired. In LA, I blow off my boss over text and get this in return: *Dude I think I smoked too much weed whoa peace out talk soon.*

Living is so easy in LA and Love tells me to hang on as we veer onto the 101. Hundreds of cars clog the arteries and it reminds me of that *SNL* sketch where they talk about the 101 and the 405. I can't imagine growing up in this madness, in cars.

Love's mom calls and I look at pictures of Love on Facebook. She's at the beach a lot, but she doesn't post full body shots. She drinks but she never looks wasted. I think I was wrong this morning. I think maybe this *is* my lucky day.

23

PEOPLE who pay thousands of dollars to board Glamorous Germ Boats (aka cruise ships) are trying to embrace a philosophy about life, the idea that it's about the journey, not the destination so you best *enjoy the ride*. I have always had a hard time with that philosophy. I am goal oriented. I put a lot of pressure on myself to be a productive member of society. Even now, I do my best. I keep one hand in Love's vagina and one hand on my phone. I am a multitasker. I don't bask.

While Love drives, I review my accomplishments. Because of me, Benji's Home Soda label was dissolved. Because of me, no publishing houses are wasting electronic ink writing to Guinevere Beck to say no to her stories, and because of me, someone more deserving has Peach Salinger's job. Because of me, Dr. Nicky Angevine is not practicing, not licensed to manipulate patients into blowing him. Because of me, Henderson's talk show does *not* go on and someday this moment will be remembered as the initial end of the age of narcissism in America. Because of me, Mr. Mooney was inspired to go away too. He's in Pompano Beach, happy as fuck, banging a broad named *Eileen*.

I also deserve a vacation. I came all the way out here and as the wind burns my cheeks and pulls my hair back and as we get closer to the ocean, I decide that this is the road away from everything bad, from Amy, from my self-destructive pursuit of her, from my paranoia and my lies. Everything with Love is good and everything bad is in the past. I look out the window and I let Amy go. Let her fall off a ladder into a chute or let her hang herself with a resistance band. I have better things to do with my time. I put down my phone.

"Finally!" Love says. "I was starting to worry your eyes were gonna pop out of your head from looking at that thing so much!"

"I know," I say. "I had to take care of some work stuff. But fuck it. *Ima* be here now."

She laughs. "I like this plan."

"I like this view," I say.

"So beautiful, right? I love the Pacific. You've been out here, right?"

"No," I say. "Not yet."

"What?" she shrieks. "Wait, wait, wait. This is your first Pacific Ocean experience?"

I admit that she is correct and I love the way Love is like love itself, boundlessly enthusiastic. My first time here is her first time here and she is crazed with joy, veering into the left lane, gunning it and blocking traffic to squeeze into a space on the shoulder.

"I thought we were going to your parents' house?"

"We'll go after," she says.

"After what?"

"After you put your toes in the Pacific, of course!"

She opens the car and strips off her tiny T-shirt. "I'll race ya," she says and all this time, my whole life, I thought horny white people in bathing suits only raced each other to the water in movies and Don Henley music videos. I let her win and when I get there, she takes my hand in hers and pulls me in for a kiss.

"Close your eyes," she says.

I hold her hand and close my eyes and it's not like I'm some poor farm kid from Nebraska. I've been in the ocean. But never like this. The stretch at the shore is so wide. The waves are loud. The seaweed is oversized, like the ocean itself. And then a wave comes and hits us and I pick her up and run through the wall of white water into the thick of it.

"Have you been to the Maldives?" she asks, when we resurface.

"Don't do that," I say.

She looks at me. She wipes her mouth. "Do what?"

"You know I haven't been to the Maldives," I say. "So don't ask me if I've been to the Maldives."

"How do I know you've never been to the Maldives?" she asks, and she's not being sarcastic. Love Quinn must be the least judgmental woman alive. She swims up to me and embraces me before leading me back to shore. She has towels in the trunk—are rich people always prepared to get in the water?—and puts on a new Pantry playlist. The first song is Eric Carmen's "Make Me Lose Control." I tell her I love this song and she says she knows. She says she took some of my songs and some of her songs and made *a bunch of infinite musical nesting dolls.* I don't know what this means, but she explains that each song mentions other songs.

"Oh, so after this comes 'Be My Baby' and 'Back in My Arms Again,'" I say.

She nods. "You really are the *Professor.*"

I wish we could keep going, all the way up north, through summer, away from Amy, from Henderson, from Delilah, from LA. But then she puts on her turn signal and veers off the highway, and we take one dirt road to another dirt road until we approach a gate. Hanging over it is a brass sign in the shape of a half-moon: *The Aisles.*

"Your home has a name?"

She laughs. "You know I like to name everything."

Love smiles into a camera and the gates open and I hear Elvis—"Never Been to Spain"—and holy fuck, wow. The road is paved with patchy grass and seashells and white sand that must have been shipped in from Bermuda, and is shaded by canopies of trees they don't have in Hollywood. We crunch along, passing Maybachs and Ferraris.

"Are your parents having a party?" I ask.

"Not exactly," Love says as she dabs her lips with gloss. "Forty's in tonight's episode of *True Detective* so my parents got the family together to watch it in the screening room."

"He's an actor?"

"I mean, not an actor-actor," she says. "He doesn't work that much. Just once in a while. I think he and Milo have a friend who is doing music on it and got him on? I don't know." She sighs and puts her gloss away. "I can't keep up and I don't try to keep up." She pats my leg. "Don't look so nervous."

"I'm not nervous," I say. But I am nervous. I know how to worry about getting betrayed by Amy Adam or judged by the police. I do not know how to worry about being a bookseller on an estate.

"You don't have anything to worry about," Love assures me. "Everybody already loves you."

A little barefoot girl with a popped collar chases a barefoot boy who will never work in retail or file for unemployment. We've entered some upscale Rob Reiner world of Rich White People and I don't think I've seen children since I was in New York. What strikes me more is the safety. In New York, you're constantly vulnerable. There could always be a psycho on the subway, on the fire escape, in the dark near the stoop. I've had my fair share of mentally ill, potentially violent patrons in the shop. My Hollywood apartment is on the first floor with bars on the window and I walk to and from work. I get into Uber cars and Lyfts with drivers I don't know and they could always be crazy. But this is so safe and it's gonna take me a minute to get used to it, the total absence of criminals.

We pull over to a sandy embankment and she leaves the keys on the dash. I offer to help with the bags but she says *the helpers can do that* and she takes my hand and leads me onto a path that's been landscaped to perfection, to make it seem like God and wind made this when really, it was Mexican laborers.

We are closer to the water, bright and blue, impossibly close, just beyond the grass tennis court, green, bright, and Love tells me about *The Aisles.* There are four houses on the property, one grass tennis court, one clay court near the main gate, and two swimming pools. There is a boathouse and I see the Donzi Love's dad told me about and I want to drive that thing. I *will* drive that thing! They have a private beach and a shed that appears to be made of actual gingerbread cookies. A sign on the thatched roof reads MINI PANTRY.

"Mini pantry?" I ask.

"Nothing mini going on in these parts." She squeezes my balls and begins to give me a hand job right here, right now, about fifty feet away from where the kids have set up a lemonade stand. She gets down and feels me up and maybe this will be when she blows me. We could get caught at any second. I tell her this and she grins, Cheshire.

Love strokes me and cups my balls and I am her clay and she works her fingers to my bone and her face is so close. I put a hand on her head but I don't push. I won't push. I will take the hand job but the hands make me want the mouth and I push the littlest bit and she takes a hand away and opens her mouth. Yes. Yes. On the tennis court someone calls: *Out!* She licks her fingers and palm instead of licking my dick and she takes that wet hand back to my cock and I come. She wipes her hands on a palm frond and I pull my shorts up.

"You okay? You seem a little tense," she says.

I shake my head. "Of course I am. I was just worried about those kids."

She smacks my ass. "Well, even if they did see, they gotta grow up sometime, right?"

We walk. No wonder Forty calls me *Old Sport.* This place is *The Great Gatsby*, new and improved. Paul Simon sings; only it's actually Paul Simon, the human being. He's sitting on a lawn chair strumming a guitar for Barry Stein and Forty, a strange sight in so many ways, three men, one guitar, no Garfunkel.

"Barry Stein knows him," Love explains. "Barry Stein knows everybody. I think that's why my parents put up with him."

"What do you mean?"

She tells me that Barry Stein is kind of a self-important douche, but her parents love the movies. Her dad wishes he were in that business but they don't invest in movies because they're too risky.

One of the million maids on staff emerges with a tray of vodka lemonades in Mason jars and Forty is quick to grab two. He offers one to Barry Stein, who shakes him off and Paul Simon says no too. Nobody wants to drink with Forty and Love sighs. "I wish Forty would get it. He always thinks Barry is gonna produce one of our stories. And it's not going to happen."

"Why not?" I ask.

She laughs. "Cuz they suck."

I love that Love isn't self-deprecating or self-aggrandizing. What I don't love is how she pulls my head toward hers and lifts her iPhone.

"Afternoon selfie," she cheers. "Hashtag, Summer of Love."

I smile. "Cheese!"

24

PAUL Simon left while we were settling into our suite upstairs in the *main house* and I'm not used to it, any of it.

"Where's the bathroom?" I ask Love.

"There are some in the cabana and some in the main house but I *love* the ones in the blue house," she says.

I try not to seem so astounded, but sometimes, the difference is too much. The French doors of the blue house are open and the bathroom is straight ahead and it's the size of a studio apartment. A fat tabby cat meows and exits.

I can try, but I will never be at ease in this. I look outside and watch Dottie hug Pierce Fucking Brosnan. A fat child picks his nose. I close the door and sit on the toilet. When I was a kid, my mom used to leave me at Key Foods. Literally just fucking dump me there. She would say we were playing hide-and-seek and I knew we weren't but I would play along. I would hide in the bathroom or sneak upstairs where they paid people to watch out for shoplifters, like ghetto *Casino.* The managers all knew me. They knew my mom. They didn't call the cops on her. The nice manager would make me my favorite meal, On-Cor Veal Parmigiana.

Eventually my mom would come back and slap me hard on the face and scream at me not to run away or pull that shit again. I promised to be a good boy and the people who worked at the store went along with the charade.

I flush and splash cold water on my face. I leave the bathroom and "helpers" (Love's word, not mine) circle in Bermuda shorts, *can I help you, do you want anything?* Love changed into tennis whites and she's on the patio by the courts. Forty waves me over and hands me a *caipirinha.* Milo is here now too. He's talking to Love, making her laugh. Barry Stein looks up Love's skirt. Fucker.

Forty shakes his head. "I told you not to worry about that."

"What's Wianno?" I ask, nodding toward Milo and his stupid tattered T-shirt.

"Wianno Club," he says. "And, Old Sport, I promise you that there is *nothing* to worry about over there."

"Where's Wianno?"

Forty sighs. "It's nowhere." He claps. "So you got any ideas for movies, Professor?"

"Not really," I say. I watch Milo, the blond hair on his arms, his Chiclet white teeth. The violence in me is like the marketing campaign for Carl's Jr., the way the signs change when they have some new jalapeño fat burger to promote. Instead of killing Amy I want to kill Milo.

Forty crunches on an ice cube. "Oh, come on," he says. "You gottta have one idea. Everybody's got one. What's the last great thing you saw?"

"Nothing," I reply. "This guy I work with always forces me to watch all this crap on Funny or Die."

"You ever have anything produced?" Forty asks.

"No," I say, and it would be socially inappropriate to pull Milo by his shirt into the water and drown him. Instead, I play along. I tell Forty about an idea I have, where you would show that part of *Love Actually* where Liam Neeson tells his stepkid that they need Kate and Leo.

"And then," I say, hoping that Love can hear me, that she'll leave Milo to see what she's missing. "Then, they're on the couch, only instead of showing that scene from *Titanic*, you show the scene from *Revolutionary Road* where Kate and Leo are fucking in the kitchen."

Forty cackles. Love doesn't notice.

"That is genius. Old Sport, you need to make that." Forty looks to see if Barry Stein has been eavesdropping but he hasn't.

I shrug. "It's just something I think would be funny."

"You gotta think, it's something that *will* be funny, Old Sport."

And then Forty has to go *field some calls* and he leaves. Love comes over and sits on my lap. "You having fun?"

"Yes," I say, and I am. With Love on my lap, I am calmer. I can love it here now that she's not talking to Milo. The light in Malibu has power that you can't buy on Instagram. Everyone looks more alive than they did at Chateau, clearer yet grainier. The Aisles isn't a home; it is a village and I wonder if any of the people who work at the Pantry know about this place and if they want to get together and storm the gates. I can picture them all shrieking, *WE DON'T WANT LOVE—GIVE US MONEY!*

Dottie says we've got to get ready for dinner and I didn't realize time was passing. Love says that happens in Malibu. "Beach brain."

Forty returns, iPad in hand. "Check it out, Old Sport," he says.

And it's like Calvin redux. I recognize the Funny or Die logo and I groan but Forty promises this is *gold.* The opening titles roll, followed by Liam Neeson and son in *Love Actually* and my heart rate quickens—that's my idea—and they're on the couch, watching Kate and Leo in *Revolutionary Road*—my idea!—and the screen rolls black and I see words I like, words that belong together, the way happily married people do:

Written and Directed by Joe Goldberg

Love is laughing and clapping and I hug Forty and shake his hand and thank him but he tells me not to thank him. "This was all you, Old Sport!"

"But I didn't do anything," I protest. "I just had an idea."

"Bullshit," he says. "You had an ending. Everyone has a beginning, but you are the guy who knew how it ended."

He hands off *my film* to Barry Stein. A new life is possible for me and I see how it is possible to become infected with aspirations. I might be *discovered* like Mark Wahlberg in *Boogie Nights* before he fucks it all up. But Barry Stein calls my video *cute.* I seethe. Once upon a time in New York I was

Different, hot

And in Malibu according to that dirty old fucker, a purveyor of hokey, dated, prefab rom-comedies, I am

Cute.

It's a buzzkill. The conversation drifts away from *my movie.* Barry Stein taps his cigar, then hands them out to Ray, Forty, and Milo. He doesn't offer one to me. Forty picks mint leaves out of his teeth and runs his hands through his hair. He is hurt; he didn't like *cute* either.

"So I have this idea," Forty says, and Barry says he needs to use the restroom and Milo needs to find his sun block and Love needs to help her mom.

I look at Forty. "Cute my ass."

Forty smiles. "Right on, Old Sport, right on."

He starts telling me about a script he's working on and I want to believe in us and I want to believe this is the start of something. But Forty's idea is terrible. In the irredeemable, maybe-he-needs-a-shrink kind of way where you know there is no possibility of him ever having any kind of success as a storyteller. Love was right when she said their ideas are terrible. This "idea" is called *The Third Twin.*

"Not me and Love," he says. "Two guys, identical, they both have tattoos on the backs of their hands from when they were babies and their mom couldn't tell them apart."

It's a special thing, when someone who can't tell a story tries. First the twins are in their mid-twenties and they're in Los Angeles and then he's describing a scene on a dark street in New York.

"And the title card smashes, boom," he shouts. "*The Third Twin.*"

Oh God, we've only just begun. Love and Milo head out to the tennis courts and I am in the right place, in the wrong place. "I think you mean triplets," I say. "There can't be three twins, but there can be triplets."

"But that gives the whole plot away," he gasps.

He runs his hands through his hair and somehow the screenplay moves forward and *we're in Vegas* and *The Hangover* walks into Scorsese's *Casino.* "You feel me, Old Sport?"

No wonder Forty has never sold a script. I glance at his iPad where he has drawings and notes. Not all messy people are geniuses. Some are just messy. My heart breaks. "Vegas," I say. "Who's getting married?"

He stands. He hoots. "You know it! Psychic! Instincts! Professor Old Sport!"

He looks around to see if Barry Stein is watching and Barry Stein is still not watching. On the court, Love allows Milo to drink out of her water bottle. Forty keeps talking and the *third twin* emerges out of nowhere in the desert to kill the twin who's driving to Vegas, trying to save his brother's life and then we backtrack again. Forty forgot a *critical scene.*

"Joe," says Forty. "Picture this. The third twin"—and JUST CALL IT A FUCKING TRIPLET—"dives into a swimming pool and we stay with him as he sees the brightness above, the pool party, the music soaring from eight-tracks."

"I thought the movie was set in the present?"

He doesn't miss a beat. "Sometimes," he says. "And other times we're in the future. Or the seventies. It's a nonlinear narrative." Love whispers something in Milo's ear. "So the third twin emerges from the pool reborn. And this is when it gets scary. You ready for this?"

Dottie rings a cowbell and Love waves at me to come but she doesn't wait for me when Milo prods her to go inside. I tell Forty we should follow and he looks at me.

"Dude," he says. "I got cut."

I raise my eyebrows. "You're not in the episode?"

"My mom digs a celebration," he says. "Everybody's stoked. They'll watch it, they'll think they missed me. Everybody wins. I mean, I read for it, I could have *nailed* it but it's just as well. First agent I ever had, he warned me. As a writer, it can fuck up your shit if you act."

Dottie rings the bell again and Forty promises we'll be there in *two minutes.* He says we have to run out to pick up a prescription for me and Dottie says we can send someone to do that and Forty says it's a *new drug* and Dottie sighs. "Be fast, boys."

Forty and I walk to the embankment where the cars are all tossed around like hungover partiers. Forty says *eenie meenie minie mo* and he settles on his Spyder.

"Where are we going?" I ask.

He grabs the keys and revs the engine. "Mexico, Old Sport. *Meh. Hee. Ko.*"

We leave.

25

OF course, Forty was being hyperbolic and we're not *actually* going to Mexico. We are leaving a paradise of canapés and fish tacos and *caipirinhas* to go to Taco Fucking Bell.

I picture everyone back at the Aisles in the screening room. I hope Love isn't sitting on Milo's lap and why does there always have to be a Benji, a Henderson, a Milo? Milo is going to be a problem and when I Google him, it's a string of irritating things, screenwriting awards, contributions to *Vanity Fair*, his *psychotically eligible bachelor* status in *Nylon*. I hate knowing that Milo *made it in Hollywood* and anyone who says he doesn't get jealous is lying. We pull into Taco Bell and Love texts: *Are you on the way back?*

I read it out loud to Forty.

"Tell her we hit beach traffic."

I look at the open road. "Seriously?"

"You're right," he says. "Tell her I'm being an asshole. She'll know what that means."

"Forty," I say. "Maybe you should text her."

"I'm driving," he says as he pulls into a spot and turns off the engine. "Seriously, tell her I'm being an asshole. She'll know what that means. It's all good, Old Sport."

So I tell Love that Forty is being an asshole and she writes back *ughghhghhhghg* and says she will cover and we get out of the Spyder and amble across the parking lot into Taco Fucking Bell. Inside, we sit at a booth and Forty tells me about his other script, *The Mess.* "It was on the Blacker List," he says. "That's a more top secret list than the Black List."

I look at him. "What's the Black List?"

He laughs. "The best unproduced scripts in town," he says. "And the *Blacker List* is the even better scripts. Only like *ten* producers get the Blacker List and *The Mess* made it."

"Cool," I say, and I wonder if schoolteachers in LA ever try to instill modesty in their kids.

Forty tells me that *The Mess* is about a kidnapping.

"Wow," I say. "I've been working on a kidnapping story too."

"No shinola?" he asks. He's trying so hard, all the time.

I tell him we should read each other's stuff and he says this is an *epic* idea and forwards me *The Mess* and *The Third Twin.* I scroll through my own stories in my phone, the ones I write when I can't sleep, when I think about her, about what the fuck happened, when I make like Alvy Singer and try to correct it all with my imagination. I tell Forty about one of my favorite Amy stories, where we go away together and use fake names. Only in this version, I catch her in the cage while she's stealing the books. I lock her up in there and force her to become my slave.

Eventually she falls back in love with me and we keep using those fake names. We become friends with the people we ripped off in Little Compton, Noah & Pearl & Harry & Liam. Forty calls it Stockholm Syndrome but he's wrong; she was *hoping* to get caught.

"Ah," he says. "Naughty girl. Nice again."

This is why people like writing. You visit old friends without having to go on Facebook and see what they're up to and deal with what idiots called FOMO. You make them into what you want them to be, the people they could be if only they were braver, smarter.

"What's this script called?" he asks.

"*Fakers*," I say. "But at this point it's really more of a description of a story than a story. I haven't worked it all out."

"Every story begins as a story," he says, as if this makes any sense. *Hollywood.* He tells me to check out *The Mess*. "Great minds," he says. "*The Mess* is very much on theme with your *Fakers*."

"You want me to read it now?"

"Send me your *Fakers*," he says. He pops a pill. "I'm in no rush to go back to the fucking Aisles. Believe me, we're not missing anything."

"*Bueno*," I say, because that's what a dickwad successful LA writer like Milo would say.

We read. We both agree that our respective works are *genius*. Forty is *blown away* by my vision in *Fakers* and I give it right back to him. I claim to be impressed by structure in *The Mess* even though *The Mess* is incoherent nonsense.

And this is when I know I've caught aspirations. Nothing good can come from them. I knew this before I moved here. Already, I have violated Mr. Mooney's advice. I am not getting my dick sucked. I fucked an actress. I swam in a pool. But I also know the way it felt to see those words on the screen of Forty's iPad: *Written and Directed by Joe Goldberg.*

I need Forty to get my foot in the door and show *Milo* how it's done. I sure as hell need more than a *cute* Funny or Die video to put that pompous fucker in his place and I read enough acting manuals to know that you don't get anywhere here unless you know someone. Now I do. I know Forty Quinn. I tell him we could combine *The Mess* and *Fakers* and his eyes bulge.

"Super script," he says. "Fuck yes. The bones are there."

"Let's do it," I proclaim.

"Should we get our agents on the horn?" he asks.

Instead of admitting I don't have an agent, I tell him we should wait. "Let's make sure we have something great first," I say. "We only get one shot here."

He slaps my back. "Wise move, Professor."

We agree to wait until the scripts are *in the hopper* until we tell anyone, Love, agents, anyone, everyone. I don't want anyone to tell Milo that I'm *trying* to do anything. I want to tell that fucker that I *did* something. Also, Hollywood is stupid, so if our scripts don't sell, then it will be like we never failed.

Forty slaps my back and we head to the counter. "Make it real with a meal," he says, and I take in the menu: Doritos Locos tacos, gorditas, something called a *quesarito* that was not concocted by an *abuela* in Mexico City but by a corporate scientist in the middle of America.

Forty starts talking *chalupas* with the stoner at the register. Then we go into the kitchen so he can introduce me to his *amigo supremo*, Chef Eduardo. Forty orders a ton of food—*dos* loaded potato grillers and *tres gorditas*, one beefy five-layer burrito, and *all the fire sauce that you can spare.* While we wait for the bill, he reaches into his pocket and takes a bump of blow and I am officially living in *Less Than Zero.*

The guy at the counter smiles. "That's thirty-nine dollars and eighty-two cents."

"Thanks, bro," Forty responds. "Don't forget our fire sauce." He whistles. "Eduardo!" he hollers. "You gotta tell the brass that they need a tip option here. How am I supposed to tip you boys?"

Eduardo laughs. "You funny, Mr. Forty."

Eduardo is probably Forty's closest thing to a true friend and Forty takes out a hundred dollar bill and crumples it and pretends to sneeze and throws the hundred over the counter. The guy at the register has seen this before and he laughs and says what Eduardo said, what Forty likes to hear: "Thank you, Mr. Forty."

Forty nods and we go back to our booth and treat *The Third Twin* like it's redeemable even as I kill his ideas and re-create it from scratch.

"Take it to the desert," I say. "The third twin is an interloper who shows up and fucks it all up for the twins."

Forty nods, hooked. You can tell he goes back and forth between thinking of Milo and himself as the third twin and I am suddenly so happy I am an only child.

"Now, the twins have their lives set but this fucker messes with everything," I go on. "He screws their women and messes with their jobs and yet it's all fucked up because he betrays both twins and it turns out they're not as close as they thought they were."

"Ah," he says. "Act Two."

"And then eventually, the twins find a way to trust each other. They're sure that it's them, the originals, so they make a plan and they bring the third twin to Vegas."

Forty pounds the table. "Location shoot. I love it."

"But they don't get there," I tell him. Idiot. "They pull off the road and they knock out the third twin and leave him for dead."

"Fuck," he says. "That's dark."

"But then." I grin. "Last shot of the movie, high above, you see the car pull over, and a body is thrown onto the side of the road."

Forty's eyes gleam. "The third twin fucked them both."

I nod. "There's your movie."

Forty says this could work and he tears into a packet of *fire sauce* and squirts it into his mouth. "Next up," he says. "*The Mess.*"

He thinks it's *Tarantino meets Nora Ephron in a classic kidnapping caper* but I've read it and Forty isn't a writer. He just likes to put names together. Of course it's a Vegas story—Forty will do anything to go to Vegas—but the characters are all over the place and sometimes the kidnapper is the guy and sometimes it's the girl and it jumps around. (Drugs.) But I can fix this; I'll just replace it with my *Fakers*.

He clicks his jaw and leans back in his seat. "Oh boy," he says. "There is one thing I didn't think about."

"What?" I ask.

"Can we do what happens in the booth stays in the booth?"

I nod. "Fuck, yes."

"Love got pissed about *The Mess* last time around. She thought it was about her."

Now I'm listening. I wipe my mouth. "Why did she think it was about her?"

Forty sighs and pulls back the curtain. He explains that Love's a *relationship girl* and she's *incapable of being single*, which is why she married young and fast, married again. "And then after the Doc died." He shakes his head. "Man, she was a wreck. Like, worried that she was toxic. If she's not divorced she's widowed and all she wants is to be with someone."

I don't think she's like that. Maybe she was. But she's not anymore. "Uh huh."

"Anyway," he says. "She swore she would never go out with anyone again unless it was gonna last forever. So I used to joke that the next time she meets someone we just gotta like tie him up and trap him in the Aisles so he can't go away, can't pull bad shit, can't go to the doctor and find out he's got cancer." He laughs. "So anyhow, that's sort of an inspiration point for *The Mess.*"

"Wow," I say.

He smiles. "You're freaking out."

"In the good way," I say. And it's true. I feel special. Love was hunting for something real and she found it and it's me and it's early and absurd and we've known each other a few days but fuck it feels good to be wanted. "This is all good by me," I say. "I'd just as soon never date anyone but Love again, but please don't tell her I said that."

"Of course not," he says. "I would never. And I mean that both ways. I would never settle down in my thirties and I would never tell Love that I told you that she *wants* to settle down."

"So Milo . . ." I say, the itch that can't be scratched. "There's really nothing between them? I mean, nothing recent?"

Forty sighs. "It's all so boring," he says. "You have to understand my sister. She is deeply, profoundly, erotically, supremely, wholly sexual."

I nod. "Okay."

"So if you mean to ask did they ever hook up, well, obviously, yes," he says. "Back east, a hundred years ago, when we were babies. But I assure you, Old Sport, the girl does not love the boy." He leans in and burps. "Don't take this the wrong way, but Love only likes guys who are rough around the edges, ya know, wrong side of the tracks."

I can't believe people still use that expression but before I can respond, Forty claps his hands. "Back to the good stuff." Meaning business and he says that Plan B is all over him for a new draft of *The Mess* and this is LA where everyone is always making everything up, but I like the idea of being one degree of separation away from Brad Pitt.

The food comes and the burritos smell like the *gorditas* smell like the grillers taste like the *chalupas* and I don't know why we got so many different things when Forty's intention was to smother all of it in fire sauce, an unsophisticated simple heat that drowns out whatever meats and cheese and veggies were defrosted and packed into these tortillas. The only saving grace is that we're facing the Pacific Ocean.

Forty eats like a starving orphan, giant bites that make his cheeks flare. He never makes eye contact while he describes, in vivid detail, his bungalow at the Bellagio, his gift for counting cards, his passion for *the moment*, and his adoration of the '70s. It's a truth that most people never want to own up to that some people were born at the wrong time. Forty would have been better off in the seventies, before AIDS and Twitter, when it might have been enough to have cool jeans and a great coke connection and a slight resemblance to *Hopper, Nicholson, fucking DeVito.* I feel extremely sorry for Forty because without a time machine, he will never be happy.

We finish gorging and head outside to the Spyder. Forty doesn't start the car.

"Here's the thing, Old Sport," he says. He pops the glove box and pulls out an envelope. "I met a *very* kind black jack dealer this past week." He lowers his voice. "I am flush and I am on deadline to get *The Third Twin* to my guys at Sony. And I can't have you slowed up because of that day job you have."

He hands me the envelope. It's full of cash. "I'm okay," I say. I don't want his charity.

"It's nothing," he says. "It's ten K I honestly forgot about."

He left ten thousand dollars in the glove box. Rich people. Stupid people.

"Love is going to wonder where it came from," I point out.

He has an answer for that. "You're dealing in books," he says. "You're a noble small businessman with an admirable work ethic and a solid start-up business. You are, therefore, the farthest thing in the world from a *gold digger*."

I've been waiting for him to use that phrase and I was going to keep working anyway because I am *not* a fucking gold digger. "I get it," I say. "Right."

"You throw pages at me and I'll do my thing in 'em and we'll get a round robin going. Bang these babies out by the end of the summer. Make the rounds and pitch 'em when the kiddies go back to school. Sound good?"

"I can get started right away," I say.

He winks. We're both aware that this partnership is a bit corrupt. But what union isn't inherently uneven in some way? I don't know any perfect couples, true partners who share the load equally.

He asks me to hand him a bottle of codeine that's on the floor and it's disgusting in here, Taco Bell wrappers and muddy bottles of Sprite, Fanta. Forty is a fuck-up—drug dependent, living in a past that wasn't even his in the first place. When we're featured in *Variety*, I'll be the hot one and he'll be the other one.

He sips his medicated Fanta and starts the car. We might die on the way back to *The Aisles.* But we also might live. We're singing along to the fucking Eagles when we take the sharp left into the estate.

Forty hits the brakes and lowers the volume. "One thing," he says. "My parents are Quakers about my gaming. They call it *gambling*, as if I'm a sorority girl from Pennsylvania who can't count cards. So let's not mention my score."

"Deal," I say.

"One more thing," he says, and I hate when people do that. He pours the rest of his *lean* onto the grassy sand and I imagine the squirrels stoned. "If you hurt my sister, I'll fucking kill you."

It's the first time I respect him. We pull up the driveway and half the cars are gone. We missed most of the party and Milo fell asleep on a chaise longue and he's an ugly sleeper—another win.

Forty goes to his *bungalow* and I go to Love's. The upstairs bedroom is a dream, a topsy-turvy place with a sodded *terrace.* Love says they copied it from a resort in Maui. I walk outside because I have never stood on grass in the sky and she asks me to come to bed.

"Forty got cut from *True Detective.*" She breathes me in. "You smell like a taco."

"Guilty," I say.

"It's really great of you to go with the flow," she says. "Forty gets bummed when he gets cut and I feel like if you weren't here he might have disappeared to Vegas or something. Thank you."

"He's a good dude."

She kisses me. "I think he needs a break from it," she says. "That stupid business is poisoning him and he should just be here this summer, not trying to cast that thing that's not even done."

I squeeze her hand. "So, let's do it. Let's stay."

"What about your job?" she asks.

I tell her I'm selling more valuable books on my own than I am at the store. I can set up a PO Box and form an LLC and go for it. Love is thrilled for me and says I can borrow an old Prius no one uses anymore so I can hit estate sales and stock up on merchandise. I love that she thinks this is a wonderful idea and I love that she does not use the phrase *yard-sale-ing.* She kisses me. She straddles me and I live here now, in Malibu, in Love. Hunting season is over. I will not think of Amy. I will not worry about Amy. I will not beat myself up. Now it's time to rest. That's what you do when you find love. Amy couldn't. I can. I'm the lucky one, not her.

26

TWO weeks into the Summer of Love and there's only one time of day I dread. *Tennis time!* You have to understand, I am living in a dream world. Every morning begins with Love riding my dick. After we fuck, I put on one of the new shirts I bought at the stupid expensive stores on Abbot Kinney in Venice and drive to Intelligentsia and buy an overpriced coffee. I sit with my back against the wall of this coliseum-style coffee shop, so austere, so clean, so California cold that you never see anybody smiling and you get dirty looks for ordering iced coffee.

I go back and forth between working on *The Mess* and *The Third Twin* and then, around lunchtime, I mail books if I have inventory that moved. Then, every day at four P.M., I wish for rain so I can get out of *tennis time!* I suck at tennis. My forehand is too big and the balls go soaring over the fence. My one-handed backhand never makes contact. My two-handed backhand makes Forty piss his madras shorts. Sometimes Milo is here, calling out, *Loosen your grip, kid.* And sometimes Love walks all the way around to my side of the court as if I'm a fucking child.

Today it's just me and Love because Love's parents have gone to Europe and Forty and Milo are out on the Donzi. Love is feeding me balls and I am missing them or whacking them to China and finally we decide to just walk on the beach.

"Okay," she says when we reach the water. "I just need to say that I know you hate tennis but you wouldn't hate it so much if you actually tried to get better. And I love you but you are stubborn and I've never seen anyone *refuse* to get better at something. You need to make an effort."

I look at her. I heard all of it. She's right. And buried in there, in the middle of all her earnest frustration, there were three little words. She didn't mean to say it. I mean I have been feeling it, the love, but I wouldn't say it either, not this early. We've only had two weeks. And yet in two weeks we have built a thing between us, a bridge, a shorthand, and I never had this with anyone. Amy and I had sex and heat. Beck dangled a carrot and I bit. But Love and I grow the carrots, peel them, and eat them together.

"Look!" she cries, pointing to a dolphin out in the ocean. "Did you see it?"

"Yeah," I say. "I see it. And don't worry. I got a gun."

She bursts out laughing and falls back onto the sand and I laugh too and she rolls onto her side, giggling, and I smack her ass, payback, and that's all it takes with Love, one joke, one smack and she's slipping out of her little skirt and climbing onto me and pulling me out of my shorts and holding my head by the temples and looking into my eyes, close.

"Are you deaf?" she asks.

"No," I say. "I was being nice."

"Well, don't be," she says.

"Okay. I love you too," I say.

She kisses me as my cock delves into her and we are perfect together and I am better for knowing her and I'm still convinced that there's a special department in heaven where they build vaginas and if you're lucky like I am, one day you happen upon the one that was built for you. I tell her this when we finish, when we're lying there on the sand.

"You should write," she says. "You say some good weird shit sometimes."

I want to tell her that I do write but it can wait. "Thanks," I say. "Maybe I will."

She nudges me. I turn to her. She smiles. "You realize you still have to get back out on the court, right?"

Yes, the *Summer of Love* is a dream. My skin is glowing thanks to Henderson's products and fucking Love. My screenplays are coming together. Forty and I meet at Taco Bell every couple of days to talk about "our work." He reads, he raves, and then he tells me the buzz he's building.

I really am proud of myself that I'm *finally* on a true vacation. You can't even call the screenwriting work; I love it too much. I'm better at tennis after Love's big lecture and I almost think it's a good thing that she won't suck my dick because if she did, I might become so happy that I wouldn't be me anymore.

The Corinthians are right and *Love is patient.* We go horseback riding and I don't know how to ride a fucking horse so here we are again, Love teaching me.

"Robert Redford is a good learning horse," she says.

"Robert Redford?" I ask, and her mom named all their horses.

Love says it's a miracle they're not all named Robert Redford. "My mom is kind of obsessed with him," she explains.

We trot along and now she wants to know how I lost my virginity and I tell her to go first.

"It was with Milo," she says. "We were staying on his family's boat and were docked at Wianno Club and the three of us, me and Forty and Milo, we used to sneak out and steal the flags off the golf course." That's why he's always wearing those shirts, Martha's Vineyard, yacht clubs, all that cocky pink and green. "And then one night, Milo was like, let's hide from Forty and freak him out. And then, you know, and it was terrible and it *hurt* and did I mention that it hurt?" She gazes upward and all the pain in her life, she's found a way to process all of it. "And then Forty got nailed for stealing all the flags." She laughs, and of course the three of them collectively refer to that night as *the night they all got nailed* and I am so happy I grew up poor and that there is nothing so *cute* about my coming of age. Love elbows me. "I showed you mine," she says. "Your turn."

"Well," I say. "I was having dinner at Chateau Marmont and this waitress came up to me with a piece of paper."

She smacks me. "That's not funny."

I shrug.

She pats my leg. "When you're ready," she says. "No rush." We are quiet together. Like I said, *Love is patient.*

Love is kind. We ditch plans to go to a ceremony in Culver City where Love is supposed to get an award because Milo calls from Commerce Casino. Forty trashed a room and they're holding him.

"Can't Milo take care of it?" I ask. And I worry about my business partner, but at the same time, this is what I expect from Hollywood.

Love says it's better we go. "Why?" I ask.

Her eyes well with tears. "Because with Forty, you have to step in or people get sick of him," she says. It's a long drive to Commerce. It's ugly in Commerce. It's not glamorous. It's vinyl. I watch Love stay up holding her brother all night. He's a blubbering mess. She tells him it's okay. When he realizes this was the night of her award, she tells him it's okay.

"They canceled it, honey bunny," she says. Her voice is aloe vera. "I didn't miss anything. Try and sleep."

The next morning, on the way back to Malibu, I worry that Love is a better person than I am. I am quiet and grumpy and pick a fight about Milo, the fact that he's texting her, that he's at the Aisles waiting for us to get home.

"Joe," Love says. "I can't ever get mad at anyone for needing a break from Forty, okay? Milo is here because we need him. Because I need him. Please don't be jealous. He's dating a really nice girl named Lorelai right now and you have nothing to worry about."

"I'm not jealous."

"Look," she says. "Forty is drawn to everything bad. It's like whether it's people or writing or his drugs or anything, you know, he has the worst instincts of anyone. I don't know what's gonna happen to him."

I want so badly to tell her that Forty is going to be fine because he's discovered a talented writer. I want to tell her that I am *The Third Twin* and that she makes me want to be kind too. I know we'll have to take care of Forty. I know he's never going to get by on his own. I know he's insecure and unhappy and negative. And I see the way Love cares for him.

"Listen," I say. "I know you keep putting off going to Phoenix and visiting the charity volunteer coordinators. Why don't you go tonight? I'll hang with Forty."

Love smiles and texts Milo to go home and she mounts me when we get back to the Aisles. She doesn't wait until we park. She presses on my leg for me to brake and she attacks me in the car, in the driveway. She thanks me for staying with Forty and I tell her it's no big deal and she raises her eyebrows. "It's Thursday," she cautions me. "It's summer."

Love was right. Forty is demanding and drunk at Matthew McConaughey's, where nobody really wants to say hi to him. He is rude to a bartender who's doing the best she can. I apologize to her when she's on her break and she says it's *totally cool.*

"Dude," she says. "You look spent."

I tell her about Forty and she does that California thing where she waits for her turn to talk and then tells me her name is Monica and she's housesitting in a place near the Aisles and bartending and surfing. She asks me if I surf and it's a question that offends me but I don't even get to finish the boring conversation because the other bartender is tapping my shoulder.

"Are you the one with the wasted friend?"

That's me, and my wasted friend is looking for me. The surfing girl bartender tells me to lighten up. "Try and find the fun," she says. "It's, like, all you can do."

The Californian refusal to accept that sometimes things just fucking suck—like getting into the car with high Forty and making our next stop an S&M hooker who lives on a ranch up in Topanga. I sit on a couch near too many dogs barking and try not to listen to him fuck her or call her *Mommy*. It is the darkest, longest night of my life and knowing that Love has had countless nights like this makes me love her so much more. A lot of girls, they would have left by now.

When I have to drag him out of his Spyder and into his house, his slumbering body is so dense and unresponsive that I worry he might be dead. But he isn't and something has to change. I need to find a babysitter for this kid, someone who will put up with his shit, someone mellow and needy.

The next day, while he sleeps it off and my girlfriend teaches the children to Swim for Love in Phoenix, I prowl the beach looking for the bartender who told me to *find the fun.* She's where she said she would be, on all fours, scrubbing her stupid *board.* She's different when she's off-duty, more stripperish, with one of those decorative bandanas wrapped around her head and a necklace glistening around her waist. Her body parts are taut and brown; she is a stereotypical LA girl and she's too hot for Forty, but anyone who gets this dressed up to scrub a surfboard is blank and hungry. She looks over her shoulder constantly. She's perfect. I go to her. I wave.

27

AS Love says, Monica might be the most *chill* girl in the world and I'm so glad I recruited her. Monica is unflappable and calm. As Love says, you could punch her in the face and she would just keep smiling. She eases into a relationship with Forty automatically, which means Love and I are off the hook. Monica is super common, with brown hair that is always parted on the left and bangs that fall into her eyes, bangs she is constantly fingering, licking, pushing aside. I want to take a razor and shave them the fuck off but I would never do any such thing. Monica is my savior, Forty's pacifier. He pets her. He likes her consistency. He tries to talk to me about her open mind in the sack but I tell him I don't want to know about her lack of nerve endings. I'm still trying to forget what he said last week: "You can pee on her, Old Sport! On her *face*!"

Monica is a severe Californian, a Beach Boys kind of girl who smiles all the time and follows Forty around trying to get him to drink coconut water. I picture her alone in the middle of the night cutting her inner thighs, but it's possible that I'm wrong, that some people are just free of demons. She is always exactly the same and she doesn't bloat or get moody or crave burritos instead of sushi. Everything is *chill* and one night we are all nestled on floats in the pool, watching a movie outside—this is how it is here, you live in an *Esquire* spread and you are the star—and Love gasps.

"It just hit me," she says. "We're *Friends.* You guys, you're Monica and Chandler and we're Rachel and Ross."

Monica hasn't ever seen a whole episode of *Friends* but she says that sounds cool and Forty says he stopped listening to Love talk about *Friends* several years ago and I dive off my float and swim over to Love and let her celebrate her epiphany.

Love's parents go off to Europe and Milo goes off with his Lorelai chick who lives in Echo Park, and Forty hires a housesitter to cover for Monica, which means she's here all the time. These are the last four weeks of summer and we couple up and do things, big things. We take a *helicopter* to Catalina and we hop a *jet* to Vegas and we eat in the pool and we swim in the pool and Monica brings home *veggies* from the farmers' market and Love calls them *vegetables* and I wish this was it, indefinite.

But then Robert Frost wasn't fucking around and there is a new nip in the air, an increasingly noticeable one. The beach isn't quite as densely crowded as it was yesterday and motherfuckers at Intelligentsia are starting to trickle in wearing scarves. It's a sign. There is change ahead. Our heavenly summer is going to end.

The days are getting shorter and Love is wrapped up in blankets, looking at *Boots* and *Puppies* online but now there are actual boxes of boots arriving every day, piling up in the kitchen, in the bedroom, on our grass patio. Love tears into the boxes and tries on the boots but she doesn't wear them, the way she doesn't adopt any actual puppies.

She says this is her favorite time of year, when she puts "Boys of Summer" on all the Pantry playlists. I remind her that it's kind of absurd in California, where it's not going to start snowing. She looks at me and tells me I'm getting a little red. She is critical lately. I tell her I already put on lotion and the sun doesn't feel as strong. There's friction between us now that wasn't here a day ago and I don't know if I'm a summer fling.

"Joe," she says. "You need to put on more lotion."

"I really think I'm okay."

She rolls her eyes. "But you're not," she says. "The sun stays strong here."

"I'm fine," I insist.

An hour later, I am a fool. I am crisp and cold and hot and burnt and my skin has been destroyed. She doesn't say *I told you so* but she does cross her arms and wear a floppy hat. We move to the shaded area of the pool and she says if I had put on the lotion I wouldn't have gotten burned. I *did* put on the fucking lotion but clearly someone left it out in the sun and all the protective power of it was destroyed. I am not going to fight with her. This is the Summer of Love and I have to believe in the Fall of Love even though it has an ominous tone. I look at Forty, asleep in the chair; Monica is inside getting ready, as if you need to get ready to lie by the fucking pool.

"Too hard," I say when Love rubs aloe on my red shoulders.

"Sorry," she says, and she lightens her touch but that hurts too and I flinch. "Joe," she says. "Maybe you should do this yourself."

I take the bottle. I can't do it myself. I can't reach my back. The thing about a true sunburn is there is no quick fix. I lie on my belly and Love puts a sheet over me and kisses the back of my head. She says she's gonna go change.

"Change?"

"Yeah," she says. "I have a meeting."

"About your charity?"

She scruffs my hair. "About a movie."

"The one you and Forty were working on?" I ask, and I don't like this.

But she doesn't have time to change her clothes or her attitude or answer my question because Milo is here, whistling, in a Black Dog Martha's Vineyard T-shirt and it's like he *knows* New England is my hate place, where Beck was born, angry and unsolvable, where Amy fooled me with *Charlotte & Charles*, where Love lost her virginity to Milo, undoable and indelible, a cherry popped on old sand.

"You sick, buddy?" Milo asks as he hugs my girlfriend.

"He forgot to put on sunblock," Love says. "Also you're early, Mi."

"Sorry," he says, and he looks at me and winces. "Hey, you should put some aloe on that."

"I did," Love says. "But it's that burn where all you can do is wait."

They're both standing over me and even though it hurts, I have to tear the sheet away and sit upright on this fucking chair. My own skin burns me, a localized panic attack on my largest organ. "It's not so bad," I say. "What's up, Milo? Where's Lorelai?"

"Lorelai's on her way to New York to go to a wedding in the Hamptons," he says.

Love nudges him with her foot. "You should go," she says. "She seems like a good one."

"She is a good one," he says. "And I had every intention of accompanying her. Who doesn't love a Hamptons wedding?"

Me, fucker, and Milo pulls something out of his pocket. It's a piece of paper folded up into a tiny triangle. He passes it to Love, who takes it and laughs. "This is so old school," she says. "This is how we used to pass notes."

Milo eye fucks her as if I'm not here. Shameless interloper, and I imagine a pack of black dogs ripping into him, eating him alive.

Love unfolds the note and she is quivering and I remain invisible. "Omigod omigod omigod!"

"I take it that's a yes."

She runs to him barefoot and straddles him and he's spinning her around and I'm sitting here in splitting pain and somehow Forty is sleeping through all this. I refuse to ask to be let in on the conversation and Love pats Milo's back and he puts her down.

She comes to me and takes my hands. "Joe," she says. "Joe Joe Joe Joe Joe."

And then she kills me. The news is disgusting. Milo got funding to direct a feature he wrote and he's going play the lead opposite Love.

"What's it called?"

"*Boots and Puppies*!" she announces.

"Ah," I say, because I am too shocked to say actual words. All this time she was searching for news about Milo's movie. She loves boots and she loves puppies but she loves Milo's movie more. Milo is the Third Twin, smug as fuck. I wonder if he got her first husband thrown in jail and I wonder if he was in a wetsuit, waiting underwater to murder her cancer-stricken doctor husband. Forty is waking up, yawning, going for the Veuve. Milo is a bad guy. And wait. Love is an *actress.*

"I'm so confused," I say. "You're gonna *act*?"

Milo lights a cigarette and relocates his Wayfarers to the top of his blond Jewfro. "Love is an amazing actress," he says. "But she's not for sale, you know? We know she's too good for that. But this is our baby. *Boots and Puppies* is ninety-five pages of straight-up sex and conversation. It's gonna change movies. It's a horror movie without any blood. It's about the sanctity of the human heart. It's the kind of stuff they *used* to make movies about. Barry Stein says it's like *The Big Chill* only in this case, the dead body is sort of us, you know, as a society. "

The level of bullshit, and I look at Forty—our movies have plots—but he's on Team Milo. He plays along and very quickly I know why. Forty says he had no idea that he would be brought on as a producer and he high-fives Milo and Milo says the script wouldn't be as good as it is without his insights and I want to kill everyone and my skin, on top of all this, *my skin.* Love wraps up in a beach towel, as if she needs to cover up suddenly. Already she is different, self-conscious, a simpering actress, overthinking her words, pursing her lips. My Love sounds like a fucking asshole as she simpers, "Our perfect little baby."

"Where are we gonna shoot?" Forty asks, clapping his hands.

"We nabbed a great house in the Springs," Milo says.

Forty says *nice* and Love is awestruck. "It's *real*," she says. "It's really *real.*"

My skin burns and my heart burns and the three of them talk more about the movie as if I asked. Milo started writing it when they were at Crossroads and you can love someone all you want, but you can't go into her past and become a part of her formative years. *Boots and Puppies* is the baby Love and Milo are going to make together while I sell old books.

Monica appears, hair blown out same as ever, stomach taut, same as ever. Forty tells her the good news and she is predictably *stoked.* She and Forty pop two bottles of champagne and Forty is also *stoked* for his buddy and it's a celebration and I'm relieved that I'm sick. At least I don't have to fake it. Love feels my forehead.

"I think you have a fever, baby," she says. "Classic sun poisoning. You should go lie down."

Love the girlfriend would want to go with me; Love the actress wants me out of here. Forty offers me some Vicodin and Milo agrees with Love, saying I should get out of the sun. He means that I should get out of this world, their life.

Love is impatient with me, leading the way up the stairs, prattling on about her identity, how she's not an *actress-actress* and the movie's not a *movie-movie.* "It's the kind of story nobody in Hollywood tells anymore," she says. "A really small love story."

Love story. "Great," I say.

She crosses her arms, classic California cold. "You don't seem all that happy for me."

"Of course I'm happy for you, but right now mainly, I feel like I'm gonna puke."

She winces. "Don't hate me, but it would be so great of you to do that in the bathroom," she says. "This guy puked in my old bed once and the smell never really went away."

I'm gonna let that one slide. I promise to vomit in the toilet and she tells me to rest and take a cold shower if I can stand it. She says she'll check on me in a little while when I'm not *Sick Boy*, the debilitated obligation upstairs. I listen to her trot down the stairs. A few minutes later, *Boots and Puppies* arrives in my inbox, a read-only PDF, and the party outside begins and the first song to start it all is “Boys of Summer.” I can’t read *Boots and Puppies* in this frame of mind and I have another new e-mail: a Google alert for a *holy fuck, no* article in the *Boston Globe.* Everything is falling apart at once, my skin, my life, my love, and I am prostrate on a bed I don’t own.

I open the link and there’s a picture of Dr. Nicky Angevine. Prison agrees with him. His hair is short and he’s a little thin, but toned. Dr. Nicky tells the reporter that his work as a therapist prepared him for incarceration—*bite me*—and the article goes into great detail about his ongoing pursuit of an appeal. Dr. Nicky says the authorities have tracked down all his patients except for one man whose name they can’t print in the paper for reasons of confidentiality and *fuck me.* They’re looking for me. Well, they’re looking for Danny Fox, the name I used when I went to talk to Dr. Nicky in his beige office and sat on his beige couch. But it’s me all the same. I read on.

The facts are disturbing: NYPD cannot locate this former patient. Dr. Nicky tells the paper that Patient X was *a good kid, a real kid, late twenties.* But he also says some cunty shit about me. He says I was obsessed with a young woman. And then I read the worst sentence I have ever read in any newspaper:

Dr. Angevine concedes that he is not a detective. “But I do wonder,” he says. “Did Patient X find me through Guinevere Beck? In my gut, I think he did.”

Dr. Nicky—the paper can fuck off, he’s not a real doctor, he’s an MSW—has done pretty well for himself. A lot of his patients are getting together online, trying to find Patient X, convinced that Dr. Nicky is innocent. His ex-wife is on his side too, telling some bullshit story about how Nicky "nurtured" tomato plants in their garden upstate and never could have killed someone. *Fuck you, wife.*

And fuck doctor-patient confidentiality, because in the thirty-two comments below, some asshole named Adam Mayweather reveals that Patient X went by the name Danny Fox. And this, *this* is why you have to kill people. If you don't, they don't learn anything. They just reemerge, more muscled, more manipulative, more hell-bent on taking you down, maneuvering reporters into furthering their agenda. Fucking *Boston Globe* and fucking Danny Fox, I should have refused to give a last name. I leave the computer and run into the bathroom and splash cold water on my face. I vomit. I stay there, slumped. Love comes into the bathroom and kneels down behind me.

"Poor, sick baby," she says.

"Nah," I manage. "I'm fine. Just a sunburn. How are you?"

"Is it awful if I say I'm great?" she asks. Her voice is different and I don't like it. There's more Kardashian in there. "I just feel like *yes*, you know?"

"Yeah," I say. And this is how summer love crumples. How it deflates like a helium balloon in a hospital.

She kisses the back of my head then retreats. She says she doesn't want to get sick, as if I'm contagious, as if you can catch a fucking sunburn. "You have to feel better by tomorrow," she says. "There's a tribute to Henderson at the UCB and we have to get people hyped on *Boots and Puppies.* Do you feel like you'll feel better by then?"

My girlfriend Love would have wanted me to feel better because generally, if you love someone, that's what you want. But actress Love is like the fashionable cunt Andrea who drinks the Kool-Aid in *The Devil Wears Prada.* I don't like this new Love. *Do you feel like you'll be better by then?* Fuck that question. Fuck the way she's standing in the doorway instead of stroking my back. I vomit.

28

I insist on driving to Henderson's memorial. Love fights me. She wants us to have a *driver* but I say I want to take *my* car and of course I need a car. Oh, there's more good news. Fucking *Milo* is with us because they're *bonding* because of *Boots and Puppies.* As if they aren't already bonded, as if she didn't lose her virginity to this fucktard sitting with his legs spread in the backseat. They're both back there, as if I'm a Lyft driver, as if I'm the servant, and every time I glance at them in the rearview mirror his knee is a little bit closer to hers.

Monica's riding shotgun. She's *psyched* and I can't imagine her enjoying UCB humor, getting any of the jokes. She wears too much makeup and she's too athletic for the Franklin Village UCB crowd, where the idea is that girls have messy hair and patterned leggings and long tongues they stick out in pictures for Instagram. I don't miss the Village. I don't want to go back. Everything is wrong and I ask Monica why she didn't ride with Forty.

"He had to do some stuff," she says. "And I needed to get ready."

She always *needs to get ready* and Forty had to pick up drugs and Monica sprays foundation onto her cheeks and Love *bonds* with Milo and the car smells like Monica's makeup. Everything is wrong. To think of Dr. Nicky amassing an army behind bars in Rikers and me, escorting this group to a goddamned Henderson tribute. I crack my window to get a little air and Love asks me to roll it up.

"Hang on," I reply.

Milo chimes in. "Joe, it's really windy back here."

I want to ram this car into a truck. "Hang on," I say, fussing with the button.

"I'm good with whatever," Monica says. Typical valuable fucking contribution.

Love laughs a new laugh, her actress laugh. "Well, I have fall hair." She giggles. "Joe, please shut it now."

"Your hair *does* look cute," Monica rejoices. Monica's hair looks the same as always and the three of them are in it together now, talking about hair.

I finally get the window shut. Love doesn't thank me. She looks at Milo. "You don't think it's too done? I feel like it's an obvious blow-out."

"I feel like she might have gotten a blow-out," Milo responds.

Monica nods. "I feel like it could go either way, like you can do that yourself if you follow directions from *Allure* or something. I can send you some videos!"

They're all idiots and Milo says he's gonna do character breakdowns of the characters' favorite books and magazines and Monica loves the idea and Love says it will be fun and I am the quiet one, the silent driver, I may as well be wearing a fucking chauffeur cap. Milo slyly manages to cut Monica out of the conversation by running over the game plan for pimping the movie tonight and I wish I could think of anything to say to Monica but she's already taken off into her phone, chatting, and I can't think of a fucking thing to say to her anyway.

I'm not going to survive this ride and I turn on the radio and Love asks me to turn it off. "Sure," I say. "No problem."

"Joe," she says. "Are you pissed about something?"

"Not at all," I say.

Milo: "You know you didn't have to drive."

Love: "He insisted. I don't know why."

"I like driving." I catch Love's eye in the rearview. She has on so much eyeliner. She looks like a stranger.

Milo squeezes Love's knee. "It's okay," he says. "We all got this. Right, Joe?"

I almost want to laugh. But instead I just smile, big and juicy. "You know it, Milo."

We hit traffic and I will not let any of it get to me. Los Angeles is a giant high school cafeteria sometimes and I survived real high school. Surely I can deal with my girlfriend morphing into a mystery bitch and icing me out.

It's not like I want to participate in their conversation anyway, the two of them droning on about how sick of Malibu they get every year, how they can't wait to get back to civilization and restaurants and awards show seasons and steakhouses and *shows at the Roxy and the UCB.* But if Monica had manners, she would stop texting and engage with me. She would quell the pervasive atmosphere of rejection overwhelming me in this fucking car and then maybe if I were lost in conversation with her, Love would get jealous and want to join our conversation. But no. Monica fucking texts. Love and Milo talk and I interrupt them and tell Love that I have some great Pantry playlists but she says she's gonna turn on some Steve Miller Band through her Bluetooth.

"Why Steve Miller Band?" I ask. "It seems so random, like someone passionately demanding a grilled chicken sandwich."

Nobody laughs at my joke and Love says she loves grilled chicken sandwiches and there's a scene in *2012* when Amanda Peet is in a grocery store during an earthquake and the floor splits and this is how that is. Love is more distant with every eighth of a mile. No wonder the divorce rate in this industry is so high.

Soon we pull off and we're on Franklin and it's the same old gas station and there is the same old Scientology Celebrity Centre and there is the same old Franklin Village and Love pouts when I hang a left onto Bronson and drive toward the canyon.

"You don't want to valet?" she asks.

"I'd rather park myself," I say.

She huffs. "Look, if you need cash for the valet, I have it."

Milo bites his lip and if this scene winds up in anything he ever writes, I will kill him. Monica is still ignoring all of us, choosing the people in her phone. I veer into a spot, like the scrappy, rough-around-the-edges villager that I am. Love yelps, overreacting, lurching. Oh, *please.* Love can't get out of the car fast enough and I tell Monica it's time to go and she is confused.

"We're here?" she asks.

Love smiles at me like I'm a third cousin she hasn't seen in years. "So," she says. "You must be excited to reunite with your friends from the neighborhood. Or wait, are they all stuck working?"

"They wouldn't be into this kind of thing," I say.

She links her arm through mine, halfheartedly. "I might be able to get some SRO tickets," she says. "That means Standing Room Only."

I pretend to sneeze and pull my arm away. "I know what it means," I say. "I'm from New York."

"Oh, I know," she says. "There's no forgetting that."

We walk in silence. And I won't be seeing my four fucking *friends*. I learned online that they're all pretty busy. Calvin got a DUI and he's working crazy hours. Harvey Swallows got throat cancer and he's trying to embrace the humor and the irony. Dez is having a party for his dog, Little D. Delilah is doing *on-air* coverage for some wannabe *Entertainment Tonight* kind of show on a network I've never heard of.

We are almost at Franklin when Love tugs on my arm. "Are you mad at me or something?"

"No," I say.

"Then why were you such a dick in the car?"

"Why was *I* a dick?"

"Don't make it about the word," she says. "You know what I mean."

"Love, you're the one being a dick."

"Very mature," she says. "Look, something is just fucked up and you're shutting down and it's bullshit and I can't take it right now."

"So don't," I say.

"You're still gonna try and tell me you're not being a dick."

I shrug. Forty's up ahead on the corner, waving to us.

She sighs. "I don't have time for this."

"For me," I say. This is happening so fast and her eyeliner looks like war paint.

"Joe," she says. "This isn't good."

"What the fuck does that mean?"

"It means I have so much pressure on me right now and you're adding to it instead of helping me."

"I'm adding to it," I repeat. I want to throw her over my shoulder but she doesn't want that anymore. She doesn't want me anymore.

"After the show, we need to talk," she says. And that is how you know it's over. Need is not want. Your girlfriend wants to talk to you but the girl who doesn't love you just needs to talk to you and I guess I should have known. She picked me up so quick, so smooth. Now she'll drop me, so quick, so smooth.

I tell her to go and she says *whatever* and runs to her brother and Milo and the three of them start talking *Boots and Puppies*. Monica is here now, too late.

"What's up?" she asks. I can't deal with her generic shit right now.

"Nothing," I say. My heart hurts.

"Cool," she says. "I have been so crazy getting ready to jam, you know? My temp agency is not very cool about people going away and stuff. They need to chill."

"Where are you going?"

She is puzzled. But she is always puzzled. "Location," she says, like I should know. "Aren't you coming too?"

I look at her. I don't know about *location.* And this is how I know what Love needs to talk to me about. She needs to tell me that it's over, that she's not bringing me to *location.*

Monica bites her lip. "Oops," she says. "I assumed Love told you. Forty asked me to go yesterday. Dude, don't get all worked up. Let's have fun!"

But I can't have fun. I am too good for this shit. I want to end this first, beat Love to the punch. I want to smash all her fucking tennis racquets into the grass court until they splinter. We spent the whole summer together and she doesn't even have the decency to *not* invite me. She doesn't look back as we round the corner and her new jeans are so tight, I hope she gets a yeast infection.

She links arms with Milo and they greet Seth Rogen and his wife, air kisses, hugs. She isn't motioning for me to come over. And now I have to have a reunion with *Calvin.* He has the night off and he's here, hugging me. There's a new small potbelly underneath his Henderson shirt and I'd like to think that Love is watching me reunite with him, wishing that I would make an introduction, but I know better. Her friends are famous. She doesn't need me. Calvin cracks a tasteless joke about how I hit the *jackpot* and I don't laugh.

Monica checks the time on her Google wristwatch. Calvin grabs her arm. She giggles. "It's a present," she says. "I could never, like, get this."

"From your boyfriend?" he asks.

She nods. But she flirts. "He saw it on my Pinterest. He can be really sweet when he wants to be."

Calvin looks at me. "Where's your watch, JoeBro?"

I tell him it's in the shop and he starts to hit on Monica and they're talking surfboards and eBay and it's increasingly obvious they're going to fuck. There is so much change, too much change, and everything I built is falling apart and Calvin is programming Monica's number into his phone. I should have left when Love said we *need to talk*. She is laughing too hard at James Franco's jokes as Milo accepts congratulatory hugs from Justin Long. This is supposed to be a tribute to a dead man and instead it's a bunch of boy-men in moth-eaten T-shirts laughing at their own jokes, cocky fucks who get paid to make jokes, get pussy because they get paid to be funny. I can't breathe.

It's time to go inside. I don't sit with actress Love. She's in the Important People Section directly across from me with the James Franco people, between Milo and Forty. Milo is wearing the Four Seas Ice Cream T-shirt he was wearing the first night at Chateau. I bet they went there after he popped Love's cherry. Everyone around me is going on *Insta* and Twitter and Vine to share snapshots of the people across from us, the *celebs.*

Monica elbows me. "Grab and pass," she says.

I grab and pass and it's a single sheet of paper with the lyrics to "Coming Up Easy" by Paolo Nutini, a hipster Scotsman who fucks models and makes cool music. I look at Monica. "It was Henderson's favorite song," she says. "We're all gonna sing along. He made a joke about it once, like he wanted a singing thing. Amazing, right?"

It's bullshit and Henderson's favorite song was either "Oh What a Night" or "Sherry" and I want to tell them they're all wrong. I knew him best because I killed him. His tastes were more in line with middle-aged Americans who drive Buicks and buy Disney vacation packages on Expedia and I am so sick of this city, everyone pretending to be cool, even in death.

The lights go down and the "tribute" begins with Milo jogging onto the fucking stage. Monica finds Calvin on Facebook and Love claps for Milo onstage. He waves for more applause instead of telling everyone to stop and Love hoots and everything is ending. I don't know her anymore and we don't *need to talk*. I'm not dead or blind.

I see her cheering for him, choosing him. This black box cage is real and I barely recognize her anyway with her hair. It's ending, our relationship, the applause.

"Welcome, friends and fans," Milo begins. I hate the word *fan.* It's almost as bad as follower. He raises the sheet of paper with the lyrics. "We're gonna start this night out the right way," he says. "The way Henderson would want it, in song."

The screaming. I think my ears are broken. Love laughs at Milo's bad jokes and Monica whispers that Twitter is *blowing up* and Love is going to dump me after the show. She's lost interest in me. She became an actress. Or maybe she was always an actress, like Amy was. Maybe I got stupid the second I got *aspirations.* I cringe to think of the movies I wrote, the way I jumped into business with Forty. Fuck it. Fuck all of it.

The house lights flicker, the show's about to start, and Love licks her little lips, the ones that never met my cock. I clench my program. In that book *A General Theory of Love*, the good relationships are defined by two chairs, side by side. Love and I are facing each other and yet she is not looking at me. Instead she's leaning into Milo. Her shoulders are relaxed and she was probably dying for this moment. She's got her movie. She's got her *director.* She doesn't need me now. Milo elbows her to look at something in his phone and she laughs at it, whatever it is. I don't know. I'm too far away.

We need to talk. No, we don't, Love. You want to ice me out and make me sit on the other fucking side of the room while you look in Milo's phone and let him put his hand on your thigh? Fine. Have it your way. Love takes Milo's hand as she sings along to "Coming Up Easy" and I bury my face in my hands. Monica asks what's wrong.

"Nosebleed," I say.

"Yikes," she says. "I told Forty his coke is not as good as he thinks it is. Calvin says you guys have a pretty good hookup here."

I'm too depressed to discuss Dez's talent as a drug supplier and I tell Monica I have to go and she says *cool* and the Villagers are irritated as I squeeze by. It's tight as an airplane and my dick is in all their faces and when I get outside onto the street, I send Love a text message: *I got a nosebleed. I'm gonna go to the Pantry and get a coffee. I miss you. I don't know what happened.*

iMessage relays that the message has been read but Love doesn't write back. Silence received. That's it. The end. I don't know what I did wrong, but I know what she did wrong; it all goes to hell when they want to be actresses.

29

I yank the door to La Poubelle. It's cool and dark and fairly empty—everyone is worshipping Henderson or waiting for the after party at Birds, in honor of his old stomping ground—but at the bar, there is one girl in a Band-Aid dress nursing a glass of vodka and trying to flirt with the disinterested bartender. I've never wanted a blowjob so bad in my life.

"Delilah," I call out. She turns. She smiles.

"Well, look what the cat dragged in." She pats the empty seat beside her. I order a vodka double. No mixers. No time for that.

Delilah introduces me to the new bartender as her *old friend, Joe.* And this means that Delilah still wants me. I refresh the Google search on Dr. Nicky when she goes to the bathroom. A feminist blogger has picked up the story. She's calling for Change.org to remove his petition and GO FEMINISTS GO! They are all horrified at the idea that this *murderer* who was in a position to help people is trying to use a patient as a scapegoat. They think it is misogynistic to speak ill of Guinevere Beck, who was a thriving and intelligent woman, a writer, an MFA candidate, a *happy, well-adjusted New York woman.* They want Dr. Nicky to shut up. They want his wife to seek counseling. They want the police department to accept that desperate men like Dr. Nicky do things like invent patients named *Danny Fox.* Thank you, feminists, and fuck you, Love, and hello, Delilah, sidling up to the bar, patting my leg, telling me I look good, tan, smacking her blowjob lips together, unabashedly hungry. I am hard. I smile. "You look good too."

If all my suffering has a purpose, and I don't yet know that it does, then the purpose can be boiled down to this: Delilah's vacuum cleaner mouth inhaling my cock on the loading dock in back of the Pantry. She said I was weird for wanting it here. It's dirty, it smells like trash, it's *a grocery store parking lot ewww.* But I know what she likes and I told her to get on her knees and suck it and the miracle of life, the sperm reaches the egg, the tennis ball teeters and falls to one side, not the other, Delilah did it. She sucked me the way I like, the way I want. I missed that. I needed that. Love is not all you need.

Fuck Love. Fuck love.

Don't Fuck Delilah and I are walking back to my place and she's grateful to be with me and I like this better, the way she clings. As we fall in step together, it becomes possible that this could be my life, that it could be one of those classic love—*fuck that word*—stories where the right girl was upstairs all along. In this quarter-mile trek, Delilah holds on tight to my hand and describes an argument she had at Oaks Gourmet with a guy who was rude to her about asking for ketchup. She is funny, all worked up, and this could be us together. We reach my building, her building, our building.

There is a brand-new door at Hollywood Lawns. "Yeah," Delilah says. "Someone got fucked up and fell into the door."

Home trash home and I unlock the door and Delilah takes charge and throws me against the wall of mailboxes. She feels my dick underneath my pants. She licks my neck. "Now," she says. "I want you inside of me now."

I unlock the door to my apartment and she tears off my shirt and I shred her Band-Aid dress and this is *fucking*. Rage mixed with sex and I wonder what set her off and at the same time I don't care. It works. She wants me and I want her and I need to fuck the love out of my system. I pull on Delilah's hair and I bite her nipples and smack her ass hard and she scratches my back and this is Hollywood fucking. You can't get mad in Malibu, not really.

Delilah salivates over my balls and she is not a cheater like Love, Love who gets to act in a fucking movie without trying to act, Love who gets to star in a fucking movie without suffering through auditions, without waitressing or striving or watching the Oscars on a futon, burning with desire to be there, spending night after night at the UCB trying to learn, to hone a craft. Fuck Love. I like Delilah and I try to be a gentleman. I stay in bed with her when it's over. I feign interest.

"So how was your summer?" I ask.

"My summer was my summer." She shrugs. "Not really any such thing as summer in LA, you know? Only difference is some of the parties are at beach houses, but what a pain, going out to the beach. Ugh. East Coast water is so much better, right?"

"Fuck, yes," I say. Delilah may think she didn't have a summer but she is wrong. She did. There is something more settled about her. Something changed inside of her and she doesn't seem as tormented. She's like the kitten that got neutered. She's calm. She isn't as sick with aspirations now that she's *moonlighting for this pseudo–*Entertainment Tonight *show.* We lie in my bed, gazing at the ceiling that used to get on my nerves, the bubbling, lowly barricade that once seemed so literal, a roadblock to a higher life. It all doesn't seem as bad as I thought. I forgot how nice it is to be contained. I know the boundaries here. I know what's mine. I don't have to feel like I'm eating someone else's Frosted Flakes and I don't have to say thank you all the time.

"I'm hungry," I say.

"Wanna order a pizza?" Delilah asks.

No. I want to dive under the covers and kiss her thighs and lick her and feel her hands in my hair. I do this and she reacts the way I want her to react. She calls out my name. Her legs shake. She sounds like she's crying and laughing at once. She sounds like an animal, like she found the *afikomen*. I am good enough for Delilah. She treats me like her Milo, telling me how great I am, how big I am, how much she missed me. She does not mention her mother and she does not try to parlay this romp into future meetings like some desperate ne'er-do-well at a blackjack table trying to make it all back. She has learned a thing or two and I could do anything to her in this bed. She gives me her ass, her fingernails, her vigor.

Afterward, we order in chicken and French fries and we watch *Hannah and Her Sisters*. I pay for the chicken and I hold the remote and we don't need a screening room. We don't need an ocean out the window. We just need my forty-two-inch TV, my dick, my futon.

Delilah scratches my chest. "What's it like?"

"What's what like?"

"The Quinn mansion," she says. "I've only seen pictures on *Curbed LA*. Is there really a bowling alley?"

It was the wrong question. I close the box of chicken. She's supposed to be basking. She's supposed to be fantasizing about our future. She is not supposed to be *reporting* and I don't like the way she sits, on her side, elevated, like she's doing yoga, like she's Molly Ringwald in *The Breakfast Club*, so blasé.

She wants to know about Love and I deflect. I tell her that it's complicated but over—and she wants to know where we met and when. I tell her I don't want to talk about it and she says she needs it in order to move on, have a fresh start. She says she has been seeing someone this summer too and she will tell me *anything* I want to know about that and now I remember everything wrong with Delilah, with Franklin Village, and I check my phone. Still nothing from Love but Monica wrote to say Love got wasted. They all passed out at Milo's house. She says Love is mad at me. I remind Monica that I *told* Love I was sick. I am waiting for a response from Monica when Delilah starts in again on Love, like a fat kid trying to get another cookie.

"Please," she says. "I'm a big girl and this is not about feelings. I just like to know these things. Tell me where you met her. Where does someone like Love Quinn hang out?"

"She came into the shop," I lie.

Monica texts: *Passing out everything will be fine Love is out cold Forty is high as shit and Milo is*

Her phone must have died because that's it. Delilah prods me. I put my phone down. "What?" I ask.

"The bookstore?" she says. "You're trying to tell me that Love Quinn came into that *bookstore*?"

"Yeah," I say, defensive. "She reads."

She pulls her hair back and looks away.

"What's wrong?" I ask.

"Nothing," she says. "It's just that I think you actually met her at Soho House."

I have nothing to hide. "I did," I say. "I don't know why I'm being weird. I feel weird talking about her to you."

She says I don't have to feel weird and she tells me about the guy *she's* been seeing and she can't tell me his name but he's an *actor* and he's someone I would have heard of and he has something you can't buy with all of Love's money. Her words, not mine.

"He's famous," she says. "Like, legit famous. And it's good but sometimes he freaks out and pulls shit like he did tonight and stands me up."

"You were waiting for him at La Pou?"

She nods and this is why she changed. She didn't evolve. She didn't grow. She didn't forsake her aspirations for a healthier outlook on life. She got some famous dick inside of her and some famous dick called her back. Between us we have no money, no fame, no power, no butler, no boxes of Frosted Flakes that just appear without having to go to the grocery store, no elevated lawns under starry skies. Between us we just have negativity. We both got dumped, fucked over.

I tell her I'm exhausted and she asks if she can stay. We both check our phones and we're both still losers. I don't need to be on this futon alone, so I tell her it's fine. We don't spoon. We're both too wounded and I fall asleep wondering if there will be more angry sex in the morning.

WHEN I wake up at five A.M. I'm still a loser, and there is no message from Love. I sigh but as long as I am here, I could go for another blowjob. I roll over. I'm ready to go and I reach for Delilah. But she's not here. I rub the sleep out of my eyes and head toward the bathroom and there she is, in a bra and panties, like some drug-addled victim of human trafficking, hunkered down in my bathroom.

And in her hand is a reusable Pantry bag, *my* reusable Pantry bag, the one I brought to Henderson's.

30

“DELILAH,” I say. My heart gets loud in my throat. What the fuck is she doing?

She whips her head around. “Joe,” she says, her eyes wide. “I was looking for toilet paper.”

“There’s a roll on the counter.” I step toward her.

She cowers. She hunches forward, as if she’s praying. “Is there?” she asks, nervous, insincere.

“There is,” I say. “I don’t see how you could have missed it.”

“Oh, you know,” she says. “Guys, a lot of the time, you don’t have toilet paper.”

I don’t like the high pitch of her voice and she turns around and scoots backward, as if she can cover the Pantry bag, as if she can backflip into my tub and escape through the drain. She went through my things. She is a self-destructive fiasco of a person. She couldn’t just stay in the bed with me. She couldn’t be content to suck my dick and cheat on her not-a-boyfriend boyfriend. Nope. Like an addict who loads the syringe even after she knows the batch is bad, that it killed a bunch of people, Delilah got out of my bed and went into my closet, where she doesn't belong. She is an addict. And you can't go to rehab for what has stricken her, a star-fucking disorder where she risks her own life and security and happiness to find out what Love Quinn's home looks like.

"What are you looking for?" I ask again. I taunt the cat. I poke the tiger.

"Nothing," she says. "It's okay."

"You said you were looking for toilet paper," I remind her. Dumb girl. Can't keep her own story straight. "Did you find any toilet paper in there?"

She stands up. "I think I should go."

"I think you should stay."

She stands in front of the Pantry bag, as if her legs are cover. "Find anything good in there?" I ask.

"Joe," she says. "I am not like that. I was just looking for toilet paper."

"Delilah," I say. "I don't think you're telling the truth."

It's always the same with these fucking people, bad people when they're caught. They try to sell you. In Delilah's case, she actually tells me that she knows people who could make a *documentary* about all this. "Like *Serial*," she pitches, as if this is what I want. "I mean, I'm not going to jump to conclusions about this bag and the way you were at Henderson's and all the ways things are adding up but, Joe, this could be very interesting."

"I don't think so," I say.

"Let's just talk about it," she says.

"Get in the tub."

She whimpers. "Please no. I'm sorry. I'll go."

I point. "Get in the fucking tub."

She cries and I had a feeling this would get loud and she yammers again. "I know people," she says.

"No," I remind her. "You fuck people."

I knock her back into the tub and she falls. I use some of the tape from the bag to seal her mouth shut and tie her arms together. I close the bathroom door and block the doorknob with a chair. I turn on some music—Journey's greatest hits—to drown out her muffled cries and I tear the Kandinsky off the wall. She doesn't know art. She doesn't know anything but celebrities and she is an empty person, a mean person. She will never be happy. She won't stop shooting for the stars, sucking them off, trying to pull them down to her futon, to her chicken bones.

I am not going to kill her just because she knows I killed Henderson, because she's crying about it in my bathroom, as if this is the path to freedom. No. I'm also going to kill her because there is no happy ending for a star-fucking girl like Delilah, a girl who actively refuses to embrace her talents, celebrate her insides, lead with her brain. After this "famous" guy, whoever he is, finishes with her, she'll go tramping for someone else until one day she realizes she's too old to be taken seriously by these motherfucking pricks. And then she'll either spend her savings on surgery or pop pills or move away and try to sell her secrets to a publisher.

Oh, the sadness of the Angeleno with a bank account dwindling, a forehead creasing, a self-esteem level deflating. I wish Delilah were a little more like me. I wish she were more confident. I wish she never stopped believing in herself, like her tattoo, but she did. She thought she needed someone famous in order to feel worthy. She could have settled down with Dez or Calvin or me or any of the guys she met. But she wanted fame more than love. She will never be happy, and really, I'm doing her a favor. She will never find what she's looking for. I pull an orange Rachael Ray knife out of the butcher's block. LA kills women. It's a shame that Delilah moved here. She should have gone back to New York. You don't belong here unless you're tough, beautiful, or talented. What I am doing is a kindness, a mercy killing. I am putting her out of her misery.

I open the bathroom door and she's cowering in the tub, on her knees. Sad cat. Poor kitten. Her face is a wad of chewed-up gum. All the joy is gone. Somewhere along the way she broke her own heart and without a heart, you can't get better.

"I know," I say. "I know how sad you are. I know how sick you are. But it's over."

Steve Perry's unmistakable voice crescendos and Delilah hyperventilates. She cries and cries, and how badly she needed this. How much more of this there would be for her were she to stay on this long and lonely road ahead. The girl who paid someone to inscribe words on her thigh, words that she could not live by, words she did not understand. The key is not just to continue believing, after all, but the key to life is to believe in something that matters, something big and beautiful, something more profound than fame, money.

I grab her extensions and smash her head into the tub and that's it. No more tears. Blood trickles down her forehead. I was right. She isn't beautiful. She was pretty. And I don't feel sorry for her. It's like they say about everything in this world. You can't feel sorry for yourself. A lot of girls, they would have loved to be so pretty.

31

IT'S a good thing I brought that giant duffel bag to LA. I don't know how else I'd get her the fuck out of here. But first I have to get dressed and find my keys and run all the way up to Tuxedo Terrace and get my car. I throw on sweatpants and a shitty old T-shirt I wore when I worked at the bookstore. It's cold. My lungs hurt. And when I get to my car, it's all fogged in and I don't have time for this. This is LA, there shouldn't ever be any bullshit with the weather. My teeth chatter as I defrost the windshield and Henderson is a bad luck charm, even dead.

When I reach Hollywood Lawns, I put on my hazards and put the car in park. I jog up the steps, back inside, and get my giant empty duffel bag out of the closet and unzip it and the zipper is loud, stuck, no. I yank. *No.* I know for a fact that I don't have any trash bags big enough to hold her and I pull again and I cut my finger but the zipper behaves. I lift Delilah out of the tub and set her inside the bag. She looks like she's being swallowed by a giant black flower and I pull the zipper over her feet, covering her legs, past her Journey tattoo. I zip more, obscuring her cheap panties and her cheaper bra and her too-short neck and her too-big mouth and her closed eyes and her rounded forehead and her hair. She never needed extensions.

I try to lift the bag but I'm going to have to drag it—and fast. This is a crowded neighborhood and everyone wants to be skinny; soon there will be exercisers. I carry the bag out to my Prius and Wolfe is fucking right. You can't go home again. Not if you live in an apartment building.

I haven't been in the Donzi alone. A few weeks ago, we were at this bar in the Marina and I ran down to the dock to get Love's sweater and I remember standing on the boat thinking about how different it is being alone than it is being with other people.

I wanted to take the boat out and push it. I wanted to drive it to Japan. I had this moment. The cover band inside was doing Toto—that "Africa" song—and I was so fucking happy. It was enough to choose Love inside on the dance floor over the great sea, the unknown. And then there's also the fact that I don't have a fucking license. Love's family can get out of anything; I know this. But Love has warned me not to take the boat out on my own.

"It's infinitely easier to deal with boat cops if Forty or I are there," she said. "And if we're not, you know, it's harder."

I am on my way back to shore after burying Delilah at sea, watching the weighted-down bag make its way to the center of the Pacific, far from the world she couldn't quite fit into. I will always think of her kindly, her unfulfilled potential, how she extended her arm for that blender that was just out of reach. She embodied the danger of aspirations and I will always wish she hadn't turned into a menacing fame monster.

I feel bad for her parents. I feel terrible for all the guys who genuinely offered their hearts. Mostly, I feel terrible for her. I picture Harvey showing someone Delilah's apartment full of her things and I sit. This one hurt. It did. LA consumes people. Able-bodied, intelligent people like Henderson and Delilah move here and turn into oversexed monsters and it didn't have to be this way. They both could have been a little kinder. I don't feel so bad anymore. My body count in LA: one star and one star fucker.

I slide into the Marina at the thirty-degree angle. I don't turn too early or too late. I learned so much this summer. I am a boater, a writer. The Donzi is in the slip. And then I hear someone calling my name.

Love.

She is wrapped up in her hooded bathrobe. I am in last night's clothes and it's a good thing I'm already parked because now my adrenaline is going and my body is shaking. She is not smiling and I have no idea how long she's been here, if she saw me go out to sea with my bag, and return with nothing.

"What the fuck are you doing?" she demands. "You bail on me and go out on my fucking boat?"

The hairs on the back of my neck stand up. "I just went for a ride," I say.

"Alone?" she asks. And fuck. My eyes scan the floor for blood but I'm good; no mug of piss here, nothing to see, folks.

"Obviously," I answer. "Do you see anyone else here?"

I can tell by her demeanor that the answer is no, she does not see anyone now; she did not see anyone when there was someone to see. She doesn't know what I did, that I cheated, that I let Delilah into my bed, onto my body, that I put her out to sea. More secrets, more bad things, but I am safe.

"I'm kind of surprised to see you," I say, and turn the tables.

"What the fuck is that supposed to mean?" she says.

"I don't know," I say. "I wrote to you. I didn't hear back."

"Yeah," she says. "I didn't write back to you because I don't write back to people who treat me like shit. I'm not a doormat, Joe."

"Me neither," I snap. "Did you have fun with your little friend Milo?"

"You mean my director?" she asks. "Because that's what he is, Joe. My director. He's not my boyfriend and he's not the enemy and we're in *business* together. Business that matters to me, goddamn it. Business you walked out on. Business that is *mine*."

She trembles and I know. She didn't fuck him and she didn't dump me and *fuck* I overreacted. I fucked up. The Donzi shimmies and what I wouldn't give to be on land. Instead I'm on this boat, this vessel that belongs to her family. She gets to be the steady one, on the dock, entitled, land ho, and fuck me.

Love folds her arms. "Just throw me the fucking line," she says, my teacher, my boss. I toss it to her and she ties a knot fast, so smooth, such a rich girl. I climb off the boat, clumsy as all fuck. She stomps along the dock and onto the beach and I follow her onto the sand. Me, the follower.

"Love," I say. "Let me just say I'm sorry. I know I have no excuse."

"Joe, when something good happens to me and you *shit* on it . . ."

"I'm sorry," I proclaim. I reach for her. She backs away. I say it again. "I'm sorry, Love."

"It's not enough," she says. "You were *such* a dick, Joe. The second we got the green light, you turned into one of those dickhead guys who doesn't like it when his girlfriend gets attention."

She continues to blast me. She says I let her down. I should have been a man and I should have congratulated her and I should have meant it. I should have expressed interest in the script and I should have been up front about my *obvious jealousy issues*. I should have called her instead of texting her because that was *a bitch move* and I should have hung around the neighborhood and waited for her after the show. All the things I should have done and we can't go back in time.

"I know," she says. "But do you get it? Do you get that it's not going to be like this?"

"Yes," I say, and I've never loved her as much as I do right now and I want the chance to be the good guy, the best guy, the talking guy. I want to clean my dick and scrub my skin and start over. I love her too much to let this be the end.

"Love," I say. "I am so sorry. You have to understand. You are right. I acted like a fucking douche."

She looks at me. I beg her with my eyes and my hands and I am as strong as she is. I apologize again and again and something transforms inside of her and my hands and my eyes did the work that I was unable to do with my dirty mouth. Love nods.

"Okay," she says. "We're okay."

And somehow we are hugging and we kiss, just one kiss, a make-up kiss, a no-sex-yet kiss, and then we flop into lounge chairs. The fight is over and she tells me about Seth Rogen's weed and her costume fitting and that she has news.

"More news?" I ask.

"Forty and Monica broke up," she says. "This was almost a record for him though. I mean, girls are like shoes for him, you know?"

"I'm sorry," I say.

She shrugs. "I know this will sound dumb but I really thought it was gonna stick. Because of the stupid *Friends* thing."

"It's not stupid," I say. "It's sweet. You want the best for him."

She nods and checks her watch. "We should go get packed. The jet leaves at noon."

I look at her. "*We* have to pack?"

She rolls her eyes. "Joe, come on. What do you mean? You think you're not going?"

"You didn't invite me."

"Didn't invite you?" She balks. "We've been seeing each other the whole summer and we practically live together. I don't have to *invite* you. You should know you're invited."

"Well, Monica said that Forty invited her."

She rolls her eyes. "So? We have our own way of talking and our own thing. Why don't you get that, Joe?"

I don't know and Love says it's going to be intense in Palm Springs. We won't last unless I *communicate*.

So I try. "Okay. I guess I also wasn't sure because of Milo."

She sighs and now she explains her dynamic with Milo. They are best friends, to an extent. She uses the phrase *third twin* and she says it's hard to talk about because it's friendship steeped in guilt. "I'm closer with him than I am with *Forty*," she whispers. "I mean, do you know how wrong that is?"

"You can't help who you love."

"Milo and I both want the best for Forty. So when you see us together or whatever, I mean, no guy I ever dated liked it. I get it. It sucks. But we're just friends."

Love is essentially asking me to tolerate her bond with another man, a good-looking fucker she's known for longer than she's known me. It's impossible, like snow in Malibu. Absurd. But what can I do?

She takes my hand. "I wish we could stay here all day," she says.

I want to fuck her in the sand but she says we have to pack. She stretches and pulls her robe tighter and I know her well enough to know that she is closing a door on this fight, that the war between us was transitional.

Love blows a kiss to the sea. "Good-bye, ocean," she says.

I stay for a moment longer, staring at Delilah's giant blue grave. It would be impossible to find my bag in there and the permanence of decisions made at sea is bigger than all of us. The wind whips, waves crash, and I head inside.

Summer is over.

32

BOOTS *and Puppies* is already on IMBD: *Best friends and former lovers Harmony and Oren are both engaged to other people. They spend forty-eight hours together trying to learn from the past, live for the present, and decide on their future.* But *Boots and Puppies* isn't a movie—it's a FUCK YOU to me and Love, a ninety-five-page torture chamber of increasingly graphic love scenes between Oren (Milo) and Harmony (Love). Spoiler alert: Harmony and Oren—the only characters in the whole fucking movie—finally decide to get married when Harmony realizes that she needs to let go of the *white puppy* she rescued who keeps chewing on all her boots. FUCK YOU, MILO. Harmony runs to Oren, who knew she would come to her senses. FUCK YOU, MILO.

On the jet to Palm Springs, Love asks what I think of the "script." I deflect. I ask her when Milo finished writing it.

"This summer," she answers. "He hit it out of the park, right?"

I contain my rage. I will not let him win. Not when I've just gone to war for my relationship. "Love," I say, pointing to the script. "You're not even a little offended by this?"

"Joe," she says, definitive, as if she'd been preparing for this. "If you're going to tell me that you think you're a *puppy*, then I'm going to tell you that you need a shrink. I am not Harmony any more than you are a puppy. Milo is not Oren. This is a *story*. A made-up story."

"I know I'm not a puppy."

"You are *not* a puppy." She sighs. "And anyway, Milo started this script ages ago. He's been rewriting it for a while. You know, Jake Gyllenhaal was going to play Oren, up until the very last second. That's how good the script is."

I do not remind Love that he *finished* it after meeting me and I do not call bullshit on Jake Gyllenhaal. We land and I try to focus on the positive. Our fight is behind us, and I've been wanting to go to Palm Springs. The desolate road from the airport snakes through a desert where the houses are giant UFOs from the sixties, spread apart, like dice rolled onto a craps table.

"We're shooting here and living here?" I ask.

"Yep," she says. "How gorgeous is this house?"

"Striking," I say, and I mean it in a bad way. The house is midcentury, ice cold, plastic and pink and orange and white, like a ceramic bowl of sherbet left in the middle of the desert during an atomic meltdown, empty as Forty's mind. We park and she knows I am disappointed and she pushes me.

"Sorry," I say. "I just thought we were going to Palm Springs."

"We are," she says, her voice fresh with indignant attitude that only comes from being cast as a *lead* and studying a *screenplay* in a *jet*. "Milo is amazing, getting us this house, right?"

I am sick of hearing that Milo is amazing. He isn't. And this house sucks. We're several miles from the hotels and the stores and the stuff I read about in *Less Than Zero*, the stuff I wanted to see. My head started pounding the second we walked into this cold house and we're only *three hours* into the day. I get the chills. It's so hot outside and it's so cold inside. There is no ocean, no relief, no shabby chic sectional, no sand on the floor of the kitchen, no crunch, no texture, no depth.

But we *had* to shoot here because Milo is desperate to get footage of some something he calls "Indoor Coachella." Coachella is a festival fashion show where people dress up like hippies and pretend that Passion Pit is as good as the Rolling Stones. So the idea of taking that mess and shoving it inside a casino is loathsome to me.

Barry Stein nixes it right away. He says Coachella is too big of an insurance risk and Milo pleads with him. "I just need a night there," he says. "I'll go in guerilla style, Barry. I just want those jagged lights, the feel of it. We *need* that flashback. And it's not Coachella for real."

"Yeah," Barry says. "It's more of a shit show. No is no."

Milo sulkily moves on, and we "shoot" all day, every day. Milo karate chops the air at the end of every take, as if he never saw a Ben Stiller movie, as if he doesn't know that chopping the air is an asshole thing to do. I wish Ben Stiller were here. I wish anyone with a brain would come and take over.

While we shoot, I have to sit in *video village*, another misnomer; video village is not a village. It's just a bunch of folding chairs shoved together in front of the monitors. I have no purpose. When we move locations and relocate the village, I'm not even allowed to move my chair because I'm not *union*.

It's day four and "Harmony" and "Oren" are fighting because Harmony's puppy ate Oren's boots and then making up because they hate fighting and Love kisses Milo *again and again.* I hate set. There's too much clapping, and bullshit with nicknames. They call the second to last shot "The Abby" and the last shot "The Martini" and the level of self-importance is unbearable. When my scripts get the green light, I won't spend all my days on set. And when Milo begs to visit, I'll say yes and then I'll "forget" to give his name to security.

"Cut!" Milo yells after they finish kissing for the thirtieth time. He grabs Love's hands. "That felt *good.* Did that feel good?"

"That felt *great*!" she says. She bounces and I die.

It's the little things that make you want to kill someone, the way Milo drinks *Diet Dr Pepper* and ties his Jewfro in a *bun* and lifts his shirt to show off his stomach and wipes his glasses down even though they're not dirty. Yes, Milo got glasses, and seafoam green Topsiders, and a navy blue Polo-style shirt with a popped collar, and didn't I already kill this guy when he was schilling Home Soda and fucking Guinevere Beck?

Milo calls *action* again and kisses Love. My muscles tighten. All I can do is eat and wait, eat and watch—and this is day four of *twenty-eight days*—and they're improvising the dialogue—bite me—because he just wants to mount her.

I want to be anywhere but here and I ask Forty about nearby restaurants. He slaps my back. "This is a *shoot*, Old Sport. We don't go *anywhere* until we get this baby in the can."

I lower my voice. "Well, what about those *other* movies?"

He whispers, "Bad news is fast. Good news takes a while. Hurry up and wait. It's your job, you're the boyfriend."

And that's what people call me. *Can Love's boyfriend bring her a Diet Coke? Can Love's boyfriend find Love's charger?*

It's bad and it gets worse on day seven when the hairstylist asks if *Love's boyfriend can grab the pickles.* Milo laughs. "'Love's boyfriend' is kind of awkward," he says. "Let's just call him *Loverboy*!"

The director gets what the director wants so now my name is *Loverboy.* Forty says I have to lighten up. Love thinks it's *cute.* Milo shows us a picture of the Restoration Hardware table, home of The Big Sex Scene on page twenty-seven. "The table represents real love," he says. "What Oren and Harmony have, the way they forget it around new people, plastic people, but then they get on this table and man, there's nothing like it."

"I love it," Love says.

He avoids my eyes and licks his lips as he leafs through his *script.* Milo is definitely trying to take her away and I will kill that table. Instead, I go to *craft service*—why can't they just call it the food?—for the fourth time in two hours. I dunk a slice of cornbread into the chili and I hear someone: *Is Loverboy at crafty again?*

And that's when I decide. I am going to get ripped here. Hot. Jacked.

I toss my cornbread in the trash and tell Love that I'm going for a run. She reacts. "A run? That's new."

"Yep," I say. "I gotta start taking better care of myself."

IT'S day seventeen and the title of the movie should have been *That Time When Milo Tried to Win Back Love.* Our sex life dwindles because of the long shooting days, and because we don't have a lock on our bedroom door. Love spends more time with Milo running lines in his room, which *does* lock. Every time she goes in there, I go for a run, and every time Milo speaks to me, he says things like, "How are you surviving?" and "You know, if you're bored, we're good. You can go back to LA."

He doesn't say this shit in front of Love and I want to kill him but I can't. He's the *director* and Love's *third twin* and people will notice if he just disappears. So I try not to dwell. Nobody will download this movie except friends and families. And anyway, they may be making a *movie* but I'm making a *body*. I downloaded an app that tracks every morsel that enters my body and every step I take. I do sit-ups and pull-ups and I sprint and I am becoming the hottest man alive while most of the people around me are getting bloated, soft.

I arrive in Video Village after my second workout on day twenty-three and Love notices my arm. "Hello, biceps," she says. "Wow."

Milo says one of these days he wants to hit the gym with me.

I tell him anytime. "You'll get rid of that paunch in no time," I assure him. "Or you can go on a run with me."

Love walks away to *makeup* and Milo smiles. "Loverboy," he says. "I wanted to thank you. I didn't want to make a big deal in front of Love, but guy to guy, if I were in your shoes, with the new scene, the rewrite, I would have gotten it if you said no. So thanks."

I don't know about this new scene and he knows it and he winks. He ambles away to check on that Restoration Hardware table and I ask a production assistant for the addition. She avoids eye contact and gives it to me. I read.

INT. KITCHEN – MID-AFTERNOON, LAZY, LOVELY TIME

We are TIGHT on HARMONY eating strawberries. Watching Oren. Her nipples pop. She says she's hungry. She licks her fingers. OREN says to eat a berry. Harmony says she doesn't want a berry. 3, 2, 1. Boom. Harmony gets onto her knees. We go TIGHT on her mouth as she takes him.

Milo knew better than to be around while I read. And all I can think is:

INT. MY BRAIN – RIGHT NOW – FUCK YOU FUCKING MOVIE FUCKING MILO

There are two days until Love blows Milo. But that's not true. Because Love is not blowing Milo. Because I am gonna do whatever it takes to get that motherfucking mouse out of my motherfucking house.

33

I lay the groundwork for my extermination. It is the most painful, derivative thing I've ever said, for so many reasons, because of my ex, because I'm not a follower, because I fucking hate concerts and Urban Outfitters and Porta-Potties. But it has to be said. If I want to kill the mouse, I have to lure him away from the house. We are on set. It's the day before the blowjob. This is it. "So, Milo," I begin. And here it comes. My anti-truth. "How cool would it be to get outta here and go to Indoor Coachella and see Beck tonight?"

"Yeah," he says. "But we have a big day tomorrow."

"But still." I lean in. "If you could intercut some of that pop and the color and the sound with the oral element, I mean, I'm just saying, that would be dope."

Milo nods. "Mm hmm," he says. "Yeah."

"I go jogging every night," I remind him. "You've been saying you want to go with me . . ."

Milo tugs on his bun. "Not a word to Love," he says.

So it's on. A plan is made. I'm relaxed just knowing that he's going to be dead soon. Granted, it sucks that I have to go to *Indoor Coachella*. But at least that festival of fanny packs and MDMA will be good for something. People die at festivals all the time. And Milo's been wanting to go to this fucking festival since day one. I'm the innocent one who just tagged along to make sure he'd be okay.

And I'm not heartless. I spend the day trying to save the poor kid's life. I try to kill the blowjob scene. At lunch, Love and I go upstairs to our bedroom and I try to make her see things my way. I hold her hands. I tell her that this is turning into a cult. "Milo even looks like Charles Manson, with those stupid beads he's wearing now."

"Joe," she says. "You need to process your own emotions. I can't do that for you."

"I'm not processing my emotions," I say. "I'm trying to stop you from doing something stupid."

She cups my face in her hands. "My job is to make things work," she says. "My job is not to tear them down."

"We're talking about a blowjob," I remind her. "Not world peace."

She smiles. "You're jealous because we don't do that. Harmony and Oren are different. I'm not Harmony, Joe. And it's not my vision. It's Milo's vision."

Everyone has been brainwashed by this fucker. Still, I try nonviolent measures of extermination. I continue my anti-blowjob mission after lunch, but everyone wants the blowjob. Forty says it's bold. Forty says people are still talking about *Brown Bunny* because of the blowjob scene but Forty is wrong. Nobody is talking about *Brown Bunny*. Milo says we *need* it. He says it elevates the material and ensures that the movie won't get lost.

Barry Stein shows up on the set—it's amazing, the way fellatio changes everything—and that's when I know there is no getting out of it. Barry Stein says the blowjob will get them into festivals. It will make Milo an auteur. The only people on my side are Love's parents on Skype.

"I don't understand the movies anymore," Dottie says. "Doesn't this make it a porno?"

Ray sighs. "You don't see anything like this in *Fast and Furious.*"

Love pleads. "That's because those movies aren't about anything real, Dad."

In the end, Ray and Dottie *send their love* to Love and they're not going to stop her and they trust her and Milo and they think she looks beautiful. We have sex, missionary, it stinks of obligation. Then Love is sleeping and I text Milo:

You ready?

He says he needs twenty minutes, so I go downstairs and pour a bowl of Frosted Flakes. I go outside and look at the stars as I eat my cereal. I can't bear the thought of the car ride with Milo, all smug, so I fantasize about what happens when he's dead. Someone will step up to the plate and save the movie and that someone will be me. In my version of *Boots and Puppies*, Love will wake up and look for Milo. (I refuse to buy into this Harmony and Oren bullshit.) She will realize he left her. Some Peter Gabriel song will play and she'll walk into the kitchen and grab her phone.

"Yeah," she'll say. "I have this big old table I have to get rid of. Can you guys help me out?"

I hear someone open the door and come outside and I turn around but it's not Milo.

"Love?" I say.

She motions for me to be quiet. She's wearing a transparent nightie I've never seen. She isn't wearing any shoes, any panties. She grabs my hand. "This way."

She leads me onto the set, into the kitchen.

"Love, what the hell is this?" I hiss.

She whips her head around. "I'm Harmony," she says. "You're Oren, right?"

Ah. *Ah.* "Yes," I say. Love gestures for me to sit on the table. I do. "I'm Oren."

"What do you think?" And she planned for me. She left a bowl of strawberries on the table. She holds my eyes. She picks up a berry. She bites. "I'm still hungry."

I warn her. "This is a hot set."

"I know," she says.

"We're not supposed to touch anything."

"I know," she says. "But I can't help it anymore."

My phone is buzzing and this isn't supposed to happen. I'm supposed to kill Milo and he's texting and he probably woke Love up accidentally, banging shit around. And I don't like this. Love's barely spoken to me all month and she knows how I feel about the blowjob scene and she thinks she can just fuck her way out of anything. And no.

"Love," I say. "What is this?"

"I'm just having fun."

"No," I say. "What is going on with you and Milo? And don't say nothing."

Love puts her hands on mine. "Well," she says. She bites her lip. Her hands are shaking. "The truth is . . ." My hands are shaking. She presses. "Milo and I hooked up at Chateau that morning, that day that you and I met."

It is worse than I thought and better than I thought. It is a lesson in instincts. I knew he was my enemy from day one. I knew it. He showed up at Chateau that night and he wanted me gone and he must have felt blindsided. One minute he's fucking Love, the next everyone is gushing over *The Professor.*

"Did you shower after?"

"Did I shower?"

"That first day," I say. "When we met. At Soho House."

"Of course," she says.

"Did you bring me to Chateau to get rid of him?"

"No," she says. Then: "Yes." She looks down. "Is that terrible? But I also really liked you. I mean that was early."

Love says I'm right about everything. Milo *is* trying to get her back and she has been uncomfortable but she isn't mad at him. "He's one of my best friends," she says. "I mean, we always go back to each other and I beat myself up, why don't I love him like that? He is not a bad guy, Joe. I have led him on. I feel awful."

Love hugs me and she is naked underneath her nightie. She puts her hands on my shoulders and moves me to the Restoration Hardware table. She unbuttons my pants. She pulls them down. She kneels like she's supposed to in *Boots and Puppies* and I am harder than I've ever been. When she takes me in her mouth for the first time, it's like being inside her vagina, her pink brain, her bloodstream. I think of God again, that section up in heaven where they build bodies to match and I knew that her vagina was for me and now I know her mouth was made for me too.

As I get close, I open my eyes for just one second and Milo is there at the edge of the set, staring. I wonder how much he overheard. Everything, I hope.

I close my eyes again, and I hear a car start. Milo is going to Indoor Coachella alone and maybe I don't have to kill him. Everything is different now. I'm not jealous. I'm logical. The mouse left the house on his own and we won't have any problems again.

I come.

34

THE next day, we wake up in a new world. We kiss and Love e-mails Milo to say she won't do the blowjob. She admits that she's relieved. I win. Milo does too. He's alive and he says Beck was great and that he respects Love's decision as an actress.

Love goes down to set and when I get out of the shower, I have a new text from Forty: *Old Sport! Tell Love u gotta go to town, books or something. Big news. Ask for the Deuce suite at the desk. Ritz. Pronto.*

I drive over there and I've never seen so much cocaine in my life. There are mountains of it on every surface of this ornate suite and I worry about the police invading but Forty says to relax.

The suite is enormous and it seems that rich people go to Palm Springs to be in big, empty rooms with shiny lamps. Everything is black and white and electric green. Green pillows abound, like the one RIP Beck used to hump in her shoebox apartment, window open. It's that kind of layout where you're inside and outside at once. We have our own private patio.

"What am I doing here?" I ask. "What's up?"

"Having a drink!" Forty says, and he hands me a flute of champagne and he's wearing pink and yellow jams and an open hooded bathrobe.

"Did you want to talk about the scripts?" I ask. His agent was supposed to be sending them out, but there hasn't been any news, any action.

Forty motions for me to sit by two half-naked hookers. "Go on," he says. "Nobody's telling on anybody."

Instead I sit in a wicker chair with electric green pillows. "I'm fine, thanks."

Forty laughs. He wants to shoot the shit about *Boots and Puppies.* He thinks it could get into Sundance but he doesn't see it getting a theatrical release. He thinks Barry Stein isn't what he used to be and he thinks Milo should have hired an actor instead of taking the part.

"Was Jake Gyllenhaal really interested?" I ask, because it feels like this is an honest zone, a sacred space, the opposite of a set where the movie is God.

"Fuck, no!" he says. "That's just Milo stroking his dick and calling it a hand job. Jake isn't into that kind of shit. I don't even think he read it."

"Wow," I say. "Does Love know?"

Forty shakes his head. "It's a boatload of hell, getting a movie made, especially one like *B and P.* You gotta believe your own bullshit, ya know? It's like when you go to Promises and it's the last day and you've been there for three weeks and they're like 'Do you feel ready to go?' And you say yes because you were there! You fucking did it.

You tried. What the hell are you gonna say? 'No, gimme an eight ball'?"

He laughs and watches a hooker dance to no music. "When did you go to Promises?" I ask.

But Forty doesn't answer. He puts out his cigarette. "Earlier today, I had Ariana eat out Shelly while I fucked Shelly in the ass."

These are things I don't want to know. "Hey," I say. "What did you want to talk to me about?"

He hoovers more cocaine. "What did I want to what?"

"Why am I here?"

"The million-dollar question," he effuses. "Why are we here? Why? Personally, I think Satan sent me here to fucking fuck shit *up*. The way God sent Love to *love* shit up."

"Forty," I say. "Maybe you want some weed?"

He points at the hookers. He tells me again about things he *got them to do* and he might be lying about all of it. I decide I will not feel sorry for myself as Forty raves on about his sexual exploits. Everyone has something. Some people have a difficult child and some people have a sick child and some people have a limp and some people have an impossible mother and there is nobody on earth who has *nothing*. I have a mug of my DNA in a house in Rhode Island. And this is what Love has: a brother. A nightmare. A coked-up maniac who is now jumping on his bed like a ten-year-old, telling me about a birthday party he and Love had as kids.

Forty jumps off the bed and falls into the credenza and bangs his head. He's too fucked up to feel it and he's on his feet again. "So are you psyched or are you psyched?"

"Forty," I say. "I think you better sit down."

"No," he says. "I think *you* better sit down."

"I am sitting."

"Fuck, yes, you better sit," he rails. He claps. "And fuck you, Barry Stein." He does more coke. "You know, he's just gonna look fucking *stupid.*"

"Forty," I say. "I think maybe you've had enough."

He wipes his nose. "Megan. Fucking. Ellison."

I put down my champagne. "What are you talking about?"

"Are you deaf?" he shouts. "Megan Fucking Ellison. So fuck *you,* Barry Stein."

My heart beats. *Megan Ellison.* She made *Her* and *American Hustle.* The hooker who was dancing is now sitting on Forty's lap, feeding him a taco.

"Forty," I say. "Are you telling me that Megan Ellison is interested in *The Third Twin*?"

"No," he says. "I am telling you that Megan Ellison is interested in *The Third Twin* and *The Mess. Both of 'em. Boom!*"

Forty found out this morning; his agent had a meeting with Megan Ellison and Megan Ellison can eat Barry Stein for breakfast. The agent says the offer will be coming any day now, and Forty and I clink glasses of champagne and his hookers flop on the bed and watch *Wendy Williams* and make out periodically and this is not my kind of party but at least Forty knows himself. He jumps in the middle of them and they both roll toward him.

"Now listen here, Old Sport," he says. "Just remember it's only interest and we don't want to jinx it."

We agree to wait until the news is official before we tell anyone, but I don't know how Forty's going to do it. He's bouncing on the bed again, shouting, "Remember this moment, Old Sport. It's going to happen, it is. And the second that this is out there, your life isn't yours anymore. This is out there, and you're the guy, the man. Everyone is gonna wanna piece of you. Everyone is gonna love you. So like, take this for *you* man, you know? This is *your* success and this is the magic hour, the golden time before the time. Just be in it. You earned it. Don't spread it and don't pull on it and don't push it and don't share it and don't examine it. This is it. If the big one hits right now, you die a writer. You die discovered. Live like that. Live right now."

It's true; cokeheads can be annoying, but they also have this knack for knocking you the hell out of your head. Forty is right. This is my success and I put up with *Boots and Puppies* and I spent all those days at Intelligentsia and Taco Bell and I *did* earn it. I jump onto the other bed and I don't remember the last time I jumped on a bed. Forty howls and turns on the *Boogie Nights* soundtrack and I jump and pounce and bounce and the hookers laugh and I did it. I captured the flag. I moved to Los Angeles. I found Love; I fell in love. And now this, the hardest thing to do in this world, one of the hardest things, and I'm about to do it. I'm going to make it in Hollywood.

Love texts: *Have you heard from Forty? He disappeared. Sorry. Welcome to my world.*

She writes again a second later: *I love you.*

I take a screen grab. I'll have this image stitched onto a pillow, dozens of pillows, written into the sky, engraved into the walls of our home. It's impossible for me to distinguish the Love high from the Hollywood high and there might even be a contact high from being in this cocaine den but

I don't need to separate one from the other. I am happy. I am here. All the fear inside of me, the *CandaceBenjiPeachBeckHendersonDelilah* of it all, has been sublimated by the joy of *LoveTheThirdTwinTheMess.*

I call Love. I assure her that Forty is safe because he's with me. Love is relieved. Forty and the hookers decide to go for a swim in the giant pool and Forty shows off, doing the crawl and the butterfly and the breaststroke. He could be out there teaching kids to swim with his twin sister, but then, some people prefer hookers over poor children.

The whites of his eyes are red. I don't know if it's chlorine or cocaine. "You're a good friend," he says. "You know I think if I grew up without all this pressure and all this excess, I think I'd be more like you."

I start to tell him he's a good friend, but before I finish the sentence, he's submerged.

IT'S the last day of *Boots and Puppies* and I sit on this set a changed man. Love is a ball of feelings, overjoyed, sentimental, excited. Her movie is ending and she doesn't know it yet but mine will begin soon. We get to have a life like this, on sets, always creating, then wrapping, then toasting. I catch Forty's eye and wink but he motions for me to stop. He's back. He's hungover. He's not sure if we have a deal. He hasn't heard from his agent all day. I tell him to relax. Let today be about *Boots and Puppies*.

"You're a good man," he says. "You see the big picture."

"Always," I say. "It's the only picture."

I am good on a set and I have come to love it here, shooting the shit, working out in the desert; I am the only crew member who will leave this location in better physical shape than I was when I arrived. I love my chair with my name on it and I love our squeaky bed. I love the way a set makes you live in the moment. Now I am excited when Milo calls *action* and I feel like I moved forward in life every time he calls *cut.*

I will miss it here. I love the kitchen table where Love first blew me; now she sucks my dick every chance she gets. I love Love. I love our movie family even if I don't know all their names. People on a set all seem interchangeable, with dry hair and tan pants. But I love that too. I love it when it's time for the martini shot and you get to clap and the day is over and you *did it.* I love the time before that too, the sweet building exuberance of the Abby—named in honor of first AD, Abby Singer, you learn things on a set, history—the almost of it all, *two more to go!* If we all die right now, we have a movie in the can.

Love's parents saw some dailies and they're so thrilled with Love's work that they're insisting on flying us all to their place in Cabo for a wrap party. Most movies like this wrap out at a dive bar with two-dollar beers, but because of Love, we're going to La Groceria for two nights. Love says I will love La Groceria and she says Cabo is "gentle heaven on earth."

I laugh and she smacks me. "Watch it, wiseass."

"Love," I say, grabbing a water bottle from craft. "Come on. When you hear Mexico, you think *gentle*?"

Milo laughs. "Lovey, Mexico is pretty much the murder capital of the world."

It's funny. Now that Milo accepts his fate, that he's not going to be with Love, he's infinitely more bearable, likable even. I relate to him, with his fucked-up parents and his creative impulses. "Yeah," I say. "Milo is right. I mean, they *behead* people in Mexico."

Just then a PA approaches. "Hey, Milo," he says. "We have a visitor."

Love and I turn our heads. And indeed, we do have a visitor. I drop my water bottle. The visitor is Officer Robin Fincher.

35

I am not jaywalking and this is not Officer Robin Fincher's territory. He has no right to be here in uniform, standing on my set, looking at my girlfriend. I pick up my water bottle, and stay on the ground a moment too long, and curse under my breath.

Milo shakes his hand. "Officer," he says. "Did you need to see our permits?"

Fincher laughs. "I just need one or two lines and a close-up."

Poor Milo can't tell whether or not the fucker is serious, but this is serious for me. What the fuck is he doing here?

"I wish," Milo says. "But it's a two-person cast. Hopefully we'll be back up this way for a sequel though, yeah?"

Fincher swallows. "I was kidding," he says, and he narrows his small blue eyes at me. "I popped by as part of a courtesy. We're just cruising through the area, addressing a theft situation," he says. "A couple places nearby have been robbed and we see you're rigged up pretty good here. We just wanted to make sure you lock down tight tonight."

Milo shakes his hand. "A horror movie within a movie, right?"

I touch Love's arm and tell her I have to go to the bathroom but what I really have to do is figure out why the fuck Fincher is here. I sneak out of the house through a side door and run around to the front where I see Fincher's car. He has headshots in the front seat but before I can explore further, I hear footsteps and turn around. Fincher lowers his sunglasses and I wish I had a pair.

"Officer," I say, sweat beading the back of my neck. "I'm a little confused."

"Did you get a California license yet?"

"No," I say. "I've been here."

"Hmm. So you haven't been back to your apartment?" he says. "Because neither has your neighbor."

Delilah. Fuck. "Which neighbor?"

He takes off his sunglasses and wipes them down with a handkerchief. "You know, your friend Delilah. She has a California state ID, lives in the same building as you. Well, not that you're official yet."

"She's missing?" I play dumb.

He nods. "You know anything about that?"

"I barely know her," I insist.

He punches me in the stomach and he is not allowed to do that and I buckle. I am in the dirt. My gut is nothing but muscles and I have no fat there, no padding to soften the blow. The fucker spits and his loogie lands next to my face. "Get the fuck up," he says. "I went easy on you just now."

I haven't been punched since Nanny Rachel and I don't like the feeling, the way my muscles are all individual things again with singular nerve endings. He kicks my knee. "I said, get the fuck up."

I stand. I will not give in. I will not reveal anything and his steely little eyes can't possibly hold anything important. "You're a fucker," he says. And it's a generic word, *fucker*.

"I don't know what you think," I say. "But I didn't do anything."

"Except kill Delilah," he says, and we have a problem. I can't allow those words to come out of that mouth where someone might hear them. "You did that. So you know, that matters to me, an officer of the law. I imagine it matters to your little fuck doll in there and I am sure that it matters to Delilah's parents. Jim and Regina, by the way. You ever think about that, Goldberg?"

He steps closer. If he hits me again I will kill him. I turn my head.

"Jim and Regina," he seethes. "Jim and Regina, Mom and Dad. They love their baby."

I turn my head and I meet his eyes head on. "I barely know Delilah," I say. "And I'm sure her parents will do everything they can to find her."

"You barely know her?" he asks, squinting at me.

"She's a neighbor," I say.

He raises a fist and he comes at me and I cower and he backs off. He laughs. "According to your neighbor Dez, you actually knew Delilah pretty well."

That drug dealer fucker. I will not be unnerved. "If you mean that I slept with her, yes," I say. "But I didn't know her very well."

"Phone records, Joe," he says. "Do you forget that I'm an officer of the law and that I have access to the missing persons database? Do you think her parents don't go out there and see to it that the LAPD talk to each and every individual who communicated with their daughter? The State of California cares about its residents. This isn't *Bed-Stuy*. We give a fuck here. We care."

He pronounces it incorrectly, *Bed-Stooey*, and I hate this kind of Californian, the type who doesn't know anything about the East Coast, the type who thinks Rhode Island is adjacent to Maine.

"I knew her a little bit," I say again. "But I didn't even know she was missing."

"I was surprised to learn that you're an opiate man," he says, assessing me. "You with the early morning jaywalking. You seem jacked up now, if I were to guess, I would have said coke. Speed. Maybe juice, but then no. You'd be a hell of a lot bigger if you were juicing."

This is taking too long and Love is going to wonder where I am. "What do you want?"

He sighs. "I want to know how to work the headphones you gave me," he says. "Do you have the instructions?"

"No," I say, and now I'm sweating. But it's not possible that the police linked me to Henderson through those headphones. Every asshole in Los Angeles has Beats headphones.

"That's too bad," he says. "Do you know how to adjust them? See, my head's bigger than yours. You have a tiny head. I bet you hear that a lot."

"I don't know how to adjust them." I give him nothing.

"You don't know how to work your own headphones?" he asks. "Don't you think that's kind of funny, Bed-Stuy? I mean, they're pretty worn in. You've had them for a while. You don't know how to work them?"

"I should get back in there," I say, edging away.

He smiles. "No, you shouldn't," he says. "You're not on the IMDb page. You're not doing anything in there but hanging out. The only way I even knew you were on set is because your buddy Calvin showed me your girlfriend's Instagram page."

Fucking social media and he is jealous and he drove all the way here from LA, working himself up. This is probably illegal but it doesn't matter. The police protect their own. "So," he says. "I'm asking everyone in the Lawns, particularly those who were close with Delilah, you haven't heard from her?"

"No," I say. It's the truth.

"You haven't reached out to her?"

"No," I say. It's the truth.

"When's the last time you bumped into her?"

And it is with great joy that I tell him more truth. "The night of the Henderson memorial I was at the UCB," I say. "I had a fight with my girlfriend. I left the UCB. I went to La Pou. I saw Delilah at the bar. I sat down with her. She was waiting for her boyfriend to get there. She wouldn't tell me his name. She said he's famous. She made it sound like he lives in the neighborhood. He didn't show up. She was inebriated. I helped her get home."

He is deflated, like a fat kid who just got told the Oreos are all gone. And I bet he *was* a fat kid. I bet he got picked on but what they don't want to tell you about bullying is that sometimes, the kid deserves it.

He tries again. "You helped her get home."

"We live in the same building," I remind him. I love it when the facts are on my fucking side. He, however, does not.

He walks up to me and gets in my face. "I don't like your attitude,

Bed-Stuy. And I don't like the fact that you've failed to apply for legal residency in this great state."

"I will," I say. "I promise."

"I don't think a promise from a piece of shit New Yorker means anything."

"Are we done here?"

"No," he says, and he should have said yes. "But you can go back inside."

I turn and walk up the driveway toward the house. My stomach is pounding and he had no right to hit me. He had no right to accuse me of anything either. He has no evidence. All he has is *hate* and he will pay for that.

I feel his eyes burning into the back of my head, stronger and more cancer-causing than the sun above. I'll have to get rid of him, there's no other option. You just can't have a fair shot at life if there's a cop out there who wants your ass behind bars.

36

INSIDE, nobody asks where I was. Everyone's too excited about the big Cabo announcement. Love's dad needs my Social Security number so that he can expedite a passport. The movie wrapped and I missed the last shot. A lot happens while you're being wrongfully interrogated.

Champagne flows and music comes on and I say that I'm gonna take a nap. Love understands. "You've been running so much; I'm worried you don't get enough rest lately."

She hugs me and I flinch. "Sorry, went overboard with sit-ups," I cover.

"You don't need sit-ups," she says. "You're perfect."

She kisses me and I go upstairs. Unfortunately, Love *should* fucking worry about me. The movie is done but my nightmare is just beginning. I close the bedroom door. I pace. I have to kill Fincher. But this is America: If you kill a cop, you die. That's how it is. I try to be calm. Be positive. We are going to Cabo, so there's that. Mexico's the kind of place where people just go around cutting heads off and shit, so I have that in my favor.

Knowledge is power. I need the lay of the land. I Google *La Groceria.* If I know Love's mother, she would have invited some sort of upscale website or magazine in to shoot her home, same way she did with the Aisles. Sure enough, I find an article about La Groceria and already I feel more centered, more focused, the way the sniper finds his target in the crosshairs. I find the address of La Groceria and take a fast course on the development where Love's family makes another home, the *famous residents* who live nearby, and the houses up for sale. And boom. Axl Rose lives in the development. Axl Rose is the type who would have a secure home. He has nut job fans and he's been around. His home has been on the market for years—and his schedule is good news too—he hasn't been to Mexico in a while. As in, not going any time soon, as in, the house belongs to real estate agents.

It gets better. Axl's home is a perpetual project, unfinished renovations, a pool that's not done, landscaping indecision, a cobbled cornucopia of yellowing lawns and half-formed cupolas. Real estate websites supply me with pictures of this house that showcase an ongoing conflict about whether to tear it down or continue with the nouveau riche terra-cotta thing.

Another point of contention, according to the comments section of a high-end real estate blog: the *home recording studio.* "Home recording studio" is real estate jargon for a soundproof fucking cage and some anonymous commenter likens this airtight box to a *panic room* and this is good news. I could use this. I could put Fincher there. But first, I have to get him there.

So now I have to convince Robin Fincher to come to Mexico. But you can't seduce anyone without knowing what they're into. Because of the headshots in his car, I start at IMDb, where he has a comically long bio in comparison to his few credits. He moved to LA to be an actor, downgraded his dreams and worked as a stunt man, a stand-in, a crew guy, and then finally he gave up and joined the LAPD. But Robin Fincher also has a website. And it is immediately clear that he did not become an officer of the law to protect and serve. Robin Fincher became an officer of the law to get back at Hollywood for kicking him to the curb.

He crossed his IMDb-LAPD streams in 2011 when he started moonlighting as a *celebrity bodyguard.* He brags that he *can protect you and hang out with you all at once*. And yes, that phrase is trademarked. The most recent picture is of him and Teri Hatcher.

I lean back in my chair. He claimed he's on a mission to find Delilah, California, that he *cares about our girls.* Well, we'll see about that. I search for projects currently shooting in Mexico and there's nothing but a remake of *Romancing the Stone*. No, I need to appeal to his obvious desire to be *friends* with these beautiful fucking people. I create a new e-mail account: *MeganisaFox@gmail.com*.

She's the perfect bait. She has a family to protect, like Teri Hatcher. She's hot. I learned from the Sony hack that people in this business don't bother to spell check so here we go:

> *Dear Officer Fincher this is out of the blue but my friend Teri Hatcher was raving about you going bed bath and beyond to help her. I'm going to cabo and would love some extra protection. Not sure if you do this. Feel a little silly like the singer in Taken but you sound like the best ther is. We r going*

tomorrow can you possibly be there? Of course we will reimburse u 4 all travels. Hope u r available fingers crossed Xx megan fox

If I got an e-mail from someone claiming to be Megan Fox, I would assume it was spam. I would think someone was fucking with me. Fincher is a cop. He's not a moron. But maybe he is because look at his fucking response, almost immediate:

Dear Ms. Fox,

WOW! I am a huge fan. I am so honored 2 help u. Yes! I am the best. Teri is the best too. I'm glad she knows I'm using personal resources to keep track of her stalker. There are so many sickos out there. I am honored 2 serve and protect. I am attaching my headshot and résumé so you know what I look like. (no objection if you want to pass it on to your agent either! I'm in SAG/AFTRA). See you tomorrow!

Wow is right. LA is a mirage. Robin Fincher is a *police officer.* The man carries a weapon. And we all know the stereotype of the bad cop—racist, violent—and we know the good cop—the one who pays for the poor mom's groceries and winds up in a viral news video. But what about this cop? What about this Angeleno, the one who pushes his headshots on Megan Fucking Fox, the one who isn't even savvy enough to maybe wait until getting to Mexico to start pimping his no-talent ass?

We need some sort of awareness program about aspirations, the way they degrade the brains of Los Angeles. *I am honored 2 serve and protect.* No, Robin. The word is *to.* No, Robin. You don't serve or protect anyone and if you did, you'd be hunkered down over a cloudy cup of coffee, reviewing every step that Delilah ever took. Obviously, this fucker is never going to find her. And while this is good news for me, it's also devastating for the population of the city he loves so much. We Angelenos are not served. We are not protected. The city can't afford to look after everyone and the county is just too spread out. I would kill Fincher even if he weren't hell-bent on putting me behind bars. I will kill him because he failed us all when he chose Megan Fucking Fox over the young dead girl, the one whose whereabouts will remain unknown, forever.

37

IT'S nine A.M. but the other passengers on *The Love Boat IV* are already drunk. The Quinns own four boats in Cabo and this is the one they use for fishing for marlin, which is what we're doing, supposedly. It's a *guys go fishing while girls get mani-pedis on the cat boat* arrangement. We have enough food and beer and tequila to feed fifty people, but it's just me and Forty and Milo and a couple of guys from production whom I didn't know all month, don't want to know now.

I'm sitting in a plastic bucket seat holding a fishing rod and Captain Dave is telling me what Love and Forty were like when they were kids. Captain Dave is a salt-and-pepper guy who looks older than forty-six. He doesn't have kids of his own. Some people are born to be uncles and Captain Dave is that kind of people. He's also a recovering alcoholic who's obsessed with what everyone else is drinking at all times. Life is hard for some people.

"But you know," he says, segueing from a story about the first time they jumped off the boat, holding hands. "It's really hard to talk about Love and Forty without talking about Milo. I mean, he was always there too, and you should have seen his hair back then." He laughs. "Huge."

"I gotta see pictures," I say, and kissing ass is hard work, but I need Captain Dave to be on my side. I'm gonna need his help this weekend. And lucky for me, he's likable enough.

"We got pictures on all the boats," he says. "I just don't know where exactly on this one. There are more on the yacht." He twists the cap off another O'Doul's. He sips. "But yep, that's why I called Milo the third twin."

I look at him. "Did you say you called Milo the third twin?"

He answers through a burp. "Yawp. You need another drink?"

I shake my head, and he continues to yammer on about Love and Forty and Milo always together and I stare at the water. I thought Forty came up with that phrase and Captain Dave finishes his fake beer. He stands, stretches. "All right," he says. "I think it's about time we chum up."

"Aye aye, Cap," I say, as if I know what that means. I offer to help Captain Dave with the barrel he's messing with, but as always, he says he's *all set.* He peels off the top of the barrel and now I smell death and decay and I cover my mouth and he laughs. "Boy's first chum," he says. "Don't worry. Ya *don't* get used to it."

Then he whistles and his assistant First Mate Kelly, a fat guy from Georgia, rings a bell and blasts Jimmy Buffett. Apparently it's time to go fishing and Captain Dave scoops chum into the water. All I can think about is Fincher and how I can drive this boat out here and drop him into the water, just like I did with Delilah, the girl he's supposed to be looking for. Done and done.

Forty is plastered and he barely makes it to his chair and Captain Dave stuffs his fingers in his mouth and whistles. "Nope," he says. "Give it a sober ten and then come back."

Forty whines but Captain Dave isn't having it. "My boat, my rules," he says.

Forty goes back down while First Mate Kelly helps Milo and me set up our rods. We dangle them in the water and Milo hums along to Buffett and tells me about Johanna, the makeup artist from *Boots and Puppies.* They slept together last night and she's young and hot and I guess he deserves to rub it in my face a little. Forty returns and asks for a rod and Dave says no and Forty lunges for the chum bucket and nearly falls in.

Captain Dave screams. "Wheelhouse," he commands. "Now."

Forty obeys and Milo laughs and I shake my head. "That captain is something," I say.

"What do you mean?" Milo asks. And it's funny to me that I was going to kill him a few days ago.

"I mean, he's on a mad power trip."

"Well," Milo says. "He's Cap. He can be."

"Yeah, but it's Forty's boat."

Milo turns his reel. "No," he says. "The Captain controls everything. It doesn't even matter if Ray is here. Boat owners say it's better because when you're messing with Mother Nature, you want someone who respects that above all else."

"Huh," I say. *Boat people.* I pretend to care if a marlin nips at my line while I think about Fincher. He arrives later today. My plan is simple: get the keys from Captain Dave when we dock. Meet Fincher at Axl Rose's house. Knock him out. Get Fincher onto this motor vessel and drive out here and dump him. Then, go to the Office with Love and eat fish tacos and drink margaritas and dance.

Milo gets a bite. He has to hand the rod over to Kelly to reel it in because he's too weak to do it on his own. But then, when Kelly reels in the fish, he hurriedly hands off the rod to Milo so that Milo can pose, as if he alone caught the fish.

Captain Dave comes back and says we should probably head back to shore because they've been having issues with pirates.

And that's when the *girls' boat* comes up on us and all the girls are dressed up like pirates, firing with squirt guns, drunk, squealing. Captain Dave drops anchor and laughs. Love cannonballs into the water.

"Come on!" she says. "It's beautiful!"

It is, but none of these people understand that I'm not on vacation. I've got to get on the burner phone I bought before we left and call all the realtors who have attempted to sell Axl Rose's house in the past two weeks. There are twelve of them and one of them has to know where the house key is.

I beg off, and while everyone else swims, I go down into the cabin and go over my spiel. I'll introduce myself as Nick Ledger, a legendary bicoastal realtor to the stars. I've seen him on shitty reality shows and I do his voice pretty well, thick Bronx, like he smoked a thousand cigarettes. I'll tell them that I'm down in this *sand pit for two goddamn days* and I get to Axl's house and there's *no fucking key because you people are so sun-stroked you fugghet how this works.*

I've watched a lot of shows about real estate. I know the way they name-drop and talk to each other and swear at each other. I know they all have different phones for different purposes. I practice the key phrases: *very famous fuck you money times ten client and I know who you know who I'm talking about* is here. She's *more private than your wife's dildo collection* and she is *pissier than your wife when you cum in her ass* and I am standing here without the key to the *one fucking pagoda that might be good enough for her, given her unique requirements.*

I call the first realtor, a woman who looks slutty and stupid, like she would bang Nick Ledger, but she tells me to fuck off. I call a guy with big ears who looks like he was bullied most of his life. He can't remember who has the listing and he wants to know if I'm shooting. I call another woman, older, probably went into this business after she saw *American Beauty* on cable. She has a New York accent too, Long Island. She says *honey, the key is up my puss. Good luck getting there.*

She hangs up on me. I growl. Nick Ledger is an asshole and a bridge burner and I should have impersonated someone dopey and happy, but they don't have people like that in high-end real estate, at least not on TV.

This isn't working, so I go into the real estate directory and look for brokers without pictures. The real fuck-ups who can't even get it together and show their faces. There is a guy named William Papova and this is harder, calling someone when you haven't prejudged them based on their proclivity for neckties or earrings.

He drops the phone before he answers, *stupid phone*, and his voice is abrupt: "Who is this?"

"It's Nick Fucking Ledger," I say.

"From the TV show?" he asks. YES. "*Rock Star Realtor*?"

"Excuse me, are you giving me shit about a project that *benefits* my fucking business?"

"No, no, no," he says. "I know you is all."

"Well, listen, I got your number from that piece Sonja."

I don't know a Sonja but I imagine realtors in Cabo know Sonjas. "Sonja," he says. "Okay."

"I'm here twenty-four fucking hours and my team drove the car off the cliff and they don't have a key to Axl's and I need a key to Axl's."

"For the show?"

"Fuck you and answer the question."

He puts me on hold a minute then returns to the call, out of breath. "I can get you a key and leave it in the outdoor shower but you can't fuck me here and tell anyone at Caldwell. I'm trying to make things right with them."

"Deal," I say. "Just make sure you leave the fucking gate open, too."

I tell him good-bye and go above deck and tear off my shirt. *Rock star realtor.* I put my phones into my seat pocket and cannonball off the boat like Love did. Under the water I open my eyes and look around the Sea of Cortez for Delilah.

But that's ridiculous. I left her in the Pacific.

THE water was beautiful but the situation is irritating. I still don't have Captain Dave's key. He keeps them looped to his belt; they may as well be attached to his dick. He's *that* guy and it would just be nice to have the keys in hand. I don't know how I will get the keys. But I will get them. It just means I need to get to know Captain Fucking Dave a little bit more than I would have liked. And it's not the end of the world, but I'm sick of small talk. We're back at Love's Mexican mansion for *disco naps* and Love is trying to convince me to stay with her instead of going for a run. "You don't need to," she says. "You look great."

"Thanks," I tell her, antsy. "But it's more that it feels good, you know? I'm used to it now."

"Maybe I'll go with you," she says, and flops onto her back. She's in the center of our round, heavenly bed. She's drunk and beautiful and this house also feels drunk and beautiful, cavernous and curvy like the Pantry, with random dramatic chunks of coral suspended on the walls.

I check the time on my phone. I have an hour until Fincher arrives and Love is begging for it so I undress and tend to her on the bed. She's good even when she's slurring her words and I feel revived. I needed that. I shower. I get into my running clothes—no shirt in Mexico—and I go downstairs and Cathy, the housekeeper, startles me. "Are you going for a run?" she asks.

"Yeah," I say.

"Evian or Fiji?" she asks.

I smile. "How about both? And then they can be like hand weights."

She brings me two bottles and I thank her and she nods.

"Hey," I say. "If I wanted to take a boat out . . ."

And the woman who was so eager to hydrate me is a different person. "Nobody drives the boats except Captain Dave or one of the first mates," she says. She softens. "But you let him know where you want to go and you got it."

Fucking fuck. But I nod and take Captain Dave's number—I've been able to convince people to do what I want before—and outside the uphill battle continues, literally. It's hotter now and I have to run *uphill* to get to Axl Rose's fucking house and I am losing my breath and this is not like the flat, forgiving terrain of Palm Springs. I'm not even there yet and already both waters are gone. I stop in front of a giant ugly house, hands on knees to catch my breath. There is concrete everywhere, jackhammers, unfinished business. I always loved all this shit when I was a kid—dump trucks, concrete pourers—but now it irritates me. You can't tell if they're renovating or starting from scratch and sometimes rich white people remind me of teenagers who can't stop picking at their scabs.

I wipe my mouth and keep going. My thighs are on fire and my eyelids twitch but I make it and the gate is open—thank you, William Papova. Axl Rose's house is a Spanglish mausoleum and no wonder it's been on the market for several years. It looks like there were battles here and maybe an explosion. There is this fucking stupid cactus in the middle of the front patio. I imagine some cunt interior decorator digging a shallow hole at the last second, as if the cactus were going to make the buyers fail to see the incomplete landscaping, the frozen-in-time fiasco of it all. I walk around to the side and sure enough, I find a little hideaway with an outdoor shower. There's an overflowing ashtray and bottle of shampoo and a leather satchel and realtors are people too. You can feel the frustration, the many salesmen who smoked and showered and fucked and whined about this odd fucking house.

I jog around to the front of the house and unlock the door and it's like that moment when the lights go down in the theater. It's starting. It is.

The house has marble floors and high ceilings but it's not inspired like La Groceria and you can tell they're trying to stage it to appeal to Mr. and Mrs. Middle America, which seems counterintuitive, as Mr. and Mrs. Middle America generally can't afford a mansion in Cabo. I go into the kitchen and help myself to bottled water from the fridge. Then I reach into my fanny pack and begin preparations. First, I e-mail Fincher:

Hey Robin cant wait to see you! left the gate open for you. we're with the babies downstairs sooo cute. When you get in, come down and join us. xoxo Meg

I don't know if she goes by Meg but Robin will like the familiarity. And now for the real fun. I use the fishing line I grabbed on the boat today to set a trip wire at the stairs, affixing them on either side with Bliss Poetic Waxing wax strips; Love won't notice they're gone. Then I go back to the kitchen, take out two more generic water bottles, and crush several Percocets into them. I stick them in an empty ice bucket along with three expired Kind Bars, then take the spiral staircase down into the basement and here it is, the panic room/home recording studio, a soundproof box with two leather chairs in it.

There's a second key on the chain William Papova left me, and it fits in the lock on the door. And *yes*, it locks from the outside, because sometimes you need to lock Les Pauls and Grammys and recording shit up.

I bring the bucket inside and set it on the floor. I pick up a microphone and tap it. I turn on the biggest red button and I tap it again. It works. Finally, I wheel one of the leather chairs just outside the studio and I wait for Fincher and sure enough, he does not disappoint. Fifteen minutes later, I hear him drop his bag by the front door.

"Hola!" he screams. The front door slams shut. He calls out again.

"Hola!" *Asshole.* I wait with my back against the wall next to the bottom step. "Hello?" he asks, and he is a terrible actor. Anyone who reads acting manuals knows that good actors *take direction* and he didn't. I hear a rustle and I picture him delving into his phone and rereading the e-mail where I specifically ordered him to report to the lower level of the house. And I am right.

"Ah," he says. And now he crosses the marble foyer and looks for the basement door. I can smell him, hairspray and suntan lotion. He whistles. "Knock, knock," he says. "Anybody home?"

I disguise my voice and call out, "Down here!"

It's one of those fundamental things about being a human. The sound and the sight of someone falling down the stairs is inherently funny, especially when it's an asshole like Fincher. He lies in a heap on the floor, knocked out, and I can't help but laugh as I drag him into the soundproof studio and lock the door.

I stare at him for a moment, and my laughter stops as I notice how vulnerable he looks. His shirt has pineapples and palm trees on it. He's wearing board shorts and sandals and I'm pretty sure he dyed his hair. He has chicken legs. He needs to do more leg presses. Well, he needed to. It's too late now.

I call Captain Dave.

"Yo!" he says. "This is the Captain."

"Hey, Captain Dave!" I say, all cheery and respectful. "It's Joe Goldberg. Love's boyfriend."

"Hey, Greenie," he says. "What can I do ya for?"

"Well," I say. "I've got a little situation. This buddy of mine showed up and he's wasted. He passed out. Love's not a big fan. Anyway, I was thinking he could crash on the boat tonight."

"Ah," he says in a grave tone. "Sorry, but no can do."

I fake a laugh. "I didn't ask if he could *drive* the boat," I say. "I just need to get the keys, get Brian up there."

"I understand what you're asking for, skipper, but the answer is still no."

I can tell that he's in a bar. I hate alcoholics like that, the ones who want to be near liquor. And I know his kind. I bet he goes to this fucking bar every day, just to prove that he's sober. "Dave," I say. "I'm asking you to work with me here. My buddy is out cold. You know, he lost his room key, he can't even remember the name of his hotel."

"I'm sure Love would let him stay at La Groceria," he says.

"Love hates him," I say. "So that's really not an option."

"Well, then I guess you're gonna have to get your buddy a hotel room," he says. "Cath can get you a list of your best options."

"Captain Dave," I plead. "We're just talking about one night."

He sighs. "I remember when my ex-wife fell off the wagon. She said, 'Dave, I only had one drink.'" He sighs again. "Rules are rules, Joe. Good luck."

He hangs up on me and the line is dead. Fuck. Fucking AA slave with his O'Doul's and his restraint and his desire to impart the rules on me, same way he gave it all up to *God* as if he doesn't sit here every day, all day, just wanting a beer, just a taste.

I thought money was power. Isn't that how this godforsaken world is supposed to work? Captain Dave does what I say because Love chose me? I pace. I don't have the money to get my own boat and I can't very well leave Fincher in a fucking house. I learned my lesson: You clean up. You get rid of the body. You don't leave a mug of piss, let alone a *cop's corpse.* But what the fuck to do?

Fuck Dave. He was supposed to say, *yes, sir* and Cath was supposed to be wrong and I was supposed to call a cab, request a wheelchair, get to the marina, grab the keys from Dave. I can't believe I didn't make a backup plan. I have a two-hundred-pound failed character actor in a soundproof box and right now, he's pissing himself in his sleep.

Love texts: *hello?* ☹

I twisted my ankle on the run home. That's my story anyway. I took Tylenol, which is why I'm not drinking, and I'm limping and I'm not myself. Love insists that I come to the Office with everyone even though I'm a mess. She won't take no for an answer, and the Office is surreal, a bar on the beach, in the sand. We sit at a long table. A tsunami could take us at any moment and Love tells me to relax.

"This is Mexico," she says. "You can get beheaded or kidnapped or shot or mugged or swept away by a riptide, but come on, Joe. A *tsunami*?" She laughs. "I don't think so. Though I appreciate your imagination."

That's my dark little girl and I look out at the Pacific that took Delilah so completely, so willingly. She helps me even when she doesn't know it. Mexico is the murder capital of the world, the land of shallow graves and dead bodies. Fuck you, ocean. Fuck you, Captain Dave. I don't need a boat. All I need is a shovel.

38

LOVE got drunk at the Office. I left her in bed along with a note that my ankle was feeling better so I went for a walk to stretch it out. She'll never know that I left at 4:42 A.M. or that I stopped off at that big house, the one where they're doing the most construction. None of the workers were there yet and I roamed around the lot, checking out the nails, and planks of wood, the slabs of marble, the cement mixers. I went around back and saw that they're building an infinity pool. And it wasn't the worst idea, Fincher resting, *in infinity.*

But now that I'm at Axl's house, I know I have to do better. This is rock 'n' roll. This is time frozen and so many people out there have so many keys. Fincher has to stay here. I can't be dragging him all over the neighborhood. I mean, yes, it's *Mexico* but Mexico is like LA. There are so many different parts of it. This isn't the area where you can casually behead people and drop them off in a neighboring pool. I have to be discreet. I'll be sweating today because of that fucker. For now though, it's time for him to learn a lesson. I'm rummaging through his duffel bag. The contents alone are reason enough to kill him. He brought *headshots* and *five-pound weights* and condoms and Jimmy Buffett T-shirts (tags on, asshole) and banana hammocks. Didn't he get the memo that this was *work*? But that's not even the bad part. The bad part is that Robin Fincher keeps an old-fashioned secretarial Rolodex of celebrity encounters. I'm serious. He bought this thing at Staples and I can just picture him in line on his day off. This Rolodex is jammed with home addresses of famous people. When I get back to LA, I can now visit *Cruise, Tom* if I want or my latest alter-ego, *Fox, Megan.* And again I say, that's not even the bad part. Turn over an index card, and shit gets real.

Fincher clearly started this project ten years ago, when he joined the force. Some of his references are dated—*Pattinson, Robert. Told him that I loved Water for Elephants and that he and Reese seem like they're meant for each other. He seemed like the real deal, salt of the earth, more British than you expect him to be. Tell agent to send him reel.*

Yes, Fincher has dutifully catalogued his celebrity encounters, all of which happened while he was supposed to be protecting and serving. He has a simple routine. He pulls over celebrities to talk to them and kiss ass. Sometimes his notes are self-interested—*Piven, J. Pulled over for jaywalking. Friendly, funny. They say he's a jerk but he was cool to me. Seemed genuine. Says to call his manager next week. Says he has a feeling about me, says I need new headshots.*

Sometimes his notes are sad—*Aniston, Jennifer. Said thank you for letting her know about robberies in neighborhood. Told me to stay hydrated. Sweet!*

And sometimes they're downright disturbing, like when he told *Adams, Amy* that someone ran over the neighbor-up-the-street's dog.

So you get the idea. Robin Fincher, who alleges to be so protective of California, is in fact, a level ten Celebrity Stalker. I turn on the microphone.

"Hey," I say. "Wake up."

I can be loud when I need to be and Fincher rolls over and sits up and blinks. When he sees me, he bolts for the glass. He bounces off it, then, undeterred, body slams it again and again. I put my feet up and ignore him and continue to work my way through his Rolodex. The idiot is so busy trying to shatter unbreakable glass that he doesn't even seem to realize that I found his secret stash. When he finally exhausts himself and kneels on the floor panting, I turn on the mic again.

"Sit up," I say. "Well, first pick up the microphone. Then sit."

He takes the microphone and he hasn't learned anything yet. He starts by ranting at me that he's a cop—as if I didn't know this—that he's an American—as if I'm not—that he's gonna see to it that I wind up behind bars—as if he's in a position to do this.

"Listen to me," I say. "It's not too late to make things right."

His nostrils flare. "Where's Meg?"

Wow. I don't respond to that, it's too fucking pathetic. I pick up a card from his Rolodex. "I'm gonna ask you a question."

"She's supposed to be here," he says, not listening.

"Fincher," I interrupt. "I'm Megan Fox."

He storms the glass again and I have to let him work it out, kick, punch, kick. He settles down, screams. When I think that's it for now, I continue. "As I was saying, you can make things right by telling the truth. It's pretty simple. I just want you to explain some of your choices."

When he ticketed me for jaywalking, Robin Fincher repeatedly reminded me that I had made a *choice* to jaywalk. And he's right. I did. But now I know that he made a lot of bad choices himself.

I spin his Rolodex and land on *Heigl, Katherine*. I take her card and turn it over and I see that he approached her at Little Dom's, a restaurant in Los Feliz. He told her that she had some fans getting aggressive out front and that she would be wiser to go out the back. He says she was *pretty, grateful, took a selfie with me, said she'll follow me on Instagram*. I pick up the mic. "So, does Katherine Heigl follow you on Instagram?"

"Put that down." Fincher stares at the Rolodex. His eyes are a ride in a theme park, two beady little balls to hell. "That's police business."

"Really?" I ask. "Because unless there's a special division dedicated exclusively to stopping imaginary celebrity crimes, I'd say this feels more like personal stuff to me."

"You have no right to look at that." I laugh. He doesn't. "I have eyes on a lot of people. That's not my only file."

"I'm sure," I say. "Anyway, did she follow you on Instagram?"

"She was very nice." He sidesteps. "Listen, you sick fuck, this is a big mistake."

"Robin," I say. "Do you know you could go to jail for this?"

"Put it down."

"What the fuck is wrong with you?" I ask. "Why would you ever bring this on a *plane*?"

"That's none of your business."

"It is now," I say. "As a concerned citizen, I have every right to look out for my fellow countrymen. This is a breach."

"Tell me what you want," he pleads. "Just put it down and tell me what you want."

"What do I want?"

"Anything," he says. "This is crazy. You gotta let me out of here."

That's not happening and he should realize that and I ignore him and I spin through his Rolodex and thank God that I am me, that I didn't get sick like this, that I don't covet imaginary friends and pry into places where I don't belong. What a dreadful existence, to be the man in possession of this Rolodex.

"Fincher," I say. "You do realize that these things are supposed to have the names and numbers of people who know you too?"

"Fuck you."

I shake my head. They always get like that when you reach the truth. The way a fish nips at the bait after circling. Robin is breaking. Biting. He is boiling down to his *fuck you* self. This is his mug of urine, his mistake, and his is infinitely worse than mine. His mug of piss may not contain his DNA, but it reveals so much more, his demented ego, his emotional core. He's no different from a thirteen-year-old girl writing a letter to Justin Timberlake, thinking he might write back. Fincher's Rolodex is a motherfucking hope chest.

"Robin," I say. "Was Eddie Murphy making a big mistake when he didn't think it was funny that you pulled him over for having a banana in his tailpipe."

Robin turns red. "Stop it."

I shake my head. "I just think *Beverly Hills Cop* was a long time ago and he's probably a busy guy, you know? He probably had somewhere he had to be. Do you think it was a great choice as an aspiring actor? Did you think he would find you *funny*?"

"Stop it," he says. He pumps his fists and you can tell he's used to carrying a weapon.

"You know you're supposed to be looking for *Delilah*," I remind him. "You just *swore* to me that you were gonna find her, but you, motherfucker, you took off to Cabo three days later. And we both know you only tracked me down because I was on a *set*." I laugh. "You actually had me scared a little. Your whole bad cop demeanor and the way you were sniffing around about me, threatening me, stealing my headphones."

"As if you didn't steal them first," he says, eyes blazing.

"Of course I did," I reveal. And he smirks, as if he figured something out, as if he won. "But what you don't realize is that I stole them from Henderson when I killed him."

Fincher starts to turn purple. "You sick fuck."

I sigh. "Says the man who travels with a Rolodex of celebrities' addresses. Do you know what would happen if this got into the wrong hands? I mean, not that you'll be around to deal with the consequences."

He's on his feet now, and he throws the ice bucket at the glass. He throws one water bottle, then the other. He falls to his knees and he's not crying because I'm going to kill him. Oh, sure, you assume that because he's locked in a cage and about to die—but Robin Fincher is crying because all he ever wanted was for this Rolodex to be his, truly. He wanted to be buddies with these people. He wanted Katherine Heigl to follow him on Instagram—he even noted with an asterisk on the back, *friends call her Katie*—and he's crying because none of that is going to happen.

He will never be friends with *Katie Heigl.* And in spite of all the red carpet events he crashed with his uniform—you should see this picture of him at an *Oblivion* event where he's with Tom Cruise and the security guards in back look like they're gonna fucking kill him—well, the point is, Fincher met a lot of people. But that was it. You can't have a conversation with an autograph and you can't go out to lunch with a group selfie and no matter how grateful Julia Roberts is that you alerted her to some problems with the elevator in the Chateau—*bullshit, bullshit*—she is only going to close the door and lock it because she doesn't fucking know you, Robin Fincher.

Now he wants me to leave him alone. But we're not done yet. "Oh come on," I say. "This Rolodex is *thick*. I mean, we haven't even gotten to *Efron, Zac*."

"Stop it," he says. "I mean it."

"No," I say. "We're gonna get to the bottom of some of these choices. Same way I acknowledged my bad choice when I crossed the street. Yes, I have authority issues. I concede that I should have waited for the *walk* signal, Robin. I can be a punk. I am a little fucking New York that way and you were right and I accepted my responsibility."

He cries. "Please let me go, please, please."

I flip over *Crawford, Cindy*. He punches the glass. "Stop it!"

"Wow," I say. "You really think she was flirting with you? Because I don't know, Robin. I'm gonna guess that she was trying to get out of a ticket."

"Stop it."

"That's what is so great about your stories," I tell him. "You don't even understand who you are, Robin. You're a police officer."

"Fuck you."

"An officer of the law."

"Fuck you."

"These people are just like me," I say, and I point to his Rolodex. "All of us, we're just trying to get out of a ticket. Don't you get that?"

He spits. I point to him. "You cop," I say. I point at myself. "Me citizen." I do it again, repeating that Tom Cruise is like me, a citizen, and that Jennifer Aniston is like me, a citizen. He screams and shakes like a monkey and I won't let up. "No, no, no," I say. "You chose to be a cop and you don't get to be a cop slash actor because you can't *be* a cop and an actor and deep down you know this or you would have *gone* for it, Robin. You would have taken your classes and waited tables and dedicated your *life* to your dream, but no. You knew he didn't have it. And this is life, you fucking shithead. You don't get to be anything *slash* anything."

"You don't know," he whimpers. "That Chinese guy, the one from *The Hangover*, he was a *doctor* before he got into the business."

I look at this sad man, comparing himself to a brilliant comedic actor. The pure absence of self-awareness is enough to kill me. "Fincher," I say. "Ken Jeong is talented. You're not."

"Fuck you."

"That's why Ken Jeong tried to break into the business the old-fashioned way, the honest way," I explain. "He quit being a doctor to become an actor. You're a cop. These people in here, they all have talent. You don't."

He looks like he might start crying again. But it's wrong of him to use his badge to harass celebrities and it's downright disgusting of him to ditch his legitimate police work to go down to Cabo and meet

Megan Fox. I don't feel bad for this fucker. You get a job, you do the job. No slash. The end.

He pounds the glass and his words bleed together, merging into a whiny plea. "Let me the fuck out of here! This is wrong! You are sick and I want out—I want out now!"

"I can't do that," I say. "You're a bad cop. You know where all these famous people are, but you didn't try to find Delilah."

He stares at me. "You sick dick," he rails. "You won't get away with this."

"Of course I will," I say. "If you were a better cop, you'd realize that by now."

He kicks and he is trapped and he is still correcting his fucking shirt when it gets stuck, still self-conscious about his appearance, still convinced that his appearance matters. Fucking Angelenos. I need a laugh. A break. I kick back and scroll through his Rolodex and I flip over *Efron, Zac.* I smile. He hits the glass.

"Okay, Robin," I begin. *Robin*, not *Officer.* "I want to know, when you pulled Zac Efron over because his left rear tire looked flat, did you seriously choose to do that because you thought you guys look enough alike that you could play his father in a movie?"

He does not nod this time. He does not yell obscenities. And maybe I should have started with a different celebrity, maybe *Unknown, Rihanna* (driving without a seat belt) or *Nicholson, Jack* (flickering headlight). Then, I might have gotten to hear the details behind Robin Fincher's life of celebrity stalking. But there's so much I'll never know because Robin Fincher is so angry at me, the person holding the Rolodex with all the celebrities he wanted so badly to know, so angry at himself, that he becomes a bull. He becomes a zombie. You can see what brains he had evaporate as his eyes shine. His skin is raw, red. He runs headlong into the glass, like a football player whose brain is already gone. He spatters against the walls and falls back, dead.

IT turns out that I have a talent for landscape design. Someday, when Love and I have a place together, I'll oversee the yard. Sure, we'll have workers doing a lot of it, and maybe even a professional designer, but I'll have the final say. I am good at this, at knowing what belongs where. I never would have known this if I had stayed in New York. You don't really get to go to the park and relocate a tree. You don't get to take nature into your hands when you live in concrete. But I did great today. I took that fucking cactus that didn't belong out front and I brought it in the back to the Zen garden. I dug a hole. I went deep. I sweated. I liked it. I miss work. And digging a hole for Fincher doesn't make me feel the way digging a hole for Beck did. He never broke my heart. He was just a bad cop.

I finish and I return inside to the cool air in the panic studio. I drag Fincher's body outside and toss him into this hole and I am sweating so much now. I bury him, his Rolodex too, both of them so deep, deeper than Beck. And then the fun part. I plant the cactus above Fincher and his Rolodex. The cactus belongs here. It works here and unifies the space, establishes it somehow, more green, less brown. It's the right size for this garden and there are other cactuses nearby, so it doesn't look so lonely and idiotic anymore. It doesn't stand out the way it did in front.

I drink water and look around this yard and at this cactus, with fat pads and its proud, confident stance. I like it. I swear the thing is even smiling at me. I think it knows that I brought it home. I give it one last look and turn to go. I have so much to do. I have to clean up the mess Fincher made when he killed himself. I have to get back to Love and act like a guy who went for a run. And I will do all this and I will do it soon, but I think it's important to give yourself time and space to celebrate the work you do.

I think that's why people in LA fall apart, why they get so needy, so desperate for validation, for their cars, for their body parts, for their talents. They forgot that the sweetest thing in life is to be alone, as you were born, as you will die, soaking in the sun, knowing that you put the cactus in the right place, that you don't need someone to come along and compliment your work, that someone who did that would, in fact, just be getting in the way. I am at peace here. Fincher is too.

39

THE rest of Cabo passes in a blur of tequila and boat rides and waiting for news from Forty's agent, and soon we are back in the States but I am still in foreign territory: Love's home. I've never been but it's like I've lived here all my life. It's new and old in all the right places, with customized red appliances and lush, gargantuan part-leather, part-fur sofas. It's just where you want to be when you fly back to America after burying a dead cop, unlike my apartment, which is so dated and tarnished.

It sucks to know that Dez sold me out, but then, a friendly neighborhood drug dealer is, at the end of the day, a drug dealer, out for himself. I can't even hate him for it. I'm just happy to be in Love's home instead of mine. I could sit here for hours, just looking at her same old Instagram photos: "Love in an Elevator," "I Just Called to Say I Love You."

She smiles. "I like this one because of the old school curly blue phone cord."

"Yeah," I say. "Old school."

She says no more pictures. She's tired of her face. I obey her wish and toss my phone on another part of this voluminous sectional. Oh, to breathe, to know that I did it. I got rid of Fincher.

Love leaps off the couch. "Come on," she says. "I want you to see everywhere."

And I do want to see everywhere, I want to sit everywhere. This is a dream house with neon signs like the ones in the Pantry. Love has a *playroom* with board games and a PlayStation and a karaoke machine and a stage, instruments flung about. The neon sign here says SEX IS BETTER WHEN YOU'RE IN LOVE and she says every room has a sign. The kitchen is MADE WITH LOVE and the dining room is LET LOVE RULE and her bedroom door is closed and the neon above the frame reads AND IN THE END . . . Then she opens the door and her bedroom is the perfect hybrid of our intimate squeaky cell in Palm Springs and the too-big luxury of Cabo and the oceanfront seasonal breeze of Malibu.

Love flops onto her bed and I look at the art above it, John Lennon's lyrics in neon, the ones he famously misquotes from Paul McCartney.

It is a miracle that she is not a vapid nitwit and this is the rest of my life, under the covers, where we could be in a shitty rat-infested walk-up in Murray Hill or anywhere. It doesn't matter. *We found love* and then out of nowhere, the lights go out. *Homeinvasionearthquakeendofworld.* But then music blasts and Love grabs my hands. "Surprise!"

It's my song, my *Pitch Perfect* pool mash-up, and she remembered when I mentioned this way back when we first met, in her Tesla, that first ride. When you are in love you listen. Strobe lights come up and

Love starts running and she is tearing off her top and she is slipping out of her skirt and she is unsnapping her bra and she is opening a sliding door onto the patio and she is naked and she is running into the pool and I am naked, following her. Splash. Skinny-dipping, making the pool our own. I am inside of Love in her pool and my song bleeds into her song, bleeds back into her song, and this is perfect and there is nothing but our songs and our bodies and our water and our future and the lemon trees, the orange trees. We fuck and we talk, our songs are on a loop, our life is on a loop, and suddenly my favorite word in the English language: *We.*

Love has plans for us. *We're* going to go to Chateau—she is dying for those truffle fries—and *we* are going to watch *Pitch Perfect*—she hasn't seen it in a while—and *we* are going to go to my apartment and get my things, assuming it's not too much too fast.

I kiss her. "God, no."

Then there is a loud sound in the house; the pop of a bottle of Veuve. *Forty.* Love calls out to him and he doesn't answer and then he comes running, fat feet padding, and he cannonballs into our pool and he doesn't belong here.

Love squeals. He emerges from the water.

"Forty, this isn't really the best time," I say, looking at my naked girlfriend, who elegantly swims to the stairs and reaches for her bikini and covers herself with the ease of a Bond girl. I can do no such thing. My shorts are far away, on a fucking chaise.

Forty flops like a sea lion and Love looks at me and I shrug. He swims to the other side of the pool and picks up a waterproof remote control and now a projection screen begins to open on the far wall. I look at Love. "We watch movies here," she says.

Forty fumbles with the remote. I think he's on a fair amount of cocaine. His fingers jitter. But he is able to find his destination: *Deadline.com*

And there, on the front page, on the giant screen, a headline:

FORTY SELLS TWO: MEGAN ELLISON'S ANNAPURNA TO PRODUCE TWO ORIGINAL SCRIPTS BY DEBUT SCREENWRITER FORTY QUINN

I rub water out of my eyes and force myself to stay calm. It's just a headline. A mistake. That's all. We'll call the paper or the website or whatever the fuck it is and they'll change the headline, put my name in it.

I motion for the remote and he tosses it to me. I refresh the page, because maybe Forty already took care of that. Maybe he thinks they already fixed things, got my name in there. The remote is slow. The world is fast, loud. Love and Forty scream and splash each other and I can't be in this fucking pool waiting right now and my stomach is whirling and I get out of the pool and I streak across the Spanish tile floor and grab my shorts and get into them. I get my phone and I drip on it and I have to protect it. I shiver. My nipples are hard. I turn away from Love and Forty and I go to Deadline but it's the same shit and then the article itself loads and it gets worse. The article reports that both scripts are written by Forty Quinn and there is no mention of brilliant newcomer Joe Goldberg anywhere. I read the first paragraph over and over, as if my name might be buried in there in some sort of cryptogram *Da Vinci Code* bullshit but no. I scroll down and scan the screen for the words *Joe* and *Goldberg* but again, no. I am breathing fast, like I'm running, like I'm fucking and I'm fucked. He stole my scripts and fucked me.

"Joe?" It's Love, my girlfriend, the one whose twin brother fucked me. He fucked me. I clutch the phone.

I turn back around. Love is on the deck, squeezing her hair. Forty is still in the pool, treading water. I want a harpoon. I want to end him. Love clears her throat. At some point in the last thirty-five seconds, she put on a hooded bathrobe and picked up her iPad.

"Go on, sister girl," Forty says. He sucks Veuve out of the bottle. "Let me hear it. Come on, Lovey."

"And I quote," she begins. "'Megan Ellison tells Deadline that she has discovered a *major talent* in Quinn and plans to fast track *The Third Twin* and *The Mess* and . . .'" Love squeals. "'The bidding war, which lasted all summer—'" Love balks. She stares at Forty. He laughs.

"You always think the worst of me," he says.

"Every time you disappeared I assumed you were holed up at the Ritz," she says.

Forty laughs. "Well, not *every* time, but sometimes women can prove to be very inspirational."

Love reads to us about the *hot property* and summarizes the comments. People are saying that Barry Stein is a fool; he's washed up. He could have had these scripts early on but he has no eye for talent anymore. Not that anyone would ever choose to team up with Stein over Megan Ellison. Megan Ellison is *the best* and they're saying Forty Quinn is *the best* and apparently there's a murder scene in the desert that will *make you see the world in a whole new way* and Forty Quinn has been *pitching for years* and it's one of those situations where *talent and hard work and perseverance* pay off and you can't *make it in Hollywood without all three* and I am rubbing my eyes again and they sting.

Love strokes my head. "Are you okay?"

"The chlorine hit me hard," I say.

"It's a saltwater pool," she says. She kisses my head. "Maybe you should go inside and wash up?"

All I want is to get away from Forty but I know what I have to do first. I have to put on a fucking show. I have to stand up and walk over to the pool and I have to extend a hand to him. I have to shake his damn, wrinkled hand.

"Congrats, my man."

"Thanks, Old Sport," he says, and tears off his sunglasses. "The best news is, this is only the beginning." I think he winks. I don't know. Maybe that's his resting face and I never noticed it. I blame my aspirations, the ones I fed every time I sat down at Intelligentsia to write. Fucking *idiot* I am. I am so much better than this. I should have spent my summer writing a *book* and Forty lowers his voice. "Megan says we have a big future together. *Huge.*"

The pronouns are discombobulated. *We* as in *he and Megan.* I am not in the *we* even though their *we* could not exist without me. *ME.* Megan Ellison. My skin crawls. "That's awesome," I manage. "You did it."

He nods. Slow. "Yes," he says. "*I* fucking did it."

Love squeals. "You guys, it's on *Variety* now!"

The news is everywhere and I am nowhere and Love doesn't know it but she is celebrating my demise. I go inside but I don't go to one of the seven bathrooms to wash up. No. I go to Forty's knapsack where I find his iPad and pull up his Gmail. I read the e-mails, so many e-mails, between Forty and his agent, this dumb fucker who thinks Forty *grew into his voice. I don't know what you did this summer, but whatever it is, it worked. Well done, 40. Here's to 40 more.*

And there are more e-mails, here's one from Barry Stein. He wants to know when Forty became *so fucking funny yet also so goddamn original, are people saying Tarantino? This feels like Tarantino* and that compliment is mine. I *wrote* these scripts and here's one, someone at CAA, someone who wants to know how he came up with this *CAGE! TRAPPING THAT GIRL IN THE CAGE AFTER THAT BEACHY WEEKEND, TO GO FROM THE BEACH TO THE CAGE. FUCKING AMAZING FUNNY TWISTED SHIT MISTER MAN YOU ARE GOD. HOLY FUCK ALSO CAN WE GET BACK TO THE THIRD TWIN? BECAUSE HOW DOES YOUR BRAIN GO THERE AND HERE?*

Outside, you can see that Forty has drunk his own Kool-Aid and crossed over to the dark side. He believes it, all of it, he brainwashed himself with compliments and coke, hookers and agents. And he didn't even come up with the fucking title—Captain Dave did. Outside, Love gets all hoppy and bouncy when "Love Is a Battlefield" begins to play and she is correct. This is war.

I go upstairs and step into Love's giant shower. I have to believe in myself. I will fix this. I try to have my own celebration. People said those things about me even if they think they were saying those things about Forty. But then I think of the way my neck ached, the way I wrote at Intelligentsia and suffered through those other people around me, the motherfuckers with MacBook attitudes and loud voices—*So I just had a meeting about directing that McDonald's commercial and I'm thinking I might just do it*—and it was me slaving, rushing like a mad man to my PO Box to keep up my cover, the bookselling business that *Forty* suggested as a way to allay suspicions of my being a *gold digger.* The door opens. It's Love.

"Hey," she says. "Got room for me?"

I nod and all this time, I was concerned about the wrong man. I wasted my time worrying about Milo when I should have been keeping eyes on Forty. Milo was never a threat. He loves Love and she doesn't love him back and most of the time in life, I'm starting to realize, love is not the problem. It's the people like Forty, like Amy, like Beck, the people who are loveless. And it's possible to know this right away. Forty labeled me *Old Sport* because he didn't want me to have a name. It is possible to know people. They show you who they are. You just have to be looking.

Love says if I still want to be a writer, Forty could give me pointers and I love her too much to tell her the truth. They were in the womb together. They remember the '80s together. They were born together and they will take it to the grave together.

Just the same, I step out of the shower. I text Forty: *We need to talk.*

40

FORTY never wrote back, not just to me. He didn't write back to Love or his mother or his father or Milo. He fell off the face of the fucking earth, which is odd behavior for someone who just scored a two-picture deal. His absence is a wrecking ball and Love is a tired, brittle, worried mess and *this* is what I cannot allow. I can't let him do this to her, to us. He can steal all my scripts. Fine. But he can't torture Love. She knew right away what he was up to. Four days ago, eight hours after I texted him, she made a declaration: "I'm calling it," she said. "He's not sick. He didn't break his phone. He's on a bender."

Love's parents came over, worried, pacing. *Are we sure he isn't in Malibu? What about that loft downtown he bought a while back?* Dottie is such a mother. She didn't want to think it was a bender. "I'm sure he's off celebrating," she insisted. "Don't jump to the worst conclusion."

"Celebrating with who?" Love asked. "Mom, I won't jump to conclusions but please don't go into denial already."

Ray told Love not to get so worked up. "He's thirty-five years old," he said. "He's not a baby."

They left and I tried to make Love feel better but it was impossible. "I *hate* the way they go into denial," she said. "He's my twin and I know when something's wrong. He goes on benders."

Love texted his dealer, Slim, but the text bounced back. She threw her phone down. "Fucking Forty," she snapped. "Of course his fucking drug dealer has a new fucking number. That's what they do! They're drug dealers."

That was four days ago and Forty is officially on a bender. He hasn't answered calls or texts or e-mails and he is an even bigger asshole than I realized.

"I miss him so much I feel crazy," she says when we wake up. "I literally feel like I'm going crazy."

"Me too," I say, but she blows up at me. She's in a terrible mood, worse every day, and whatever I say is wrong. And she doesn't know that he fucked me over and I have to sit in this house and pretend to care about him, pretend that I'm not sitting here in shock.

There's a knock on the door.

"Babies?" It's Love's mom. Again. Because this is how it is now. They show up in the morning and they're here puttering around all day, all night. "Are you decent?"

"Yes!" Love shouts, with no regard for my morning wood.

Dottie comes into the room and flops onto the bed. "Did I not love him enough? You know, your daddy and I found out about his big deal from the trades."

Every day we go over the events. I have to listen to the same fucking conversation, with Love assuring her mother that she did most certainly love them enough. I've grown too familiar with Love's mother's habits, the way she nervously twists her rings around her fingers, the way she brings a different purse every day even though all we do is sit in the house and speculate. I picture her at home, in *Bel Air*, moving all her pills and credit cards and blotting papers and lipsticks from one purse into another.

Ray calls from downstairs. "I got eggs!"

Yesterday it was *I got French toasties* and the day before that it was *I got huevos rancheros* and Love gets out of bed without looking at me. She slips into her robe and helps her mother off the bed and they walk away, telling each other how wonderful they are, how great a daughter Love is, how loving a mother Dottie is.

Downstairs, Ray tells me to have a seat and now it begins again, his questions about my business. Ray loves me. Ray wants to invest in me. Ray believes in books. Once upon a time, before Forty got a two-picture deal and disappeared, Dottie loved me too, but now she resents me. She doesn't like Ray treating me with such love and acceptance. She doesn't eat her eggs. Ray sighs. "Whatsa matter now?"

"Sometimes you don't sound like someone whose *son* is missing," she says. "Sometimes you sound downright chipper."

"Pardon me for not being surprised," he says. "I missed the memo where we were told to act as if there's anything surprising about this mess."

"You shut it," she says. She looks at me, at her husband. "Have some respect for your *son*."

Ray slams the refrigerator door shut and Forty has destroyed them. They were so happy before and the only thing that makes them stop fighting is Love, who starts crying and banging her fists and begging them to stop. "I can't take this! You can't do this now, you just can't!"

And now her mother is soothing her and her father has them both in a bear hug and they promise her it's going to be okay. "We'll get through this as a family, Love bug," he says. "We always do."

I learn that Forty's favorite game as a child was hide-and-seek. He never stopped playing. When things go well for him, he self-destructs. He hides. The day he got into grad school at UCLA, he went to a racetrack and drove his car into the wall. It was an accident, but at the same time, we all know what's possible when we get into a fucking *sports car.* Two days before Love's wedding, a happy time for all, Forty took off to go *skiing* via helicopter. He fell, of course, and no one could locate him for days. Love's wedding had to be postponed. Forty was found in the woods and he claimed he was too disoriented to use his phone. One of the guys on the rescue squad lost a *finger* trying to find him.

After breakfast, Love and I go outside so she can water her plants. "Love," I say. "Maybe we should get out of the house, you know, go to a movie or something."

"A *movie*?" She lashes out at me, brandishing her hose. "How can I go to a *movie* when my brother is missing?"

"Because he always turns up."

"You don't get it because you're not . . . close with your family," she says. "I don't mean that in a bad way, but just, just please don't say things like *how about we go to a movie*? I need to be here. I can't be in a movie theater and get a call that he's . . ."

And she's crying again, and I swear, she's crying because she feels guilty because she wishes he would die and leave her alone already. He is tedious and he lacks imagination and he stole from me and he is a vampire, sucking the life out of his sister. I hold her.

"Joe," Love says. Here we go again.

"Yeah?"

"When he showed up and we found out about his deal, you didn't look happy."

"Love, we were in the fucking pool. We were literally *in the fucking pool.*"

She tosses her hose. "No," she says. "It's not about that. You looked *mad.*"

"I wasn't mad," I say, and I want so badly to tell her I wrote those scripts, but if I tell her now, while Forty is gone, she will bury me.

She sprays her cactuses, as if they need water. "No," she says. "You were definitely mad."

I have no choice here. "Okay," I say. "You're right. You just told me how you're done with the business and you don't want to act and he walks in and he sold his movies and I was like, well, there goes that. Now you're gonna wanna be in his movies."

"Because I can't think for myself?"

"No," I say. "Because you're twins. Because you work together, because of course he'd want his sister to be in his movies."

"But I literally just told you I was done with that," she says. "I literally told you I never want to act again. Just tell me why you weren't happy for him, why you went off and skulked into the house. I mean, there's *something* going on."

"I love your brother," I lie.

"Then why didn't you hug him and be like *yes*?" She drops the hose. She paces. "Never mind," she says. "This happens every time I go out with someone. At first you act like you love my brother and it's cool and you want to be friends but then the minute he, I don't know, *needs* something from you, you turn your back on him."

"He didn't need anything from me," I say. "He got a fucking deal."

"He needed you to be happy for him." She sniffles. "He needed you to love him. I mean, why couldn't you have just *hugged* him and been there for him? Why did you have to run away?"

So now it's *my* fault that Forty ran away and Love's father is calling us in for another feeding. I try to talk to Love but she says now isn't the time. She isn't the same girl she was four days ago and if this keeps up, she won't love me anymore. She is a snowman melting, a phone dying, a plant wilting. I go inside and eat my *guac* and talk about books with her parents and I am a limp dick. Her parents decide to go to a movie—ha!—and I don't say *see I told you so.* They go and we're alone and we sit on her giant sectional and once again whatever I say is wrong.

If I tell her it's going to be okay, she says I have no way of knowing that.

If I tell her I love her, she says she can't deal with me right now.

If I ask her what I can do, she tells me there's nothing anyone can do.

If I try to make her laugh, she says she doesn't want to laugh.

If I get upset, she says she can't deal with *one more person* losing their shit.

Her parents come back. "Any word?" Ray asks.

"No," Love says.

Dottie tells us that it finally hit Ray. They didn't make it to a movie theater. They just went to Forty's condo above Sunset. They think he's dead. They can feel it. I try to be positive because that's what they say to do in these situations, but it doesn't work. I try to cheer up Ray and watch *Fast Five* with him and Love says I'm abandoning her. I leave Ray and the movie and follow her and she snaps at me. "Well, now you're abandoning *him.*"

I can't cure Love when she's sick like this, sitting in the dark with her headphones on, blocking out the world, watching things, as she was when we met, and I understand now that she was sad that day too. She had just had sex with Milo; she was hating herself, blaming herself for leading him on. And right now, Forty is the one who ran away, and he did that, but she is blaming herself, as if his fuck-ups are her fault. There is a codependency between twins that can't be broken. And then I get a text.

It's Forty.

The first thing I do is look around to make sure Love and Ray and Dottie are all far away from me and they are. I unlock my phone. I read: *Feel like grabbing some grub, Old Sport?*

Unfuckingbelievable. His family is on a vigil and he doesn't offer any explanation. Does he not care about them? Does he not remember when he stole intellectual property from me?

I write back: *Where and when?*

He writes back: *Now and the 101!*

I put my hands on Love's shoulders. She takes her headphones off and looks up at me.

"I'm going to go find Forty. I can't just sit here and do nothing."

She reaches out to me. "How?" she asks. "What do you even mean?"

"I mean I'll find him," I say. "I'll drive around. I'll go to his haunts."

"Joe," she says, brightening. "You're amazing. Thank you."

"You don't need to say that," I say, and I kiss her hand. "You're the amazing one and the least I can do is get in the car and try and bring him home."

Love nods. "I'm so sorry. I know I'm being a royal fucking bitch. I don't know how to control it and I hate myself for not having figured out how to control it yet. Thirty-five fucking years."

I kiss the top of her perfect head. "Life is long," I tell her. "You're gonna be fine. I'm going to find him and sober him up, whatever it takes, I'm gonna be with him. And then we're gonna come back here and he's gonna be with us and I'm gonna take care of him so I can take care of you."

"I love you, be safe," she calls as I leave the house.

The person she should worry about is her brother. He's hit my last nerve and if he isn't calling to apologize for stealing my scripts, fucking me over, and torturing his family, then he is going to be roadkill on the fucking 101.

41

I drive fast and when I get to the 101 Diner from *Swingers*, Forty's already in a booth, red-faced and high, feet up, dirty toes in old huaraches and he's flirting with a waitress and nursing a beer. My least favorite song in the world comes on, the song that was playing in LAX when I arrived, that stupid fucking Tom Tom Club song, and as I walk to Forty's table, the song feels like an omen. Just the same, I am a fair person. I give Forty the benefit of the doubt. Surely he's been squirreled away, wracked with guilt over what he's done to his family, to me. Surely this is the scene in his sad life when he comes to Jesus, when he begs for forgiveness.

"Forty," I say as I sit down in the booth. "We're all having a nervous breakdown looking for you. What the fuck?"

"Whoa," he says. "I sense a little hostility."

"Yeah," I say. "Call your sister."

"You look a little piquant, Old Sport."

Only assholes say *piquant* and I know that this is not the moment where he sees the light, where he becomes a human and cops to his horrible behavior. He called me here because he's full of cocaine and he hums along to the frothy, bratty pop as he peruses the menu. I order a blackened chicken sandwich and he orders a *BBB—bacon, bacon, and bacon* sandwich—and puts down his menu.

"Joe," he begins. "I have to say that I'm hurt."

"I'm sorry to hear that," I say. "But do me a favor. Before we get into anything, call your sister."

He shakes his head. "I know you think I screwed you over somehow, but you need to remember that I've been working on these scripts for *years*."

"Let's not get into that now," I say. "I just want your family to know you're okay."

"Well, I'm not okay," he snaps. "You couldn't even *congratulate* me properly. I get the news of my life and you turn into a jealous little bitch."

"Forty, we had a deal . . ." I stop, I take a deep breath. This is not why I came here. "It doesn't matter. What matters is call your sister."

But he's exasperated. "A deal? Do you *know* how many people have pitched in on these projects over the years? That's what this business is. We read each other's shit. There was no *deal.* A deal is what I have with Megan."

Every time he says *Megan* my aspirations flare. I won't let them do me in and distract me. I'm here for one reason: He either gets to call his family and have one more shot at life or he gets to abuse his family and suffer the consequences.

The music is too loud and he goes off on how the scripts are his. He paints a picture, wherein I am the shady one, the one who didn't even want to tell Love that we were *talking about maybe doing something together.*

"You know, I'm actually kind of impressed. Separation of church and state." He winks. "My dad would have told my mom in a fucking *heartbeat*. But you didn't let your dick get in the way of your brain." He smacks my shoulder.

"Whoa," I say. I want to bash his face in and set him straight. I count to three. "Love has nothing to do with the deal we made."

And I should have told Love; I regret not telling her. I want a time machine. Secrets erode trust and that's how I got into this mess. Had I told Love about Forty's proposal she would have lifted her little hand to her chest and said *ooh, Joe, I'm not sure that's such a good idea.* But you can't go back in time; I know this from the mug of fucking piss.

"Old Sport, can you fucking just *believe it*?" Forty says. "How cool is it, right? Megan Fucking Ellison! I still can't believe it. But at the same time, I can, you know how that is? How unlike the lottery it is, meaning that there's nothing random about the good fortune. You do the work. Eventually, you get paid. Then you get laid!" He twiddles his thumbs and looks at me so directly, like a bear facing a human in a backyard in New Hampshire.

"You maybe want to call your sister?" I ask him.

"I never use my phone during a meal," he says.

Forty whistles at the waitress and asks her for a bottle of their *worst* champagne and she laughs, as if he's so funny and comes back to us with two small bottles of white wine. "What are we toasting?" she asks.

"My career," he says. "I'm blowing up."

She says the drinks are on her and she winks. "I would eat that ass," Forty says. "And I generally don't do that."

I slam the table. "*Forty.*"

He looks at me and moans. "Old Sport, I did not invite you here to be lame," he says. "Now, you should be thanking me. You did some beautiful tweaks on my work. You're well on your way to a great career."

"I didn't *tweak* anything," I snarl.

He slumps, like I'm so boring, like I'm stupid. "*When Harry Met Sally. Jaws.* Do you know what these movies have in common?"

"Fuck off," I snap. I know where he's going.

"I'll tell you what they have in common," he says. And he tells me what I already know: The famous lines about orgasms and big boats were improvised. "But do the actors get credit? Hell, no. Do they get cowriting accolades? Fuck, no. Are they earning royalties on that gold? Hell, no."

"That's different and you know it."

He shakes his head. "You just don't get it," he says. "You waltz into this town and you think it *owes* you something because what? Because you fuck my sister and you have a flair for dialogue?"

The waitress brings beers. "These are for you guys to keep up the celebration."

Forty grins. "You are a doll. Porcelain doll."

She smiles. "No," she says. "I'm slightly more flexible."

She leaves and his eyes are gone. "Wouldn't it be aces if the waitresses in here were on Rollerblades?" He squirts ketchup on a napkin for seemingly no reason. "You should work that into something. Roller skates are killer on film. *Boogie Nights* meets I dunno, you know."

The waitress returns with a shake. "On the house," she says. "The chef read about you in the *Hollywood Reporter*."

Hollywood, where the rich don't have to pay for anything and Forty thanks her and lowers his chin and nods. He pulls his straw out of the case and sips his shake. "I drink my milkshake," he says. "Get it? Like, you think I'm drinking *your* milkshake but see, the chef knows, the waitress knows. They know what's up."

"Fuck you," I snap.

He shakes his head and tells me I need to watch out for my *ego*. He says I didn't kiss Barry Stein's ass the right way. He preaches about my lack of respect. I don't know what it is to pitch and pitch and hear the word *no* and go back and try again.

"Fifteen years I've been at this," he says. "For fifteen years I have been developing my brand. Getting my name out there. Generating buzz. Fifteen years of driving to studios and telling my stories to executives and producers who have told me they *love me* and they *love it* and they *want it* and then a week, two weeks later, nothing." He's fuming now. Give a miserable person an ice cream cone and the miserable person will nosh, digest, and go back to being miserable. "I just can't wait to see the look on Milo's face. Right?"

"You should really call Love," I say. "She's literally worried sick."

He's brittle, pissed. "She's fine," he says. "They're all fine."

The food comes. He's happy again. He plows into his bacon sandwich and I don't touch mine. He's failed his test, and I tried, I really did. But this codependent twin saga existed before I got here, Forty fucking with Love, Love forgiving him, no matter what. My job is to end it. I see that. I will do that, for Love, as an apology for the mess I made, the way I enabled this selfish louse.

I can't decide how I'm going to kill him but I do know that when rich people die, the cops actually care. The first thing they try to figure out is the motivation. I can't risk those e-mails we exchanged biting me in the ass. "Forty," I say. "You should delete all of our e-mails, you know, about the scripts. Just in case someone were to hack into your account. You want to make sure that there's nothing, well, you know what I mean."

He laughs and chokes and sips beer. "See, only someone fresh off the boat would say something like that," he says. "You can go to a lawyer right now. Have fun. Good luck paying the retainer. Oh, and good luck finding anyone who wants to work with a guy who lawyers up like a fucking baby when his girlfriend's brother gets a sweet deal." He burps. "You can be litigious or you can be creative but you can't be litigious *and* creative. Nobody wants to get in the sandbox with the guy who *sues* people."

I tell him I'm just looking out for him. "I know a reporter who tries to hack into shit all the time," I explain. "You don't want a paper trail."

He nods. "I do see your point," he says.

Now he's in his phone, swiping. The waitress comes back with a platter of sweet potato fries *just because*. Forty is sobering up. "That was good advice," he says. "But it's also a bummer. This is the kind of shit you learn from a lawyer, not a writer. We *could* get something going together but then I'm not bringing a litigious prick anywhere. I don't like litigious pricks. You need to tell me that you're not going to be a litigious prick."

At the counter, a different waitress flirts with an *aspiring* writer who's probably been trying to fuck her and finish his screenplay for months. He asks for a side of *guac* and she tells him that it's two dollars extra. That's how it works here. The guy who deserves free *guac* doesn't get free *guac*.

Forty wipes his mouth and pushes his plate away. "You know," he says. And now he reaches for the big guns. "My sister loves me very, very much."

"I know that, Forty," I say. "I do."

He runs his hands through his greasy hair. "You got Love," he says. "Don't be a pig. Stop looking for money. It doesn't make you happy. All the money and all the fame, it's nothing without love."

I remind him of his family hunkered down at Love's house. His eyes are empty. He is the boy named Forty, the hapless, hopeless brother of Love. "Yeah," he says. "There's nothing Ray and Dot love more than a party, even a search party. My fam-damn-ily, they're something, right?"

He's an outsider and he knows it and he'll never stop punishing them. When I tell him they love him, I sound like I'm lying. Lies sound like lies and it's impossible to know which came first, the selfish, repugnant nature of this man or the missteps of his nurturers. What I do know: If he stays around, he will destroy everything between me and Love. His family is right. He is self-destructive. But he is also outwardly destructive. Killing him will be the greatest risk of my life—I could lose Love—but it will, of course, yield the greatest reward. I will have Love without Forty.

I pick up the check. I pay cash; I've learned.

Outside, Forty picks at his teeth with a toothpick. "Well, I'm off to Vegas to bang out another script." His car pulls up, big and black.

"Forty," I say. "I know you're not going to write."

He laughs. "Oh right. Ha. But it's good, you know, good practice for the talk shows and shit," he says. Fucking asshole.

"Hey," I say. "What do you want me to tell your family?"

That vacant stare again. He knows they love Love more than they love him. I'm sure that's true in most families, and some kids shrug it off. But other kids, kids like Forty, I bet he made this same face at every birthday party when Love got just a *few* more presents than he did and when her mom hugged her and just held on for a *teensy* bit longer. Forty did not get enough love. A lot of people don't. But the thing is, he's *twinned* with someone who got so much love that she *is* Love. And that's got to be hard.

He shrugs. "Let my mom stress out and starve for a few more days," he says. "She's been starting to pork up, Old Sport. We don't want that, right?"

My sympathy evaporates. "So you don't want me to tell them you're okay?"

"They need to back off," he says. "I'm not in fucking high school." Reverse psychology 101 and his eyes pop. "You know what I *do* want though," he begins. "Old Sport, you should come to Vegas. We can bang out a new script, *Hangover* meets *Hangover*!"

The *Hangover* can't meet the *Hangover* because the *Hangover* is the *Hangover* and I tell him no, maybe next time, *definitely* next time.

He shrugs. I see a *bag of drugs* in his car, literally, a bag of drugs. He raises his hand for a high five and the next time I touch him, it will be different. I will be strangling him.

42

SEVEN thousand hours later, I am getting close to Vegas and the lights of the city twinkle in the distance the way they did in *Swingers*. I made it. And it wasn't easy. When I told Love that I had a "hunch" that Forty was in Vegas she was befuddled.

"Joe," she said. "I'm his twin. We have that psychic twin thing and I think I would be the one to know if he was in Vegas."

"I know what you mean," I reasoned. I folded my shirts into one of Love's black suitcases. "But I think when you're upset like this, it has to affect your radar."

She sat on the bed. "Should I go with you?"

I kissed the top of her head. "No," I said. "I got this."

"You really want that Boyfriend of the Year trophy, don't you?" she asked teasingly.

So I fucked her good and hard and then I went to Hollywood Boulevard to pick up some items for my Captain America costume—not the superhero, the generic Vegas bro. I got a Colts jersey and a baseball cap. I let the guy at the store choose. I was feeling lucky. I was going to *Vegas.*

And now I'm almost here, I see it in the distance, getting closer. My balls drop. It's *Vegas*; it really is. It's brighter than it is in the movies and it's uglier as I get closer, every sign a threat. *Last casino for twenty miles* and *last gas* and I pull over. I put on my Dodgers hat. I tear the tag off my Colts jersey and pull it on. Mr. Average America! I get back on the road.

On the strip, at a stop light, I see a woman pull her pants down, squat, and defecate. Tourists abound. People smoke cigarettes and push their babies in carriages and it's *hot* and I want to stare at all of it, the sheer volume of lights, the width of the sidewalks, the throngs of people, young and old, fat and American. I allow myself a few minutes to dork out and blast Elvis and the fountains at the Bellagio are grander in real life. I tell Love I made it and she tells me to start at Caesars.

"This isn't a twin thing," she says. "It's a Forty thing. He says they have the best tables."

LOVE was wrong. Forty is not at Caesars and everything here is so grandiose. The floor of the casino is a sprawling wide pasture and the slot machines are immovable cows, blocking my view. There are pods of blackjack tables, people everywhere, blasting music, machines making noise. I have a burner phone. I could call him. But I don't want to call him until I have eyes on him. Love calls again.

"So my dad got word from our host at the Bellagio," she says. "Apparently he's over there."

"Okay," I say. "I'm going there now."

I walk fast. The air is dry and random dudes high-five me—*Colts!*—and I listen to my pool mash-up and I reach the fountains. There is so much pomp leading up to the front entrance—oversized revolving doors, giant glass flowers on the ceiling, behind the front desk. Businessmen and hookers fill a lounge. I pass a bay of blackjack tables where the minimum bet is ten dollars. I move on, weaving my way through cocktail waitresses in skimpy sequined getups, couples fighting, a woman on the phone with her bank—*CASH ADVANCE*—a toddler crying, a mother telling him to *hold on baby, Mommy's almost done*, as if gambling is a job.

It's disorienting the way every area is identical, tables and slots, tables and slots. I reach a clearing and I see a *Hangover* slot machine and he's not there and I walk toward another mess of tables, white leather chairs, more of a palace than Caesars, and that's why Forty is here, sitting in a white chair at a blackjack table. His hair is a wreck. He's wearing two pairs of fucking Wayfarers, one pair on his head, one on his face. His collared shirt is wrinkled and his feet are grimy and he's got them propped up on two chairs, like he owns the joint. He's playing three hands, smoking two cigarettes. Chips fall out of his pocket and he doesn't bend over to retrieve them. I want to bash his head into the table but the ceilings are high and the cameras are everywhere. I sit down at a slot machine. Texas Tea. I put in ten dollars. I text Love: *I've looked and looked and I haven't seen him but I'll keep looking.*

She writes back: *My dad says thank you. You are the best.*

I write back: *We'll find him.*

I play two cents a round on Texas Tea and Forty plays *a thousand dollars* a hand on his three hands. He's losing. He is loud. Even several feet away, I can hear him. He sits with a hooker and he periodically grabs her neck and licks her chest. A Chinese lady stares at him disapprovingly. "I'm sorry if I offend you, honey, but this is Vegas and if I want to blow lines off Miss Molly Tupelo's lovely, enhanced chesticles, then I will do it all night long."

The Chinese woman gets up and walks away and I can't believe this city is so crowded.

Forty loses a hand. "Is that cuz I pissed off the Chinawoman?" he asks. "Because if that's the case, then you're gonna have to call the pit boss." He smashes the table with his drink. "Fuck this!"

Forty walks five feet and sits down at another table. And it all happens again. A girl in a short skirt sits down next to him. A new old Asian woman tries to sit down too. Forty grabs the seat. "Does it look like I want company, lady?" He knocks back his whiskey. "Fuckin' A. Back off."

The girl in the short skirt laughs and tells him he's funny. He says she can stay but only if she's lucky and she says she hopes so and I officially hate it here.

The dealer tries. "Maybe a little lady luck would do you some good, sir."

Forty sneers. "I'd rather have some face cards. You know what? Fuck this."

And he's up and I leap to follow him but no. He sits at a neighboring table. He lights up next to a pregnant woman.

"Do you mind?" she asks. She points at her protruding belly.

"You should be at a non-smoking table," he says. He blows smoke into the air. "Or really, you should be *home*. You fucking pregnant people, you own the whole world. Do you really need to own this too? I can't smoke anywhere because of you and you really need to tell me I can't smoke in fucking *Vegas*?"

The dealer asks him to quiet down and Forty rises. "Do you know who I am? Motherfucker, I *own* this city. I just sold a screenplay that takes place in this fucking city for more money than you'll see in your whole fucking life."

My hat itches and I have lost nine dollars at Texas Tea.

The dealer is trying hard not to laugh. Forty knocks his drink onto the floor and snaps his fingers at a waitress. "I'm empty, sweetheart."

She looks tired. In Vegas they force the waitresses to walk around in sequined bathing suits and panty hose. The woman says she's delivering drinks and she'll be back to take orders after she drops off her drinks. Forty is irate. "I don't care what you're doing," he says. "Why the fuck do you think I care what you're doing, honey? Do I look like I care? I told you I want a gimlet. Goose. Gimlet. Now. As in now."

"When I come back I can—"

He barks, "GET ME A FUCKING GOOSEY GOOSE GIMLET."

She walks away and the boss man in the pit—I've seen *Casino* a thousand times—approaches Forty. "Mr. Quinn," he says. "We're so happy to have you back. I hope you're having fun gaming with us."

"Rocco!" Forty says. "It's a helluva lot more fun to *game* when you've got a nice big Goosey gimlet. What the hell is going on here?"

Rocco tries to resolve the gimlet situation while Forty loses a few thousand more dollars and I win fifty-two cents at Texas Tea. Forty is on the move. I follow him. My pants itch.

He cruises around the casino and every few feet, he ducks into a row of slot machines and takes a bump of blow. He stumbles up to a depressed-looking leggy girl in a tight dress at a slot machine and pulls her hair. She yelps.

"What the fuck, dude? Get your hands off me!"

"How much?" he asks. "I wanna go for a ride."

"I'm not a fucking hooker, motherfucker," she says. "I'm a *teacher*."

"I can get hot for that," he says. He reaches for her. "How much?"

She smacks him with her purse. "Stop it."

He laughs. "Honey, honestly, by the look of your dress, you could *use* the money and what happens in Vegas stays in Vegas, you know what I mean, jelly bean?"

She spits at him and he doesn't wipe off her saliva. He sits down at the machine. He loses a hundred dollars. A hooker witnesses his fight and approaches, so obvious—Vegas! Why didn't Delilah just move here?—and she tells Forty she wants to party. He looks her up and down.

"I'd love to sweetheart, but I'm not a homo."

She stares at him.

He slips her a hundred dollar bill. "Take this C-note to the craps table and get it up there and do yourself a favor and go buy some tits."

She doesn't register any emotion. She says *thank you, baby* and walks away and this is the most depressing place I've ever been. There are no clocks or windows and the people are either incredibly sloppy or incredibly overdressed.

Forty walks up to a craps table and spills a drink. People boo him. "Yeah," he says. "Boo fucking hoo. Do you people know that I have a two-picture deal at Annapurna? Yeah. Have fun with your boring fucking lives."

He walks away. Nobody at the table knows what *Annapurna* is. He sits down at a new blackjack table and gets a marker for fifty grand. People are gathering to watch and he is bragging about being a huge writer. When people ask if he's here alone, he says, "I'm with my girlfriend, Love. She's upstairs."

My girlfriend, Love. I shudder. The song "Born in the U.S.A." comes on and he groans. "I hate Bruce Springsteen," he says. "Can we do something about this? Goddamn whiny Democrat, we *get it. You're from New Jersey and you think it's cool to be poor.* Just fuck *off* already."

The dealer says he prefers the song "Thunder Road."

Forty huffs. "You also probably think a Chevy is as solid as a Beamer. No offense . . . but there is such a thing in this world as fucking *wrong.* Like these cards. Is there a rule against giving out tens in this shithole? And about a hundred years ago I ordered some gimlets."

He sat down ten seconds ago but nobody tells him he is wrong and "Thunder Road" is a great fucking song. I sit down at a *Hangover* slot machine. I lose ten dollars in a few seconds and Forty splits tens. I know this because the dealer calls it out to the pit boss and the people standing around are gasping.

He loses.

A newly married couple enters the bar and everybody claps and Forty stands up and whistles with his hands. He motions for the band to stop playing. The lead singer looks at the doorway where a man stands with his arms crossed. He nods. This really is Forty's playground. Forty goes onstage and grabs the mic.

"First of all," he says. "Congratufuckinglations!"

Everybody cheers. He is the good guy. Fun guy. He high-fives the groom. He kisses the bride on the cheek. "Now, let's have some fun," he says. "As it happens, I am here to celebrate too. I just sold *two* scripts to Megan Fucking Ellison." He waits for a reaction. Still nobody knows her name. "Point is, I made some money and I wanna spread the love around!" Applause, obviously. "And this is what I wanna do. Groom, get the fuck up here."

The groom *gets the fuck up here* and he is a small guy, shorter than his wife. He seems shy. He has a big smile, big teeth, they're too big for his face. His wife cheers. "What's your name, son?"

"Greg," he says. "Mr. and Mrs. Greg and Leah Loomis from New Township, New Jersey!"

Greg has probably never said that many words out loud to a group this size. Forty motions for everyone to quiet down and he waves the bride onstage. He puts his arm around Greg. "Greg," he says. "You got a beautiful bride. And you got a long life ahead."

There is a mixed response. Some laugh. Some are disgusted.

"So why not let me give you guys a wedding present you'll remember forever," he says. "Greg," he raises his eyebrows up and down and up and down. "I'll give ya ten if ya let me kiss your wife. Right here. Right now."

Greg the groom doesn't punch Forty. People boo. They hiss. Some people whistle. They want to see it. Forty takes five thousand-dollar chips out of his pocket.

"One, two, three, four, five!" he exclaims.

More of the same, booing and cheering—America—and the bride is pleading with the husband. I think she's saying something about the mortgage. The groom is turning redder by the second and the bride does a shot and Forty plays with his chips and finally the bride wins; she is the alpha, she will choose their vacations, program the DVR, demand him to renovate the *man cave* he undoubtedly has where he roots for his teams, eats his salsa. No *guac* for these two; they're not from that part of America.

She finishes slapping on lipstick and she gets up onstage. Forty kicks, *yes!* He dips the bride. He grazes her boob and he never said anything about feeling her up—booing and cheering—and he leans over and grabs her ass, hard, and he shoves his tongue down her throat. I watch the groom. He looks broken; ten minutes ago he was in love, he was *just married.* And now he's *just fucked over.* Forty releases the bride and she wipes her mouth and she puts her hand out and Forty tosses the chips on the floor and pumps his fists.

So now, of course, there are a million people who would kill this guy. The lead singer takes the mic and the bride hugs the groom but you can tell Forty ruined their marriage. Their odds of happiness are lower now than they were before they met Forty Quinn.

Forty takes off again, meandering through the floor of the casino. I follow him and text him from my burner phone: *It's snowing at the Sapphire.*

Forty writes back: *?*

Me: *It's Slim. New phone. Your sister's looking for you.*

Forty: *Heavy snow? Better than last time I hope*

Me: *Yes. Sapphire in twenty.*

Forty: *Leaving Bellagio now*

But he's not *leaving Bellagio now.* He's settling into another white leather chair, motioning for the dealer to deal, as if he doesn't know that the dealer can't deal to him while he's texting. He writes: *I heard there's hella ice out there too.*

I confirm that I have *hella ice* and I park myself at a slot machine with a lobster theme. I insert my ticket, now worth only $2.11. Forty is the world's least interesting man, bragging to the disinterested players around him about his *career* being *on fire*, as if people came to this place to talk about work.

My machine goes berserk. The screen changes and an animated lobsterman introduces himself to me. The woman next to me says it's a bonus round and the fisherman reaches into the water and pulls out cages of lobsters. My $2.11 turns into $143.21. The house doesn't always win and I know when to walk away. I take my ticket to a machine and cash out. I text Forty: *Snow ice and snow bunnies too gotta come now.*

Forty gets off his ass and leaves the casino. He lost a lot of money but I walk through the casino a winner. I find my car in the garage and I text Love: *Any word?*

She writes back: *Nothing. But he's probably passed out in some hooker's bed by now.*

I write back: *Don't worry. I'll find him. Things are gonna change. They are.*

And it's the truth. If anything, this trip to Vegas has opened my eyes to what it's been like for Love all these years. She is back in LA texting him and here he is ignoring her, feeding her fear, eating away at her life. He's a parasite, a user, and I think he enjoys torturing Love.

I can't blame Ray and Dottie. No parents do everything right. No parents can control how they love their children. But this isn't about blame. This is about the love of my life, the pain in her eyes, the weakness in her voice, the way she is choking on his silence. I can't let him smother her anymore. I love her too much for that.

43

TWENTY minutes later Forty slips out of his cab and moseys to the back of this off-strip, derelict gas station. He's wearing a stupid backpack, like a kid going to camp, expecting to see his counselor/dealer. I step out of my car and smile, especially at the security camera that hangs by a thread, decimated, cracked, the reason I chose this particular spot.

"Old Sport!" Only joy registers on his bloated face as he gallops toward me and throws his arms around me. His hug is too hard and he reeks.

"What are you doing here?" he yells.

"It's a long story," I say. "What are *you* doing here?"

"I was supposed to meet my dealer, but he didn't show. Luckily I'm well equipped." Forty shrugs and pats his backpack. "Does this mean . . . are you finally good with everything? Down to party?"

I nod even though I hate drugs, hate the way people get around them, the need that comes through.

"Fucking Goldberg!" he sings, and then he's on about his Molly and his blow, his this and his that. He wipes his fat hair off his stretched face. "You know, I know we had some talks, some iffiness with the business, but that's what it is, my friend. Business gets whack and shit happens and then what do you do? You smoke a little crack."

He winks and slips into my car with his fucking backpack. "We need this," he goes on. "I bet this is your first time in Vegas right? Professor Goes to Vegas! I love it!" His eyes narrow, curious. "Where's my sis?"

"At home," I say. "With your parents."

"Nice," he says. He cracks open a forty-ounce can of malt liquor. It pops and fizzes. "You relationship people, I don't know how you do it." He burps and beer dribbles down his chin. "You feel like you need to bring home the bacon and the big dick and make them babies and dance that dance and it's like, fuck that. I answer to me and me alone. Fuck love." He laughs. "You know what I mean. Not Love love. I love my sister. She's my rock. Do you know how many times she texted me today?"

I count to two. It doesn't help. "Did you write back to her?"

He shakes his head. "It's that twin thing, she's my rock. She knows I split sometimes. She gets me. You want a bump?"

SelfishmotherfuckingpigdruggieLovewrecker

"I'm good," I say. I think about those situations, when women are pregnant with twins and the doctors have to go in and remove the fetus that is sucking the life out of the other. It's the humane thing to do. Sometimes, one must die so that the other can live. Biology isn't sentimental. None of Love's other boyfriends had the balls to end Forty. But I do. I look at him, scrolling through his texts from her. He only feels loved when she's a wreck, worried about him, consumed. Some people are strong enough to share a womb and a birthday. Love is. Forty isn't.

"Check out the ass on that ass," he says, pointing to a high school girl looking for the bathroom. "Should we take her with us?"

I want to kill him. Now. In this rental. I start the car. I can't kill him here. I grip the wheel. He pounds the roof. The schoolgirl found the bathroom. She's safe. We go. Silence only lasts for two lights and then he's at it again.

"You and my sister are my fucking *rock*," he says. "You take care of her or else, right? You know that, right? Like, you get that you are a dead man if you fuck her over?"

I clench the wheel tighter. "You're a good brother."

"I'm the best brother," he says. "The motherfucking best."

He pulls a little baggie out of his pocket and sniffs. I pull onto the freeway and he is so high that he doesn't ask where we're going. He only rants about how he's *never getting married* and how he's gonna live with me and Love and all the fun we're gonna have. He's sealing the deal on his death and the car hums and we are farther and farther from the bright lights, and there are fewer cars all the time. The inside of Forty's mind is a grave place and it's right next to me, soaking up the oxygen. He is the anti-Love and he confesses that he shops at *Ralph's*.

"It's fucking *groceries*," he sneers. "It's food. And you know what food is, Old Sport? It's pre-shit. That's all. It's pre-shit and we need it to survive. And it used to be a fucking pain for the cavemen, right, my friend? I mean, you had to get out there with your club and whack at woolly mammoths and drag that shit home before the flies got all up in it and *that's* why food was a fucking pain. But come on. It's modern time. Food is fucking easy."

He rubs his nose and shakes his head. "All you do is go in, you get your tacos, and you fucking eat. People like my parents, they want to act like it fucking *matters* so much, like what you eat for dinner is so interesting but it's not! It's fucking food! Just eat it and shit it and be done with it and don't feel special cuz you eat that shit *with* someone because in the end we all shit alone! Who the fuck cares that you ate the pre-shit *with* someone if you shit alone, on a toilet, door closed, whammo!"

He snorts more cocaine. I could pull over and roll him out the door but he's on so much blow right now that he would probably just turn into a roadrunner, catch up to me, and jump back in.

"I could eat a taco," he says. "Fucking chomp right into that thing."

He wants to call Love. I panic and my hand slips on the wheel. I sweat. I tell him we had sort of a fight.

"Then maybe we *shan't*," he says. He rolls down the window, all smiles, like a dog searching for fresh air. It's telling, how his spirits lift the second he thinks I'm on the outs with Love. He doesn't want me to be happy. He doesn't want anyone to be happy. Especially Love.

He brags about his time in Vegas, one lie after another, twisting it all, a mile a minute, deranged, and we can't get there fast enough but I can't speed—the mug of piss—and he won't stop talking about table minimums and hookers refusing to take his money. He doesn't say one true thing for the entire journey through all this brown land, blue sky, and he's so fucked up, so full of himself, verbally expunging, the loneliest man on earth.

I can't tell you what a thing it is to see our first stop glimmering, tiny, in the distance, finally, the place where I can begin to kill him: the Clown Motel.

"There it is," I interrupt him mid-rant about his host at the Monte Carlo.

He drums his backpack, happy dog. And he tells me he has been here before—he has been everywhere, I get it—but this is my first time and it's the greatest thing I've seen in the west so far. It's the Wild Wild West I wanted. The blue-and-white motel is decked out with clown signs, and the giant Nevada lettering above the building is straight out of a ghost town or a Tarantino movie: WELCOME TO THE CLOWN MOTEL. The lobby is supposed to be a tightly packed swarm of clown dolls from different eras, but I won't get to see it because I'm going to murder Forty today, so I can't very well go into the fucking lobby.

Forty is finally calm and his backpack is closed and he puts his baggie away. He checks himself in the mirror and he says this was a good call. "I love clowns," he says, and of course he loves clowns. He's an imbecile, a clown himself, with his puffy red nose and his wild swath of dirty hair, his belly fat jiggling in his turquoise shorts; a nightmarish thing that frightens Love, haunting her, weighing her down, the thing that she's supposed to love, the way the world initially instructs children to love clowns even though we all know deep down that they're creepy, old, puffy men in masks leering at children.

"Hey, Forty," I say. "You should look online to make sure they have rooms."

"Old Sport, you and me are for *sure* shooting something here." He sighs. "That will be aces. We could even call it *Aces.* Like *Ocean's*

Eleven but with *Saw* and the clowns are the victims and the bad guys are those fucking tourists, the fucking little boyfriend and girlfriend holding hands and shit."

"Right," I say. "So the clowns are the good guys."

"Exactly," he says. "The couple gets here and the girl is like *I hate clowns* and the doofus boyfriend is like *I do too* and they complain and then eventually, they get a machine gun and just spray the clowns."

"Forty," I snap. "Did you look to see if they have rooms?"

He ignores me. "You know," he says. "Last time I was here, it was with Love and Michael Michael."

I feign surprise, as if I didn't already know this, as if we aren't here because I know this. Love posted a #ThrowbackThursday photo a few months ago, harkening back to another era, when she did drugs and had a *tongue piercing* and eyeliner below her eyes, not above. The three of them came here on the way to Burning Man—God, am I glad I didn't know her then. The comments told a story: Love and Forty and Michael Michael Motorcycle traveled here, lured in by the gigantic clown boards promising FREE WIFI and WELCOME BIKERS. Forty disappeared with the car. He showed up a month later. He didn't apologize.

In minutes we are there. I pull into the parking lot and drive around to the back, the part of this tourist trap that I wanted to see most: the early American cemetery.

"Do you know what a travesty it is that we have no shrooms?" Forty asks. "You can't be in this cemetery without shrooms."

"Fuck, yes," I lie. I park in the farthest corner. I don't see any cameras but the mug of piss I left in Rhode Island is with me at times like this.

"Solid," he says. "You know, Old Sport, I knew you had it in you, the cool."

I offer him a hundred-dollar bill, my Vegas winnings. "If you use a credit card in there, your whole fam-damn-ily is gonna show up."

"You think I'm an amateur?" He laughs and whips out a fake ID. "I'm Monty Baldwin, motherfucker! Get it? The lost Baldwin brother. Fuck yeah."

And, of course, that would be Forty's dream in life: to be a Baldwin brother, surrounded by brothers instead of Love. "This Baldwin will be back," he says. He jogs toward the manger's office, his backpack bouncing, and I remember that first night at Chateau when I wondered if he and *Joaq* Phoenix were buddies.

I get out of the car and walk into the cemetery. The sun beats down on me and the dead people are nothing but bones under the dirt. The causes of death are listed: suicide, gunshot, plague. The cause of Forty's death will be me, but it won't say that on his tombstone and I wonder how many of these stories are true.

There's a shovel against the side of the motel. I wish I could bury him here, but there are too many people around: truck drivers, hippies with GoPro cameras, a family fighting over whether this is too much for the kids. I just need Forty to check in, to talk with the manager. I read about the manager online and he's the kind of guy that remembers *everyone.* He will remember Monty Baldwin. He will confirm that he seemed *on something*. Even if he says Forty was talking with someone in the parking lot, I am unrecognizable in my baggy clothes and Colts jersey and rental car.

I trudge back to the car, keeping my head down. I take out five Percocets. I mash them down and dump them into a bottle of water

I bought at the gas station. As I shake, Forty emerges from the manager's office and returns to the car.

"Want to check out the hot springs?" I suggest when he slips into his seat. I Googled the springs when I was learning about the Clown Motel. It's true. You really can kill people in the desert. "They sound pretty crazy."

"Alkali," he says. "Fuck, yes. I have some iowaska and oh, Old Sport, you haven't lived until you get in that water and you just *see* shit. This is what we were missing." He belts up. "Just straight-up road trip, writing all Kerouac and what's the guy, the one with Johnny Depp, the one in Vegas with the backpack and the drugs and the sunglasses."

Jesus fucking Christ. "Hunter S. Thompson."

He claps. "Hunter S. Thompson."

"Yeah," I say, and I can't get out of this parking lot fast enough. I hand him a bottle. "Here," I say. "We gotta hydrate before we trip."

He tears off the cap. He didn't notice the broken seal. He gulps. "Old Sport," he says. "I like the new you. Fuck all that shit in Hollywood and the family and the pressure and the nonsense. We're artists, man. My sister isn't. God bless her but she's not, you know."

He turns on the music, my *Pitch Perfect* pool mash-up. He laughs at me and says my horrible taste in music is proof of my creative genius. "This is it," he says. "Freedom."

I put the car in reverse. "Yeah," I manage. "Freedom."

He unzips his backpack and takes out a *butter knife* and dips the soft-edged blade into a bag of blow. He sniffs and this might be another Fincher occasion. I might not have to kill Forty. At this rate, he'll do it to himself.

44

THE alkali springs are disgusting, just two brown holes in the desert, like something you'd see in *Little House on the Prairie* or some Charles Manson documentary. It's disgusting in every way you can imagine. There's a fucking Magnum condom on the ground nearby, used, crusty. The wrapper is here too, along with a can of Bud.

Forty swipes the can and sips—I might vomit—and he strips down and there's blood on his shirt—somehow he managed to cut himself with his butter knife—and I turn away. I never wanted to see him naked but I did want to see him here, alone, in the middle of nowhere, near Area 51, nothingness filling the land for miles.

He screams and pounds his chest as he steps into the water. "There it is!" he cheers. "Fucking springs, baby! Woo!"

He drank the Percocet water on the way here and not only is he still alive, but he talked the entire car ride here. He's not Henderson and apparently it takes a pharmacy to kill a pharmaceutically enhanced person like Forty. I hope I have enough.

Forty settles in and someone else's ass was there and animals probably dip into this and people are foul. "Come on, Professor," he calls, waving. "I know you're all New York and shit but there's nothing gay about getting into a spring with another dude."

"I'm good."

"Come on," he says. "This is God's hot tub. This is home, Old Sport. Get in here. Man up. Live up! Feel the fire! You get in here, this is how you make a movie. You let your mind go."

He waves his arms at the blue blanket sky and howls. I sit down in the dirt. "You know," I say. "There are just as many creative people out there who aren't into this sort of thing. Woody Allen would never get into dirty hole of hot water."

Forty laughs. "He'd fuck a tween though." He smiles. "He's an artist! We're weird! Professor, you need to get your weird on. Stop being so safe. You think, you bear down, but do you ever just *go* for it? Honestly, you're a great writer. But I think you'd be *golden* if you had the guts to get *in* it."

This coming from a guy who sold my scripts in his name and I go back to the car to make him more Percocet water. Every time he does coke, he fights my downers. He's making this so much harder than it has to be and we can't stay here forever. I shake the bottle and offer it to him.

"I'm fine," he says, waving me off. "Get in!"

It's my turn to tell him I'm fine and he attempts to swim in his little hole, as if there's room. It's fitting that he will drown in two feet of water when his sister appointed herself a national advocate for water safety. I sip my water, no drugs.

"You sure you don't want some?"

"Fuck, yes, I want a sip!"

His memory is eroding. I read about wet brain. Maybe that's what it is, Forty swallowing the water he said he didn't want a minute ago. I need him lower, weaker. Henderson had no tolerance. He went so quietly in the end but this is ridiculous.

"What else you got in your bag of tricks?" I ask.

"Iowaska, baby!" He reaches in for his tea. He drinks. That's a good boy. Let that tea mix with the Percocets. Let the poisons collide. He passes me the bottle. I pretend to drink. I am a good boy.

In *Closer*, Jude Law tells Natalie Portman, "This will hurt," and then it does hurt. That is where I am right now, no matter what a dick he is. It's starting to hit me. Killing Forty will hurt Love. In a fucked-up way, she won't know how to live without the drama and this is going to be harder than I thought. But then, all change hurts. In the end, Love will be a new person without her brother. She'll sleep better. She won't have to find a way to forgive him every time he fucks her over. She won't have to let him into her home or rationalize her feelings. Imagine what she could do with the power, the power I'm giving to her by doing away with him.

Forty flips onto his belly, a baby whale. He dips his butter knife into his bag. "I feel whoa," he says. "Like whoa."

"Just go with it," I tell him. "Ride the wave."

"Wouldn't that be cool if there were waves in here?" he asks. "You ever think about that? How there can't be waves without a lot of water?"

This is the part of college I never wanted: a self-important fuckwit contemplating *the sea.* I get my phone. I can't listen to this shit. It's only going to get worse as he slips away and loses access to his brain, what's left of it. I have a new e-mail, a Google news alert. My chest tightens. I click on the link and it takes me to the *Providence Journal Bulletin.* There is a picture of Peach Salinger, looking happier than she ever did in real life. Peach's parents love her more dead than they did when she was alive. They whitened her smile and enlarged her eyes and now they are seeking justice.

"A wave." Forty pontificates. "A wave never goes away. Like, what if the ocean just stopped? What then?"

Forty blathers. His words aren't words anymore, just sounds, as I read the news, the unbelievable news.

The Little Compton Police Department received an anonymous tip regarding local girl and Brown graduate Peach Salinger. Authorities won't reveal details about the tip but they do confirm that they have reopened the case. They were wrong that it was suicide. Or at least, they think they were wrong. The language is delicate, hesitant, but the message is clear. They think Peach Salinger was murdered. And they have started a brand-new investigation. Oh, fuck. Double thousand triple fuckity fuck. Forty starts slapping the surface to create waves and I have no patience for the whale in the water anymore. I have to get out of here. I have to deal with this.

I put my phone in my pocket and I walk to the hole in the mud. He's half gone, pupils warbling toward the underside of his skull where that poisoned pink brain slows to a halt. He's going, but I can't wait. I can't sit here, not with an investigation open on the other side of the country.

"Hey, buddy," I say. And when he swims toward me, I lean over and push Forty Quinn's head under the water. My hands are on fire. The water is at least ninety degrees and the air is hot and I feel my body become a furnace, the heat rises, curling around my arm like something out of a Dr. Seuss poem. He isn't like Henderson. He doesn't struggle. He is weak. Dark yellow piss whispers out of his soft, vile dick. Dehydration. I look up at the sky and I wait for his unconscious body to stop flailing.

Finally it's over. Monty Baldwin is dead. His fake ID is stuffed into his brick of coke. The condom wrapper is a godsend, more DNA, not mine. I pull my hands out of the water. I catch my breath. At some point the butter knife fell into the water with him and it's there, glistening at the bottom. I've never tried cocaine before. I dip my finger into his bag. I do like he did, one tiny bump. I shake. But maybe that's just that feeling you get when you're next to a brand-new corpse.

45

THERE is no way around it. I have to lie to Love. I am on the phone with her while I wait in the JetBlue Terminal at McCarran Airport. They have slot machines here too and I am leaving Las Vegas and I am going to Little Compton but I can't tell Love that.

I have no explicit plan. It's probably stupid of me to return to the scene of the crime. But I can't stay in Vegas and wait for the police to find Forty and I can't go to LA and sit on the sofa with Love and refresh the search engines for information on Peach Salinger. Because the truth is that I fucked up. I left the *mugofurine,* my one loose end, and I won't let it be my undoing.

Besides if I'm going to be caught for murdering that depressive, vicious Salinger, I'd rather it happen there. This is why dads don't let their kids visit them in prison, why people dying from cancer don't want their picture taken. This investigation could expose that mug of piss and I don't want Love to have to see me in handcuffs.

Love is on the phone, silent, sighing every few seconds, a signal

that she wants me to stay on. It is never a good thing when a woman is silent. I have to keep asking if she's there.

"Yes," she says. "Why?"

"'Cause you're not saying anything."

"What do you want me to say?" she asks. "I'm irritated. I'm sick of this. I can't get anything done and I don't know if my brother's dead and it sucks."

"I'm sorry," I say. "I'm trying."

"Did you start at Caesars like I said?"

And I say yes and we retrace my steps again and I promise to keep trying. "You know he'll turn up," I say.

"Which casino are you at right now?"

"Planet Hollywood," I lie.

She sighs. "He doesn't like their tables."

"I know," I say. "I remember you said that, Love. But I'm trying everything. Unless you want me to come home . . ."

"No," she says. "God, no. I'm sorry. I'm just tense."

"I know, it's okay," I say.

I know she wants to stay on the phone and say nothing, but my flight to Providence, Rhode Island, is boarding.

"You there?"

"Yes! Joe! Stop asking me! Are *you* there?"

"I'm here," I say. "I'm not going anywhere."

She cries. I tell her it's okay and now I'm gonna have to wait. I can't board with Group A. People are real assholes about their suitcases and I'm nervous there won't be room for mine, but Love comes first. Suddenly she is laughing.

"I'm watching *Friends*," she says. "It's the one where—"

"Shit," I say. "I think I see him."

I hang up and rush to the Jetway. It's a shitty thing to do, but watching *Friends* while you're on the phone with your boyfriend is also a shitty thing to do. I text her: *Sorry. False alarm. I love you.*

She writes back: *XOXOXOX*

I wish she had said *I love you* but then again, I have to prepare myself for change. I go online again because I still can't believe it. I watch a press conference with Peach's parents and her mother is identified as Florence "Pinky" Salinger. She is an old version of Peach, with fuller lips and broader shoulders. "I repeatedly told the police that while my daughter battled depression, she was not suicidal." She breathes. "While it is comforting that the authorities are now treating my daughter's disappearance as a crime, a murder, it is deeply disconcerting that the police declined to investigate until someone called in an anonymous tip." The woman heaves. The woman has no soul. No wonder Peach was so terrible. "It is a sad state of affairs when a mother's instinct and knowledge means *nothing* to a detective. But we are grateful that my daughter's murderer will at last be brought to justice."

She straightens her jacket, as if it matters what she looks like, and steps back from the podium. I wonder what it's like to be a mother and you're going to give a speech for reporters about your dead daughter and still, you go and get your hair and makeup done.

The broadcaster explains that the Salinger family intends to use *all their resources* to resolve this homicide case and the video ends.

We take off and it's strange to be going back to Little Compton, to think of a time when I was so in love with Amy. I haven't thought about her or our trip in so long, about Noah & Pearl & Harry &

Liam, about *Charlotte & Charles* and all that food and all that sex. I remember the way she tasted and I remember the blueberry-stained sheets and the sound of her voice when she said she would try to learn to trust. If I never took Amy to Little Compton, would we still be together? Is life predestined or do you change it by shoving your way into small, quaint towns because you're fascinated by how out of place you feel there?

It's a risk, going back to Little Compton. But I'm doing it for Love; our love can never be safe so long as the *mugofurine* is out there taunting me. And really, it's like love itself, like drinking. We all get our hearts broken. We get fucked up and throw up and we cry and listen to sad songs and say we're never doing that again. But to be alive is to do it again. To love is to risk everything.

WE land in Providence and no flight was ever this fast. I text Love: *My phone died and I'm gonna crash. Nothing yet, wish I had better news. Love you.*

She writes back immediately: *Ok*

I buy some crap in the airport. A candy bar that's too big, a copy of *Mr. Mercedes*, and a Red Sox cap. I walk directly to Budget Car Rental. There's no way to rent a car without showing an ID and providing a credit card. I do these things. What I have going for me: I was only here with Amy this summer, a vacationer. That guy who was here in the winter, that guy who smashed up his car and killed that girl? His name was Spencer Hewitt.

I don't get a convertible. I get a Chevy. I start it up and I drive into my life, into my past, my future, my genetic coding, my mistakes, my possible salvation, my probable doom, Little Fucking Compton.

46

THE theme of my life appears to be working vacations. Like so many Americans, I appear to be incapable of taking a fucking break. And it's bad for you. This is where Europeans are healthier. They relax. They rest. They turn off their phones and leave their work in the office and when they go to the beach they take off their tops, they show their tits and their hairy chests and they drink and sunbathe and they fucking go for it. I, on the other hand, am one of those fucked-up workaholic Americans plodding on an empty beach, not savoring the sunset, not romping in the waves—though it's too cold, it's autumn—and I am working hard, deciding how the hell I am going to get into that motherfucking house.

After I checked into my shitty motel, I went into a sleep coma. Vegas will fuck you up. I think I went twenty-eight hours without so much as a nap. I woke up on the cruddy, low-thread-count bedspread in a pile of my own drool. I showered in the stifling, tiny shower and I used the terrible small rectangles of bad soap, and I drove to the public parking lot that's closest to the beach near the Salinger house. And I started walking. As if you can just walk into a fucking crime scene. Before I even got there, I saw the activity, the police cruisers and the TV news vans, the various Salingers in their winter clothes, and I had to back off.

I pretend to be a guy walking on a beach relaxing and meanwhile, that fucking house fills up with people who might find my mug of piss. I need to get in there so I try to get in there.

I drive to Crowther's and order a shit ton of food to go. I buy one of their T-shirts. I go to the Salinger house and park as close as I can. The TV vans are gone—news is only news for a little while—and there is only one cop. I put on my Red Sox cap and I lift the heaving box of food and I trot toward the house, the way any delivery guy would. I knock on the door, the way any delivery guy would. Nobody answers so I ring the bell, the way any delivery guy would.

A guy who can't be more than twenty and looks exactly like Peach walks up. He's wearing a Yale T-shirt and scratching his head. He looks like he's never held a rake or scratched a lottery ticket in a 7-Eleven. "What's up?" he asks.

"I have a delivery," I say, as if this isn't completely fucking obvious. "Can I get in there and put this down?"

The Salinger's eyes roll to the side of his oval head. "Mommmmmm!" he calls out.

"Buddy," I say. "My back's breaking here. If I could get in there and get this down."

But now his mother is here. "Trot," she says. "Don't scream." She looks at me. "I'm sorry," she says. "We're requesting that all flowers and food and gifts be sent to the battered women's shelter in Fall

River. Peach was very passionate about women's rights and we just don't need the food."

Peach was not very passionate about women's rights. She was passionate about women's pussies. She wanted to fuck Beck, which is why I killed her. *Salingers.* This bitch just stares at me. "Do . . . you . . . speak . . . English?" she asks.

NO, BUT I SPEAK CUNT. "That's so great of you," I say. "But my boss would have my ass if I drove to Fall River. You sure I can't just get in there and leave this with you?" Meaning, get in there and steal the keys that are undoubtedly on the kitchen table because rich people, particularly the ones on the East Coast, really like to throw their shit on the kitchen table.

The bitch sighs. "You poor thing." She reaches for her purse. She thinks I want a tip. "You take this and you keep that food." She slips me a *five-dollar bill* and gives me a fake smile, the kind people do when they want you to know you're faking it. She closes the door and locks it and now I've been made by not one but *two* fucking Salingers, so it's not like I can show up here tomorrow in a UPS uniform. Not that I have a UPS uniform. All I have is a heaving box of food.

I drive to my shitty motel room. I eat. I text Love: *Still nothing and yes I am the asshole who got sucked into a blackjack table for hours*

She writes back: *I'm not your parole officer. You don't have to report to me! I know you're working hard. I'm helping my dad with some Pantry stuff.*

This was the wrong time for her to use the phrase *parole officer* and I don't want to talk to her until I've destroyed that mug of piss. I wish I could change things. I wish I had taken care of this mug before we met.

Miss you, she writes, and most girls would throw hissy fits if their boyfriend went into silent mode in *Las Fucking Vegas* for several hours, especially while said girl was in the middle of a family crisis.

My phone buzzes and now she's calling me.

"I just wanted to hear your voice," she says when I answer.

"How you doing?" I ask her. She starts in about a difficult woman at work, Sam, and I yawn and the room is cold and I walk to the window to close the blinds and I left my headlights on. "Fuck," I say.

"What's wrong?" she asks. "Are you okay?"

"Yeah," I say. "I left my lights on. It's fine."

I grab the keys and go outside—the bitter cold—and I turn off the lights and I run back inside and Love asks me where I am. "A diner," I say. "The Peppermill."

She says she's glad I'm eating and she wants me to rest. She says I sound tense. I tell her I sound tense because I am tense. She tells me that when they were in college, Forty disappeared for *two months.* "Right after I got married," she says. "*Two months*, Joe. You know you can't stay in Vegas for two months."

"I won't, but I can't give up yet," I say.

"Promise me you'll take care of yourself," she says.

I promise her. And then I make shitty motel coffee and go on Tinder. Fortunately, there aren't *that* many girls in the area. I swipe and I swipe and I swipe. I swipe while I piss and I swipe in the bed and I swipe in the car and then I find her. *Jessica Salinger.* I recognize her from a picture of the family in the article. She's a prettier version of Peach and she's *less than a mile away.* This is what I needed to know, that she was still here; her fucking Facebook and Twitter are private but her pussy, apparently, is open. Humans. I will never understand.

I shower. I shave. I dress. I run out to my car and thank God I noticed the lights because my battery works and I need it to work, I need to get to Scuppers now, the place I went with Supercunt. It's the only joint in town, really, this time of year and I go in and the first thing I notice are the tall chairs at the bar, brown as opposed to the white leather chairs at the Bellagio. And two chairs are of particular interest to me because one contains Jessica Salinger, the other has the friend I was banking on, and there is plenty of room for me at the bar.

It's quiet—some fucking Sade in the background; really, Rhode Island?—and I have no competition. There are two other dudes here, construction workers I think, they're both wearing rings, more interested in the news than the girls. There's no band to get in the way of things and tease the young girls, there's no crowd, not even with all the excitement involving *the dead girl.* New Englanders are stingy and they hibernate at night, as if going out makes you into some kind of whore.

Of course I am not gonna go for Jessica Salinger. That would be too creepy since I was just at their house today. I have to put the moves on the friend, the one I knew she'd be out with, because girls like Jessica *always* have a friend around, and she's always a little shorter, a little more drunk, a little more down to earth, literally. This friend is tapping her straw and removing it from her cocktail. This friend is bored. This friend is gonna be mine. Easy.

It's been so long since I hit on a girl in a bar, but I know how it works. All you do is stare into the girl's face, reflected in the mirror ahead. You let her friend notice you staring. You don't look away. She meets your gaze in the mirror and you crack up and you apologize—

it's so good to start with *sorry*—and you tell her that you didn't mean to stare but you couldn't help it.

"You're just so gorgeous," I say. "And I don't mean that in a creepy douche kind of way and I'm not gonna try and pick you up when I see you're very clearly here with your friend."

And then I take all my marbles away and flag the bartender and order a *gimlet*—I want to know why Forty was so into them—and now the girl puts her hand on my arm. "What's your name?"

"Brian," I say. Like Brian from Cabo. "Brian Stanley."

"Well," she says. "I'm Dana and this is my girlfriend Jessica. Are you here by yourself?"

"Yeah," I say. "What about you girls? Are you here by yourselves?"

Jessica rolls her eyes and this is exactly what I want. My gimlet comes. I sip. I ask Dana what she's doing here and she tells me she's here to provide moral support for her friend Jessica. Jessica is feeling more invisible by the second—it won't be long now—and I sip my gimlet slowly. Dana is Jessica's roommate in New York and Dana is a first-year law student and Dana loves this cute little town and Dana loves this song and she loves this bar and Jessica does not love being a third wheel. She stands. "Do you guys mind if I get out of here?"

I apologize—I am Mr. Manners—and Dana says she should go and Jessica says that's ridiculous. She says she's tired. Dana doesn't know how she'll get home. "It's not like New York where you can just call a cab," she says. "No, I should go."

Jessica says she'll be in the car. Jessica Salinger has no use for me. I tell Dana it's unorthodox and presumptuous but I *could* give her a lift home if she wanted to stay.

"Thank you," she says. "But I don't even know you."

"Yeah," I say. "I'm sorry. I wasn't trying to . . ."

Two hours later, Dana is a teetering drunk girl and she's in good hands with me. I help her out of the bar. I open the car door for her. "Just like *Say Anything*!" she says.

I start the car. This is it. I'll have to keep up the gentleman act and escort her into the Salinger house. And she's so drunk, she won't be able to make it up the stairs alone. "So," I say. "Where am I taking you?"

"Ugh," she says. "Hang on. I have to find the address in my phone."

I almost fuck up and tell her I already know the address. But she unlocks her phone—1267—and she bites her lip and she scrolls through her e-mail. "Got it," she says. "Thirty-two Starboard Way."

My head snaps up. That's not Peach's address. "Are you sure?"

She raises her phone and shows me the Airbnb page and I am fucked. A whole night wasted. "I usually stay with Jess and her family," she says. "But they have some crazy shit going on right now. Did you see the news about the girl who they think was *killed* here? That was her cousin."

"Really," I say. And I look both ways and I use my blinker and I curse Tinder. "That's some scary shit."

When I escort Dana into her Airbnb, she tries to kiss me. I tell her I'm sorry. "I'm getting over someone," I say. "I'm really sorry. I just can't now, you know?"

Dana gets it. She says she's been there. But she has no fucking idea. I go back to my shitty motel. I should have gotten an Airbnb.

47

I go down to breakfast the next morning and why in the fuck would I ever want to make my own waffles? Do I look Belgian? I itch and I think my room has bedbugs. And the number one thing I did not miss about the East Coast: the *humidity*. After the brisk chill of yesterday, Little Compton, Rhode Island, is suddenly in the midst of an unplanned natural event they call *Indian summah!* The girl at the front desk beams, sunburnt, small-minded: "Didja come heeah foah the Indian summah? It's a wicked pissah!"

I came here to get my *mugofurine*, thank you very much, and my hole in the wall is a fetid hot zone of bacteria, I know it, and this morning when I showered, I felt like I wasn't alone. I feel very cramped in here, as if my civil liberties have been chopped up by the bitch at the front desk, by the eleven-year-old kid who cut in front of me in the waffle line.

I am nervous. The kid's fat dad whistles. "I think you're beeping."

I yank the top of the waffle iron and my waffle is blackened and there is a long line; it would be a dick move to make another. I remove my raw-on-the-inside, black-on-the-outside freebie carb from the old machine and stick it onto a plate that is sticky, that clearly didn't make it into the dishwasher. There are kids everywhere, talk of water parks and a drive-in an hour out and isn't it *October*? What are all these people doing here? I didn't anticipate the crowds, the talk of blueberry syrup and gas prices, the *New England* of it all. The coffee is weak—no shit, Sherlock, I know—and the dad plops a waffle onto my plate.

"You look like you could use a lift," he says, and he winks and it is a kind world, a fair world. I need my energy. I eat the waffle and I drink the coffee and then I do a drive-by at Peach's house. It's more crowded today than it was yesterday and I can't go anywhere near it now that I fucked up with my special delivery and Jessica Salinger thinks my name is Brian. Is someone finding that mug of piss right now? I get out of the car. A couple of old ladies are power walking.

The skinny one: "And you know apparently she was a *lezzie*."

The skinnier one: "Do they think that awful mother of hers might have killed her? You know I wouldn't put it past her."

The skinny one: "She's putting on weight."

The skinnier one: "She shouldn't be going around in those flats. She needs lift."

At least Peach didn't come from one of those happy families where nobody can conceive of anyone in the family committing a crime. New Englanders like murder as much as they enjoy the music of Taylor Swift and the antics of the Kennedys. I want to hear more parking lot banter so I go to town, where it's more crowded.

I enter the Art Café and Gallery and immediately I know this was a mistake. Heads turn. Elderly locals bemoan the *nosy New Yorkers sniffing around* and look me up and down. Were it not for my California tan I'd probably be strung up on the flagpole outside but fortunately there is a distraction. A flock of grown men in spandex enter, *cyclists*, and they are regulars here and they are welcome and I am invisible again. I purchase a coffee. I wrestle with the bad pump on the milk dispenser and a cyclist advises me to hit it once, hard. It works. My luck is turning.

"Thanks," I say. I look at him and my luck is turning back again, the way every session at a blackjack table eventually concludes with the dealer making twenty-one. Luke Skywalker knows that he might die in battle and Eminem knows that he might get too choked up to make rhymes and I, Joe Goldberg, know that when I fly to Rhode Island and reenter my bad place, Little Fucking Compton, it is possible that I might wander into a store, let my guard down, and find myself face to face with the cop I met on my first visit. Yes, it's Officer Nico, in purple spandex and a blue helmet. Already, his eyes are narrowing.

"I know you," he says.

And he does. He knows me as Spencer Hewitt, the boy he found in the boathouse next to the Salingers' after he crashed his car. He knows my Figawi hat. He is going to remember me and he's going to remember that cold December night. He might even read the file on Peach Salinger and realize that she disappeared right around the same time as that Hewitt kid was freezing in that boathouse.

I take a step backward. "Thanks for the milk. I owe ya one."

He is unperturbed. "I never forget a face," he says. "Hold on."

The other cyclists need milk, too and he motions for me to follow him outside—Indian summer!—and even off-duty, he has the authority of an *officer of the law.* He is the reason that Robin Fincher never should have made it through police academy and he is biting his lip and taking the lid off his coffee.

"Do you live around here?" he asks.

"No," I say. "I'm just up from Boston."

He is as kind as I remember and I wonder if he ever fucked that nurse in the hospital in Fall River who seemed so into him. The other cyclists are trickling out onto the lawn and they are dullards mostly, white dentists, they want their black cop buddy back. I raise my hand to make my escape and raising my hand sparks Officer Nico's memory and that's right, this is *New England* where people watch because they like to watch, where memories are intact, primed because the people here are not bogged down by *aspirations.* The only thing Nico aspires to do is save the fucking world and he snaps his fingers.

"The Buick," he says. "You were that kid, poor kid, you totaled that Buick."

The cyclists are interested now and I am a part of this world in the worst possible way. If I lie, if I say that wasn't me, Nico will know it. He's a real cop.

"That's *you*?" I say, and I put my coffee down and move to shake his hand. "You saved my life."

Never mind the absurdity of me, a white guy who passed through the whitest place in America in the dead of white winter not remembering the very black officer who found me in a boathouse and drove me to a hospital. I am fucked. Or maybe not. Nico shakes my hand, solid. "I'm surprised you remember any of it," he says. "You were banged up."

"I remember the important parts," I assure him. "I didn't recognize you with your gear on. You guys all ride on the reg?"

Now I have included the dentists, provided them with the chance to tell an outsider about their weekly *rides* with their cop friend, their banal adventures, the dings with bad drivers, the roadkill, the time that Barry rode over that hose and fell and everyone is belly laughing, *oh, Barry.* Officer Nico is relaxed, involved in a few conversations, none about me. I am okay. I pulled it off. I will stay a while just to prove that I am at ease, and when one guy asks what brings me to their *sunny seaside hamlet* I don't hesitate.

"Indian summer," I say, and I call upon the amiable demeanor of Harvey Swallows. I open my arms. "Am I right or am I right?"

I am right and soon, it's time for the cyclists to move on. Nico waves good-bye; he hopes my stay this time around doesn't involve a trip to the emergency room. I knock on the table. He squints. "Son," he says. "That's a metal table."

He laughs and he goes and I find a birch tree. I knock.

I am still itchy. It could be psychosomatic. But it could be real. I might have picked something up from Dana. God knows what germs were crawling on me in Vegas, on the plane. I am uncomfortable in my skin in Little Compton. I never should have gone to the Art Café and I never should have come here. I strip the bed. I search for bedbugs and I don't find any. I flip the mattress but there is nothing wrong with the mattress. There is something wrong with me. Love lifts us up but it also makes us roam around Little Compton like we didn't murder the girl in the news.

I'm hungry. The motel doesn't offer a continental dinner and I am starving and marooned here, unable to will myself out the door for a Burger King run, too itchy to sleep, too potentially fucked to attempt to relax. If I can't get that mug of urine then the police will get that mug of urine. If the police run tests on that mug and connect the dots, I will go to prison, and I won't be able to get back to California and marry Love. I stop itching. I didn't realize that until now.

"I want to marry her," I say.

And suddenly I know what I'm doing here. I am being that person who runs away from love, the one who self-sabotages. I don't think I can sleep in this room, in this township, in this universe, and I drag the sheets into the bathroom, the only sterile vortex in this musty pit. I rankle at the sadness of it all, the granite countertops and the little shitty soaps, the non-organic shampoos. Love wouldn't want any of this and all I want is her.

I dump the sheets in the tub and I wash my hands and I hear a knock at the door. My heart races but the rest of my body freezes and I picture Officer Nico's face. I panic. There is another knock. It feels like the end. On the way to the door, I trip. I bump my knee against the bed. My body is protesting. I reach for the handle. Steeling myself, I swing the door open. But the person standing there isn't Officer Nico. It's someone worse.

Love.

48

LOVE'S arms are folded across her chest. "You said you left your lights on," she says. "But it was only five."

"Love," I say. "I can explain."

"I hope so," she says. "Because you should also know that *Pitch Perfect* is not, and never was, on Netflix."

She enters my room. "Anyone here?" she asks.

"No," I say. "I'm alone."

She looks at the stripped bed. "What's this all about? Destroying the evidence?"

"No," I say, and I can't keep up with her questions. "Love, let me explain."

She raises her voice. "Yoo-hoo! You can come out now?"

"Love," I say. "There's nobody here."

"You know, we all live in the world, Joe. You think I can't figure out that you *flew* to Rhode Island and rented a *car*? And I don't mean this is in the asshole way, but you know who my father is. His people couldn't find Forty because Forty knows how to hide. Because we grew up in this and we know how to disable our phones and pay with cash. But you think I can't find you? Jesus Christ. Where is she? Hello!"

"Love, please stop."

"No," she says. She is wearing a navy raincoat, bell-bottom blue jeans, and a shrunken pink sweater. I want to hug every part of her, even now, while she accuses me of cheating on her, especially now. She isn't going anywhere. She isn't afraid of me even though she knows I was lying, even though I disappeared on her while I said I was looking for her *brother*. She isn't the police. She is Love, which is why she is crying.

"Why won't you tell me things?" she says. "I tell you things but you—you shut down, you won't tell me the real deal. Why don't you tell me how you saw *Pitch Perfect*? Because no, Joe. You didn't see it randomly on Netflix. It's not *on* Netflix and even if it was, a lie just *feels* different. I know you know that. And I *think* about this shit, you know, in the middle of the night, when you're asleep, this is the kind of shit I think about. Why won't you tell me?"

"Love," I say, and I can't explain it but I want to tell her. I want her to know.

"You know," she says. "When you do stuff on your phone, I mean since the very beginning, like the whole time we've been together, I know you are *doing* something. Sometimes I think you have cancer. I actually console myself by thinking *he just has some disease and he's gonna die and he doesn't know how to tell me that I'm gonna get my heart broken.*"

"I don't have cancer," I assure her. But then I do; I have the *mugofurine*. It is a tumor spreading, malignant, infiltrating my love, my Love. She's still wearing her coat.

"I know you don't have cancer, Joe. That's the point. But I have to know what you have. I can't take it anymore. I have enough problems. I have a brother who disappears and a father who can't even pretend he wants him to come back and a mother who wishes he wasn't here in the first place. I can't do this." She is crying. I go to her but she doesn't want me. "No," she says. "You can't be in this with me if you won't be in this with me." She wipes her eyes. "What the fuck are you even *doing* here? Why are you in Rhode Island? Is my brother here? Who *are you*? Because I can't fucking ask you anymore. I can't ask you anymore."

"I'm sorry."

She's right. You can't be in love, not fully, not eternally, if you can't tell the truth. It builds up on you. She told me about fucking Milo in the Chateau. But how can I tell her my truth? I killed her brother. It's like the atomic version of that universal truth: you can talk shit about your mother, but nobody else can, no matter what you say, no matter what she does. I can't tell Love what I've been up to and to talk to her is to lie to her.

"I should just go. I don't know what I'm doing here."

I kneel at her feet. "Please stay."

"Why?"

"Because I love you."

She shakes her little head. "Love isn't enough, Joe. It isn't nearly enough. I want more."

"I know you do."

"I don't know what else to say," she says. "But I can't stand the way you make me feel so good, like, better than I ever felt, and then you tear it all away, like deep down, you don't want me to be happy."

"Of course I want you to be happy."

"Then tell me who you are. Tell me why you said you watched *Pitch Perfect* on Netflix."

"Love," I say, and if we were married, if I had let her go with me to Vegas and we had eloped, she would not be able to testify against me in a court of law. But we are not married and the justice system does not acknowledge relationships like ours. I want to marry this girl. I want to stay with this girl. I want our ashes mixed, our crumbling bodies buried side by side. I want her to know how badly I want that. I don't want to live without her. I don't want to let go of her. If she leaves me, what then?

"So that's all you have to say. That's fine. Fine." She sounds cold and she is inching away from me. "Joe," she says. "It's over."

I look up at her. This is like *Homeland* when he's going to cut a wire and the bomb might explode. I might kill us, everything we have. But maybe I can live with that because without her, I will die. I know it. I accept that she might hit me, call me names, run to the cops. This could be the end. But this could also be the beginning.

When you get baptized, you fall back into the water, your entire body. Some people hold their noses. Some people don't. But there is no way around it; you have to get wet if you want to be in God's hands.

I take Love's hands. I choose love. I accept risk. I breathe. I speak. "The first time I saw *Pitch Perfect* was when I broke into a girl's apartment."

WHEN I am done, when I have told her everything—everything but Forty, of course—she just sits there. The minutes tick by and her face gives me nothing, the way Matt Damon's face never looks all that fucked up when he's being Jason Bourne.

I think about what I've done, about how it all must seem to her. I did not do that thing where you leave out the grotesque details to make yourself seem like some kind of unstained, impervious hero. I told her how I stole Beck's phone and strangled Peach on the beach. I told her about the blood of *The Da Vinci Code* in Beck's mouth when she slipped away, how I buried her upstate. I told her about the mug of piss.

I gave her as much as I had, but it's like the difference between a movie and a book: A book lets you choose how much of the blood you want to see. A book gives you the permission to see the story as you want, as your mind directs. You interpret. Your Alexander Portnoy doesn't look like mine because we all have our own unique view. When you finish a movie you leave the theater with your friend and talk about the movie right away. When you finish a book you think. Love grew up on movies and I have just read her a book. I give her the time to digest.

I am preparing for the worst, for Love's face to change, for her to run out of here screaming. In a funny way, all the women in my life helped me brace for this moment. My mother. Beck. Amy. Women leave me, and Love will leave me. She has to. She believes in love and decorates her home with it, carries it on her passport, in her heart. She is going to walk out of this room and feel like she's done it again, chosen the wrong man, blown those other two out of the saltwater infinity pool we'll never go in again.

I've never opened up like this, never said it all out loud before, and I hold my knees to my chest and tell myself that what happens next is out of my control. I can't make Love love me. But I did the right thing. I told her what she wanted to know. I stopped lying.

The wait is eternal, and her eyes are fixed on a stain on the floor. I think of all the people who stayed in this room before and wonder if any of them have been like me.

And then, finally, she looks up.

"Okay," she says. "I'm gonna tell you about Roosevelt."

Roosevelt was a puppy they had when they were babies. Forty named him. She didn't know why then, doesn't know why now. "He's weird that way," she says, as if he's still alive. "I mean, what six-year-old calls a puppy Roosevelt? And also, it's not like he was precocious and into politics or whatever. He just liked the word Roosevelt."

"It's a good name," I say.

She ignores me. "Anyway," she says. "Roosevelt disappeared. And we looked everywhere and put up signs and all that. But then Forty woke me up in the middle of the night and he took me outside and showed me that Roosevelt wasn't missing. He was dead."

"Oh dear."

She looks at me. She holds my hands. Now she is the one who's not blinking, staring at me directly. "He tied Roosevelt to the wall," she says. "He was mad at him because he kept wanting to sleep in my room instead of Forty's. So he punished him. He starved him and muzzled him."

"Love," I say. I've never harmed an animal; I can't imagine being that sort of monster. "Jesus Christ."

She takes her hands away. "You have no idea what it is to be twinned with someone who does things like that."

Her voice quavers when she says *things like that* and Roosevelt is not alone; there are other crimes, I'm sure. "Love," I say. "I'm so sorry."

"So it's like this," she says. "I love that fucking sicko. I know he is demented and I know he tied a dog to a wall but you know what? I didn't tell anyone. And you know what else? Fuck that dog for ignoring him. Fuck that Monica for bailing on him for that *loser* friend of yours and fuck all the girls who act like there's something defective about him, who don't even pretend they want his money. Fuck my parents for not even *pretending* to think he's talented and fuck Milo for being better at everything. Fuck everyone who's, like, *who was born first, you or Milo* and fuck people who are never surprised when I'm like, *I was born first* because they're like, *of course you were, you seem so together.* Fuck everyone, Joe. I mean, I will defend my fucked-up brother all day long because life isn't fair. It isn't. Roosevelt *cried* when Forty tried to hold him and Forty was the one who wanted Roosevelt in the first place. Who makes a world like that? Where you can't hate anyone because ultimately everyone has some god-awful fucking thing they put up with and you have no way of knowing what it is exactly. I mean he's got to be Forty but I've got to be his fucking sister. Who has it worse?" She shakes her head. "Tell me. Who has the right to hate anyone?"

Love is breathing heavily. It's clear she's never talked about this to anyone; you know when someone is opening up a box so private that there isn't a key.

She looks at me. "All I know is how to love," she says. "So I can deal with you."

"Ouch."

She takes my hand. "That's a compliment," she assures me. "This is why I hate it when people keep getting married like it's so simple. It's not. Finding someone who gets you is special."

I kiss the back of her hand. "What kind of dog was it?"

"Golden," she says. "Roosevelt was a golden."

"I love you, Love."

"I love you," she says.

I flinch when a car brakes outside, the screech. I'm still nervous, still can't quite believe it.

She smiles. "Look, Joe, I wouldn't have come here if I didn't know that it might be bad."

"Bad," I repeat.

She squeezes my hand. "This is it for me. In this messed-up way, I feel like this will work. You did all those awful things, but you also fell in love with a person who can forgive you."

"I don't know what to say," I say, and I think of six-year-old Love staring at that dead puppy.

"Joe," she says, and my name belongs to her now. There's more. She says she knew when Trey died that if she ever found anyone again, it would be forever and she looks at the floor and then she looks at me. "I'm pregnant."

Did I hear that right? "Pregnant?"

Yes, I heard that right. "Pregnant!"

Now there is permanence between us and it means her forgiveness is whole. True. If she were afraid of me on any level, she would have run out of this room and never told me about the baby, our baby.

And then it hits me. We're gonna have a baby! We're laughing and I'm kissing her belly and she's telling me about taking the test—it's early—and she had to come tell me in person and she's glad she did.

"Me too," I say. This baby is great equalizing force between us, the definition of the future. No matter what I did, a part of me is inside of Love. It's the most beautiful thing in the world and Love and I are fixed, locked together, our genes intertwining, a little human, part me, part her, wholly triumphant. Watching Love doze off, I feel love like I have never have before.

"Sweet dreams," I say, and I kiss the place between Love's slumbering breasts, the hardness above her heart.

I go into the bathroom and turn on the shower and the cramped stall feels larger to me somehow. The whole world feels bigger now that someone else knows everything, someone who loves me. I understand why Peach Salinger was in such a dark place. Beck knew her. She did not love her.

I turn off the shower and tear the curtain aside, but I when I try the door, it is stuck. I didn't lock it and it locks from the inside and I don't understand. I push the door but it won't budge. Alarm bells go off and I try the knob again but the door is clearly blocked from the outside. I panic. I bang on the door. I call out to Love and hurl my body against the door. No answer. She trapped me in here and she probably invented Roosevelt and our baby and all that empathy just so she could safely get away from me. It worked.

49

I am a monster now. I live in the white, tacky bathroom and I am a monkey on steroids. I know I can't get out but still I pound into the door. I use my body and I am bruised. I am blue. I am black. I am swollen. When my ribs won't stop stinging I use my feet. I kick. I have broken the shower stall and I have torn the lid off the toilet. I have screamed help and it's a shitty motel and someone must hear me. The people below, if there are people below, they don't care. I run the shower and the water and when it's cold it stings my wounds and when it's hot it scalds me. There is no love for me in Little Compton and I knew this going in and that's the thought that drives me to my feet, which are streaked with blood. I slam into the door. Bad Joe. *Gently, Joseph,* Mr. Mooney used to caution me when I was a boy, when there was hope. Was there ever hope?

I don't know. *Bam* goes my torso and that time I think an organ moved. I will not use the shattered glass from that shitty mirror to kill myself. I want to go out with a BANG and I drive my other side into the door. The door is my enemy, stronger, more powerful, always ready for me, always locked, always hard, always NO. I breathe. I do cry.

There is no baby. I know that now. The Corinthians tell you that love is patient and kind, but Love is also smart. She is older, wiser. She was married twice. She knows things. She knows men. She knew how to win my trust. And now she is with the police.

I'm stupid. I teach and I teach and I test and I test, and yet I'm the one who never learns. I choose wrong every time. I see my mother in her Nirvana shirt, the one Beck is buried in, and somehow it is there, the way you can do that in a dream, in a nightmare. *BAM.* I hurl myself into the door and my mother is only betting five dollars at the five-dollar minimum blackjack table in Florida, New Jersey, does it matter where? She is laughing and she likes Forty and he is laughing and I did this. I came here. I told Love all of it and now I don't get to have love and I don't know how to stand. My feet don't work. Bad feet. Bad Joe. *Gently, Joseph.* I jiggle the handle. I slap the handle. I can't break the handle. I try. I pull. I push. I fall back and hit the toilet and I flush it and I listen to the water go away and come back and I am not like that. I am not coming back from this.

I breathe and I see Beck, in the ground, smiling, clawing her way out, the *Mona Lisa*, smiling, can a skeleton smile? Does it matter? She says to Amy *omigod I need a drink, that was so crazy, I need to tweet that shit now.* She is gone into the woods and I am here in the bathroom. The ceiling has a yellow stain. I can't reach it. I tried.

I am not going to leave the bathroom. I am not going to be a dad. I am going to die in here because I was dumb. I believed her. *Don't date an actress*, Mr. Mooney said, and Love is an actress. I wonder if she recorded me and I wonder how I sound and I wonder how long it takes to die and I liked it better when I was *BAM* going into the door but there is so much pain now and it's hard to move. My skin is the sky in a storm, squalls of black and blue and white, and the red is hot and I know it's the end of the world. I close my eyes. I bleed for Little Compton. I am nobody's father. I am a killer and I'm going to jail and there is no love in my life, not anymore.

Will they let me watch *The Third Twin* and *The Mess* in prison? Will Mr. Mooney give me advice? Will they let me choose where I see my time? Will they put me in the electric chair and will the food be as bad as it looks in *Locked Up* on CNN? Will I work out or get scrawny? Will I be in Wikipedia? Will they give me a nickname in the media? JoeBro? TaxiDriver? Old Sport? The Professor? Loverboy?

Will there be a trial that drags on for months and will Dez bury his bricks under his bed and take his Dodgers cap off and shake his head and quiet Little D and tell *Dateline* that I was *kind of shady, not a bro*? Will Harvey be on IMDb if he's on Deadline talking about how I was never late with rent? Will Calvin cry alone in his bed but laugh about it with other people and use his connection to me as way to seduce Tinder whores?

I cry out: "Help!" I punch the door. My hand bleeds.

Will the LAPD send someone on the inside to beat the life out of me? Will my *Love Actually Revolutionary Road* directorial debut on Funny or Die go viral now that my name will be out there? Will I be famous?

Will Officer Nico be on the local news in front of the bullshit coffee art house with his spandex crew in the background, telling them all about running into me here and our drive to the hospital in Fall River last winter? Will the doctor who treated me at the hospital last winter see it all on the news and shake his head in disgust? Or will he not even remember me because of how many patients he sees every day, because I was just some guy, it's not like I was someone he knew, someone he cared about. I drive my body into the door again and again I get nowhere.

It goes without saying that Milo is, by now, on a jet headed out this way, wearing a *Wianno* T-shirt and watching an early cut of *Boots and Puppies* and speculating on how much time needs to pass before he puts the moves on Love. Is he drinking or is he so fucking happy to have me out of the picture and be the knight in fading pastels that he doesn't even need to drink?

Will Dr. Nicky's wife take him back when they let him out of prison? Will he disclose details of our therapy sessions? I charge the door, elbows and ribs. Nothing but pain.

Love. Will I ever be inside her again? Will Love ever love and trust again or will her open heart and her beating vagina be the worst casualties of my capture? The worst loss?

I bring my ear to the door. A new sound. I am still. A plastic keycard unlocking the door. The door closing. My heart is too loud. Fuck the question. Fuck the police. Fuck Love. I will plow. When this door opens, no other door will close on me ever again and I stand guard. I prepare. I have my hand on the doorknob. When the cops so much as even start to unlock, I will pull back. I will fight. I will go.

I hear them take away the bureau that Love used to keep the door closed and they are here. This is it. I feel the doorknob start to turn and I pray to God that he is with me—this is how that happens, how you find God in jail—and I roar and I yank the door and it's . . . Love. I stop.

She covers her mouth. “No,” she says. “What happened to you?”

I swallow. “I fell.”

“You fell hard, huh?” She steps toward me and kisses my chest. She looks up at me and I was wrong.

I think I smile. I don’t know. My face hurts. My body pulsates in different places. “You locked me in.”

“I know,” she says. “I’m so sorry. I just knew you would try to stop me and I wanted to make sure you were safe. And, well . . .” She trails off.

And that’s when I notice how different she looks, like Halloween, with painted pink lips and Jennifer Lopez hair pulled back in a high bun. She wears her trench coat and beneath, a dress with every pastel color in the rainbow smushed together, overlapping in flowers. Then she reaches into her coat and she is a magician pulling a rabbit out of a hat. It’s the mug from the Salinger house. It’s bluer than I remember and I would know it anywhere and it’s dry and it’s in my hands, my freedom, the traces of my urine grainy and visible in the interior.

50

I wanted to get the fuck out of Little Compton and I do have a morbid curiosity about Brown University because of Guinevere Beck and it's so strange, to speak *openly* of these things. Love parks near campus and it looks like you'd think, like an Ivy League school, an idyllic setting with trees and old buildings. On Thayer Street, the main drag on this campus, there are a few bars, a University Bookstore, an Urban Outfitters, and a fucking Starbucks—America is America is America—and we duck into a Greek restaurant that is more New England charm than it is Orthodox baklava. Love orders chicken and salad and I'm starving. I feel like I just got out of prison. I order calamari and spanakopita and leg of lamb and moussaka and Love laughs. "Do you need to order some food with your food?"

I swat her hand. "Watch it, Mom."

She does a happy dance and says her mind is blown and I tell her we have to talk about our baby but first she wants to tell me how she got the fucking mug.

"All right," she says. Deep breath and she begins, so much more articulate than her brother. Her first order of business was to do a drive-by and stake out the Salingers to get their *vibe.* She then drove all the way to a boutique in Newport for new clothes. "I needed a Lilly Pulitzer dress," she says.

"What's that?"

"That pink-and-green thing I was wearing," she explains.

Love then beat it back to Little Compton and parked at the Salinger house and put on *big fat Chanel sunglasses* and stormed past reporters, past cops. She burst in the Salinger house. She started sobbing.

"I mean, I guess I *do* kind of like acting," she admits. "But I still don't want to do it professionally."

"What did they do?" I ask. "What did you even say?"

"I told them I was Peach's lover, of course," she says. She is proud. Our calamari arrives. She grabs a tentacle, pops it into her perfect little mouth. "I did a whole monologue about our secret love and New York and all this stuff about the way she wouldn't let me meet her family or come out for real and I mean I went *off* and told them I knew she didn't kill herself. I knew she'd *never* kill herself and if you ask me, it was that fucking titty tease Guinevere Beck."

"You did not say titty tease."

She dips squid into cocktail sauce. "Maybe I did," she says. "Maybe I didn't. I mean I was so *in it*, you know?"

"Jesus," I say.

I have yet to eat any calamari and Love licks her fingers and tells me how *amazingly uptight New England Puritanical bullshit* it was. "This is where I am such a Cali girl to the bone," she says. "We don't care, you know? We're like, do whatever. Chill out. Be gay. Be straight. I mean, what is the big deal? We're all gonna die anyway, you know? Who wants to spend their precious life hating?"

I understand now the depth of Love's love for me. I have unlocked some cauldron of confidence inside of her. No longer is she content to sit low in a dark room and watch the monitor. Love is *alive* and she feels more connected to me than she does to her brother. Listen to her talk about her scam and there is not *one* mention of Forty and she credits me with this newfound freedom, here in the Greek restaurant.

The rest of our food arrives. We eat it. All of it.

Love continues her story. She says she dug deep. Her inspirational performances were Rosalind Russell in *Auntie Mame* and Goldie Hawn in *The First Wives Club*. "I knew one thing," she said. "These people, who hate gay people and who essentially hated their own *family member* for being gay, they don't want to think about her grinding on me. They don't want to think about *any* of it. I mean, maybe they go to a benefit once a year and tolerate it, but they don't want this fucking *preppy lesbo* in their house crying over Peach's beautiful body."

She drinks her water and continues. She told them to let it go, all of it, because you can't prosecute the dead. She said that Peach was *incontrovertibly in love with Guinevere Beck* and that Beck for sure killed her.

"See," she says. "The magic of this is that they won't even *breathe* a word to anyone, because they don't want Peach to be gay, let alone be murdered by a gay chick, you know?"

"That's kind of brilliant," I say.

She nods.

Our baklava arrives. I dig in and give her the first bite. "Mm," she says. And she is happy. "You should have seen their faces, Joe. I was like, 'I just need to go upstairs and be in our bed for a moment.'"

"*Our bed.*"

She nods. She opens her mouth. I stuff flaky Greek pastry inside of her and I can't wait to fuck her. "That's also pretty brilliant."

"And then, obviously, I knew there was no *way* any one of them was coming upstairs to see what the preppy lesbo was doing up there, so I went room to room and I found the mug and tucked it into my Kate Spade purse and then I went downstairs and offered to make a statement to the police about my relationship with Peach."

I choke. "Holy shit," I say. "That's hysterical."

"Yes," she says. "They almost lost it, then helped me leave out the *back door* and asked if I wouldn't mind going back to my car from the public parking lot. You know, so it can feel like none of this ever happened."

"Brilliant," I say. "But there's one problem."

She wipes her cheeks with her napkin. "What's that?"

"When *Boots and Puppies* comes out . . ."

She rolls her eyes. "You mean when it's dumped on Netflix."

"Either way," I say. "They're going to recognize you."

"Who the fuck cares? I never said who I was or how I knew Peach, and I can say I am bi or something. I don't care. The girl is dead and we were secret lovers. What can you ever do about that?"

There is no more baklava left and I get a Google alert and the Salingers are preparing to ask the Little Compton Police Department to stop the investigation for *personal family reasons that have come to light.* There is light, fluttering Greek guitar on the stereo and the goblets on all the tables are New England blue. My belly is full. My love is real.

"We should talk baby stuff," I say. "I don't know the first thing."

"You seem to know how to make 'em pretty good."

I know what she wants and I want it too and we pay the check and sneak into the bathroom and it's the strongest sex we've ever had.

Outside, we pass the Brown Bookstore and college kids walk and we are so lucky to be older. They are all either drunk or nervous and I can't imagine having *homework.* I put my arm around Love and she pulls me tighter.

"Should we get one of those *What to Expect* books?" I ask.

Love says yes but holds up a finger. Her dad is calling. "Hi, Daddy," she says, and it hits me. Someday my child will call me and say that, *hi, Daddy.*

The crosswalk turns white. It's our turn to go. But we don't go. Love trembles. "Daddy, Daddy, wait," she says. "One second." She puts her hand over the phone. She looks like she's had a stroke and her face is a battlefield. Her muscles spasm.

"Are you okay?"

"Joe," she says. "They found him. They found Forty! He's alive!"

I hear her dad faintly coming through the phone, *Love! Love!*

And now I feel like I'm having a stroke, but I have to fake it or else I'll seem like a psycho and I grin and pull her into a hug. "Yes!"

We run back to the car, no books for us, no time. Forty's alive. Alive! I may as well be back in that bathroom hurling my body at the door. He's alive. *How?* I picture a couple of shrooming college kids imitating *Boyhood* and roaming the desert, finding the hot springs. *He's alive.* I picture one spotting the body, unsure if it was a hallucination or if the body was real.

She tells me it's a miracle. "Some girl found him and he's in a hospital in Reno and he's fine." She smacks her lips. "He's fine. This is *so* Forty, just like the time he disappeared in *Russia*."

"Reno?" I say.

Love nods. "Apparently this girl found him in the desert, I don't know where. She picked him up, he was passed out, dehydrated, and she brought him to the hospital and they put him on an IV and he's gonna be fine."

It's the worst diagnosis in the world. And I am not gonna be fine. I am fucked. I think of my acting manuals. I must not ask questions. Love unlocks the car. "The guy has nine lives," she says. "And I mean *phew*."

"I can't wait to talk to him," I say.

"Well, you will," she says. "My dad says he's talking up a storm."

"That's crazy," I observe, in my peppiest voice.

"Right?" she asks. "I mean, of course he doesn't remember a damn thing about how he got there and his last memory is at the Bellagio but, you know, that's my brother."

We drive to the airport. We don't talk about our baby. We just gush over Forty. And this is my fault. I did not check for a pulse. I did not finish my job. In spite of everything I've learned from the mug of piss, I didn't put that knowledge into action. I'm like an asshole in a sitcom who learns the same fucking lesson every week and this is my *life*.

My phone buzzes. It's Forty:

See you soon, Professor.

51

IT'S a long flight to Reno. I pretend to read *Mr. Mercedes* and we talk intermittently about the baby but mostly it's all about Forty. Love shares the good news on Facebook and writes back to various worried friends. Love e-mails with her mom about whether or not he needs rehab. The answer is no. Ha.

I don't mention Roosevelt; it's like our conversation never happened. It is unbearable, the way she smiles about him surviving, the way he sits in a room in Reno, conscious, aware that I am the one who put him there, who left him in the hot water to die.

We arrive in Reno and there is a car waiting for us at the airport and the driver says it won't be long until we get to the hospital and I pray for a crash or an earthquake on the inside and I deserve an Oscar because I'm so good.

Love says we shouldn't tell anyone about the baby just yet and I say okay and my prayers are unanswered when we reach the fourth floor. The building doesn't crumble or shake and I can already hear him in the room, loud, cognizant, on the phone. "Reese is interested? That's bananas!"

I smell hand sanitizer and chicken broth as we walk toward his room. Love squeezes my hand. "Yay!"

"Yay!" I say.

Dottie steps into the hallway and does a double take. "Lovey!" she says.

Love runs to her and they hug and I stand in the hall trying not to stare into the room where an old man screams *help me.* Dottie whistles. I hug Dottie as Love disappears into Forty's room. My heart pounds. "You feel hot," Dottie says. She puts her hand on my forehead. "Are you sick?"

"No," I say. "It's just the desert, I guess."

"Well," she says, linking her arm through mine. "We *have* to talk. Forty has the most wonderful idea about what we can do with you."

Murdermefeedmealivetodogstrapmedrownmeinapoolintheoceantiemeup-starveme

"Really?" I say. "What, um, what did you two have in mind and, my God, how is he?"

"Come see for yourself," she says, and leads me into Forty's room. Music plays and trays of food abound and Ray must have brought his own chair because he's in a recliner and Forty sits up in bed laughing with Milo, who sits in the other bed.

I walk toward Forty Quinn and he meets my eyes and he smiles. "There he is," he says. "Good to see you, Old Sport. Have a seat if you can. Settle in for story hour."

Ray stands, yawns. "I don't think I need to hear it again," he says. And whatever the story is, it's bullshit and Ray would rather leave than go on indulging his son. Dottie takes the recliner and Love joins Forty in his bed. I sit in a shitty, hospital-issued folding chair.

"Well," Forty says. "The first thing you guys have to understand about me, going forward, is that I'm a *writer.*"

I might vomit. "Okay."

Forty takes a pompous breath. "What this means, is that writers write. We shut off our phones. We take off. We get lost in the *narrative.* You guys, I know I have pulled some crazy shit in the past, but that was then. This is now. Now I'm a working writer, which means I didn't wanna fucking stay in LA and rest on my laurels and pat myself on the back. I wanted to hunker down in a quiet hotel room and *think* and *do* and *make.*"

Dottie moans. "Sweetie, I'm on your side and I love you. But you could have called."

Love: "Mom! *Enough.*"

Forty: "And next time I will call. I was just dying to start in on a new script because that's how this town is. You're only as good as what you've got coming up."

Milo now with an *amen, brother.* I might faint.

"What were you writing?" Love asks.

He looks at me now, intently. He smiles. "Another kidnapping story," he says. "I pretty much sold it in the room at Paramount a while back, but they got cold feet and now that I'm a thing, you know, they want in again. So I promised them I'll have a script soon."

Love is perplexed. "Well, how the hell did you wind up in the desert? Mom says you're starting to remember more? That a girl found you?"

My heart pounds. He looks up at the TV. "I went on a walkabout," he says. "I needed to do research. Sometimes, you just have to get out there and see shit if you want to write about it, you know? If you want to write about the outer reaches of the desert, where there's nobody around, you have to see it."

Maybe I could get a nurse to kill him and why can't anyone ask what we all want to ask: Where is the new script? He can't explain what happened to his computer or his notes because he didn't bring notes and a computer. He brought cash and coke.

My brain hurts. My palms sweat. "Who found you?"

He smiles. "That's the thing, Old Sport," he says. "It's all kind of a blur. One minute, I'm sitting in the buffet, giving five grand to a couple of newlywed kids who look like they can't afford to eat in a real restaurant"—FUCKING LIAR—"and the next minute, boom"—MOTHERFUCKING LIAR—"I'm in the desert and this blond girl." He sighs. He flails. "I just got a flash of her."

Dottie runs across the room. "What did you see?"

"A sweatshirt," he says.

Dottie pleads with Forty—*try, try to remember*—but he can't remember anything. All he can see is the girl, her shirt.

"And then I woke up here," he says. "Splat."

Love kisses his hand. "We need to give *her* five thousand dollars."

"We can't," Forty says. "She's gone. The nurses say she took off. She didn't even come in. They found me outside."

Dottie starts to cry and Milo puts an arm around her. Love asks Forty how the staff has been here and he says *it's not the Ritz* and he looks at me and asks how *I've been.* I look him dead in the eye: "Worried about you," I say.

"We were *so* scared," Dottie says, and she stands. A nurse appears and says she can come back later when everyone is gone and Love runs after her and it's just me and Milo and Forty and Dottie, who is pacing, worked up, wrung out, hands on hips. Imagine how well I would have done had I had a mother like this, the kind who cares, the kind who is here, no makeup, bags under her eyes from worrying. "Well, remember this," she says. "You can't write *anything* if you're dead and your father and I need to know where you are."

"I'm thirty-five years old," he says. "Where does it end?"

"Not in a desert!" she says, and now she is sobbing. Forty crumples up a paper towel and throws it at Milo. He points toward the door.

Milo obliges. "Come on, Dot," he says. "Let's go for a walk."

"Joe can stay here with me, right, Old Sport?" Forty offers.

I feel myself being murdered, slowly, the way they used to drain the blood out of people. "Sure thing," I say. "You guys take a break."

Dottie kisses her son on the head. "Don't make it so hard for me," she says. "I love you. Daddy loves you. Let us love you. Let us be there."

"Mom," he says. "It was a few days."

Milo ushers Dottie out of the room and when they're gone I turn to Forty. "Shut it," he says. "First the door, then your mouth."

I get up and walk to the door and I close the door and I return to my shitty chair. He does not encourage me to sit in the recliner and he does not suggest I get in the bed. He points to the chair next to the bed. "Here," he says. "I'm suffering from exhaustion and dehydration and I don't need to be yelling."

I sit in my chair. On the muted television, *The Cosby Show* begins. Forty opens a drawer in the tray table and pulls out two open bags of M&M's. He reaches into one for candy. He reaches into the other bag for pills. *Fucking Forty.* He pops a bottle of *Veuve.* He pours his apple juice onto the floor, as if he's in a parking lot and he pours champagne into his cup.

I don't want to be the first to speak, but I can't help it. "Is that gonna help with your dehydration?"

"No," he says. "It won't help with my exhaustion either, but it's fine. I'm not the one with work to do."

I look at him. "Did you call the cops?"

He ignores my question. He looks at the TV. He laughs, demented fucking sicko. "I love this episode," he says. "You know this one, right, where Theo wants the fucking shirt? Never gets old. He wants that shirt. His fucking know-it-all dad wants him to *work* for that shirt and his sister tries to make him the shirt at home but at the end of the day, the only way to get that fucking shirt is to pony up and buy it."

"Forty," I say. "Maybe we can talk."

He snaps and throws an M&M at me. It hits my nose. "You fucker. You left me in the desert, in the middle of fucking nowhere."

"I'm sorry."

"I could have died."

"I know, I'm sorry."

"*Maybe we can talk*?" He pours M&M's into this mouth. "Maybe you can go fuck yourself."

"Did you call the cops?"

"None of your business," he says.

"Look," I say. "Obviously, we're both upset."

He is exasperated. "Did you seriously just say that we *both* have reason to be upset?"

"Just hold on."

"Look, psycho, I know you're from a broken home and I know you came here with no friends and no family and no nothing, but my God, *Professor*, you are not a fucking retard."

"Don't use that word, Forty."

"You're right," he says. "Professors graduate from college. They *work* at colleges. You never even went to college."

I seethe. Forty eats another M&M. "What the fuck do you want?"

"Number one rule of Hollywood," he says. "Shit I learned when I was an intern at CAA for two weeks." Only Forty would have a *two-week-long* internship. "Don't burn bridges."

"Just tell me what you want."

"I want you to listen," he says. "You can't burn bridges because LA is not like a hospital. The fucker mopping up this floor, he's not gonna be operating on you next month. It doesn't work that way. In this business, people get places and you don't know how they got there but they get there. And then the guy wiping the floor, he's running the studio."

I hate it when he has a point. "Forty, they're all gonna be back any minute," I say. "What do you want?

"I've always wanted a dog," he says. *Roosevelt.* "A white fluffy dog but my mom is allergic. That's where the title of *Boots and Puppies* really comes from. We had this puppy for like a minute, and we loved the shit out her. We named her Boots and Mom made us get rid of her because Mom was allergic. Fucking broke Love's heart."

Liars lie and I can't betray Love and families do this. Each person gets to invent a history, a version of the injustices, the pets, the names. I will never know the Quinns the way Milo does, Milo who is probably sitting in a Quinn sandwich right now. "What are you trying to say?" I ask.

"That I'm a fucking grown-up," he says. "A hot shit screenwriter and I'm my own person making my own bucks so I'm getting a dog. And you know what I'm gonna call that fucking dog?"

I know what he's going to call the fucking dog and I don't want to say it out loud. But I think of my child. This is what parents do. They sacrifice. "You're calling it Professor," I say.

He nods. "Professor," he repeats. "Prof for short. Here's the deal, *Prof*. You are gonna write what I tell you to write, when I tell you to write it."

"Forty—"

He talks through me. "You are gonna churn out shit like you're the guy in *Misery* fucking chained to the bed by the fat chick," he says. "You will write and I will earn and if you ever even so much as *think* about telling my sister what we're doing, you fucking dog, I will put your ass in prison so fast you won't know what hit you." He barks at me, as if he's the dog, and he's too fucked up from pills and Veuve to keep his analogies straight. "And you will be fucking loyal or I will *kick* your ass. I own you now. The end."

I try to breathe. Forty throws another M&M at me.

"I said, did you hear me?" he asks.

I look at him. "You expect me to believe you're not going to the cops?"

"I hate cops," he says. "It's tedious and there are so many questions and lawyers."

"You could have died out there and you want to *work* with me? You expect me to believe that?" I shake my head. "Forty, here's what I expect. I expect to walk out of this room and get clocked and come to in an hour tied up in some fucking basement."

He grins. "There it is," he says. "That imagination."

"I left you in the desert," I say. "So don't fucking tell me we're gonna be *business* partners."

"You're not a good killer," he says. "Obviously. But you're a hell of a good writer." The sick fuck eats more M&M's and proceeds to tell me that I'm worth more alive than dead. "Look," he says. "I don't care about any of this shit. I don't care about getting sick and getting better and I don't care about getting married and having kids and getting healthy." He breaks. Choking. He's back. "All I care about is gold. I want an Oscar. I've wanted one my whole fucking life. You can't buy 'em, I mean, not technically. And I sure as hell didn't come close to getting one for the last fifteen years and now you, motherfucker, *you're* gonna get me *my* Oscar."

And he goes back to his Cosbys. He really doesn't care about Love, about any of the Hallmark human joys we're programmed to want, family and holidays, joy. He knows what I am, what I did. And he would still allow me to fuck his sister, but then, his sister knows about me too and still she wants me and of course she does. Of course he does. "I'd fuck Denise," he says. And of course he would. *Twins.* And my child shares his genetic coding and this is why we have war, because no gene pool is perfect.

A nursing assistant barges in to take Forty's vitals and she is cheery and pretty and she thinks it's *so amazing* how Forty has such a *big and loving family.* "I wish everyone could have what you guys have," she says. "It's so sad when people are here and they don't have anybody."

"You know what I'd like to do?" Forty asks.

The nurse cuffs him. Blood pressure. Not real cuffs. I wish. "What's that?" she chirps.

"I'd like for you, when you have time, to take all of these flowers and all of these balloons and disperse them to all the people on this floor who have no family around."

She looks at me. "Could you just die?" she asks. "This family is the best, right? If they're not bringing in sushi for us then they're showering the whole floor with flowers." She puts a thermometer in Forty's mouth. "I hate to say this, but I wish you could stay with us forever."

"Me too," I say.

Forty looks at me. The nurse says he has no temperature and he'll be out of here *in a jiffy* and Love and Milo and Dottie and Ray return and the party continues. Forty reminds his mother about their *plan* for me and she says that they want to start a book club at the Pantries. "You'll choose one book a month to spotlight," she says. "We can even use you in the signage."

Love squeezes my hand. "I love this idea," she says. "Don't you love this?"

"I love it," Forty says. "Dad, do you love it?"

Ray nods. "Professor Joe," he says and now the Quinns are debating what the first book should be and Love elbows me and says it should be *The Easter Parade* and I cringe and I should not have told her that detail about Amy. I do not want her referencing Amy, ever. Forty says it should be *Misery* and Ray thinks that's a good idea and Dottie only ever saw the movie and Milo says the book and movie are both great and this is my life now. Or it is until Forty's memory miraculously comes back. He could do that to me at any moment, turn me in, take it all away. And I can't kill him, not now that Love knows what I am, not when she could suspect me. He's my new mug of piss, alive and well and wiping his nose. Love may have forgiven me for everything else, but she would never forgive me for hurting her brother. *Professor Joe* would be a terrible moniker for a serial killer.

IN the hotel room that night, Love is moody, slamming drawers. I ask her what's wrong.

She sits on the bed. "Well," she says. "Why should I even bother? I mean, do you know what the nurse says *really* happened?"

Fuck fuck fuck. "No," I say. "I thought he can't remember."

Love sobs. I hold her. It goes on like this for hours. She says her father told her Forty burned through a hundred thousand dollars in a few days.

"Jesus, Love. I don't know what to say."

She looks out the window at Reno, which looks like Vegas and yet also looks nothing like Vegas. It's lesser, smaller, worse. "It's never going to end," she says. "My mom is going to sit there and act like he's clean and my dad is gonna run away grumpy and I don't know." She wipes her eyes and looks at me. "How do you think he even *wrote* those screenplays if he's so fucked up to the point of winding up in the desert coked out of his mind?"

"I don't know."

"And who is this girl?"

"I don't know."

"Do you think she's even *real* or do you think maybe drug dealers fucked him up?"

"I doubt he owes anybody any money."

Love looks out the window. "Michael Michael Motorcycle said he's the kind of guy people just want to hurt."

"Michael Michael Motorcycle is in prison," I remind her. "You and me, we're gonna take care of Forty. And . . ."

She nods. "Believe me," she says. She brushes her hand over her belly. "This is saving me."

I look out at the lights and I see my future—*arf arf*—and how I will clap for Forty when his movie gets cast, when it goes into production, when he gets nominated, when he wakes us up with a phone call—*I did it!*—and Love and I will dress up to go to the premiere and we will be the writer's *family.* I will smile and I will meet all the people who love my work and I won't be able to accept their love. I won't be able to tell the story of how I came to write *The Mess* or *The Third Twin* or the kidnapping story due soon.

Love pats my leg. "I'm so tired," she says. "My brother, God love him, but sometimes I think he literally drains me."

She undresses. She throws her panties into the empty trash can. She is too tired to fuck me and I am too tired to sleep.

My career is over. I will live a lie, like so many people in LA. At least there will be truth where it matters, in this bed, in so many beds. And I'll find a way to make myself known someday. I'll be a good dad; I'll raise my kids so they won't be stuck like this. Like so many great writers, I won't be appreciated until after I'm dead and Love finds a key to a safety deposit box with a letter inside explaining how I came to write all her brother's movies.

Eventually, I sleep.

52

IT'S true what they say about happiness. If you approach life from a place of gratitude, you're more apt to enjoy things. I am whole. I don't need fame; I never wanted that and I did not move here because of *aspirations.* It's enough for me to write and know that I did the best I could. I enjoy my life. *Our* life. Our baby! And I love that our baby is a secret.

We go to a premiere and meet Jennifer Aniston and Justin Theroux and I eat *guac* with them and we talk about *Cabo.* They are both narrow and kind and they treat me like an equal and the whole experience is surreal. The best part of it is what happens when the party ends and Love and I are in bed discussing it all and talking about Jennifer Aniston's hair.

I go to Milk Studios and a photographer shoots me for the Professor Joe promotions. They aren't going to use my picture because I don't want to be a public figure—Ray can respect that—but they are going to model the mascot on my likeness. Dottie *loves* that.

The first book will be *Portnoy's Complaint* and Love is chopping lettuce and she points the knife at me. "Now *that's* a good fuck-you to that Amy girl," she says. "I hope she sees the signs the day they're out."

I have a life partner, the mother of my child. She harasses me to take vitamins and tells me to brush my teeth. She sucks my dick and falls asleep before *Cocktail* is over and ignores her brother's calls when she *just can't deal.* I know the code to our alarm system and I am more comfortable driving in LA all the time. I find that it's easier to start the day by going *down* a hill than it is going *up* a hill and I tell this to Jonah Hill at a party and he laughs and says *don't tell that to my fucking date, guy.*

Love was serious about ditching her acting career and she is different now and it's hard to know the source of her power. She glows. She says it's because of me. I say it's her. We decide it's *us.* The baby.

I meet up with Calvin for beers in the old neighborhood that hasn't changed. He and Monica only went out for a few days; he doesn't know what became of her, doesn't care. He is being crushed by debt from his DUI. He is defeated now; he keeps telling me he was in jail for twenty-eight hours. He's gained a few pounds and he doesn't check Tinder. He says he might move home. I tell him to get his iPad and we work together on the *Ghost Food Truck* outline.

"Well, well, well," he says. "This is *good.*"

"It sure is," I tell him. "And you know what? Just go for it already."

"JoeBro," he says. "I feel like I've been kind of a dick."

"You weren't a dick."

"Well," he says. "I got caught up in shit. Anyway, I think we should pitch *GFT* together."

I drink my beer. I tell him not in a million years. "It's your concept, Calvin," I say. "You came up with it and you've worked it over a million times and you will be the one to make it happen."

He pats me on the back. He wants to know what I think about Delilah disappearing. "I think LA is a hard place, Calvin. I think it wishes we would all disappear and it's more of a miracle when people don't."

"Deep," he says.

We watch a commercial for automobile insurance. Calvin says his is *crazy expensive* because of his DUI. I enjoy the taste of the beer, the music in the bar—"Take It to the Limit," the Eagles, melodrama that only sounds good in a bar, when someone else puts it on—and when we're done, I drive *up* to the hills to go home and I enjoy that too.

At home, Love is making veal Parmesan. "Babies for the baby," she says. "You know, because veal are babies. Oh God. That came out wrong. Sorry, little, innocent cows. Tomorrow we'll have old, bitter chickens."

She is the one.

I hug her and kiss her.

She breaks pasta into a pot of boiling water. "How go the books?"

"They go," I say, and we are happy.

I track down Harvey. He's in hospice. I bring him flowers and chocolate cake and Eddie Murphy DVDs and he thanks me. He asks me if I saw Henderson last night. I get the chills. The nurse says he gets confused like this. I tell him he's gonna be fine.

"Am I right or am I right?"

His face contorts. I want to believe it's a smile. "I don't know," he says. "I'm scared."

I sit with him until his ex-wife returns and she hugs me and she cries. When I get home to Love, I cry. Love sends them a TV. She says the TVs in those places are never big enough. Harvey's ex-wife calls. She loves the TV. Harvey does too.

I don't go see Dez; drug dealers can all fuck off.

Every Sunday we drive out to Malibu to see Love's parents. Sometimes Forty is there and sometimes he isn't. But I see him regularly. Twice a week we meet at the Taco Bell in Hollywood.

Today I am first. I slide into a booth and when he arrives he is visibly fucked up.

"Let me get you a Coke," I say.

He grabs my hands. "Thank you," he says. "Old Sport, Professor, whatever you are, thank you so fucking much for what you did. Do you know how gold this is? I mean, I read what I wrote and I swear, I think being left in the desert is the best fucking thing that ever happened to me."

I get the Coke. He knocks it over. I go for napkins and he stops me. "They have people who do that."

"Forty, help me out here." I haven't seen him this fucked up since Vegas and I forgot how annoying it is. And at the same time, I want to save him; Love rubs off on me.

"I mean, a job's a job," he says. "You spill, they wipe."

I look at his swollen face. "You don't hate me, do you?"

"Hate you?" he says. "How could I hate you? Dude, Amy Adams is gonna do *The Mess.*"

Will that name ever leave me? No. "Great," I say. "Congrats."

"It's not for sure," he backtracks. "But it looks *good.* Amy Fucking Adams. How could I hate you? I mean, you don't even know the level of ass I am getting. Unpaid pussy, my friend. How could I *hate* you?"

I remember when I thought it would be a terrible thing to be a dog and now I fetch the chalupas and the hot sauce and the tacos and the gorditas. *Woof*!

Love wins another award for her charity work and I write a speech for her. On the way home, she says maybe we could have a winery. After the baby, of course. I can't believe this is my life, where the possibility of periodically stomping on grapes and owning a vineyard is real.

I call Mr. Mooney on his birthday and tell him about Love, about meeting Jennifer Aniston and choosing books as Professor Joe. He asks if I'm getting my dick sucked then tells me he's still in Florida. He has an orange tree and the oranges look nothing like the ones in New York. "They're mottled," he says. "Like the jelly beans with the flecks in them, never mind, I'm boring myself." He sighs. The conversation dwindles and I go find Love. She's outside, in her favorite float, the one with arm rests and drink holders and she's wearing sunglasses. I jump into the pool and push the raft over. She screams again, and falls into the water. She comes up laughing, saltwater kisses. We float.

"Sam is at it again," she says.

"Sam the work bitch?"

"Yeah," she says. "We're getting interns and she said we have to check to make sure they're not on Pinterest because she says people on Pinterest are all stupid."

"She's stupid."

"I know," Love says.

"If you hate her so much why don't you just fire her?"

Love rolls over onto her side and reaches out for me. "Because I don't hate anyone," she says. "I really don't. It's just not worth it."

We hear her phone ringing, we hear my phone ringing.

Love runs to her phone and she answers. "Mom?" she says. And then seconds later, she drops her phone. I go to her.

She stares at me. She is different. She is frozen. My first concern is the baby but how could that be? It wasn't the doctor on the phone.

"It's Forty," she says.

He went to the cops. That fucker. That louse. I'll kill him. "What happened?" I ask.

And then she starts crying. It's primal and terrifying and whatever that fucker did, he will pay for this. I grab the phone.

"Dottie?" I say, and I try to hug Love. And she's shaking. Her whole body is convulsing and this cannot be good for our baby. "Dottie, are you there?"

"My boy," she sobs. "My boy is dead."

My body goes slack. "Forty is dead?"

When Love hears me say it, she lets out another scream and I tell Dottie I have to go and I don't know if the baby will survive, but I know we will. I hug Love, I hold on to her. I wish I could make it better. But I can't. Forty's dead.

53

FORTY didn't overdose on Xanax or gorditas. He didn't get cancer and he didn't drown in the saltwater of the Pacific or the chlorinated water of the hotels he loved so much or the saltwater that his parents collected for him. A car hit Forty Quinn while he was crossing the street in Beverly Hills. The girl who hit him wasn't drunk—God is not *that* trite—and she was driving a Honda Civic. She only just moved here. Her name is Julie Santos. The people in back of her were honking. Angelenos, particularly those on the Westside, don't like to wait. Julie Santos says the guy in back of her had been riding her tail and honking. Her roommate told her that it's *basically legal* to take a left-hand turn after the light turns red because otherwise, nobody would ever get anywhere.

Forty was sober; there were no drugs in his possession or inside him. He was going to Nate 'n Al's alone to gorge on corned beef and French fries, according to the waiter who says Forty came in alone a lot over the years. We never knew that, any of us. Julie, who seems like a gentle, unsteady person, the kind who will never get over this accident, she wanted to see the *Pretty Woman* hotel and she knows it's silly and it's not even called the *Reg Bev Wilsh* anymore but . . . she cries. I resist the urge to make a joke about Forty and hookers, how even when he's not blowing money on them, they're in his domain, good old Julia Roberts.

A review of the security footage shows that Forty was jaywalking. Love's teeth chatter. She tells me he got *eight jaywalking tickets.* Forty didn't like to wait either; he wanted it *now*, his career, his Oscar, even the goddamn crosswalk. There will be charges filed against Julie Santos and she says she's going to move back to Boston. She says she never wants to drive again and it feels like a bad thing, to move somewhere and kill someone immediately.

Nobody can believe it. I can't believe it. I think about Julie Santos a lot. I find her on Facebook and Twitter and I could start a religion around her and God *does* have a sense of humor; her last name is *saint.* I did not pray for this but I am allowed to rejoice in this. Nobody will ever know about what happened between us in the desert. Nobody will ever know about our Taco Bell deals, his malfeasance. I am in Neiman Marcus and there are *two* tailors working on me at once because when you're rich and someone you know dies, you go to Neiman's and you get a new suit.

Love sits in a chair with her legs crossed. She isn't crying anymore.

"Is it awful if I say you look hot?" she asks.

"No," I say. "You say whatever you need to say."

She nods. I ask the tailors to give us a moment and they oblige and I go to her and mirrors surround us and everywhere I look, I see us. Just us. The third twin is gone. "I love you."

"I love you too," she says. "I promise I'm gonna come out of it."

"Take your time."

"It's just weird." She stares at her Kleenex. "I don't know how to not worry about him."

"I know."

"It's, like, my go-to place," she says. "What do I do? I worry about Forty. I mean, it's not even so much about drugs, even though it seems that way, it's about being a *twin.*"

I tell her again to take all the time she needs and I promise to be here no matter what and she stops shredding her Kleenex and looks instead at me. "What would I do without you?"

"Irrelevant," I tell her. "I'm not going anywhere."

She hugs me and she cries again and one of the numerous pins in my suit pricks me and I bury the pain and I savor the pain. He's dead. Julie Santos killed him. After all this time, I finally got a little fucking help from the man upstairs and I squeeze my girlfriend and I count my blessings. She pats my back. The tailors return and Love dries her eyes.

"You really do look hot," she says.

The suit will be ready in time for the funeral. Milo is too sad to write a eulogy and Ray is in shock and I am the loyal boyfriend so I step up and I don't just jot down some bullshit about his sense of humor and his big, fat heart. Fuck, no. I write the fuck out of this eulogy and it's right up there with *The Third Twin* and my kidnapping script, the one I'll volunteer to finish, now that he can't because he's dead.

Love and I emerge from the limousine and the carpet leading into the Beverly Hills Hotel is pink and green. Love says this was their favorite place when they were kids and they had their sweet sixteen party here and she is crying again and I hold her.

"I've never been," I say.

"Well," she says. "We stopped coming here a while ago, I don't even know why. We practically grew up in here. They have this soda fountain and we used to get cheeseburgers and then we would stay in a villa and sneak out and run around in the garden."

"You're adorable," I say, and I mean it. When we first met, I was uncomfortable. I thought all this shit with the palm fronds and the multiple bathrooms mattered. But childhood fucks you up, no matter what it looks like. I see that now. The closer we get to having the baby, the less hostility I feel toward my parents. I don't resent my mom for dumping me at Key Foods anymore because I found warmth there. Poor Forty couldn't find the warmth in here, this pink and green paradise, this *Beverly Hills Hotel.*

Memories are all the same at their core; it's just us trying to keep each other alive, the best parts anyway. We're all pretending that Forty was a wonderful person and Love is saying something about *Beverly Hills 90210*, abut Brandon and Brenda Walsh, how they used to call Forty the anti-Brandon.

Everyone who's anyone is here. Agents, executives, producers, *Joaq*, and I am the one who Love holds on to, the one who has held it together, the one who will eulogize the man who was like a brother to me. The lights dim. A video begins, a tribute to Forty and "The Big Top" by Michael Penn plays, the song that closes *Boogie Nights*, and there are pictures of sober Forty and clips of drunk Forty and there is Forty skiing on the water and skiing on the mountains and he is laughing and he is a child and then he is an adult and then he is a child again.

Life.

I cry. It's important that I show emotion, I realize this, but it's also genuine. The song has always moved me, the circus sounds, the applause, the blunt sadness and the fatality of life, the way the song doesn't end so much as it peters out. And now it's *his* funeral song so it can't be mine. Or maybe it can; maybe funerals are different from weddings and people don't remember them and talk about them, blow by blow. The Michael Penn orchestral dirge slows down and the song slips into silence. The lights come up. It's my turn. Love kisses me. I step toward the podium.

"I think we all need a moment of silence," I say.

It's the right move and I bow my head and everyone does what I do. I have never understood why an Armani suit should cost so much money until now, as I stand here anticipating, trying not to stare at Reese Witherspoon, and readying my pages. I take the mic. "Good afternoon," I begin. "My name is Joe Goldberg and I am so blessed to know the Quinns, my surrogate family."

I eulogize the *fuck* out of Forty Athol Quinn and it's lucky that I got a head start when I thought he had drowned in the desert. It had to be altered because of his freak end, but the rewrite is good. Great even and I should have a job writing eulogies. The best ones celebrate the person's potential; they emphasize that person's unique contribution to society. I talk about Forty calling me Old Sport the very first time we met.

My audience is loving this and I seize this opportunity to educate them. I tell them about one of my favorite books and I'm sure most of them haven't read it because most of these people focus their energies on reading fictional narratives. But there's important nonfiction out there that's useful at a time like this, particularly for Forty Quinn.

"The book is called *Life's Dominion*," I begin. "And it poses a philosophical question. Anyone could stand up here and speak to Forty's charming wit, his burgeoning brilliance, his generosity, his swagger, his madras shorts and madcap sense of adventure, his extensive knowledge of film and his idealist sense of commitment. We've seen his smile, his joy," I say, pointing at the wall where his life just played out. "But what you can't see in those pictures is Forty's philosophy about life itself, and this is where I think I can best pay tribute to him by telling you about *Life's Dominion.*" I take a deliberate, staged breath. "The book poses a question we face every day, all day. What is the right choice? A bus is packed with adults, all of whom have lived, all of whom have mortgages and children, attachments. And there is a stroller crossing the street. The bus can brake and go off the cliff and everyone dies. Or the bus can run over the stroller and the child goes."

Amy Adams tilts her head. Joaq is rapt. "Ronald Dworkin argued that there is no universal right or wrong because it's valid to say that life is valued based upon what one has already done. But it's also possible to say that life can't be qualified, that the baby might have gone on to cure cancer, to win an Oscar." I know my crowd. I see people whispering, wondering who I am. "Forty Quinn was a unique man. He was the baby in the stroller, the one with everything ahead of him, the *potential* we all know about, these scripts he sold, after working *so* hard for *so many years* to forge connections and get better. He earned his success and it would be remiss to say that anything was handed to him because he grew up running around here," I say. Amy Adams nods.

"Quinns give. And Forty gave us his stories, the ones he tried so hard to tell, year after year." I shake my head. Megan Fox uncrosses her legs. She wants me. "I mention *Life's Dominion* and Ronald Dworkin because something you might not have known about Forty Quinn was how much he read, how much he wrote, how passionate he was about learning." That's the thing about the charade of love; nobody gets mad when you don't back up your lofty statements about someone's triumphant life with tangible facts. I look at Love and she smiles. She likes this story I'm telling because the truth would be terrible. "He told me how much he learned from *Life's Dominion* shortly before . . ." I trail off.

Reese wipes her eyes and Love's tears are soaking her dad's jacket.

"Let me say what we all know. Forty was a giant. He was a force. He was one of the people on the bus, one of us, a person with deep ties in the community, a person who spread his joy everywhere he went. Mrs. Quinn, if you'll cover your ears, I can tell you how much they loved him at Taco Bell." I get laughs through tears and I wait for my silence. "Very few people are able to straddle those quadrants of life. Forty is the only person I've ever known who could do that. He could play with toys, he could make you feel like the best was yet to come, and he could make you feel like what you'd done was worth everything."

I tear up and then I am closing. "Forty Quinn called me The Professor, but Forty Quinn was my professor." Joaq smiles. We are going to be friends.

"Once I asked Forty what it was like to grow up with so much privilege. He told me that it was hard. He told me that when you have parents who embody the best of human love, parents who love each other more as time passes, who live to love, that it was hard to be constantly misunderstood by people who assumed that his wealth was purely financial. 'The thing about my parents,' he said, 'is they could have been working in the Pantry, behind the register, in the deli, and they would have provided Love and me with just as much love.'" I pause. Love is sobbing now. Reese Witherspoon is leaning forward and her agent husband has an arm around her. I fucking *win*. "Forty Quinn knew that love is all there is; everything else is transient, impermanent. If he had made it across that street, I can guarantee you that he would have gotten out of the jaywalking ticket. You could not say no to Forty Quinn. He was the other kind of yes man, the kind who makes us all want to say *yes.* Rest in peace, brother."

When I return to Love, she transfers her trembling body from her father's embrace to mine. This is *The Godfather* and we spill out into a ballroom with bottles of *Veuve* everywhere and gigantic pictures of Forty that are projected onto the walls, changing. He is young, he is old but either way, he is dead. *Yes!*

Everyone I've ever wanted to meet is here and they want to meet *me* and Reese Witherspoon wants to hug me—yeah, she does—and her husband wants to talk to me and *Joaq* wants to get a drink and Love is proud of her book-selling boyfriend, crushed and destroyed, but proud.

Barry Stein takes me aside. "Do you like cigars?" he asks.

"Absolutely," I say, and he will be useful in my negotiations with Megan Ellison. I will get Stein to offer to buy my shit and then turn around and make deals with *ME.* For now, it starts with friendship. Forty is right; I won't burn bridges. And first, I have to build them. I have to walk out onto the lawn and watch Barry Stein wrestle with his bowtie and search for a polite way to segue into business talk, as if there is a polite way to segue into business talk.

He chews his cigar. He spits. "You know," he says. "Forty and I, we kicked some ideas around lately. You and I, I think we should talk."

I nod. "Absolutely."

"I think his work should not die with him."

"Absolutely."

I smoke a cigar and *Barry* wants me to call his office and set up a meeting. Inside, the food is incredible. Kate Hudson is hugging me. There are crab cakes and antipasto and drinks that never stop, gimlets and steak tips that melt and cold chunks of lobster. Forty's favorite songs play, most of them about the fucking drugs that almost killed him but didn't kill him and George Clooney shakes my hand—*Good speech, kid*—and the greatest part of all of this is the beautiful truth of it.

I killed it with my speech and I did not kill Forty Quinn.

It's silly to play games, to wonder how he might have lived. What was Julie Santos even doing in Beverly Hills? What if she had continued to go straight on Santa Monica, all the way to the Pacific? It's like in *Match Point* with the tennis ball and then later with the ring. All of life is slightly dependent on magic. So is death. If his body had been found in the spring, if his skin had started to disintegrate, his shit staining the hot water, his body stuffed with cocaine, well, the funeral would be different. I mean, I would have killed it and found a way to bring the light, but it would have been a darker day. Thank God, if there is one, for Julie Santos and her left-hand turn.

"Joe," she says, and she is Susan Sarandon. She hugs me. She pulls away. "I just needed to do that."

I hope Reese saw and I hope Amy saw but what really matters the most is that Love saw. She wraps her arm around me. "You did so good," Love says. "Do you even know?"

It's not the time for me to brag so I am humble, supportive, stroking her arm and kissing the top of her head and she steps away, family obligations.

People like Forty Quinn are their own worst enemies, increasing the odds of an untimely death by chugging codeine, and with his death, I am liberated. I can go anywhere I want and I wander into the lobby, the pink and green of it all, freedom. I sit on a circular sofa and Love finds me. She plants herself on my lap. She strokes my hair. "Let's stay at the Aisles tonight," she says. "I don't want to stay here. I want my own bed."

When a girl wants her own bed and she wants you in it, this is how you know it's real. "Whatever you want," I say, and I will give it four weeks until I tell her that I'm inspired by Forty's work, that I think I'd like to try writing something on my own.

I put my hand on her stomach. Forty can't take this moment away, the quiet love in this ballroom and the inaudible sound of a new heart beating.

I am too happy to be still and Love is like Sleeping Beauty. Her twin is dead; this will take a while. I kiss her perfect little forehead and I put on pink shorts with whales all over them and I put on a T-shirt and I grab my sunglasses and I leave Love's room. I hum "Thunder Road" and I walk through the house that Forty will never walk through again—it's real!—and I smile.

Outside I walk down the path, barefoot on the sandy grass, the grassy sand. I hear the waves and they are slow and lazy and when I reach the beach, I am startled because there is a mist as dense as snow, a Stephen King kind of mist, thick and white. Suddenly I am a kid again and monsters could live in this mist and how surreal it is to hear the water but not be able to see it.

I remember feeling this happy once, when I was a kid. Snow covered the streets and they were perfect and white, as if the world had been coated in vanilla ice cream. My mom said school was canceled and I could go outside. I'd seen snow before, but there was something about the snow that day. It was early, before the people would come and destroy it all, and I clomped outside and it was up to my knees and I was the first one to walk in it and I was so fucking *happy* to be first, to see my footprints, giant and deep, to know that I had all day, that there would be no school, no homework. There is magic in a snow day and how strange it must be to grow up in Southern California without that possibility. It will be my first question for Love when she wakes up.

I walk into the mist toward the water and I hear a dog barking. *Boots and Puppies.* I whistle. The dog barks. He sounds afraid. "It's okay," I call out. "Come here boy."

But he only mews, sounding almost like a kitten. "Hey, little guy,

54

I wake up early. Happy. I'm still high on the funeral, on Kate's ass, Reese's eyes, Amy's intensity, my *baby*. And I missed it here at the Aisles, the tennis court, the sand and the grass forever mixing, never melding. I'm a runner now and the beach looks different to me, useful. It's my track. And what a great feeling it is to revisit the puzzle of your life and say, *ah. I know what that beach is there for. It's there for me.*

My body doesn't want to sleep. I think it has something to do with all the change. The last time I was here, I killed Delilah. Love had no idea who I was, but she wanted to find out so she invited me to go to the film set with her. She stood on that beach and watched me coming in on the Donzi and she did not know where I had been or why I had been out there. The miracle of life, of the girl in my bed; she loves me more now than she did then. And now there is so much new love in my life, meetings and opportunities and purpose. I will take care of Love. I will honor Forty's legacy and see his projects to fruition. I will be strong for my child and I will protect myself.

it's okay." I pat the sand. I am reminded of the puppy in *Single White Female* that won't run to Jennifer Jason Leigh, and then she kills the puppy because it didn't love her. And then I think of Forty murdering Roosevelt, Love's version, and Love crying when their parents gave Boots away, Forty's version. There really is no such thing as the truth but there is such thing as happiness, and I can picture the amazed look on Love's face if I brought her home this dog.

Dogs like authority, so I command. "All right, get over there, pup. Right now." But the whimpering sounds farther away. I start running, making my way through the swirling white, and fifteen yards in I stumble and stub my toe. *Fuck.* Sand is harder than you think.

"Would you just come here already? I'm not gonna hurt you!" I keep going and the puppy is still crying out there, somewhere. "It's okay! I'm here."

The ocean ebbs and flows beyond the fog and I hear the dog again, and I crouch. I want to be prepared to hug him, to get coated in puppy slobber, to be loved—this is why people in Franklin Village keep dogs—and I think I see him. He is as white as the mist, with a little black mouth and black eyes and a pink tongue coming into focus. The dog is panting, running, and I wonder what we'll call him. He looks like a Charlie or a Cubby or a George. I whistle to him. He ignores me. Fucker.

I laugh. What is wrong with me? It's a puppy. It's not a fucker. But then, maybe it is. Babies can be assholes and puppies can be fuckers. But you accept the risk when you make a baby, when you adopt a dog. I think I'll write something about an asshole baby and a fucker puppy and it will be like one of those old-school *Peanuts* cartoons, where you can't hear what the adults are saying because it's all just sonic wonking.

I clap my hands and that's when I see a flash of white linen, a bright yellow shirt and I realize the dog isn't alone. The puppy yelps and the human throws something, an electric green tennis ball. The human whistles and the human is female. I see her hair in the mist—blond, tangled—and I see her sharp shoulders and two long legs and

Amy? Amy. Amy? Amy?

She scoops the puppy that was going to belong to me and Love into her arms. She kisses the puppy and then she looks up. She startles.

"Joe?" she says. She looks terrified, guilty. Time stops. I am in shock.

She holds the puppy too hard and the puppy fights and the puppy has claws and the puppy wins. She drops the puppy and it runs and she stands there, frozen, and this bitch fucked me. Stole from me. Tricked me. Lied to me. Used me. She wronged me and the nice people in Rhode Island—Liam & Pearl & Harry & Noah—and I loved her. I loved her but she didn't love me.

Amy? Amy.

"What are you doing here?" she asks, and she thinks she's pretty and clever, tucking her hair behind her ear, pretending to trust me, but people don't change and I see her bracing to run. She doesn't get to run away from me now the way she did then, not after what she did. She turns, hair flying, and instinct takes over. I spring forward. She runs but I'm faster and I knock her to the ground. She screams and I clamp my hand over her mouth and look into the eyes I know too well.

She knees me in the groin and I react, loosening my grip, but I manage to grab her by the hair and pin her down in the sand. I cover her mouth again and she thrashes like a marlin and I can't believe that after all these months, Amy is here.

Her face has changed from all this sun, more freckles, smoother skin, longer hair, crusty mascara around her eyes, she was out last night. She is who I used to love. Who I used to covet. Who I used to want to kill, but who I forgot to worry about after I fell in love with Love.

She kicks me again and I smack her face. "Don't scream," I say. "Understand?"

She says yes with her eyes. They are as bright as I remember, even in the mist. I take my hand away.

"Jesus, Joe, what are you doing?"

"Shut up," I command. I clamp my hand over her mouth. "You are not to yell. Do you understand?"

She nods emphatically. "Joe, please," she begins.

I'm still getting reacquainted with her face, how crazy human faces are, how noses are all so different, some bulbous, some pointy. Amy's is aquiline. I used to love her nose. I used to kiss her nose. Now I love Love's nose.

"Joe," she says. "About the money . . ."

"The money?" I can't help it. It's been so long, but it all washes over me again. The humiliation I felt when I found my computer in the cage, the keys I made for her, the note in *Charlotte & Charles*. "How can you think this is about money?"

"Cuz I lifted the books," she pants. "I can pay you back."

"I don't want your fucking money, Amy," I say. "I'm not like you. I don't give a fuck about *money*."

"I get it, okay? I suck. But please, let me go," she begs.

I hold her down. "You do suck. You're a vicious empty cunt."

"You're acting crazy," she says. "Let me go."

I spit at her. She blinks. "Fuck you," I say.

"Joe," she says. "Please stop it."

I tighten my grip on her neck. I should get it over with. I should squeeze the life out of her for all the things she *did* do. Instead I am allowing her to speak, to rail on about what she did. "I took some books," she confesses. "And it sucks and I know it. And I know it must have been terrible for you to find out. But you know, Joe. You knew I was in it for myself. I know you knew."

I didn't know. And this is what hurts. I loved her and she did not love me. She doesn't think it was real, she never did. My cheeks turn red. I need to kill her because she says things like *we were just fucking* and *it was summer* and *I didn't rip you off. I ripped off the shop.* She wasn't in love with me and every time she promises she can get me the money I know I have to kill her. She wasted my heart, my time. She begs me to let her go and she can get a *cash advance* and she can *get you anything you want* and she is house-sitting and there is *art I could sell, like, a lot of art* and she is a commercial beast.

Beck never loved me either and if Love knew about this, the dark humiliating truth of it, that I love women who don't love me back, I don't know how I could look her in the eye. I don't know if I could go on, because the real horror of my life is not that I've killed some terrible people. The real horror is that the people I've loved didn't love me back. I may as well have been masturbating in the cage, telling the books about the girls because all the girls before Love, they were not there with me, not really, especially this one, this tall blond cunt begging for her life and promising me that she can give it all back to me *every last penny.*

"You don't get it," I tell her. "There's nothing you can do."

"Let me go," she pleads, she squirms.

Everything in her tone and her language and her eyes seems confused. She's acting like I'm some guy she knew and I'm looking at her like she broke my heart. But she's just talking about what a pain it was to sell books online. Does she really think this is about *Portnoy's Complaint*, about Yates?

"What about everything you wrote in *Charlotte and Charles*?"

She swallows. "What?"

"*Charlotte and Charles*," I snap. "You read it to me on the beach and a day later you run out on me and write me a letter in it and I want to know why."

"'Cause it was in my bag from the beach when I went back to the shop," she exclaims, and that is not what I was asking about.

"You read the book to me on the beach and you left me a note in the book and now you want to tell me you don't *remember.*"

"Joe," she says. "I told you. You were looking in my phone. I mean, you didn't trust me either."

"Why did you leave that book for me?" I ask.

She asks me to let her go. I ask her to tell me about the book. The air is cold and loud off the water and she groans again. "Because you're so sad and lonely!" she says. "Jesus, if this is it, fuck it. I give up." She smacks her lips. She clears her throat. "Get off me," she says. "Get off me and I'll tell you."

"No," I say. "Tell me now."

"I left you that book because I *did* feel bad," she says. "You're sad and lonely and you should be better at being alone. You're just so fucking *depressed* and you wear it like a badge the way you sit in that shop alone and you're so obviously desperate for someone to come in and change your life and it's fucking annoying. Like, take care of your shit. Pull yourself together. Stop being so self-conscious about your music and every little thing you say. I gave you that book because those giants are pathetic, the way they can't fucking deal with themselves and they expect everyone to be as decent as they are. They have no right to be shocked when the humans gang up on them. Like, that's fucking life. Get over it. You can't go around expecting everyone to be like you. That's the point."

Her words sting. "If I'm so depressed and pathetic, then why did you date me?"

She rolls her eyes. "Joe," she says. "The day we met, I was using my ex-boss-boyfriend's credit card and you didn't call the cops."

"I'm not judgmental."

"You have to see things as they are," she says. "I mean, I didn't try and fool you or anything. And you know, I was like, okay, this guy, he's so cool with my shady shit. He obviously has his own shady shit. There's no way around it."

"I am nothing like you."

I hurt her, finally, and she shifts. "Well, congratufuckinglations," she says. "Can I go now? I mean, come on. This is ridiculous. What are you gonna do, *kill* me?"

Amy Adam has no idea about me. She thinks I'm a lonely sad person with poor reading comprehension skills. She used me. She isn't smart enough to love me or know me and suddenly I feel sorry for her. She doesn't understand that *Charlotte & Charles* is about the resilience of the human spirit, that happy people get fucked over and swim to another island and buck up and go on again.

Amy is not a con artist and she's not a conniving thief. She's a sad, lonely girl. She carried a book around that she didn't even understand and she wants the world to be like a Richard Yates book, with sad endings. The only Philip Roth book she ever finished is *Portnoy's Complaint.* She isn't the girl I thought she was, talking to me now about her boss, her dog-sitting, and I am not going to kill her.

In a strange way, Amy Adam is right. I *am* incapable of killing anyone right now. I have Love. I'm going to be a father. I have changed. I move off her completely and she wipes the sand off her arms, off her shirt. She shakes her legs.

"Only thing about the beach," she gripes. "Sand."

From her end this was a lover's quarrel and so we do what all former lovers do: We revisit our past together. But our memories are so different. I bring up that last night in Little Compton.

"Remember our new best friends, Noah and Pearl and Harry and Liam?" I ask.

She is aghast. "You remember their *names*? How do you remember their names?"

She is not like me, not like Love. She is not burdened with a sensitive heart. Hers just beats. She laughs. "Remember when I busted you looking in my phone?"

I get a ripple of humiliation in my stomach. "Uh huh," I say. "You were mad."

"Yeah," she says. "Paranoid. I had already put a couple books online and looked for a sublet out here. I was like *fuck* he found out."

"Wow," I say, and I think of *Match Point*, where Woody Allen reminds us that all the best tennis players are also lucky. Amy had a lot of Safari windows open on her phone that day. I only saw the one with Henderson. If she had to wait in line, if she'd washed her hands more thoroughly, if she'd put on lipstick, I would have found those other windows. I had bad luck with her. But then again, without her, I never would have found Love.

"I know," she says. "I mean, I pitched a fit because I thought you knew what I was up to and you were gonna wanna *talk* and all that."

She asks me what I'm doing in LA and I tell her I moved here because it was something to do, because it was time to get out of New York. She says she might move to Austin. I tell her it seems like a lot of assholes talk about moving to Austin. She laughs. "You are funny," she says. "You still got it, Goldberg."

I feel nothing. I don't yearn for what we had, the way all we could do was mock everyone else. I gaze at the ocean but I can't see through the mist. She pulls her hair over her left shoulder. Her neck is bruised, proof of my violence, a new mug of piss. My heart starts to beat fast and maybe I do have to kill her. I hurt her. I did this. And if I do away with her, I will never have to worry about her ever again. She won't be a loose end, another *mugofurine.* I could do it. She draws in the sand with her finger. That could be her last act as a human. But then the tide creeps up on us and recedes, and the line vanishes, just like the redness on her neck will. Nature is an inherently forward beast; footsteps disappear, past hurts fade. I won't kill Amy. I will not remove life from this planet while Love and I are in the process of bringing life into this world. I've already confessed my past to Love and I don't want to confess my present.

I stand and I offer Amy a hand but she stands up without my help. She asks if I'm sure I don't want money for the books. I tell her I'm good and she smiles then turns and walks back into the mist. She keeps her head down and her arms crossed. I sit back down in the sand where she lay, cool and wet, and I feel the weight go, as if she's passing out of me every time I breathe, every time I blink.

I can't tell you the specific moment that I can't see her anymore, because she disappears in segments. First the mist takes her bare feet, then the back of her yellow shirt. Her hair comes back to me for a brief spell, blond, tangled, and then it's gone and then she's gone, all of her, into the mist, almost like she was never here at all.

55

IT'S so different being at Taco Bell with Love. She already has pregnancy cravings and wanted to pig out on enchiladas and gorditas. *Twins.* But we don't order everything on the menu, just gorditas and two chicken tacos. She wants soda even though she feels bad about the sugar and I tell her we'll start a better diet tomorrow.

She asks me to pick a booth and I choose one by the window, far from the one where I always sat with Forty. She fills up our cups with ice and mixes a little root beer into our Cokes. "I kind of love this," she says.

"Me too," I say. "Maybe we should get married here."

"Did you just propose to me in Taco Bell without a ring?"

I nod. She laughs. She thinks she peed her pants and I tell her you don't get to pee your pants when you're a few *weeks* pregnant. We hold hands across the table. "So will you?" I ask.

"Yes." She smiles. "But don't make me a ring out of a straw or anything, okay?"

"Deal," I say.

We wait for the feast and we talk about the baby's room and where to live and when to tell people. I tell her I think I want to write something, maybe even this idea I've been kicking around about a ghostwriter called *Fakers*. She says she likes the title—fucking right, she does—and she says Forty could tell I was a writer the day we met.

We watch the cars go by on the PCH and we rehash the funeral and she says my eulogy was the greatest thing ever and she wants to watch the video tonight. "Is that weird?" she asks.

"Not at all," I tell her. "Death is weird."

When our food is ready, I walk to the counter and I thank the guy. He's new. He doesn't know me and he'll never know Forty. Love bites into her gordita and half of it falls on her shirt and now I think *I* piss myself laughing and I pick up a chicken taco and shove it in my mouth so that half of it falls onto *my* shirt on purpose and now she's laughing.

I slide out of the booth and she keeps her eyes on me and only Love is sexy with gordita all over her shirt. I move to her side of the table and I feel her react to me. I actually feel the love well up inside of her, in her legs, in the way they shift toward me, so slightly, petals to the sun. When I kiss her, she quivers like we just met and she strokes my back like we've known each other forever.

"I love you," I say.

"Me too," she says.

I am smiling ear to ear. If this is how we are after her brother's shocking death and our surprise pregnancy, imagine how good we're going be when we don't have any stress in our lives.

"Okay, I actually do have to pee," I say, and I nod to the guy at the counter on the way to the bathroom.

It's one of those bathrooms with a permanently fogged mirror that's mostly just splinters and graffiti and I can't see my reflection. After I flush, I wash my hands more than Amy did at Del's that day in May. I press the button for the air to come out of the hand dryer but it's broken.

Someday, if I meet the owner of Taco Bell, I will advise him to renovate these fucking bathrooms. I will explain that my wife and I—*wife!*—like to go to his establishment every so often. I will tell him we would go more often if the bathrooms weren't so disgusting.

I push through the door, excited to tell Love about my plans to renovate the bathrooms at and stop short. Her gordita is sitting there as fat as it was when I left, but she's not at the booth. And the guy at the counter is gone, too. The kitchen is silent and outside the PCH is empty. Nothing. Not a single BMW. Goose bumps cover my body and I run into the women's bathroom, but every stall is vacant.

My phone rings, echoing in the vast silence of this deserted Taco Bell. It is Love, and I silence the call because I know, now, what this is. Love retrieved the mug of urine but the mug of urine was not my only mistake. I'm sure of it. The only other possible explanation for the vacuum of silence is an atomic meltdown, in which case the sky would be orange.

I turn on the faucet. The soap in here is newer, pinker. I wonder if my child will be a boy or a girl. I wash my hands with hot water and I rinse with cold water. This is my last trip to the spa for a while and I push the dryer and the hot air blows. I close my eyes and let my hands take on the heat.

My phone is ringing again. Love. They're making her call me to see what's taking so long. They do shit like that in Dennis Lehane books. But you can't hold it against them; their job is to get me.

And they must want me very badly because the perimeter has been cleared. That's why there's no one at the register and no cars on the PCH. If I had been a gentleman, I would have let Love go to the bathroom first and I would have been the one to watch the cops sweep in, stealthy and silent.

I pull the door and exit the women's restroom. I memorize the tiles on the floor of this Taco Bell and I take one last bite of Love's gordita and this is it. I pull the first door and enter the vestibule. I open the second door and enter the parking lot. The sun pierces my eyes. There is a cop on the roof above me.

"Put your hands up," he says.

I do.

He reads me my Miranda rights and cops pop up everywhere, from behind the parked cars, from around the side of the building, from the bushes. I don't care about them. I don't care that I am under arrest for the murder of Guinevere Beck and the murder of Peach Salinger.

What I care about is Love and she appears now with tears streaming down her face. She is trying to run for me but they are holding her back. If she has a miscarriage because of the ridiculous, over-the-top antics of the United States Federal Justice System, I will kill each and every one of these people.

All that evolved *Charlotte & Charles* shit about trust and optimism is good and all, but not when your pregnant wife is sobbing in the Taco Bell parking lot and she's got *gordita* all over her shirt and you can't do anything because you have to go to *jail.* But I don't have to worry. I'm one of the rich people now, the untouchables. These fuckers can't nail me. I'm gonna have the best lawyers money can buy. And let them try proving that I killed either of those girls without a single shred of evidence, without the *mugofurine* Love got for me.

I lock eyes with Love. I tell her I love her. She nods. *Me too.* The cop asks me if I'm done and before I answer, he opens the door and shoves me into the backseat. This is real. This is not a minor traffic infraction where they give you a warning and ask you about New York. This is not a jaywalking ticket by some power hungry cop. This is *two counts of murder one suspect in custody, over.*

Fuck you, radio. It's not over. Not even close.

56

THE police are so fixated on the past and I want to tell them that it's all gone. I'm a changed man. I saw Amy on the beach, Amy, the reason I moved here, the person who stole from me and broke my heart, and I didn't kill her. I'm not that guy anymore and this seems relevant, but then legally, it isn't. My brain gorges with my defense, the one that I can't reveal because the case against me is not about Amy, damn it, though I wish it were.

Here's the gist of it. Detective Peter Brinks and the New York Police Department are not like the feminist bloggers. They took the complaints of Dr. Nick Angevine seriously. One of his complaints was regarding Patient X, one *Danny Fox.* They were unable to locate Danny Fox. It was like he didn't exist.

Meanwhile, in Little Compton, Rhode Island, Officer Nico was spending a lot of time around the Salinger house. In police work, there is a lot of down time, a lot of sitting around, a lot of coffee, a lot of waiting, and while he was sitting around doing nothing, Officer

Nico decided it would be fun to flip through a sailing magazine. And in that sailing magazine, he saw a picture of a guy on a boat. The guy was identified as Spencer Hewitt. "I looked at that picture," he says. "And I thought, what are the odds that there are *two* guys named Spencer Hewitt?" Even though the Salingers insisted on closing the book on Peach, Officer Nico went to the garage that worked on my Buick. He wondered: Did they have a record of that transaction, perhaps a license plate? And they did have a license plate number on a receipt. Officer Nico found that the car was registered to a Mr. Mooney. He read about the bookstore in some BuzzFeed article about old bookstores in New York. He saw the name *Joe Goldberg* and then he found me on motherfucking Facebook.

Fucking Facebook.

He recognized me and he brought the picture to the Salingers and they knew me, of course, as the delivery boy, as the guy in the bar. So then the red flags were raised. Officer Nico is no dummy, and he knew Peach's *friend* Beck had also met an untimely end. I almost wish I could have been there on the day that Officer Nico visited Dr. Nicky in prison and showed him my photograph—*fucking Facebook*—and said, "Is this Danny Fox?"

So that's how this maelstrom came together, like any storm system in nature, a confluence of circumstances. It's as absurd as me running into Amy on a beach in Malibu after hunting her in Hollywood for months. How things come together in this universe, how they don't, is unfair. I was so judicious with Amy. I let her go. I didn't punish her. I think the justice system should see where I am now, how far I've come, all the good I have to lose. They should stop prodding into my past. It's so vengeful, so middle school, the way they want to boil my entire life down into these two dead girls.

And I had no warning of the coming storm but because of Love, I was able to batten down the hatches. I have a lawyer named Edmund and he sits alongside me through every interrogation. He is my counsel. He nods when it's okay to answer and he shakes his head when he wants me to be quiet. Edmund says to focus on the facts and reminds me that the cops have yet to produce any evidence that proves that I did anything. All they know for sure is that I like to use pseudonyms. In our first conversation, I reminded Detective Leonard Carr that *lots* of people use pseudonyms. "Look at authors," I said. "Look at famous people who check into hotels."

It's been three days and life is never how you expect it to be. The food here isn't bad. It isn't good, per se, but I'm not starving. In the newspapers they call me *Killer Joe* and it's disappointing, the failure of modern media, the lack of originality. Love visits me. Her father too. At night I worry. I wonder if there are other mugs of piss, if I forgot about them. I think about *Charlotte & Charles.* I daydream about Love. I think about the baby, running from Love to me and then back again. I dream of the baby learning to walk and I wake up ready to face my long days of cheap coffee and interrogations.

Leonard Carr is the *good cop.* He says I'm too smart to bother with *bad cop* and he says he won't bore me with head games. But of course he's boring me with head games. He thinks I'll relax and accidentally admit to killing someone. He has kids. He should know better. But then, he's human. We all are.

After lunch, he returns to the windowless room where we have our talks. He offers me water and he kicks his feet up. "So," he says. "I've been thinking about *Wolf of Wall Street.*"

There is something springy about him and I break my rule about looking at the camera, the one focused on me all the time, all day, the glass orb hell bent on capturing me as I incriminate myself. Edmund nudges my leg, a reminder to stay calm. Detective Carr has new information. I know it. He's excited, trying so hard not to show it that he's showing it. But then, maybe that's part of his strategy.

"Here's what I like about the movie," he says. "I like it when the guy eats the goldfish. It's so simple. Something about it. That stayed with me. I've never seen anyone eat a goldfish. Have you?"

"No," I say and I wonder what he knows. I am thirsty but I don't drink the water.

"Not ever?" he asks.

"No," I say. I would like to open his skull and find out what he knows so we can avoid this banter and I can get out of here and go on with my life.

He nods. "You didn't see anything like that in Cabo?"

I look to Edmund. He nods. "No," I say. "I didn't see anyone eat a goldfish in Cabo."

Fincher. What the fuck do they know about *Fincher*? My heart beats loud. I tell it to stop. It doesn't listen to me. I do not control my heart. Nobody does. Detective Carr is still nodding. Torturing me. Scratching his neck. "Hey," he says. "How's your buddy Brian?"

Captain Fucking Dave. I swallow. "He's fine."

"Now, he sounds like a party animal to me, right?" He laughs. "A guy like that, I bet *he* would swallow a goldfish, yeah?"

"I don't know," I say.

Detective Carr stares at the wall. Edmund stares at me. There is a unique silence to this room and I know what happened. Captain Dave is a fearful man—*Rules are rules, Joe*—and when the cops asked him about our time in Cabo, he forked over every detail. He told them about my imaginary friend *Brian,* the one I invented when I was trying to get the boat so I could dump Fincher's body. Now the police are going to want to talk to Brian and there are probably others on this case, cops poring over airline records, passport records, cops trying to find Brian the American who went to Cabo San Lucas. They aren't going to find Brian. But they are going to realize that a cop named Robin Fincher flew to Cabo. They are going to see that he disappeared while I was in Cabo and I love Love, but this is America. If you kill a cop, they don't let you go. Cops protect their own. They are the ultimate family, loyal to the end.

"How'd you meet Brian?" Detective Carr asks.

"At a party," I say.

"Henderson's party?"

Nice try, fucker. "No," I say. "I didn't meet him at Henderson's party."

Henderson, of course, is their favorite thing to talk about, the fact that I was there, that I was in his house, on YouTube, the night that he died. They think it's too much coincidence. But they have no evidence.

"Sounds like you guys aren't close," he says.

"We aren't," I say. The days are long in here. I will not complain when I am free, staying up around the clock helping take care of the baby.

"Why did Love hate him so much?"

I look at him. "Huh?"

He smiles. I fucked up. *Huh* was the wrong thing to say. "They're asking her right now," he says. "Just one of those things, you know, we're curious about you, Joe, the kind of people you run with and all."

"I don't know why she hated him," I say. And this is that *Newlyweds* game show from before I was born, where they test your knowledge of your partner. But it's not fair. We are not playing for a fucking vacation to Cabo. We are playing for my life, for my right to be a father to my child. My *child.* Love and I did not sign up for this but I have to play.

"Take a guess," he says. He gets a text. He reads the text. He nods. "Huh," he says. He is imitating me. He has Love's answer and I don't have Love's answer and I don't know what she would say.

"Joe, you don't have to answer," Edmund reminds me, but he's wrong, I do. Detective Carr isn't going to leave the room until I answer a question about someone who doesn't *exist* or I will be one step closer toward a life without love. Milo will raise my baby. My baby will run into his arms.

My mind swirls. Brian doesn't exist. There is no Brian. But Love answered the question. What did she say? This is like in *Magnolia* when the kid breaks down. I am cracking under pressure and Detective Carr knows it. He knocks his phone against the table and this is the sound of my life ending.

"Are you thirsty?" Detective Carr nudges the water toward me. "Go ahead," he says. "Trust me, we didn't slip anything in there."

I look at him and I am doing it again, digging my own grave. Does he know about the cactus? Was there a camera at the house? Was there a camera in the sky? A drone? He sips his water. "When did

Love meet Brian?" he asks. "Did she meet him before you left town to do the movie? Or did she meet him in Palm Springs?"

He could be lying. Love could have refused to answer the question. She might be playing the same game as I am. I try to imagine that I am Love, pregnant, in love, and there is a man asking me questions and if I say the wrong thing, the man I love so much will be gone. My heart beats faster and faster, and I wish I could carry it around in a rolling suitcase. It's annoying, the way it's connected to my other bodily functions, the way my little motherfucker pores allow sweat to weep upon my forehead, the way my asshole pupils shrink and expand and I can't control them. I'm not a fucking sociopath.

Detective Carr puts his feet up on the desk again. "Joe," he says. "What was Brian's last name? Love can't remember. Do you remember?"

Edmund looks at me meaningfully. "No," I say. "I don't remember."

I don't remember. The magic words, according to my attorney, according to Love. If I just keep saying I don't remember things, I will be out of here soon. I will not let Detective Carr break me. Love and I shouldn't be playing the *Newlywed Game*. We're not even married yet. I will my heart to take it easy and I sip the water and I can't wait for this session to be over. I look forward to returning to my cage. I feel empowered when I'm in there, locked up.

Love is the key to happiness in life, and I have no doubt that it will set me free. Love, and Edmund, that's all I need and I have it all, and I know that if I believe in Love and play by the rules—*say nothing, remember nothing, say as little as possible, say nothing*—I know I will be out of here soon, watching my child break out of Love's vagina, my favorite place in the world.

If Love were here, in this room, she would wrap her arms around me and tell me why she hates Brian, what his last name is, share with me all the elaborate and specific details of when and where they met, how he offended her. I know it's ludicrous to say such a thing. After all, Brian doesn't exist. They never met. I invented him so I could get access to one of the boats. So because there is no such *thing* as Brian, there is nothing for Love to know. And yet I know she would know because that's the thing about feeling so connected to someone, so entrenched, so attached. I believe she knows me better than I know myself, and hopefully I know her as well too.

"Joe," he says.

"Yeah?"

"How did Love and Brian meet?"

I say nothing. What would Love say?

"What's his last name?"

I say nothing. What would Love say?

"Why does she hate this guy?"

I say nothing. What would Love say? I know Love and I have to believe in myself right now. I have to walk out onto the plank and I have to jump. I stop sweating. My heart resets and my pores rest. This is it.

"First of all," I begin. "I barely know that Brian guy. And the thing is, Love doesn't hate him."

He swallows and it's an unmistakable sign that I passed the test. Love told the cops the same thing and I remember her exact words in the pool that day, talking about Sam the work bitch, our conversation in Little Compton about Forty. *I don't hate anyone*, she said. When you love someone, you listen. You remember it all.

"Truthfully," I say. "Love doesn't really hate anybody."

He clenches his jaw. "Yeah," he says. "So I heard."

Inside, I pump my fist. I knew it. I know her. I love her.

But most people in love face obstacles and here is ours, Detective Carr, back again, firing away: "But you told Captain Dave that Love hates this guy. Why?"

"I didn't want to go here. Ray and Dottie have been through enough . . ." I work up some tears. My lawyer asks for a minute but I say no. "Look, Detective, I can't stress this enough. I'd rather Ray and Dottie not know that Forty was involved in this, but well, fuck. Brian was Forty's friend," I say, and it's the money shot, my would-have-been-brother-in-law saving me from the great beyond. "I just met him in Cabo. He and Forty got really fucked up and Forty didn't want to just leave him out there, but he was too fucked up to deal with it himself." I shrug. "I was just trying to do him a solid."

"Why not let him crash at the party? La Groceria has more than a few spare bedrooms." Detective Carr is the one sweating now, drumming his fingers on the table. And this is the beauty of reasonable doubt. He may suspect that I'm making this all up, but at the end of the day, he can't prove that and Forty's not around to tell him differently.

"Because it was our wrap party," I say. "It wasn't a free-for-all."

"Who else met this Brian? Anyone *alive*, I mean?" he asks.

I shrug. "I don't remember."

I was worried I would sound sarcastic, like a senator's son at a date rape trial, but I didn't. I pulled it off. I took a leap of faith and made an educated guess on what Love said and I guessed correctly. I did it. We did it. Detective Carr is standing, irritated. He says it's odd the way I know so many people who *don't fucking exist anymore* and I let him rant. I don't tell him that the last person who said that to me wound up dead.

I have my priorities in order: Love comes first, above all. She is patient and kind as the Corinthians say and I bring patience and kindness into this room as I watch this poor bastard pace. He's older than me, more tired; he probably lives in Torrance, in some house full of Bud Light and expired coupons and firearms and soiled diapers. It can't be easy, being a cop in California and he's not very photogenic or articulate. I bet he never wanted to be an actor and I bet he wasn't even in love with his wife when he proposed to her. I bet he was just with her and I bet she was dropping hints and I bet he was one of those guys who proposes because he's thirty, because he figures it's time to get married and settle down. I bet there was no love in his heart when he got down on one knee and asked the girl to marry him, not any more than usual, I mean.

"You can't tell me *anything* else about this Brian?"

"I'm sorry," I say. "For all I know, that wasn't even his real name."

"Don't fuck with me."

"I'm not fucking with you," I say. "I met him briefly. He was Forty's friend and Forty knew some shady people, you know. He did drugs, he got around."

"It's bad luck to speak ill of the dead."

"I'm not speaking ill," I say. "I'm trying to help you guys out."

Detective Carr sits in his chair. In a way I think it would be terrible to live in LA devoid of aspirations. How would you do it? How would you put up with the traffic and the monotony of the sun, the way people use the word *hella* and lie so freely? How could you stand it here if you weren't striving for something better? Oh that's right; he liked *The Wolf of Wall Street.* He aspires to take someone down like me, a *serial killer.* But he chose the wrong guy. I am done with all that. And I will not let my past dictate my future.

He rubs his forehead. "You know, Joe," he says. "We have all of our officers looking for Brian. You do know that we will find him. We're gonna make sure he's okay. We're checking hotel records and we're gonna find out all of it, who he was, what you did with him, why."

"Okay," I say.

"Okay," he says, and I feel bad for him. He's so close. And he's going to get closer. He'll come in here tomorrow talking about *The Godfather Part III* and asking me if I heard about a cop disappearing in Mexico, a guy named Fincher who also visited the set of *Boots and Puppies.* But the thing is, it's all circumstantial evidence. It's not enough to keep me here. I was very good at killing people when I needed to be.

Was. The past tense. I'm retired.

And really, when you grow up, and get over yourself, when you *fuck narcissism* and leave the hashtags at the door, you see what really matters in life. What matters is what you do next. I get it. And this is America. You have to prove that someone did something and they can't prove that I did anything.

In *Fast Five*, Dom is in a prison bus, glum. His friends force the bus to crash so they can free him. But my team doesn't have to do that for me. They won't be able to convict me or get me on a bus because there is no evidence of my past actions. Well, aside from the baby growing inside of Love.

Prison isn't that bad and I treasure the solitude. From everything

I know about parenting, I expect that in a few months, I'll be glad I got to spend some time alone before becoming a father. We all need to be with our thoughts. Angelenos like to meditate and stare at expensive statues of Buddha, and I stare at the cement. Same difference. I learn to smile at everyone and I feel the world reciprocate.

The guards are polite. And then when I'm not alone, I'm in the room. I kind of like it in there, the way Detective Carr challenges me every day. My lawyer says I'm *damn good* under pressure. This is all great research for my screenwriting career and I can see myself writing a movie that takes place during a trial. I use this time to learn how to become the best possible father, to figure out how to provide for my family. One day Love and I will be buried together or cremated, I haven't decided yet, and Detective Carr will undoubtedly spend eternity in a plot selected by his controlling wife.

"Don't move," Detective Carr says. He leaves and this is the most awkward time for me, when I am the most afraid for my safety, when I know they are watching me, studying my face, trying so hard to figure me out, talking shit about me, speculating. I have no phone to play with, no TV to watch. I look into the orb that connects me to them. I wait. In my head, I recite Corinthians; *Love is patient, love is kind.*

This is how you get away with murder, how you get out of the interrogation room—a woman cop comes for me *okay, let's move you back*—and this how you get escorted into the safety of your cell, locked up, left alone to recover from the day's needling, to dream of what might come tomorrow or the next day. You believe in love. It really is all you need, although yes, a solid defense attorney helps too. But I do believe in love, in Love, and when it's time, I will hold our baby. The thought soothes me and the mattress feels softer.

Life puts you in cage so that you'll treasure your freedom, how lucky you were to be running on a beach, the way your girlfriend looked over her shoulder at you, the ring you did not fashion out of a straw. All time is good. No time is hard, not if you think of it as time to celebrate love.

I roll over into the fetal position and I think of my child, in the same position, so much younger, unconscious, gestating, serving time just like Daddy, waiting. It doesn't fully exist yet, but Love and I created a human, a boy or a girl, we don't know, can't know. It's too early. You could say the same thing about my fate. The future is a frontier we can't fully explore until we make it there, but then we arrive, and the distant horizon has become something else, something less romantic. It's just the present—the mattress coils in my back, the bars on my cell, Love waiting for me to come home.

You think about this stuff in jail so you don't go crazy. You realize your intuition is stronger than science, truer than a molecule. I feel it in my caged gut. I will be free soon. I also know that we're going to have a baby girl. I don't have to close my eyes to see her, a little version of Love with my dark irises on her heart-shaped face. I smile. We exist. We are both on a journey and we are both in love and that's all anyone can hope for in life.

ACKNOWLEDGMENTS

IT'S time to thank all the people who worked zealously to bring this book into your hands. Everyone at Emily Bestler Books, Atria, and Simon & Schuster, I thank you. My editors Emily Bestler and Megan Reid ask smart questions. Line for line, you care and invest. I am continuously awestruck. I count my blessings for Josh Bank, Lanie Davis, and Sara Shandler at Alloy Entertainment. Your eyes and ears mean the world to me. You get it. ☺ I'm grateful to Les Morgenstein, Judith Curr, David Brown, and Jo Dickinson. You are champions. Natalie Sousa, thank you for your astounding ability to tell a story with images. Santino Fontana, thank you for your voice.

Big thanks to the WME team. Jennifer Rudolph Walsh, Claudia Ballard, Laura Bonner, Maggie Shapiro, and Katie Giarla, you make wonderful things happen.

To my mom: You have always made me feel like everything I write is an event, like it matters. You are brave and honest. Thank you for saying *hmmm.*

To my dad: Thank you for your voice. You are always with me. Your clarity and your chutzpah, your poetic nature and your love of words, you live on.

I love the world of books. It's a joy to connect with readers, bloggers, librarians, booksellers, authors, journalists, and podcasters. The bright side of technology is a tweet from someone who was up all night reading your book. I love you guys for reaching out to ask for more Joe.

Finally, I raise my glass of vodka to my beloved friends and family. You crack me up. You make me think. Thank you for believing in me. Thank you for your love.